'My apologies for the interruption, Your Majesty—'

'Akram…?' Zahir prompted impatiently. 'I have a meeting in thirty minutes.'

'It's…*her*! That woman you married!' Akram recovered his tongue abruptly. 'She's out there in the streets of our capital city, shaming you even as we speak!'

Sapphire—the one mistake he had ever made, and the payback had been unforgettably brutal. He had endured indescribable punishment to keep her as his wife for even a year. She owed him. She definitely owed him. She had used and abused him before walking away unharmed and incalculably richer. Maybe it was finally payback time, Zahir reflected grimly. And the very thought of Sapphire being in his power was the most seductive image that Zahir had indulged in for years.

THE
SHEIKH'S PRIZE

BY
LYNNE GRAHAM

First published in Great Britain 2013
by Mills & Boon, an imprint of Harlequin (UK) Limited.
Harlequin (UK) Limited, Eton House, 18-24 Paradise Road,
Richmond, Surrey TW9 1SR

© Lynne Graham 2013

ISBN: 978 0 263 90012 5

Printed and bound in Spain
by Blackprint CPI, Barcelona

Lynne Graham was born in Northern Ireland and has been a keen Mills & Boon® reader since her teens. She is very happily married, with an understanding husband who has learned to cook since she started to write! Her five children keep her on her toes. She has a very large dog, which knocks everything over, a very small terrier, which barks a lot, and two cats. When time allows, Lynne is a keen gardener.

Recent titles by the same author:

A RICH MAN'S WHIM
   (A Bride for a Billionaire)
A RING TO SECURE HIS HEIR
UNLOCKING HER INNOCENCE
THE SECRETS SHE CARRIED

Did you know these are also available as eBooks?
Visit www.millsandboon.co.uk

CHAPTER ONE

ZAHIR RA'IF QUARISHI, hereditary king of the gulf state of Maraban, leapt up from behind his desk when his younger brother, Akram, literally burst into his office.

'What has happened?' Zahir demanded urgently, straightening to his full six feet three inches of height, his lean powerful body tensing like the army officer he had been into immediate battle readiness.

His face unusually flushed, Akram came to an abrupt halt to execute a jerky bow as he belatedly recalled the niceties of court etiquette.' My apologies for the interruption, Your Majesty—'

'I assume there's a good reason,' Zahir conceded, his rigidity easing as he read Akram's troubled expression and recognised that something of a more private and personal nature had precipitated his impulsive entry to one of the very few places in which Zahir could usually depend on receiving the peace he required to work.

Akram stiffened, embarrassment claiming his open good-natured face. 'I don't know how to tell you this—'

'Sit down and take a deep breath,' Zahir advised calmly, his innate natural assurance taking over as he settled his big frame down into an armchair in the corner of the room and rested his piercing dark-as-night eyes on the younger man while moving a graceful hand to urge him to sit down as well. 'There's nothing we can't discuss. I will never be as intimidating as our late father.'

At that reminder, Akram turned deadly pale, for their late and unlamented parent had been as much of a tyrant and a bully in the royal palace with his family as he was in his role as a ruler over what had once been one of the most backward countries in the Middle East. While Fareed the Magnificent, as he had insisted on being called, had been in power, Maraban's oil wealth had flowed only one way into the royal coffers while their people continued to live in the Dark Ages, denied education, modern technology and adequate medical support. It had been three years since Zahir took the throne and the changes he had immediately instigated still remained a massive undertaking. Angrily conscious that his brother worked just about every hour of the day in his determination to improve the lives of his subjects, Akram suddenly dreaded giving Zahir the news he had learned. Zahir never mentioned his first marriage. It was too controversial a topic, Akram acknowledged awkwardly. How could it not be? His brother had paid a high price for defying their late father and marrying a foreigner from a different culture. That he had done so for a woman clearly unworthy of his faith could only be an additional source of aggravation.

'Akram…?' Zahir prompted impatiently. 'I have a meeting in thirty minutes.'

'It's…*her!* That woman you married!' Akram recovered his tongue abruptly. 'She's out there in the streets of our capital city shaming you even as we speak!'

Zahir froze and frowned, his spectacular bone structure tightening beneath taut skin the colour of honey, his wide sensual mouth compressing hard. 'What the hell are you talking about?'

'Sapphire's here filming some television commercial for cosmetics!' Akram told him in fierce condemnation, resenting what he saw as an inexcusable insult to his elder brother.

Zahir's lean strong hands clenched into fists. 'Here?' he repeated in thunderous disbelief. 'Sapphire is filming *here* in Maraban?'

'Wakil told me,' his brother told him, referring to one of Zahir's former bodyguards. 'He couldn't believe his eyes when he recognised her! It's lucky that our father refused to announce your marriage to our people—I never thought we'd live to be grateful for that…'

Zahir was stunned at the idea that his ex-wife could have *dared* to set a single foot within the borders of his country. Rage and bitterness flamed through his taut powerful frame and he sprang restively upright again. He had tried not to be bitter, he had tried even harder to forget his failed marriage…only that was a little hard to do when your ex became an internationally famous supermodel, featuring in countless magazines and newspapers and even once in a giant advertising hoarding over Times Square. In truth a mere five years ago he had been a sitting duck of a target for a cunning schemer of Sapphire Marshall's ilk and that lowering awareness had left an indelible stain on his masculine ego. At twenty-five years of age he had, thanks to his father's oppression, still been a virgin, ignorant of the West and Western women, but although he hadn't had a clue he had at least *tried* to make his marriage work. His bride, on the other hand, had refused to make the smallest effort to sort out their problems. He had fought hard to keep a wife who didn't want to be his wife, indeed who couldn't even bear for him to touch her.

More fool him, he reflected with hard cynicism, for he was no longer an innocent when it came to women. The explanation for Sapphire's extraordinary behaviour had become clear as crystal to him once he shed his idealistic assumptions about his wife's honour: his bride had only married him because he was wealthy beyond avarice and a prince, *not* because she cared about him. Unpardonably, her goal in marrying him had simply been the rich pay-off that would follow their divorce. He had married a woman with all the heart of a cash register and she had, not only, ripped him off but also got away scot free while he had paid in spades. At that reflection, his even white teeth ground together, tiny gold flames igniting in his fierce eyes. If only he had been dealing with her in the present as a male who now knew the score, he would have known exactly how to handle her.

'I'm sorry, Zahir,' Akram muttered in the seething

silence, ill at ease with the rare dark fury that had flared in his brother's face. 'I thought you had a right to know that she'd had the cheek to come here.'

'It's five years since I divorced her,' Zahir pointed out harshly, his lean strong face impassive. 'Why should I care what she does?'

'Because she's an embarrassment!' Akram rushed to declare. 'Imagine how you would feel if the media found out that she was once your wife! She must be shameless and without conscience to come to Maraban to make her stupid commercial!'

'This is all very emotive stuff, Akram,' Zahir countered, reluctantly touched by his brother's concern on his behalf. 'I'm grateful you told me but what do you expect me to do?'

'Throw her and her film crew out of Maraban!' his brother told him instantly.

'You are still young and impetuous, my brother,' Zahir replied drily. 'The paparazzi follow my ex-wife everywhere she goes. Try to picture the likely consequences of deporting a world-famous celebrity. Why would I want to create headlines to alert the world's media to a past that is more wisely left buried?'

When Akram had finally departed, still incredulous that his brother had failed to express a desire for retribution, Zahir made several phone calls that would have astonished the younger man. It was a supreme irony but Zahir's coolly astute brain was perpetually at all-out war with the volatile passion of his temperament. While it made no logical sense whatsoever he wanted the chance to see Sapphire in the flesh again. Did that desire imply that he still had some lingering need for closure where she was concerned? Or was it simple and natural curiosity because he was currently facing the prospect of having to take another wife? Once, in a desperate search for a solution to his seemingly incurable problems with Sapphire, Zahir had read books about all sorts of strange subjects before he finally accepted that the simplest explanation of the apparently inexplicable was usually the closest to the truth. Since then events in his ex-wife's life had suggested that his sceptical convictions about her true character were spot-on. He had wed a gold-digging social climber with not an atom of true feeling for him. After all, he was well aware that Sapphire was now cosily ensconced in a live-in relationship with the award-winning Scottish wildlife photographer, Cameron McDonald. Presumably she wasn't having any difficulty bedding *him*... Zahir's dark eyes burned afresh like golden flames at that incendiary thought.

Saffy dutifully angled her hot face into the flow of air gushing from the wind machine so that her mane of blonde hair wafted back in a cloud over her shoulders. Not an atom of her growing irritation and discomfort showed on her flawless features. Saffy was never less than professional when she was working. But how many times had her make-up already needed retouched in the stifling heat? It was simply melting off her face. How many times had the set security had to interrupt filming to make the crowd of over-excited spectators back

away to give her colleagues the space to work? Coming
to Maraban to film the Desert Ice cosmetics commercial
had been a foolish mistake. The support systems the
film crew took for granted were non-existent.

'Give me *that* sexy look, Saffy…' Dylan, the photographer, urged pleadingly. 'What is wrong with you
this week? You're not on form—'

And as if someone had zapped her with an electrified
cattle prod, Saffy struggled to switch on the expression
he wanted because she hated the fact that anyone should
have noticed that anything was amiss with her mood.
Inside her head, she fought to focus on the fantasy that
never failed to ignite that much vaunted look of desire on her face. So ironic, she reflected momentarily,
so very *cruelly* ironic that she should have to focus on
what she had often dreamt of and never yet managed
to experience in reality. But when she was working a
shoot costing her clients thousands of pounds was not
the time to allow all that old bad stuff to resurface. With
the strong determination that was the backbone of her
temperament, Saffy forced the distressing memories
back down into her subconscious again and then mentally searched to extract the required familiar image: a
man with jet-black hair down to his broad brown shoulders, a man who positively oozed raw animal magne-
tism from every pore with a lean powerfully naked body
encased in warm gilded skin. In every image he would
slowly turn his head to look at her, revealing fiercely
stunning eyes of gold surrounded by black lashes so
lush they acted like eye liner on a guy already so sav-

agely masculine and passionate that at one glance he took her breath away. And all those wretched frustrating responses swam back through her taut body in a wave, her nipples beading below the scrap of silk she wore, her entire body dampening with shocking awareness.

'That's it…that's exactly it!' Dylan crooned in enthusiasm, leaping around her posed figure to take photos from different angles as she shifted position with languorous ease, that image inside her head like an indelible tattoo below her skin. 'Lower your lids a little more—we want to see that eye shadow…brilliant, sweetheart, now *pout* that gorgeous mouth…'

A couple of minutes passed before with a tiny jerk of displacement, Saffy returned to the present and was suddenly plunged back into the heat, the noise and the curious crowds, her huge bluer-than-blue eyes reflecting her discomfiture at the massive attention they were attracting. But Dylan had got the shots he wanted and he leapt around like a maniac punching the air with satisfaction. Her single-minded concentration on her role gone now, she looked out above the crowds and saw a vehicle parked at the height of a giant rolling ochre-coloured sand dune with a robed figure standing nearby holding something in his hand that glinted in the sun.

Zahir had his high-definition binoculars trained on his stunningly beautiful ex-wife. With her glorious mane of golden hair blowing back from her face like a sheet of gleaming silk and seated atop a pile of giant fake ice cubes, she would have looked spectacularly eye-catching by any standards. But in the beauty stakes, Sapphire occupied a category all of her own and the sight of her took Zahir's hot-blooded temper to new and dangerous heights. He was outraged that she was appearing in public in Maraban clad in only a couple of scraps of azure silk that displayed the surprisingly bountiful mounds of her breasts, the smooth skin of her now bejewelled midriff and the incredible svelte stretch of her very long and perfect legs.

He watched the men involved in the shoot dart slavishly around Sapphire, offering her drinks and food and fussing with her hair and her face, and he wondered with vicious coarseness which of them had had the pleasure of her beautiful body. After all, she might live with Cameron McDonald, but the UK tabloids had, nonetheless, exposed the fact that she had had several affairs with other men. Clearly she was anything but a faithful lover. Of course, it was possible that Cameron and Sapphire enjoyed a civilly negotiated 'open' relationship, but Zahir was not impressed by that possibility or even by the concept of open relationships. He didn't sleep around, he had never slept around even when he finally had the freedom to make such choices. His ex-wife had to be a bit of a slut, he decided with dark brooding bitterness, his lean strong face set granite hard at the acknowledgement. He had married an embryo slut and, worst of all, she was a slut he *still* lusted after. At that final disturbing admission, Zahir ground his even white teeth while perspiration beaded his upper lip, his tall, powerful body furiously tense and aggressively aroused by his perusal of that perfect body and even more perfect face.

Sapphire, the one mistake he had ever made and the payback had been unforgettably brutal. He had endured indescribable punishment to keep her as his wife for even a year. She owed him, she definitely *owed* him for twelve months of unadulterated hell. Add in the millions she had received from him since the charade of their marriage finally ran aground in a divorce and he had every right to feel ill-done by, every right to still be aggrieved and hostile. She had used and abused him before walking away unharmed and considerably richer. Maybe it was finally payback time, Zahir reflected grimly, his adrenalin spiking at the idea. And bearing in mind that she and her film crew had chosen to come to Maraban and film without the permission of the relevant authority, she had put herself and her precious high-flying career in his power. And the very thought of Sapphire being in his power was the most seductive image that Zahir had indulged in for years. He lowered the binoculars, thinking fast, squashing the disconcerting logical objections already trying to assail him to persuade him to restrain his primal responses. It wouldn't be the same between them now, he reasoned angrily; he was not the same man. This time around he had the weapons to *make* her want him back.

That process of self-persuasion was incredibly seductive. Throughout his life Zahir had very rarely done what *he* wanted to do, for the necessity of always considering the needs of others had taken precedence. But why shouldn't he put his own desires first for once? He had already checked Sapphire's schedule and she was due to leave Maraban within hours, an awareness that merely made him all the more single-minded. Zahir made his plans there and then with ruthless cool and the same kind of fierce, almost suicidal resolution that had once persuaded him to take a foreign wife without first asking his despotic father's permission. As that reality and comparison briefly occurred to him he stubbornly suppressed the piercing shard of unease it awakened.

With a sense of merciful release from the strain of being on show, Saffy stepped into the site trailer to change. She shed the skimpy silk bandeau and slashed skirt and peeled off the fake navel jewel before donning white linen trousers and an aqua tee. In a couple of hours she would be on her way home and saying goodbye to the joys of Maraban couldn't come quickly enough as far as she was concerned. After all, it was the last place in the world she would have chosen to visit, but civil unrest in a neighbouring country had led to a last-minute change of location and nobody had been willing to listen to her necessarily vague objections. But then the fact that nobody had a clue about her past connection to Maraban or Zahir was a relief. Thankfully that period of her life before fame had claimed her remained a deep dark secret.

So, in spite of all he had once had to say on the score of corrupt hereditary rulerships, Zahir had still ended up taking the throne to become a king. But then, according to what she had read in the newspapers, the citizens of Maraban had not had a clue what to do with the offer of democracy and had instead rallied round their popular hero prince, who had rebelled with the army against his old horror of a father to protect the people. There were pictures of Zahir everywhere: she had noticed one in the hotel foyer with a vase of flowers set beneath it rather like a little sacred shrine. Her lush mouth twisted as she questioned the thread of bitterness powering her thoughts. He was honourable, a big fan of justice and was very probably an excellent king, she conceded grudgingly. It really wasn't fair to resent him for what he couldn't have helped. Their marriage had been a disaster and even now her thoughts slid away from the memories with alacrity. He had broken her heart and dumped her when she failed to deliver and she wasn't really sure that it was fair to hate him for that when by that stage she had been urging him to divorce her for months. Everyone made choices, everyone had to live with those choices and a happy ending wasn't always included.

But she had a good life, she reminded herself doggedly as the security team cleared a path for her through the crush of spectators to the waiting limo that would whisk her back to the airport. She now had three glorious days of freedom to look forward to, and a tired sigh escaped her as she touched an admiring fingertip to the silky petal of an impossibly perfect blossom in the beautiful bouquet displayed in a vase inside the limo, while only vaguely wondering where the flowers had come from. When she got back to London, she would first catch up with her sisters, one who was pregnant, one who was desperate to conceive and one who was still at school. Her eldest sister, Kat, was thirty-six and considering fertility treatment while still being full of the newly married joys of her life with her Russian billionaire. After a sticky interview with her tough brother-in-law, Mikhail Saffy was a little less enamoured of her sibling's blunt-spoken husband. Mikhail had demanded to know why Saffy hadn't offered to help Kat when her sister had run into serious debt. Well, *hello,* Saffy thought back angrily—Kat had never told Saffy that she was in trouble and, even if she had, Saffy knew she would have found it a challenge to come up with that kind of cash at short notice. Having made a major commitment early in her career to help support an African school for AIDS orphans, Saffy lived comfortably but not in luxury.

Saffy's twin, Emmie, was pregnant and Saffy had not been surprised to learn that Emmie didn't have a supportive man by her side. Saffy was painfully aware that her twin did not forgive those who hurt or offended her and in all probability the father of Emmie's child had made that mistake. Saffy knew better than anyone how inflexible her sibling could be because the relationship between the twins had long been tense and troubled. Indeed Saffy could never suppress the surge of the guilt that attacked her whenever she saw her sister. As young children she and Emmie had been very close but events during their troubled teen years had ripped them apart and the two young women had never managed to repair that breach. Saffy would never forget the injuries that *her* reckless behaviour had inflicted on her twin sister or the many years of suffering that Emmie had endured as a result. Some things were just too bad to be forgiven, Saffy acknowledged sadly.

In any case, Mikhail and Kat would undoubtedly assist Emmie in her struggles as a single mum—certainly, Saffy knew better than to offer assistance that would be richly resented. But she could not understand why Emmie had chosen to make a big secret of her baby's paternity. Saffy winced at that thought. While it was true that Saffy had never told her sisters the humiliating truth about her own failed marriage, she felt that she had had good reasons for her silence, not the least of which was the embarrassing fact that she had totally ignored Kat's plea that Saffy get to know Zahir better and for longer *before* she married him. Just common sense really, Saffy conceded wryly. Getting married at eighteen to a guy you had only known a couple of months and had never lived with had been an act of insanity. As immature and idealistic as most teenagers with little experience of independent life, Saffy had struggled from the outset with the role of being a wife in a different culture. And while she had struggled, Zahir had steadily grown more and more distant, not to mention his penchant for disappearing for weeks at a time on army manoeuvres just when she needed him most. Yes, she had made mistakes...but then *so had he*.

Satisfied with that appraisal, which approportioned

equal blame for what had gone wrong in the past, Saffy
emerged from her reverie and noticed in surprise that
the limo was travelling down a wide empty road that
strongly reminded her of an airport runway. As the route
back to the airport entailed travelling through Maraban
city, she frowned, gazing out in confusion at the emptiness of the desert surrounding her on all sides. Strewn
with stones and occasional large volcanic rock forma-
tions, the bleak desert terrain was interrupted by little
vegetation. And so pervasive was the march of the sand
that it was steadily encroaching on the road, blurring
its outlines.

Saffy had never warmed to Zahir's natural preference for a lot of sand in his vicinity, had never learned
to adjust to the extremes of heat or to admire the aus-
terity of such a landscape. Where on earth were they
going? Could the driver be taking another route to avoid
the city traffic, such as it was? Her smooth brow creas-
ing, she leant forward to rap the glass partition to attract the driver's attention, but although she saw his
eyes flicker in the rear-view mirror to glance in her
direction he made no attempt to respond to her. While
Saffy was annoyed at being ignored, his behaviour also
awakened the first stirrings of genuine apprehension
and Saffy rapped the glass harder and shouted for him
to stop. What on earth was the stupid man playing at?
She didn't want to miss her flight home and she didn't
have time to waste.

As she withdrew her fingers from the glass her
knuckle brushed against the flowers in the vase and

for the first time she noticed the envelope attached to them. She snatched it up and ripped it open to extract a typed card.

It is with great pleasure that I invite you to enjoy my hospitality for the weekend.

What on earth? Saffy stared down at the unsigned card. Who was inviting her where and why? Was this why her uncommunicative driver was travelling in the wrong direction? Her even white teeth gritted in angry frustration. Had her lightly clad appearance at the shoot caught the eye of some local randy sheikh? Possibly even the guy in the sand dunes with the binoculars? What did he think she was? Dial-a-tart? No, no, *no!* Her blue eyes flashed like twin blue fires. No way was she sacrificing her one free weekend to pandering to the ego of yet another rich man, keen to assume that the very fact she made her living by her face and body meant that she was an easy lay available to the highest bidder! Desert Ice cosmetics was always willing to serve her up to VIPs as the face of its product and the some-what racy reputation bestowed on her by the tabloids encouraged the wrong expectations and made rejecting amorous men even more of a challenge.

No way on earth was she spending her weekend with some man she hadn't even met! She dug through her bag in search of her cell phone, intending to ring one of her colleagues for assistance, but she couldn't find her phone and only finally accepted that it wasn't there after she had tipped out the contents of her bag on the seat beside her. She had had her phone in her hand be-

fore she got changed, she recalled with a frown. She had
set it down…and clearly she hadn't picked it up again!
She ground her teeth together and just for the sake of it
attempted to open the door beside her. She wasn't surprised to find it locked and it really didn't matter, she
conceded ruefully, for she had no intention of risking
serious injury by throwing herself out of a moving car.

Conscious of the anxious glances the driver was now
giving her in the mirror, she lifted her head high, her
brain working double time. She might feel as if she
were being kidnapped, but that was a most unlikely
interpretation of her situation in a country as old-fashioned and law-abiding as Maraban. In addition, no Arab
host would want an unwilling guest in his home. Indeed making a guest uncomfortable was a big no-no in
Marabani culture, so once she politely explained that
she had a prior engagement and apologised for being
unavailable, she would be free to leave again…only by
that time she might well have missed her flight home.
Her lush mouth took on a downward curve.

Only minutes later, the limo came to a halt by the side
of the road and with a click the door beside her opened.
Saffy's brow pleated as she climbed out and she thought
about making a run for it. But a run for it to where? It
was the hottest part of the day and she would burn to a
crisp. In addition the road was still empty and they had
travelled miles through unbroken desert. As she pondered the unavoidable fact that there was nowhere safe
to run to, a large four-wheel-drive vehicle drew up at
the other side of the road. The driver jumped out and

opened the passenger door wide while regarding her expectantly. Clearly it was an arranged meeting for her to be transferred to another vehicle. Did she accept that? Or fight it…but fight it with what? She glanced back into the limo and studied the glass vase that held the flowers. It was the work of a moment to smash the vase against the built-in bar and retrieve a jagged piece of glass, which she cupped awkwardly in her hand because she didn't want to tighten her fingers and cut herself on it. Straightening her slim shoulders, she crossed the road and climbed into the four-wheel-drive. The door slammed instantly behind her.

Was she in any true danger, she asked herself irritably, or was she at even greater risk of being swept along by an over-confident belief that somehow she was still in control of events? As soon as they arrived at their destination she would make it very clear that she wished to return to the airport immediately and if anyone dared to lay a single finger on her she would slash that person with the glass. Now was not the time to wish she had taken self-defence classes.

The vehicle moved off and performed a U-turn to pass directly in front of the limo and drive down a stony track that ran straight out into the desert. That change in direction took Saffy very much by surprise and she looked out of the windows in dismay at the giant looming sand dunes coming closer to tower all around them as the rough track streaked doggedly ahead. It was very bumpy and very hot because there seemed to be no air-conditioning in the car. Perspiration beading her brow,

Saffy gripped the safety rail above her head and gritted her teeth, thinking that possibly she should have made a run for it while they were still on the highway. As the track inevitably vanished beneath the sand the powerful vehicle roared endlessly over the shallow mounds that had taken its place, forging a zigzagging path between the dunes. Finally, when every bone in her body felt as if it were rattling inside her skin, the vehicle began to climb up the steep side of a dune, the engine whining at the strain. At the top she peered out of the window and focused on the sole sign of civilisation within view: a stone fortress with tall walls and turrets that looked remarkably like an ancient crusader castle.

Oh, dear, she thought with a sinking heart, for it didn't look as though it would offer the comforts of a five-star hotel and where else could they possibly be heading? And who in their right mind would invite her to such a remote place? Aside of a herd of goats there was nothing moving in the castle's vicinity.

The car thundered down the slope towards the building and big black gates spread slowly open as they approached. Through the gates she glimpsed surprisingly lush greenery, a welcome sight to eyes strained by sand overload. The vehicle lurched to a halt and she breathed in slow and deep when she saw staff clustered round an arched entrance. Maybe it *was* a hotel; certainly it looked at least the equal of the one she had stayed at in the city. As Saffy stepped out heads bowed low and nobody looked directly at her and nobody spoke. Saffy was in no mood to speak anyway and she followed in the

steps of the older man who shifted his hand to gain her
attention. Her shoes clicked on a polished marble floor
and the blessed coolness of air-conditioning chilled her
hot damp skin but nothing could have prepared her for
the awe-inspiring sight that met her eyes. The amazingly spectacular hall stretched into seeming infinity
in front of her. Fashioned of gleaming white marble and
studded with gilded pillars and ornate mirrors, it was
as unexpected in its sheer opulence inside those ancient
walls as snow in the desert. She blinked in bewilderment, gazing up to scan the heavily decorated ceiling
far above, which rejoiced in a gloriously well executed
mural of a sunny blue sky dotted with exotic flying
birds. A few feet ahead her guide hovered to wait for
her to move on again.

Her mouth tightening, Saffy walked on to descend
a shallow flight of stone stairs and walk through tall
gilded doors into a vast sunlit room, which, although
draped in luxury fabrics, was traditionally furnished in
Eastern style with low divans and beautiful rugs carefully arranged around a central fire pit where coffee
could be made and served in the same way as it might
have been in a tent. It was a statement that her prospec-
tive host respected the old ways from the far-off years
when the Marabani had been nomadic tribesmen. She
pushed the piece of glass into her bag.

'Qu'est-ce que vous desirez, madame?'

Startled, Saffy turned her head to see a youthful
maid eager to do her bidding, and well did she recall
that sinking sensation at the familiar sound of the French

language, which was more commonly spoken in Maraban than English. For a girl who had dismally failed her GCSE French exam, communicating in French had been a major challenge five years earlier.

'*Apportez des refraîchissements*...bring refreshments,' another voice interposed in fluent accented French as smooth as honey warmed by the sun. 'And in future use English to speak to Miss Marshall,' he advised.

Tiny hairs prickling eerily at the base of her skull, her eyes huge and her slim body trembling, Saffy stared in disbelief at the man in the doorway. In the corner of her eye the maid bent her head, muttered something that sounded terribly servile and backed swiftly out of the room through another exit.

'*Zahir...?*' Saffy framed in shaken disbelief.

CHAPTER TWO

'WHO ELSE?' ZAHIR enquired silkily as she backed away small step by small step.

Saffy's heart was in her mouth and she was desperately short of breath because her every instinct for self-preservation was pumping full-blown panic through her tall, slender length. Zahir? Zahir, the King of Maraban. *He* was responsible for bringing her to the castle/fortress/palace, whatever it was? *He* was the host who wanted her to enjoy his hospitality for the weekend? What kind of sense did that make for a male who had divorced her five years ago and never once since alluded to their former relationship in public?

Yet he stood there, effortlessly self-assured in a black cotton shirt and jeans, a casual outfit that however emanated designer chic, for both garments fitted his very tall, well-built frame to perfection. He was one of the very few men Saffy had to look up to even in heels because he was several inches over six feet. Unhappily the sheer impact of his unexpected appearance shattered her renowned composure. For so long she had told herself that memory must have lied, that if she were to meet him again she would not be so impressed as she had been at the tender age of eighteen. And yet there he stood, defying her every ego-boosting excuse. Luxuriant hair with the blue-black shine of polished jet accentuated his absolutely gorgeous face, drawing her attention to the slash of his high exotic cheekbones, the proud arch of his nose, the stubborn jut of his strong jawline and the beautifully defined, wide, sensual fullness of his mouth. He had the lean powerfully athletic physique of a Greek god. And the fiercely stunning dark eyes of a jungle predator. He wasn't safe; she saw that now. Zahir was not a man who played safe or who gave his woman the freedom to do her own thing, not when he had come to earth convinced of the fact that he always knew best. She had been way too innocent at eighteen and yet already damaged, she conceded painfully, much more damaged than either of them could ever have guessed. In spite of the surge of disturbing memories, butterflies still leapt and fluttered in her tummy at the stirring sight of him: dear heaven, she acknowledged in even greater shock, he could *still* rock her world.

In defiance of that disturbing conviction, Saffy flung her head high, shining layers of wheaten blonde hair sliding like heavy silk back from her face and tumbling off her shoulders. '*You're* responsible for bringing me here?' she demanded shakily, her voice embarrassingly breathy and insubstantial from the level of incredulity still gripping her. 'Why on earth would you do that?'

Eyes of heavenly blue clung to Zahir's lean dark face. His astute dark eyes narrowed, hardened, kindled to burning gold as he allowed himself a slow steady appraisal of her lithe figure. Tall and slim she might be, but unlike many models Sapphire had womanly curves and the fine cotton T-shirt she wore could not hide the high pouting curve of her breasts or their beaded tips, any more than her white linen trousers concealed the long supple line of her thighs, the delicious peachy swell of highly feminine hips below her tiny waist or the dainty elegance of her narrow ankles. The pulse at his groin kicked up hell in response and he clenched his teeth together, willing down that threat to his self-possession. If he was honest he had expected to be a little disappointed with her when he saw her again face to face, but if he was equally honest she was even more staggeringly lovely now than she had been as a teenager. Shorn of a slight hint of adolescent chubbiness, her flawless bone structure had fined down.

Zahir surveyed her with smoulderingly bright eyes, instantly resenting her effect on him. 'Since we parted, you've cost me over five million pounds. Maybe I was curious to see what I was paying for. Maybe I even thought I might be due something in return…'

Angry resentment surged from the base of Saffy's insecurity and discomfiture. How dared he talk back to her as if he had done nothing wrong?

'Just you stop right there… Are you out of your mind?' she blazed back at him full tilt. 'What the heck gives you the right to bring me here when I don't want to be here?'

'I wanted to speak to you.'

'But we've got nothing to talk about!' Saffy scissored back without pausing to draw breathe. 'I never expected to see you again in this lifetime and I don't want to speak to you, not even to find out why you're talking about five million pounds that I certainly didn't receive!'

'You're a liar,' he retorted quietly, using that deadly quietness he had always had the power to deploy once he had got her to screaming point. It was impossible to deflect Zahir from his target.

'I have to ask—on the score of the five million pounds you mentioned—what planet are you living on? I haven't had a penny from you since I started working!' Saffy snapped out of all patience while desperately trying to recapture her cool and with it her wits.

'Denial won't cut it,' Zahir scissored back with cool contempt. 'I have paid you substantial alimony since the day you left Maraban—'

'No way!' Saffy sizzled back at him, enraged by his condemnation. After all, she was very proud of her independence and of the fact that she had never taken advantage of his great wealth, believing as she had that their short-lived and unsuccessful marriage gave her no right to expect his continuing support. 'That is a complete lie, Zahir. You gave me money when I first left and I needed to use that until I started earning. But I never wanted alimony from you…I told my solicitor that and he must have informed you.'

'No, since your departure the money has been paid every month into a trust fund and none of it has ever been returned,' Zahir informed her with infuriating certainty. 'But at this moment I should warn you that that may not be your most pressing problem.'

Saffy gritted her teeth. She was shaking with rage and shocked by the speed with which her usually easy temper had gone skyward. She had forgotten, oh, dear heaven, she had actually forgotten how easily Zahir could push her buttons. 'Why? What may be my most pressing problem?' she slung back scornfully, hot pink adorning both her cheeks.

'You and your colleagues shot your commercial without first lodging a request for permission to do so from the Ministry of the Interior.'

'I know nothing about that!' Saffy proclaimed in instant dismissal of the charge. 'I've got nothing to do with the legal requirements or arrangements for filming abroad—I'm just the model. I go where I'm told and you had better believe that Maraban was the last place on earth I wanted to come!'

Zahir tensed, an even brighter sliver of gold lightening his dark eyes. 'Why so? Maraban is a beautiful country.'

'Surely that view depends on your standards of beauty?' Saffy snapped back with lashings of scorn. 'Maraban is eighty per cent desert!'

The gold effect in his eyes heightened to flame level. 'Had you still been my wife I would have been ashamed of your narrow outlook!'

Saffy loosed a cutting laugh. 'Mercifully for me I'm no longer your wife!'

The insult made him tense even more, his big shoulders squaring, the wall of his strong abdominal muscles tightening visibly below his shirt. His eyes held her fast, held her as completely as if he had her pinioned to a wall, those extraordinarily beautiful eyes of his set below well-defined ebony brows, eyes rimmed with thick curling black lashes and stormily bright with aggression. 'Mercifully for us both,' he murmured levelly.

Inexplicably his agreement wounded her and she sucked in a sudden surge of air to fill her deflated lungs in the seething silence and decided to concentrate on basics. 'So the shoot took place without permission from some authority—what does that mean?'

'That the film was confiscated at the hotel where you and the crew were staying,' Zahir advanced grimly.

Saffy took a hasty step forward. '*Confiscated?*' she repeated in horror. 'You can't do that!'

'I can do anything I like when people break the law in Maraban,' Zahir responded levelly. 'Filming was not authorised.'

'But you have the power to overlook it. I'm sure the company just made a mistake if they didn't seek permission. The location was changed at the very last minute—there probably wasn't time!' she protested. 'Is that why you've brought me here? To tell me this?'

'No...I wanted to see you again,' Zahir confided with shocking cool.

And she remembered the shock of that honest streak of his, his ability to cut through all the rubbish people could spout and hit the bottom line without hesitation or embarrassment. 'Why would you want to see me again?' she prompted stiltedly.

'You only have to look in the mirror to know why,' he fielded without skipping a beat. 'I want you. Just once I want what should have been mine when I married you and what you have since given to other men...'

Shock engulfed Saffy in a tidal wave. She moved back from him again in dismay, disbelief and bewilderment. Her ex wanted her to have sex with him?

'Unless, of course,' Zahir murmured silkily, 'you truly *do* find me physically repulsive...'

Saffy backed away another step, thinking that there was surely not a woman alive who could find Zahir repulsive. She certainly didn't; never had, in fact. Was that the impression she had left him with? Guilt rippled through her, for she was agonisingly aware that he could not possibly have overcome her problems for her five years earlier. It had taken years of therapy for Saffy to find the solution and to come to terms with what she had learned about herself during the process.

'If you can convince me that you do, I will let you go,' Zahir purred, literally stalking her across the room with fluid steps.

Zahir wanted to sleep with her. So, tell me something new, a wry little voice said inside her head. It was like being plunged back into her marriage without warning, unable to give him what he wanted and needed. The most appalling sense of inadequacy gripped her afresh. She had failed him and not surprisingly he was bitter. But that was no excuse whatsoever for his current behaviour. 'You virtually kidnapped me!' she accused rawly.

'I sent you flowers and an air-conditioned limo. How many kidnappers do that?'

'You've got to be crazy... I mean, are you even thinking about what you're doing?' Saffy gasped, stepping back against a piece of furniture and sidling sideways to avoid it and to keep moving further out of his reach.

'I don't *think* around you,' Zahir muttered flatly. 'I never did.'

Saffy was more than willing to kick his brain back into gear. 'Zahir, you're a king...royalty doesn't do stuff like this!'

Zahir flung back his darkly handsome head and laughed with rich appreciation, even white teeth flashing against his bronzed skin. 'Sapphire...my father kept a harem of a hundred concubines in this palace. Until very recently indeed, royalty did indeed do things that were neither socially nor morally acceptable.'

'Your father? Had a *harem* here?' Saffy parroted in consternation, her heart beating so fast as he stalked closer that she was convinced it might burst right out of her chest. She refused even to think of that nasty old man, Fareed, having had a hundred unfortunate women locked up to fulfil his gruesome requirements. It wasn't a surprise though: her father-in-law had been an out-and-out lech.

'I have no harem...no wife,' Zahir pointed out.

'Those are the only positives you have to offer in your own favour?' Her voice was careening up and down as if she were on a vocal seesaw. She was locked into his eyes, those amazingly beautiful amber eyes, which had struck her like a thunderbolt at eighteen across a crowded department store. 'Stay back...'

'No, been there, done that, paid the price,' Zahir countered, running a forefinger slowly down over her cheekbone so that in some strange way it seemed perfectly normal to turn her cheek into his hand.

Saffy looked up, clashed with his eyes, experienced a light-headed sensation that did nothing to collect her wits, and swallowed painfully. How could he be so gorgeous that she couldn't breathe? Why was it as if the world had stopped turning and had flung her off into space? She was completely disorientated by his proximity, the very heat she could feel filtering from his lean powerful body towards hers even though their only connection was the hand resting against her face. 'Zahir?'

He lowered his proud dark head. He's going to kiss me, he's going to kiss me, a crazily excited voice chanted inside her head and both anticipation and denial warred inside her. And then he *did,* firm, sensual lips circling hers, the pressure steadily deepening even as a shriek alarm of shock shrilled through her trembling body. He parted her lips, let his tongue dart between and it felt like the most erotic caress she had ever experienced because the taste and the flicker of movement inside her mouth were indescribably sexy. Heat burned in her pelvis, her nipples swelling taut, abrading the cotton covering them. That intoxicating intense physical reaction was exactly what she had wanted to feel for a long time but he was the very last man on earth she wanted to feel it with.

And yet she couldn't will herself to break free while his tongue tangled with hers, touching, tasting, *savouring,* a low growl breaking from his throat while his fingertips stroked her neck where it met her shoulder. Unholy pleasure was ricocheting through her treacherous body as it awakened to sudden life, hot, damp sensation tingling at her feminine core while her breasts swelled and ached. Gathering every atom of her strength, she pushed her hand forcefully against a wide muscular shoulder and broke free. 'No...no, I don't want this!'

His gaze filled with sardonic amusement, Zahir studied her hectically flushed face with satisfaction. 'Liar,' he said thickly. 'You always liked my mouth on you.'

Saffy felt the rush of heat below her skin and momentarily closed her eyes while she blocked him out and fought for recovery. He was a demon kisser. That far, *they* had worked and the chemistry had misleadingly suggested a match made in heaven. In that instant, she loathed him for bringing the past alive again and reminding her of exactly what she yearned to find in another man's arms. Frustration filled her. Been there, done that, as he had said, although they hadn't actually *done it.* Did he feel cheated? Was that why he had brought her here? Why did he think that anything would have changed between them? It was not as if he knew what she had gone through in search of a cure. Crushing out that torrent of curious questions and musings, Saffy concentrated on the here and now.

'I want transport to the airport and the film that was confiscated,' she told him drily, straightening her slender shoulders to stand up to him.

Zahir viewed her from beneath the cloak of his lush black lashes, dark eyes bright as stars. 'It's not happening.'

'Then what would it take to make it happen?' Saffy prompted, determined to sort the situation out by taking the practical approach that generally served her well in difficult situations. 'That missing money you mentioned? I promise I'll look into that mystery and sort it out as soon as I get back to London.'

'Don't try to avoid the real issue here—I want *you...*'

Her mouth ran dry and her skin ran hotter than hot as he lounged back against the wall beside him and she noticed, really couldn't help noticing by the close fit of his jeans that he was aroused. She turned her head away, her tummy flipping even as she recognised the healthy discovery that the awareness of his arousal no longer made her feel threatened. 'But we can't always have what we want,' she pointed out tautly, hanging onto her cool with difficulty. 'And you know that bringing me here is crazy. Your people would be scandalised by this set-up.'

'I'm a single man and not a eunuch.'

'You're also intelligent and fair—at least you used to be,' Saffy countered with determination.

'Then you will understand that I seek justice.'

'Because you didn't get either the wedding night or the bride of your dreams you think you can magically turn the clock back?' Saffy lifted a fair brow. 'Good luck with that without a time machine.'

'You're *staying*,' Zahir declared with razor-sharp emphasis. 'And I don't want the girl you were five years ago. I want the woman you are now.'

'But the woman I am now is living with another man,' Saffy slotted in curtly, shooting the last bolt in her rejection routine, which she usually regarded as worth using only at the last ditch but his sheer persistence was ruffling more than her feathers

'And he shares you with whomever you choose to stray with,' Zahir retorted, unimpressed, his wide sensual mouth compressing with speaking derision.

Saffy stiffened as though he had slapped her in the face. Evidently he had come across the silly stories about her that the tabloids printed and believed them, actually believed that she slept around whenever she felt like it. But then she had only to be pictured emerging from a man's apartment for the press to assume she was engaged in an affair, but the truth was that she had some very good male friends, whom she visited, and had learned to treat the reports with amusement, for there was really nothing she could do to stop lies about her appearing in print. That, she had learnt, was the price of a life lived in the public eye.

'That is not true. Cameron and I are very close. He's my best friend,' Saffy admitted, throwing her head high, reluctant to lie to him about that relationship but happy to take advantage of his ignorance if it acted as another barrier between them.

'I don't want to be your best friend. I want to be your lover.'

Saffy's lovely face snapped tight and turned pale. 'And we both know how that panned out five years ago,' she reminded him flatly. 'Let me go, Zahir. Bringing me here is reckless and illogical.'

Zahir studied her with veiled eyes, a grimly amused smile tugging at the corners of his handsome male mouth. 'Perhaps that's why it feels so good.'

Saffy had shot her last reasonable bolt and she was stunned by his indifference. 'You don't know what you're saying.'

'I have never been so sure of anything,' he shot back in rebuttal.

The last string of restraint broke free inside Saffy. She had had a very long, hot and tiring day and now Zahir was plunging her into the nightmare of her better forgotten past. 'But you can't be serious…you can't *really* intend to keep me here against my will!'

'I will do nothing that causes you harm,' Zahir replied stubbornly.

'But keeping me here against my will is causing me harm! What gives you the idea that you can do this to me?' Saffy lashed back at him, her temper finally slipping its leash and her voice rising on a shrill note.

'The knowledge that I have achieved it. Your colleagues have been informed that you have accepted a private invitation to spend another few days in Maraban. Nobody will be looking for you or concerned that anything is amiss,' Zahir asserted with satisfaction.

'You *can't* do this to me!' Saffy erupted, infuriated by his self-assurance, his evident belief that he had covered all bases. 'And why? Nothing's going to happen between us. You're wasting your time!'

'No man looking at you could possibly believe that I was wasting my time in at least trying,' Zahir drawled with husky appreciation, his golden eyes resting on her delicate profile with possessive heat. 'It is a risk I take with pleasure.'

'But I *don't!*' Saffy slammed back at him in furious rebuttal. 'I didn't agree to this. Nobody tells me what to do or makes me stay somewhere I don't want to be and nothing on this earth is capable of persuading me to get into bed with you again, so you can forget that idea right now!'

'I will call Fadith to take you to your room…' Zahir pressed a button on the wall with a graceful brown hand, his bold profile set in uncompromising lines.

In outrage that he wasn't even taking heed of her objections, Saffy swept up a china vase on a stand and pitched it at him. It fell short and smashed against the edge of the fire pit to break into a hundred pieces.

Zahir enraged her by turning his handsome dark head and treating her to a slashing smile of very masculine amusement. 'Ah, that takes me back years. I had forgotten how you liked to throw things at me when you lost control of your temper. I will see you later when it is time to dine.'

And with that very cool and unruffled assurance, Zahir strolled out of the room and left her standing there in a tempestuous rage that she could do nothing more to vent with her target gone. Trembling from the force of her pent-up feelings, Saffy breathed in deep to find inner calm. He would pay; she would *make* him pay for this in spades!

CHAPTER THREE

FADITH REAPPEARED AND led the way down a corridor and up a flight of pale marble stairs. Shown into a room as traditionally furnished and comfortable as the room she had seen downstairs, Saffy breathed in deep. The furniture was ebony inlaid with gleaming mother-of-pearl and the bed was a fantasy four-poster hung in swirling silk that piled opulently on the floor at each corner. Saffy wandered into a bathroom with a sunken marble tub and every possible extra and suppressed a groan. As she returned to the bedroom Fadith was removing a tray from another maid's grasp to set it on a table.

'Thanks,' Saffy murmured, reluctantly lifting the mint drink she recalled from the year she had spent in Maraban. Maraban, the land that time forgot, she reflected grimly. She asked if there was any water and was shown a concealed refrigerator in a cupboard. She pulled out a chilled bottle and unscrewed the cap.

'Would you like a bath?' Fadith asked her then, clearly eager to be of service.

Saffy screened her mouth and faked a yawn before telling an outright lie to get rid of the younger woman.

'Perhaps later. I think I'll lie down and sleep for a while. It's very warm.'

Fadith pulled the blinds and scurried over to the bed to turn it down in readiness before departing. Playing safe, Saffy waited for a couple of minutes before heading off to explore. She had no intention of staying with Zahir and since there was no prospect of her being rescued she had to rescue herself. She walked across the vast landing on quiet feet, passing innumerable closed doors and peering out of windows into inner courtyards before finally heading downstairs. Ignoring the ground floor, she went down another flight into the basement, which she could see by the trolleys of cleaning equipment was clearly the servants' area. It was easy to identify the kitchens from the clatter of dishes and the buzz of voices and she gave it a wide berth. She stared out through a temptingly open rear door at the line of dusty vehicles parked outside while wondering what the chances were of any of them having keys left inside them. She wasn't stupid enough to think that she could walk out of the desert: she needed wheels to get back to the city. Without further hesitation she sped out into the heat and the first thing she saw was a four-wheel-drive full of soldiers at the far side of the courtyard. In dismay she dropped down into a crouch to hide behind a car. Of course there would be soldiers around to guard Zahir while he was in residence, she conceded ruefully. She inched up her head to peer into the car and then twisted to study its neighbour: there was no sign of keys left carelessly in the ignition. Meanwhile the soldiers trooped indoors. Saffy continued her seemingly fruitless search for a car to steal and dived behind a vehicle to avoid being seen when a couple of kitchen staff strolled out of the palace talking loudly.

One of them wished the other a good journey home in Arabic and she recognised the phrase as the young man threw his bag into the pickup and jumped into the driver's seat. He was going home? There was a good chance that he would be driving into the city. For a split second Saffy hesitated while she considered her options. The gates were guarded. It would be impossible for her to drive through them without being detected. Possibly stowing away in a vehicle being driven by a member of staff would be a cleverer move. Before she could lose her nerve, she scrambled over the tailgate and dived below the tarpaulin cover.

But the pickup didn't immediately move off as she had expected. In fact someone shouted to the driver and he got back out of the vehicle. She lay still, stiff with tension, listening to voices talking too fast for her to follow before the steps moved slowly away and she heard the driver moving back. Finally the door slammed again, the engine ignited and she expelled her breath in relief. Her original drive from the road down the track to the palace had been long and rough and lying on the rusty bed of the pickup, Saffy rolled about and wondered if the constant pitching gait of the vehicle would leave her covered with bruises. But she was willing to endure discomfort as the price of having escaped Zahir.

What on earth had come over her ex-husband? Their

marriage had been a train wreck and who in their right mind would want to revisit that?

And the answer came to her straight away. Failure of any kind was anathema to Zahir, whose callous old father had expected his son to excel in every field and who had punished him when he botched anything. Zahir was trying to rewrite the past. Why didn't he appreciate that that was impossible? People changed, people moved on…

Although she had not moved on very far, a tart little voice reminded Saffy, who was bitterly conscious that she was still a virgin. And time rolled back for her as she lay there and the pickup rattled and roared across the sands, threatening to shake her very teeth loose from her gums. Saffy had been eighteen and working at a department-store beauty counter when she first met Zahir. She hadn't wanted to go to university like her twin, had preferred to jump straight into work and start earning. Zahir had travelled to London with his sister, Hayat, who had been shopping for her wedding trousseau. Saffy still remembered seeing Zahir that very first time, her heart jumping inside her, her breath shortening as she collided with the most mesmerising dark golden eyes she had ever seen. Hayat had bought cosmetics while Saffy stared fixedly at Zahir and Zahir stared back equally transfixed at Saffy. She had never felt anything that powerful, either before then or since: an exhilarating and intrinsically terrifying instant attraction that swamped her like a fog, closing out the rest of the world and common sense.

'I will meet you after you finish work,' Zahir had told her in careful English.

He had told her that he was an army officer in Maraban. He hadn't told her that he was a prince or the son of the ruler of Maraban. She had had to look up Maraban online to find out where it was and her mother, Odette, with whom she had briefly lived at the time, had laughed at her and said, 'Why worry? He'll be gone in a few days and you'll never see him again.'

Initially Saffy had been desperately afraid of that forecast. After only a handful of dates, she had fallen for Zahir like a ton of bricks and she had been ecstatic when he told her he would be back the following month to attend a course at Sandhurst. She remembered little romantic snapshot moments from that period: sitting in a park below a cloud of cherry blossom with Zahir brushing a petal out of her hair with gentle fingers; lingering over coffee holding hands; laughing together at mime artists in the street. From the outset, Zahir had had the magic key to winning her trust, for, unlike previous boyfriends he didn't grab and grope and didn't expect her to leap straight into bed with him. At the same time, though, he was chary of the part-time modelling she was already doing, even when assured that she didn't do nude or underwear shots. She had recognised that he was old-fashioned in a way that had gone out of fashion in her country, but she had very much admired the seriousness of his quick clever mind and his unvarnished love for Maraban. Long before his course was over he asked her to marry him and he told her who he really was. And the news that he was a royal prince had merely added another intoxicating layer of sparkle to the fairy-tale fantasy she was already nourishing about their future together, Saffy conceded sadly.

Zahir had married her in a brief ceremony at the Marabani embassy without any of his family present and without his father's permission. With hindsight she knew how courageous he had been to wed her without his father's consent and she knew he had done it because he had known that his parent would never agree to him taking a foreign bride. Reality, unfortunately, hadn't entered their relationship until she landed in Maraban. Starting with the wedding night during which she panicked and threw up and ending with a daily life more like imprisonment than marriage, their relationship had hit the rocks fast. She hadn't been able to give him sex and neither of them had been able to handle the fallout from that giant elephant in the room. Any sense of intimacy had died fast, leading to backbiting conversations and even more of Zahir's constant absences.

The pickup came to a sudden jolting halt. A door slammed and a burst of voices met her straining ears. As the voices receded she began to snake out from below the tarpaulin, only then appreciating that it was almost dark. That was not a possibility she had factored into her plans and, climbing out of the truck, she soon recognised the second big drawback. It had not occurred to her that the driver might be rendezvousing with his family at a huge multi-roofed tent right out in the desert. Consternation swallowed Saffy whole as she stared round her at what she could see in the fast-fading light. There was no sign of a village, a road or anything else for her to focus on as a means of working out where she was. Biting her lip with vexation, she was pushing her bottle of water into the front pocket of her jeans when a tall pale shape clad in beige desert robes moved out of the tent.

'It's cold,' he said. 'Come inside.'

Disbelieving her ears, Saffy froze and gaped, her eyes straining to penetrate the growing darkness. '*Zahir?*' she exclaimed incredulously. 'What are you doing here?'

With one hand he tugged off the headdress bound with a gold and black circlet of cord and straightened, black hair ruffling back against his lean strong face in the slight breeze, his dark eyes bright as stars in the low light. 'I drove you here.'

'You…*what*?' Saffy gasped in disbelief.

'The security surveillance at the palace is the best money can buy,' Zahir drawled. 'I saw you climbing into the pickup on CCTV and I decided that if anyone was going to take you anywhere it should be me.'

'I've been under that tarpaulin for more than an hour!' Saffy launched at him in a rage of disbelief. 'I was so thrown about under it I'm not convinced my bones are still connected!'

Zahir shrugged without even a hint of sympathy. 'Well, it was your chosen mode of travel.'

'Don't you give me that!' Saffy flung at him through teeth that were starting to chatter because it was extraordinarily cold, but mercifully her temper was still rising like rocket fuel to power her. 'You knew I was in there!'

'Perhaps I thought a little shaking was a just reward for a woman stupid enough to climb into a car driven by a stranger when she didn't even know where the car was heading.'

Such a jolt of rage roared through Saffy that she was vaguely surprised that she didn't levitate into the air like a sorcerer. Her great blue eyes flashed. 'Don't you *dare* call me stupid!' she warned him in a hiss.

Zahir had never been the type to withdraw from a fight. He stood his ground, wide shoulders thrown back, stubborn jaw line set like granite. 'But it was *very* stupid to take such a risk with your personal safety.'

Saffy knotted her hands into fists and clenched her teeth together. 'My safety wouldn't be an issue if you hadn't kidnapped me!' she bit back.

'I kept you safe and I will continue to keep you safe and unharmed until you return to London because while you are here you are my responsibility,' Zahir countered in a tone of crushing finality. 'Now I suggest that you come inside so that you can wash and eat. I don't know about you...but I'm hungry.'

'Mr Practical...Mr Reasonable all of a sudden!' Saffy raged back at him, aggrieved by his unshakeable self-assurance in the face of her violent and perfectly reasonable resentment. 'How could you do this to me? I hate you! Get stuffed!'

Zahir expelled his breath in a slow sibilant hiss.

'When you are ready to be civil again, you may come inside and join me.'

And with that ultimate putdown, he was gone, striding soundlessly into the dimly lit tent and simply leaving her standing there. Saffy stamped her feet in the sand to express her fury and only just resisted an urge to slam her fists up against the metal side of the pickup. What a prune she felt—what a complete and utter idiot! Her bid for freedom had been seen and Zahir had stepped into the driver's seat to ruin her escape attempt. He had made a fool of her and not for the first time. It was many years since Saffy had been so angry, for in general she was the mildest personality around and quite laid back in temperament, but Zahir's dominant gene got to her every time. She gritted her teeth, stretched her aching back and legs and leant back against the pickup. Contrary to her every expectation of the desert, it was absolutely freezing and her tee was so thin she might as well have been naked. She couldn't stop shivering and she rubbed her chilled goose-fleshed arms in an effort to get her circulation going again. Seeing Zahir again seemed to have fried her brain cells.

When she couldn't stand the cold any longer she stalked into the tent, which was even larger than she had appreciated and even offered communicating doorways to other sections. Festooned in traditional kelims, it nonetheless offered sofas in place of the usual rugs round the fire pit. Zahir was being served coffee by a kneeling older man.

'What is this place?' Saffy asked abruptly. 'Where are we?'

'It's a semi-permanent camp where I meet with the tribal sheikhs on a regular basis. Although I know you would sooner be dead than sleep under canvas, it offers every comfort,' he murmured smoothly. 'The bathroom is through the second door.'

A wash of heated embarrassment engulfed Saffy's pale taut face. He was throwing her own words of five years ago back in her teeth, her less than tactful rejection of anything to do with tents and the nomadic lifestyle that had once been customary for his people.

'I suppose it's too much to hope that there's a shower in there?' Saffy breathed tautly.

'No, it is not. Go ahead and freshen up. A change of clothing has been laid out for you.'

Her gaze flickered uneasily off his darkly handsome features, her heart beating too fast for comfort or calm. Straight out of the frying pan right into the fire, she acknowledged uncomfortably as she brushed back the hanging that concealed a normal wooden door and stepped through it into a bathroom that contained every luxurious necessity. She stripped off in haste because even cold as she was she still felt sweaty and grubby, and her white linen trousers had not withstood the journey well. The powerful shower washed the grit from her skin and an impressive array of surprisingly familiar products greeted her on a shelf. Wrapped in a towel, she combed out her wet hair and made use of the hairdryer. Hot running water and electric in a tent?

Had he told her that that was a possibility she would have agreed to the desert trip he had tried to take her on soon after they were married. Or *would* she have? If she was honest, her fear of the intimacies of sharing a tent with him had lain behind her dogged refusal to consider such an excursion.

A silk kaftan lay over a chair with a pair of simple mules beside it. Leaving her underwear with her clothes, she slid into it, wondering what she would wear the following day and where he was planning for her to sleep. There were at least two more doorways leading out of the main tent for her to investigate.

'Are you ready to eat?' Zahir asked.

Eyes widening, she nodded affirmation and spun to look at him. He had shed the robes and got back into jeans. Damp black hair feathered round his lean bronzed features, accentuating those smouldering amber gold eyes surrounded by dense black lashes. Her pulses gave a jump. Butterflies flocked loose in her tummy and she swallowed hard, frantic to shed her desperate physical awareness of him. It seemed so schoolgirlish and immature to react that way after all the years they had been apart and the life she had since led. She was supposed to be calm, sophisticated...in control.

'No table and chairs, I'm afraid,' he warned her, settling down by the flickering fire with animal grace.

'That's OK,' she muttered as a servant emerged from one of the doorways bearing a tray, closely followed by another. 'So, you have a kitchen here.'

'A necessity when I'm entertaining.'

He had mentioned the tribal sheikhs he met up with but Saffy was already wondering how many other women he had brought out into the desert. She *knew* there had been other women. For a couple of years after the divorce and before the overthrow of his father, Zahir had made occasional appearances in glossy magazines with several different beautiful women on his arm. And those glimpses of the new and much more visible life he was leading abroad without her had cut deep like a knife and made her bleed internally. She had known that those women were sharing his bed, entangling his beautiful bronzed body with lissom limbs and giving him everything she had failed to give him. Divorce, she had learned the hard way, wasn't an immediate cut-off point for emotions, even emotions that she had no right to feel.

Zahir watched Sapphire curl up on the sofa opposite, looking all fresh faced and scrubbed clean just the way he remembered her, the way he liked her best, for with her stunning looks she required few enhancements. Her restive fingers toyed with a strand of golden blonde hair and instantly he recalled the silken feel of it sliding against his skin and got a hard-on. He crushed the recollection before it could stray into even more erotic areas and reminded himself that she was a beautiful shell with a cash-register heart. He was not at all surprised that she had dropped the subject of the five million pounds without any acknowledgement or adequate explanation. It might be pocket change to a member of his family, but it still mattered that she had taken so much and given nothing in return.

Perched with a plate on her lap, Saffy helped herself to portions of different dishes and dug in because she was starving. While she ate she studied Zahir from below her lashes, marvelling at the superb bone structure that gave his features such strength and masculinity. From every angle he was glorious. Sitting there, his attention on his plate and quite unaware of her scrutiny, he mesmerised her. Her breasts stirred beneath the silk, the tips growing tender and swollen. She dredged her eyes back to her food, her mouth dry, her heart hammering, images from the past bombarding her. Although consummating their marriage had proved impossible, she had learned how to give him pleasure in other ways. At that thought she shifted uneasily on her seat, moist heat pooling at the heart of her. He had never understood what was wrong with her. How could he have? But he had at least *tried,* assuring her of his patience while he did everything possible to set her fears to rest. Unfortunately her fears had been in her subconscious and not something she could control, fears from a hidden source that she had repressed many years before while she was still a child. All of a sudden she simply could not comprehend why he would bring her back into his life after a marriage that had turned into a hell on earth for both of them.

'Why on earth did you want to see me again?' Saffy demanded abruptly.

He lifted his dark head, stunning golden eyes locking to her. 'Few men forget their first love and you're the one who got away...'

Regret stabbed through her and she flinched, for they had begun with love in spite of the fact that during the year of marital strife that followed they had lost it again. The plates were cleared away and coffee and cakes served. She ate to fill the emptiness inside her, the hollow that never seemed to fill. She couldn't look at him, didn't dare look at him again, knew the temptation was a weakness to be suppressed at every opportunity.

'I wanted to see you again before I remarried,' Zahir heard himself admit in brusque addition, knowing that he would never have trusted himself to see her after that event had taken place.

Her golden head flew up, heavenly blue eyes wide with shock. 'You're getting married again?' she gasped, shattered at the idea although she couldn't have explained why.

Zahir raised a winged ebony brow. 'As yet there is no particular bride in view but there is considerable pressure on me to take a wife. Inevitably I will have to satisfy my people's expectations.'

Some of the tension eased from her taut shoulders and she lowered her head. Of course he would be expected to marry: it went with the territory of kingship. What did it matter to her? Why should the concept bother her? It was not as though she still thought of him as her husband. In fact she was being ridiculously oversensitive and it was time to grow up and don her big-girl pants. Exhaustion engulfed her in a debilitating wave then, reminding her that she had been up since five that morning. A yawn crept up on her and she stood up smothering a yawn. 'I'm incredibly tired…'

Zahir sprang upright and rested his hands on her shoulders to prevent her from moving away. Her mouth ran dry, her heart skipping a beat as she looked up at him, up over that full sensual mouth to the black-lashed golden eyes that wreaked havoc with her insides.

'Tonight you're tired.' His deep dark voice reverberated through her very bones, the husky nuances toying with her nerves like a secret caress. 'I won't touch you…'

Saffy shivered at just the thought of being in bed with him again. The image caught at her and not with the sense of threat that she believed she should have felt. A lazy brown forefinger grazed the length of her delicate collarbone, smoothed a passage up her slender throat while she struggled not to fall in a limp heap at his feet because her knees were threatening to buckle. She couldn't breathe, couldn't think while he touched her, and then he brought his mouth crashing down on hers with a hungry passion that should have frightened her out of her wits, but which instead stormed through her and set her on fire. There was a primitive sense of tightening and dampness between her legs, a sudden painful pulse throbbing through the peaks of her breasts. With every plunge of his tongue she trembled, lost in the hot, electrifying darkness of overwhelming physical sensation.

'Bed,' Zahir muttered raggedly, stooping to haul her up bodily in his strong arms, thrusting back a door with an impatient shoulder. 'I want you wide awake tomorrow.'

He laid her down on a big modern divan dressed in pristine white linen. When he had said, 'bed' in that deep thrilling tone her imagination had exploded into the stratosphere and when he released her again and moved back to the door, she frowned at him poised there in the dim light, black hair tousled by her fingers, the taste of him still on her lips, the sheer call of him to her senses overpowering. She rolled over and buried her hot face in a pillow. No, she didn't have a stupid bone in her body. She was looking for a man—had been for years— but he was not the one, although inconveniently he still seemed to be the *only* one she actually wanted, the only one she could even imagine becoming intimate with.

Angry tears of frustration stung her eyes. After the divorce had destroyed her faith in true love and happy endings, she had licked her wounds for years, terrified of getting into another serious relationship and meeting up with the same problems. But after therapy, she had longed to lose her virginity and have sex with a lover to prove that she was fully cured and had come to terms with her past. She had simply wanted to be *normal* as other women took for granted…how could that be wrong? Or selfish? Or immoral? And she did not need to compound her mistakes by being attracted to a man who had not only hurt her very badly once but who also had plans to marry another woman.

Zahir went for a shower—a very cold one. A great well of burning hunger was consuming him but it was cooled by disturbing memories of Sapphire shaking with unmistakeable fear when he had tried to make love to her during their marriage. Even with all the sexual experience he had painstakingly acquired since then, he was wary and seriously distrustful of the physically encouraging vibes she was putting out. He had been wrong before; why shouldn't he be wrong again? And while a faint sense of wonderment was stirring that he should actually have her in a bed again within reach, no sense of regret yet assailed him. In fact a merciless sense of all-male satisfaction was still driving him hard.

Saffy froze when she heard the door open again and rolled over, ridiculously conscious that her eyelids and her nose were probably pink from the overload of emotion and events that had brought overwrought tears to her eyes. She sat up in honest surprise to stare at Zahir, poised one step inside the door clad in only a pair of black silk boxers. Her throat closed over and she stopped breathing.

'There is only one bed…'

'It's not a problem,' Saffy responded as carelessly as she could contrive, rolling off the bed and yanking the bedspread off the mattress in almost the same movement. 'I'll sleep on the floor, although you *could* have taken one of the sofas.'

'I refuse to do so and you can't sleep on the floor.'

'I can do whatever I want to do,' Saffy told him, rolling herself into the spread and lying down beside the bed as well wrapped up as an Arctic explorer.

'Except when I'm around,' Zahir pronounced in direct challenge, snatching her up from the floor and planting her back on the divan with the strength that came so naturally to him.

'I'm not sharing that bed with you!' Saffy spat at him.

Zahir dealt her a derisive appraisal. 'Even when you already know that you can certainly trust me to hear the word no?' he queried in a very dry reminder.

Hot pink colour washed her lovely face and then receded to leave her pale and stricken. She was crushed by all that went unsaid within that aide-memoire, but equally suddenly she felt foolish making such a fuss about sharing a bed, and she squirmed out of the cloaking folds of the spread to slide below the sheet. 'This is all your fault—you should never have brought me here!'

Zahir almost laughed. She was shouting at him again, fighting with him, and he should have been furious at her lack of respect but he wasn't; he was too busy enjoying the novelty of being treated like an equal by a woman. Sapphire wouldn't bat her eyelashes at him, look down in submission and offer honeyed words of feminine flattery as the other women he met did. He climbed into the bed and lay back against the pillows. With Sapphire's mane of hair tossed all over the pillow beside his, the smell of the shampoo she used wafted into his nostrils, a familiar floral scent she had worn ever since he had known her, and that evocative aroma awakened too much that he would have preferred to forget. Slowly his lean brown hands clenched into fists, the tension in his lean powerful body extreme.

'Well, isn't this cosy?' Saffy mocked, determined not to show weakness again.

'Don't rock the boat...' Zahir purred softly in warning.

'Your English has improved so much,' Saffy remarked acidly, staring up at the boarded ceiling. 'Was that a by-product of your promiscuity with various Western women or did you actually have to study the language?'

His even white teeth gritted. The novelty of her backchat was fast dimming in appeal and he sat up to stare down at her. 'I was *not* promiscuous...'

Saffy stared stonily back at the lean bronzed beauty of his arresting face. 'None of my business.'

Eyes as dark a black and cold as she had ever seen them, he swivelled away from her and turned on his side and she caught a glimpse of his back, and anything else provocative that she might have said was forgotten instantly. Without thought she thrust down the sheet to get a better look. The once-brown silken sweep of his smooth, muscular back was marred with slashed and intersecting lines of scars. Before she could think better of it, she exclaimed, 'What on earth happened to your back?'

In an abrupt movement, Zahir flipped round to lie flat on his back again while colour crawled across his slashing cheekbones because he had forgotten to keep his shirt on. 'Not something I want to talk about.'

'But it looks like you were beaten...*whipped!*' Saffy burst out, unable to stifle her horror at the thought of anyone deliberately inflicting that amount of pain on him. His back must have been shredded to leave scars that deep and extensive.

In the nerve-racking silence, which only Zahir was capable of using like a weapon he switched out the light. She could recall so many times when he had shut her out like that five years earlier, keeping his own counsel, refusing to share his thoughts or even the details of what he did or where he went when he was away from her. He wasn't the confiding type, never had been, was very much made in the iron image of an army officer with the proverbial stiff upper lip. She compressed her lips on the questions tumbling on her tongue. Had he been caught, imprisoned and mistreated during the rebellion that had brought his father down? But surely his status as his father's heir should have protected him on either side of the fence?

Bewildered, even wondering why she should be so curious, Saffy closed her eyes and instead pictured him lounging in his boxers by the door and finally she smiled faintly in the darkness, the more disturbing images banished. He might have acquired a few scars but he was still a vision of bronzed masculine perfection, still her fantasy male from his perfect pecs to his six-pack abdomen and powerful hair-roughened thighs. He would either be highly amused or highly offended to learn that she pictured him when she tried to look sexy in a pose.

CHAPTER FOUR

SAFFY WOKE UP because she was too warm and then went rigid, for at some stage of the night she and Zahir had drifted across the great divide of mattress separating them in the huge bed and it was hardly surprising that she had overheated. Their bodies were welded together like two magnets and, compared to her, he put out the most extraordinary amount of heat. Even more disturbing, however, was the hard male arousal she could feel thrusting against her thigh.

He was always in that state in the morning: she had realised that while she was married to him. But the flush of awareness that shimmered through her was shockingly new, fresh and intensely energising and she shivered. Her fingers flexed against the male bicep they were resting on, colour flashing across her embarrassed face as a hunger to touch him flared deep inside her. It was a supreme irony that in the past, while she couldn't bear him to touch her, she had *loved* to touch him.

Black lashes dark as midnight and effective as silk fans swept up and she collided with stunning golden eyes and knew instantly what he was thinking. She yanked her hand off his strong muscular bicep and snaked back from him but she wasn't quick enough, for Zahir had closed long brown fingers into her hair to entrap her.

'Right at this minute,' he positively purred like a very large predatory jungle cat on the prowl, 'I'm all yours.'

'I don't know what you're talking about!' she said in desperation, a spasm of panic claiming her.

'Want me to tell you what you're thinking about?' Zahir husked. 'Or will I just tell you what *I'm* thinking about?'

'Let me go!' she gasped.

He freed her hair and rolled back.

Low in her pelvis something clenched almost painfully while her nipples tingled into throbbing beads.

'You want me to take care of this myself?' He gestured towards where his erection was evident beneath the sheet, shameless in his enjoyment of her most mortifying yet moment of recollection as if he had somehow worked out exactly what was on her mind.

No, she wanted to flatten him to the bed, kiss her way down the roped muscles of his stomach *and...* With a stifled sound of distress, Saffy leapt off the bed as though she had been bitten and fled from the room to the bathroom. He had *kidnapped* her, deprived her of her freedom and she had been lying there in that bed tempted to reach for him, touch him, caress him with her mouth, watch him reach a climax with pride and satisfaction, the only satisfaction she had ever known in the bedroom, an entirely one-sided stunted thing born of her inability to engage in intercourse.

He was cruel; no, he was gorgeous. She couldn't make her mind up to the extent that in the grip of that struggle she felt semi-insane and, refusing to think, she took care of her more pressing needs instead. A knock sounded on the door when she had finished brushing her teeth with the brand new battery-powered toothbrush set out for her use. After a moment's hesitation, she yanked the door open. Sheathed in jeans and nothing else, Zahir handed her a pile of clothing.

'I was joking.'

'No, you weren't,' Saffy snapped.

Zahir lifted and dropped his lean brown hands and sudden amusement slashed his full sensual mouth. 'Well, I wouldn't have said no…first and foremost, I'm a man and I have some very hot memories of you.'

'H-hot?' Saffy stammered helplessly, taken aback by the word, certain he must have misused it.

Zahir stared at her, taking in the tousled golden hair hanging like a veil round her slim shoulders, the brighter than bright blue eyes, and acknowledged that the embarrassment her entire stance telegraphed was not at all what he had expected from her. She wasn't an innocent any more, so why was she blushing?

'In that department you were very hot.'

Cold tainted her at the meaning of that sentence, the reminder that there had been others intimate with him since their divorce. 'Now that you can make comparisons?'

'Don't take that angle—it's offensive,' Zahir ground out with sudden force. 'If I'd known what I was doing in our bed, we wouldn't have had problems!'

Consternation slivered through her taut length. 'Is that what you thought? That it was somehow *your* fault? You are so wrong, Zahir. There was nothing you could have done to make things any different between us,' she declared with fierce conviction, her innate sense of fairness making her speak up. 'I needed professional help.'

Saffy couldn't believe she was telling him her even a little piece of her biggest secret, but then he had been the only other person who had experienced her problems with her. It shook her that he had blamed his inexperience for *her* failure in the bedroom, but then how could he possibly have guessed what was really wrong with her? Was that why he had come up with the insane idea of kidnapping her? Was that why he still supposedly wanted her? Was that ferocious pride of his still set on rewriting the past and retrieving his masculine pride?

Zahir frowned, his surprise palpable. 'Professional help?'

'Never mind. Like you last night and your back… not something I choose to discuss,' Saffy fielded, because she was extremely reluctant to share her secrets, and indeed was already wondering if he might consider her in some way 'soiled' if he knew the truth. And just at that moment, quite ridiculously in the circumstances, she really *did* value the fact that, in spite of everything, Zahir was *still* attracted to her. It made her feel better about the past, and when she collided afresh with his mesmerising dark golden eyes she was beset by a stark sense of regret and loss. After all, when she stripped all the complications away one fact stood clear: he wanted her and she was still fiercely attracted to him, the guy she had fallen for as a teenager. Did that make her sad and pathetic? Was it the pull of first love that still made her want to reach out to him? Or simply that all-important element of sexual desire that she had not so far managed to find with another man?

And did it really matter? she asked herself, for at last the opportunity to move into the adult world and be a normal woman was being offered to her with no strings attached. If she had sex with Zahir, nobody would ever know about it and she would never see him again... Wasn't this finally the chance for her to achieve the intimacy that she had always longed to experience? Sex was a physical thing, she bargained with herself, and it didn't have to mean anything, didn't have to take place within a defined relationship. Her sister, Kat, was a bit of a prude and had raised her to have a very different outlook...but Saffy had done the serious thing, the marriage thing and the love thing and had ended up broken to pieces inside herself, enduring a pain and insecurity that she had still not managed to overcome. Simple sex would be enough for her, she reasoned in desperation, suppressing her uneasy feelings while telling herself that she was surely old enough and mature enough to follow her own instincts.

'Go back to bed,' Saffy murmured tautly, the momentous decision already made and it was a choice that she felt she could live with. 'I'll join you in a few minutes...'

Zahir's cloaking black lashes lifted on frowning dark eyes of incomprehension. 'What are you saying?'

Saffy shrugged a slender shoulder, putting on a face because her pride was too great to allow him to suspect how insecure and inexperienced she actually was. 'It's only sex, not something worth making a fuss about...'

Taken aback by that blunt statement, Zahir breathed in deep. 'Passion is always worth pursuing.'

'Not in my world,' Saffy countered doggedly, thinking of the many casual affairs she had seen begin and end among her friends, and she doubted that true passion-ripping-your-clothes-off passion—had driven many of them. Loneliness and lust would be a more honest description of their motivation.

Zahir stepped forward, lean brown hands reaching up to curve to her cheekbones and centre her gaze on him. 'If that's true, I find it sad. I want to give you passion.'

'No, you don't,' she whispered. 'You said it yourself. I'm the one who got away and you can't live with that.'

'It's not that simple,' Zahir growled, protest etched in every hard, angular line of his powerful bone structure while he clashed with her beautiful blue eyes, knowing that no other eyes had ever been so very deep a blue that they reminded him of the sky on a hot summer day.

'Don't make it complicated,' she urged, her breath hitching as he angled down his tousled dark head and her lips tingled like a silent invitation.

'It was always complicated with us,' Zahir argued, stubborn to the last.

And Saffy rose up on her toes and angled her lips up to his, eager to stop him talking and treading all over her memories with hob-nailed boots in that obstinate, all-male, infuriating way of his. He kissed her and her heart seemed to jolt to a sudden halt inside her chest. He stole her breath with a kiss of such unashamed passion that she felt light-headed and her legs went weak.

He carried her back to bed, yes, *carried,* her bemused mind savoured, for very few men were physically big enough or strong enough to lift five-foot-ten-inch Saffy off her feet as if she were of tiny and delicate proportions. He captured her mouth again with intoxicating urgency, his tongue delving deep between her lips, and her body sang. Even while doubts and fears about how she would react to what came next were circulating madly in the back of her head, she could feel the supersensitive awareness of desire infiltrating her, sending prickling spasms of warmth across her breasts and a kick of heat down into her pelvis.

'I assumed I would have to seduce you,' Zahir admitted, staring down at her with those amazing eyes and the kind of honesty she had once loved him for.

'It's no big deal,' Saffy countered a tad shakily, wondering if he would assume that she was a slut, always up for the possibility of a little fling with an attractive man when she was on her travels. But what did it matter what *he* thought? she demanded angrily of herself, because what she was planning to do was entirely for her own benefit and nothing whatsoever to do with him. That he would also be getting what he apparently wanted was only an accidental by-product of her decision. She was the one in control, *full* control. This was sex, nothing to do with the softer emotions, because she simply refused to let him screw up her emotions again.

Taken aback by that statement, Zahir frowned again, ebony brows drawing together.

'Call a spade a spade, Zahir!' Saffy snapped, out of all patience. 'Isn't this why you brought me here?'

'You've changed,' he condemned.

'Of course I have…I grew up, realised fairies and unicorns didn't exist, got divorced,' Saffy recited tightly.

And then he kissed her again, his mouth crashing down on hers with angry fervour and, even though she recognised the anger, she was exhilarated by his passion. He tugged her up into a sitting position and before she even knew what he was about he had swept the kaftan off over her head, leaving her naked but for the cloaking veil of her long blonde hair.

'You're still the most beautiful woman I've ever known,' Zahir declared.

And she still wasn't comfortable being naked around him, Saffy registered in dismay, fearful that the embarrassment enveloping her was only a small taster of the discomfiture she had felt in the past with her own body. Casual nudity was the norm behind the scenes at catwalk shows where fast changes of clothing were a necessity and that didn't bother her, but being naked in front of Zahir bothered her on a much more visceral level.

As he studied her a veil of hot red colour blossomed on her skin in a flush that ran from her breasts to her brow.

Long brown fingers lifted to the rounded perfection of pale breasts topped with distended pink nipples and he stroked the tightly beaded tips before he pushed her gently back against the pillows and bent his tousled dark head to put his sensual mouth there instead, suckling at the straining peaks until she gasped for breathe, shaken by even what she recognised to be a relatively minor intimacy. Even so, it was an intimacy that sent arrows of fire hurtling to her womb and her thighs trembled at the thought of what was yet to come. Let it be all right this time, she pleaded inside her head, snapping her eyes shut, seeking to blank out her thoughts lest the old panic take hold of her again.

Zahir couldn't quite believe that this was Sapphire, lying there, admittedly passive but not freaking out. It felt just a little like all his fantasies rolling up in one go and that disturbed him. He didn't know what he had expected and could only recognise how much she had changed while wondering with dark, forbidding fury which of her men had succeeded where he had so comprehensively failed. That mystery burned through his bloodstream like acid and he had to fight it, suppress it and exert iron control not to ask questions and demand answers. On the other hand, what if she was acting like a human sacrifice because that was how she felt?

He tasted her lush mouth with driving hunger, tried and failed to squash that inner question and lifted his head again. 'If you don't want this, tell me,' he told her.

Consternation filled Saffy to overflowing as she registered that evidently she wasn't putting on a very good impression of being a relaxed and experienced lover. She sat up with a start, her pale hands fixing to his smooth bronzed shoulders, blue eyes wide. 'I want this…I want you.'

'Then touch me,' he growled low in his throat, his hunger unconcealed in his star-bright gaze.

And on the edge of fright and uncertainty, she did, smoothing her hands over his warm golden skin, feeling the rope of muscles beneath his hard, flat stomach and his sudden driving tension as she found him with her fingers. Hard and silky and so velvety smooth and large. She gulped at the very thought of what he was going to do with it…*if* she managed—and she *had* to manage, had to be normal for the sake of her own sanity and his.

Zahir groaned with unashamed sensuality, lying back against the pillows, his black hair in stark contrast to the pale linen, eyes half closed and screened by his outrageous black lashes. 'Not too much,' he warned her unevenly. 'I'm too aroused.'

So, she stayed with the touching, her hand trembling slightly while she felt her body progressively warm in a great surging wash of desire. She needed him to touch her, needed that so badly that it hurt yet she was terrified that she might lose her nerve, her control. He hooked a long thigh over hers, nudging her legs apart, and she stopped breathing as if she were a candle being snuffed out, for this was the acid test, the one she couldn't really call and couldn't afford to fail. Long brown fingers smoothed down her thigh as if he knew on some level that, even hungry as she was, she was scared as no adult woman should be scared. After all, it wasn't as though he had ever physically hurt her. She regulated her breathing, cleared her head of such dangerous thoughts, for thinking that way was surely like inviting her phobia back in. He skated through the crisp golden curls on her mound and she bit her tongue so badly she tasted blood in her mouth and she was trembling, all hyped up with expectation, wanting and not wanting in that moment to test her boundaries. *New* boundaries, she reminded herself resolutely.

He kissed her again and she squirmed against him, insanely conscious of that exploring hand touching where she had never been touched in adult memory, rubbing over that wildly sensitive little button that she hadn't even known existed for more years than she cared to recall. Sensation sparked through her, startling in its very intensity, sending another cloud of heat through her quivering length. Before she even guessed what he was about to do, he eased a finger into her and she didn't go off into a panic attack, didn't jackknife back from him as though he had assaulted her. It felt strange to be touched like that, by someone else rather than by herself, but it didn't hurt and it didn't make her feel sick or frightened, and hope rose in a heady gush inside her that she was going to be all right, after all, and the scene was not set for another disaster.

With so much frantic reflection taking place inside her head, it took a minute at least for Saffy to register that she *liked* what he was doing, the sweet rise of sensation fanning through her lower body as his mouth toyed with an achingly sensitive nipple and his fingers delved into the tender wetness of her body. She hadn't expected to like it, she acknowledged, had simply regarded it as something she had to get through, the mountain of her virginal state at nearly twenty-four years of age a complex challenge that had to be conquered solely for her own benefit.

'I want you so much but you're very tight, *aziz*.' Zahir groaned, snaking down her body, and she didn't know what he was doing and almost yelped in dismay when he put his carnal mouth between her parted thighs instead, caressing the sensitive pink folds of her femininity.

Saffy lay there like a stone dropped to the bottom of a very deep well, so far out of her depth she felt lost, indeed shattered by the gathering waves of increasingly powerful sensation that he was wringing from her untried body. The wave gathered her up and kept on pushing her higher until she was pulsing and throbbing and aching with an excitement that she had never known existed. Her hips were rising, her back was arching and then suddenly, with very little warning, the instant she had most feared was there: his bold shaft was nudging against her for penetration and she tensed, struggling not to freeze, but every skin cell in her body was gripped by nerves that her body might bottle out and let her down at the worst and most unforgivable moment.

And then she experienced the delicious friction of his entry eased by the slick dampness of her arousal.

He was pushing, stretching her inner sheath with the hard, demanding pressure of his entrance and she was briefly amazed at what he felt like inside her. Instinctively she lifted her pelvis and he plunged forward and then it was done, a sharp stinging pain flashing through her so that her eyes widened and she gritted her teeth together, contriving to rein back a cry of pain. She pushed her face up into his shoulder to further conceal her reaction. He had no entitlement to the privilege of learning that, against all odds, he had become her first lover, and there was not much she would not have withstood to keep him from that knowledge. On that ungenerous thought a spasm of intense pleasure took her quite by surprise as her inner muscles tightened their grip on his intrusion.

With a low growl of satisfaction that vibrated his chest against her soft breasts, he began to move, pulling out, pushing back in. The strange seductive sensations built and she gasped, feeling her control sliding against the onslaught of a wild excitement she hadn't anticipated. Excitement roared through her, her heart hammering while she panted for breath. He lifted her legs over his shoulders, rising up over her like a conquering god, his lean darkly handsome face flushed and taut with driving desire and uninhibited satisfaction while he drove into her hard and fast with a pagan rhythm that put her every sense on overload.

Nothing had ever felt so good or so necessary to her. Had he stopped she would have screamed. He touched the tiny button below her mound again, rubbing fast, and the golden light already expanding inside her burst through into brilliance and exploded in a series of violent aftershocks throughout her body. The waves of hot, sweet pleasure racked her with compulsive shivers of disbelief and a certain amount of awe, for she had never dreamt that he might make her feel so much. He shuddered over her with a moan of intense masculine satisfaction and then fell still, letting her legs fall back down on the bed and rolling off her to pull her close.

'That was absolutely amazing,' Zahir breathed, his diction ragged, his accent pronounced, his chest still heaving against her as he pulled her close, their bodies damp with perspiration and sliding against each other.

But Saffy's sense of perfect peace lasted for only a few seconds. What struck her as *most* amazing at that moment was how much other women must have taught him, how much practice he must have had in other beds to have gained the sexual expertise he had just demonstrated. That fast she wanted to thump him hard and kick him out of bed and her hands knotted into fists of restraint below the sheet. Careful, she told herself in fierce and bemused rebuke, for she didn't recognise the feelings bombarding her. He was her ex-husband, not her lover, and she wasn't jealous or possessive where he was concerned. He meant absolutely nothing to her and she didn't understand why he was still holding her and pressing a kiss to her delicate jaw bone as though they had shared something special. After all, she had just used him to have sex for the first time and he had been good...well, *amazing,* to borrow his word. But that was an acknowledgement that only made her fists knot tighter and her temper flare even higher, for nothing could have been more different from the tentative and inexperienced young husband she remembered than the uninhibited demonstration of raunchy sex he had just treated her to.

Without hesitation, indeed reacting on pure gut instinct, Saffy pulled free of Zahir and slid off the bed in one strong movement, a mane of rumpled golden hair falling round her pale slender length like a veil. 'Do I qualify for a car to the airport now?' she asked thinly, blue eyes cold as the polar wastes.

Raking long brown fingers through his black hair, Zahir sat up in the tangled sheets, the white linen providing a striking foil for his golden skin. He tensed and swore and, assuming his reaction was the result of her sudden exit from the intimacy of the bed, she flicked him a bitter glance. Yes, he was still unquestionably gorgeous, but she hated him, totally hated him, wanted to be gone now as fast as possible, escaping the scene of the crime. No doubt he thought *he* had used her but it was the other way round and she would have liked the freedom to tell him that, but was still not prepared to spill her deepest secrets to him.

'I want you to stay until tomorrow,' Zahir admitted in a low-pitched tone evocative of anticipation.

Her blue eyes flashed. 'No. I'm done here. I want to go home right now.'

Zahir, gloriously unaccustomed to being in receipt of a negative female response since his divorce, stared back at her with faint but perceptible hauteur while he wondered what had gone wrong. 'I don't do one-nighters.'

Her lovely face without expression, Saffy dealt him an impatient glance, eyes as unemotional as stones. 'I do and, as I said, I'm done.'

Determined not to meet his gaze, Saffy focused on the neat pile of freshly laundered clothes sitting on a chair and wondered when they had arrived, where they had contrived to get washed and ironed and when they had been returned, for all of those inconsequential thoughts were safer than thinking about the insane passion she had just shared with Zahir. She scooped her clothes up and headed at a brisk pace for the bathroom.

Zahir leapt out of bed and reached the door a step ahead of her, one brown hand bracing on the door to keep it shut. 'There's something I should tell you first.'

Refusing to look directly at him, Saffy grimaced. 'What?' she asked impatiently.

'The condom I used broke…I suspect I was too passionate. I assume that you're on the contraceptive pill and that there's no risk of conception?' he pressed with the evident belief that that was the natural order for a woman like her.

For a split second her eyes narrowed and she paled as she assimilated that shocking information, suddenly grasping what had most probably provoked his curse mere minutes earlier, and although a chill of dismay gripped her she nodded immediate agreement. 'Of course,' she lied, wanting him to believe that she was already taking that precaution against pregnancy because she slept with other men, for that belief best conserved her pride. And she also knew how much that belief would annoy him…for he was possessive to his backbone. At least, he *had* been when she knew him, she qualified grimly, but who could say what drove him now? Five years' separation, a lot of other women and possession of a throne had changed him: of course, they had. It would be very naïve of her to think otherwise.

'I'll organise transport,' Zahir breathed grittily. 'And see that the film shot of the commercial is also delivered to you before you depart.'

'Is that my reward?' Saffy enquired drily, concealing her relief that he was willing to hand over the film, well aware that the film crew and her clients would be going mad over its confiscation.

His handsome features clenched. 'If you choose to see it that way—'

'Oh, I do,' Saffy asserted, watching gold glimmer like a flame in his dark as midnight eyes and loving the burn of it, knowing she had annoyed him as he threw open the door for her to leave the bedroom section of the tent. 'And while I remember it, I would advise you to look more closely into the disappearance of that five million pounds you mentioned—because I'm telling you now, I didn't receive a penny of it!'

Zahir inclined his arrogant dark head in grudging acknowledgement. 'I will have the matter investigated,' he conceded, coldly formal in tone.

Was he offended that she hadn't appeared to want a repeat of their intimacy? Saffy stepped into the shower and washed her skin clean of the scent of him. She felt sore, every movement of her lower limbs reminding her of his passionate possession. It was done. She was no longer a virgin. She had surmounted her fears. She was *finally* a normal young woman and now in a condition to consider a relationship as a potential part of her future. That was good, she told herself firmly. She forced her stiff facial muscles into a determined smile and had just wrapped a towel round her dripping body when a knock sounded on the door and heralded Zahir's reappearance, his lean bronzed body still clad only in boxer shorts.

'Yes?' Saffy prompted tightly, not having wanted to see him again because seeing him hurt, made her think of the other women he had been with and, even though it wasn't fair or even rational when she had been unable to consummate their marriage while they were together and they were now divorced, she hated him for having found pleasure and satisfaction when she could not.

'I must have hurt you…there's spots of blood on the sheet,' Zahir informed her grimly. 'Why didn't you tell me?'

Hot colour flew into her cheeks like a banner of scarlet. It had not occurred to her that there might be any detectable physical proof of her innocence and she was mortified by his discovery. 'You didn't hurt me…er, it's been a while for me, so perhaps that explains it,' she muttered awkwardly through clenched teeth of discomfiture.

'Why has it been a while for you?' Zahir demanded bluntly. 'You live with a man.'

Somehow he contrived to voice that statement in a manner and tone that implied she regularly sold her body on street corners. 'That's my business,' Saffy responded flatly, her eyes veiled.

'You should see a doctor,' Zahir informed her curtly. 'I can contact someone—'

'No, thanks.' Her cup of humiliation now truly running over and threatening to drown her, Saffy moved towards him and opened the door for his exit. 'Excuse me, I'd like to get dressed.'

'Sapphire…' Frustration stamped on his lean dark features, Zahir glowered down at her, smouldering golden eyes alight. 'Why are you behaving like this? Is this a habit of yours? Do you often indulge in casual sex?'

She refused to look at him and her lush mouth compressed so hard that her lips turned bloodless. 'That would be kissing and telling, which I definitely *don't* do.'

CHAPTER FIVE

SAFFY RESTED BACK in her cream leather reclining seat in Zahir's incredibly opulent private jet, but beneath the skin her every muscle was tense and she could not relax.

Even so, Zahir had certainly ensured that she was travelling back to London in style. She frowned at the acknowledgement because she would have preferred to consign every image and conversation of the past twenty-four hours to a mental dustbin sealed with a good strong lid. She had slept with her ex, no big deal, she told herself with rigorous resolve. It was only a major event for her because having sex had been something she had, until relatively recently, been afraid she couldn't ever do. *She* had used *him*. That was how she had to look on what had happened. If he knew that his temper would have gone nuclear because Zahir expected everything on his own terms. In that spirit he had married her and in the same spirit he had decided to divorce her again. Nothing had ever been equitably discussed: he had been happy to make his mind up for both of them.

Five years ago, they had landed in Maraban as a newly married couple and that too had been very much on his terms, with her not having the first clue about the dysfunctional royal family she had joined. His father, King Fareed, had been livid that his younger son had married a foreigner and had initially refused to even meet her. She had met Zahir's older brother, Omar, and his wife, Azel. Omar had died in a car crash a few months after Saffy arrived. As Omar and his wife had been childless, Zahir's importance to his father had mushroomed once he became the heir-in-waiting and Saffy had seen even less of her husband as he was forced to take on the ceremonial roles that had once been his brother's.

Staying in the royal palace just outside the city limits, Saffy had been sentenced to a very boring and hidden existence. As her father-in-law refused to accept her as part of the family and was determined to keep the presence of a Western blonde in the palace a secret, she had not been allowed to go out and about in Maraban and explore freely. Indeed aside of a few stolen shopping expeditions in the company of her widowed sister-in-law, Azel, Saffy had barely gone out at all. Zahir had declared that *eventually* his father would accept her as his wife but that she would have to be patient. But twelve months living like the invisible woman had convinced Saffy that her marriage had been a major mistake, particularly when things between her and Zahir had gone badly awry as well.

'You're very unhappy here,' Zahir had acknowledged the very last time she saw him during their marriage.

'You've been telling me that you wanted a divorce for the past six months and now I must agree.'

'Just like that you *suddenly* agree?' Saffy had yelled at him incredulously, shock at his change of heart winging through her in sickening waves as she realised he had clearly had enough of her and their marriage. 'But you swore that you still loved me, that we could work it out...'

'But now I want you to go home to London as soon as it can be arranged. I want to divorce you and set you free,' Zahir had countered as stonily as though she had not spoken.

It was true that for weeks whenever they argued she had hurled the threat of a divorce at him on a fairly frequent basis. But she had never really *meant* it, had simply been dramatising herself and struggling to make her young husband take her unhappiness seriously. But she had somehow still expected Zahir to continue to refuse to even consider divorce as the answer to their problems. Coming at her out of the blue like that, his volte-face had shocked her and pleading in the face of his clear determination to get rid of her had been more than she could bear. For so long, regardless of their difficulties, she had clung to her conviction that Zahir still loved her no matter what and that what they had together was still worth fighting for. Deprived of that consolation and cruelly rejected by the divorce that swiftly followed, Saffy had been heartbroken and not surprisingly had felt abandoned.

Her older sister, Kat, who had raised her from the

age of twelve, had tried to comfort Saffy, pointing out that King Fareed's opposition to their marriage must finally have worn Zahir down while reminding Saffy that neither she nor Zahir had foreseen the very real difficulties that would arise in Saffy's struggle to adapt to life in a different country, far from family and friends. Saffy didn't want to remember how appallingly she had missed Zahir after she left Maraban or how many months had passed before she could enjoy the freedom she had reclaimed and stop thinking about Zahir at least once every minute. She had genuinely loved him and it hurt to appreciate that he had moved on from her so much more easily than she had moved on from him. Maybe he had never really loved her, Saffy conceded painfully. Maybe it had *always* been about the sex and only the sex. Certainly, given his behaviour in shipping her out to the desert for seduction, that looked like the most viable explanation. It was equally agonising to admit that had she been capable of doing what she had just done with him five years earlier they might still have been together. Or *would* they have been? Was that just fantasy land? Perhaps all along she had only been a fling in the form of a wife for Zahir.

But didn't she have rather more pressing concerns in the present? What about that contraceptive accident they had had? Saffy tensed, her appetite evaporating in front of the beautiful lunch she had been served as her skin chilled with complete fright at the idea of being faced with an unplanned pregnancy. Once she had believed she would never have children because she wasn't able to have sex or even handle the concept of artificial insemination. Now she knew differently and knew her future had opened up another avenue once barred to her. So, if she did fall pregnant, what would she do about it? She had friends who would rush to request the morning-after pill after such a mishap to ensure that no conception took place, but if against all the odds new life did begin inside her, Saffy registered that she was totally unwilling to consider a termination. In that moment she was suddenly realising with a heart that felt full enough to burst that a baby would mean the sun, the moon and the stars to her and that there was nothing she would cherish more. It might be a disaster as far as her current clients were concerned, but it would only be a short-term one and surely her earning power wouldn't die overnight. She breathed in deep and slow, both terrified and enervated by the risk she was prepared to take with her own body. If conception happened, she decided, it would happen and she would embrace it without regret.

Having dropped off the film of the shoot with the exceedingly relieved production company, Saffy caught the tube back to the two-bedroom apartment she had bought with Cameron. Cameron, a keen cook, was in the kitchen dicing vegetables, but it was the sight of the small brunette perched on the counter chatting nineteen to the dozen to him that startled Saffy.

'*Saffy!*' Topsy cried, velvety somber eyes full of warmth as she leapt off the counter like a miniature whirlwind and threw herself exuberantly into her much taller sister's arms. At slightly less than four feet eleven inches tall, Topsy was tiny. 'I wish you hadn't been away this week. I wanted to go out with you to celebrate the end of my exams!'

Saffy's eyes stung as she gratefully accepted her youngest sister's affectionate hug. Topsy always wore her feelings on her sleeve. At eighteen years of age, having just finished school, Topsy was much less damaged by their disturbed childhood and more outgoing than her older sisters. She was also exceptionally clever and overflowing with an irrepressible joie de vivre that few could resist. Yet as Saffy studied the younger woman she saw shadows below her eyes and a tension far removed from Topsy's usual laid-back vibe and she wondered what was wrong.

'How did you find out that I was back so quickly?' Saffy prompted.

'She's been phoning here every day...I texted her after you called me from the airport,' Cameron, a tall attractive man with close-cropped dark curls, told her from his position by the state-of-the-art cooker.

'I assumed you'd want to stay on at Kat's with Emmie,' Saffy remarked.

'No, Kat and Mikhail are hosting a big dinner tonight and I wasn't in the mood to play nice with loads of strangers,' Topsy confided with a slightly guilty wince. 'And Emmie has already gone home again.'

Saffy's heart sank at that news because it was obvious to her that once again her twin had chosen to dodge meeting her. Her estranged twin was *still* avoiding her, Saffy acknowledged unhappily, wounded by Emmie's

reluctance to even be in her company. Was she that
bad? Was she truly so hateful to her twin? Or was it
a simple if unpalatable fact that her past sins were beyond forgiveness?

'Emmie's gone back to Birkside?' she checked, referring to Kat's former home in the Lake District, the farm-
house her elder sister had inherited from her late father.

Kat was the daughter of their mother Odette's first
marriage, the twins the daughters of her second marital foray while Topsy was the result of their mother's
short-lived liaison with a South American polo player.
By the time the twins reached twelve years of age they
were a handful and Odette had placed all three girls in
foster care. Kat, then in her twenties, had made a home
at Birkside for all three of her sisters and Odette had had
very little to do with her children since then. In every
way that mattered, Kat had become the loving, caring
mother her sisters had never really had.

'*Should* Emmie be on her own up there?' Saffy questioned the younger woman anxiously. 'I mean, it's a
lonely house and now that she's pregnant…?'

Topsy rolled her eyes. 'Emmie always does her own
thing and she has friends up there and a job,' she pointed
out breezily. 'I also think that just at the minute Kat
and Mikhail being so lovey-dovey makes them hard for
Emmie to be around.'

Even while Saffy adored the fact that Kat had found
happiness with a man who so obviously loved her, she
too had felt like a gooseberry more than once in the
couple's company. If her twin's solo pregnancy was the

result of a recent relationship breakdown, Emmie was probably feeling a great deal more sensitive to that loving ambiance.

'Dinner will be ready in ten minutes,' Cameron announced.

'I've got time to get changed, then?'

'Yes. Let's go into your room,' Topsy urged, tugging at Saffy's arm.

A frown indented Saffy's brow at her sister's obvious eagerness to get her alone. 'What's up?' she asked as she closed her bedroom door.

Topsy, all liveliness sliding from her expressive face, sank down on the edge of the bed, hunched her shoulders and muttered, 'I found out something I wasn't prepared for this week and I didn't want to bother Kat with it,' she admitted.

Saffy dropped down on the stool by the dressing table. 'Tell me...'

'You'll probably think it's really silly,' Topsy confided.

'If it's upset you, it's not silly,' Saffy declared staunchly.

Topsy pulled a face. 'I don't know if I am upset. I don't know how I feel about it—'

'How you feel about what?' Saffy prompted patiently.

'A few weeks ago, my dad, Paulo, asked me to agree to a DNA test. I'm eighteen. We didn't need Kat's permission,' Topsy explained as Saffy raised her brows in astonishment at the admission. 'Apparently Dad had always had doubts that I was his child and since he got married he and his wife have had difficulty conceiving—'

'Your dad's got married? Since when? You never told us that!' Saffy exclaimed.

Topsy sighed. 'It didn't seem important. I mean, I've only met him a half-dozen times in my whole life. With him living in Brazil, it's not like we ever had the chance to get close,' she pointed out ruefully. 'Anyway, his new wife and him went for testing when she didn't fall pregnant and it turns out he's sterile.'

Saffy stiffened at the news. 'Hence the DNA testing...'

'And it turns out that I couldn't possibly be his kid,' Topsy confided with a valiant smile. 'So, I went to see Mum—'

Saffy gave her a look of dismay, for Odette was a challenging and devious personality. 'Please tell me you didn't!'

'Well, she was the only possible person I could approach on the score of my parentage,' Topsy pointed out ruefully. 'First of all she tried to argue that in spite of the DNA evidence I *was* Paulo's kid—'

'I doubt if she wanted the subject dug up after this length of time,' Saffy remarked stiffly, cursing their irresponsible and selfish mother and hoping she had dealt kindly with her youngest daughter.

'She definitely didn't,' Topsy admitted with a grimace of remembrance. 'She just said that if Paulo wasn't my father, she didn't know who was. Did she really sleep with that many men that she wouldn't know, Saffy?'

Saffy reddened and veiled her eyes. 'There were periods in her life when she was very promiscuous. I'm sorry, Topsy. That was an upsetting thing for you to find out. How did Paulo react?'

'I think he had already guessed. He didn't seem surprised. Let's face it, I don't look the slightest bit like him. He's over six foot tall and built like a rugby player,' Topsy reminded her companion ruefully. 'Now I'll probably never find out who my father is but why should that matter to me? After all, you and Emmie have a father who lives right here in London but who still takes no interest in you.'

Saffy groaned. 'That's different. Mum and him had a very bitter divorce. She dumped him because he lost all his money. When he built a new life and remarried and had a second family he didn't want anything more to do with us.'

'Does that bother you?'

'No, not at all. You can't miss what you've never had,' Saffy lied, for that was another rejection that still burned below the layer of emotional scar tissue she had formed. When she and her twin had been at their lowest ebb, their father, just like their mother, had turned his back on them and had said he wanted nothing to do with them.

'You're evil...just like your mother. Look what you've done to your sister!' he had told Saffy when she was twelve years old, and even the passage of time hadn't erased her memory of the look of dislike and condemnation in his gaze.

'Sorry to land you with all this,' her kid sister muttered guiltily.

Beyond the door Cameron called them for dinner and Saffy seized the chance to give her kid sister a comforting hug, wishing she had some clever reassurance to offer Topsy on the topic of absent father figures. Unfortunately, not having normal caring parents left a hole inside you and even Kat's praiseworthy efforts to fill that hole for her sisters had not proved entirely successful. Saffy had simply learned that when bad things happened you had to soldier on, hide your pain and deal with the consequences in private.

Only when Topsy had returned to Kat and Mikhail's home for the night with her spirits much improved did Cameron turn with a concerned look in his shrewd eyes to ask Saffy suspiciously, 'What—or should I say *who*—kept you unavoidably detained in Maraban?'

Saffy visibly lost colour. 'It's not something I want to talk about right now.'

'You know that's not a healthy attitude,' Cameron, who was a firm believer in therapy, warned her.

'Talking about anything personal will never come easily to me,' Saffy admitted tightly. 'I spent too many years locking everything up inside me.'

She was extraordinarily tired and she went to bed and lay there with her eyes wide open in the darkness, struggling to suppress the images of Zahir stuck inside her head. Fighting thoughts teemed alongside those unwelcome images. She would get over that little desert rendezvous in Maraban and leave Zahir behind her... in the past where he truly belonged.

* * *

Ten days later, Saffy wakened because while she had slept she had slid over onto her tummy and her breasts were too tender to withstand that pressure. With a wince, she sat up, wondering if it was time to use the pregnancy kit she had bought forty-eight hours earlier, but she was still strangely reluctant to put her suspicions to the test. Could she have enjoyed intimacy just one time and conceived when her unfortunate sister, Kat, had been trying without success to fall pregnant for many months? It struck her as unlikely and she had only bought the test in a weak moment of dreaming about what it might be like to become a mother.

Such silly dreams, *childish* dreams for a grown woman to be indulging in, she scolded herself impatiently, dreams full of fluffy, fantasy baby images and not a jot of reality. Somewhere deep down inside her a voice was telling her that a baby would be one little piece of Zahir that she could have and cherish, but she was intelligent enough to know that the reality of single parenthood was sleepless nights, cash worries and nobody else to share your worries and responsibilities with. Frustrated by her own rebellious brain, she got up and did her morning exercises, desperate to think of something else. When that didn't work she changed into her sports gear and went out for a run, returning to the apartment drenched in perspiration and on legs wobbly from over-exertion. Stripping, she walked into the shower and washed. She was towelling herself dry when she heard the doorbell buzz. She pulled on her robe and padded across the hall to answer.

She looked through the peephole first and froze, looked again, her heart rate kicking up a storm. *Zahir? Here in London?* Her teeth gritting, she undid the chain and opened the door.

'What do you want?' she demanded sharply.

CHAPTER SIX

'INVITE ME IN,' Zahir commanded.

Saffy was uneasily aware of the two security men standing by the lift, of the status and level of protection Zahir now required as the ruler of Maraban, and the very idea that he was now at risk of becoming a target for attack gave her stomach a sick jolt. She swallowed hard, mustering her defences such as they were. 'No.'

'Don't be juvenile,' Zahir urged, his handsome mouth tightening, his air of gravity lending a forbidding edge to the smooth planes of his lean dark absolutely gorgeous face. 'We have business to discuss.'

'Business?' Saffy parroted, suddenly wishing she hadn't opened the door with wet hair and a face bare of make-up for, deprived of her professional grooming, she felt defenceless.

'I told you that I would investigate the trust fund I set up for you.' Impatience edged his dark deep drawl, energised his stunning dark deep-set eyes with sparks of gold, and as she watched him her mouth ran dry as a bone. 'I have now done so.'

'Oh, the missing money,' she muttered in weak com-

prehension, and she stepped back with stiff reluctance
to open the door, for she didn't want him inside her personal space, didn't want one more memory or associa-
tion with him to further colour her existence.

'Yes, the money,' Zahir said drily, in a tone that suggested that he could have no other reason to roll up on
her doorstep.

She studied him, in a split second memorising sufficient to commemorate his image for life, and she turned
away, colour crawling up painfully over her cheekbones as she led the way into the living room. He wore
a business suit, a beautifully tailored designer effort
that showcased his height and breadth and long powerful legs. He had had his hair cut since she had last seen
him, jet black hair feathering back from lean strong
features to brush the collar of his shirt, the inevitable
stubble shadowing his sculpted mouth and stubborn jaw
line because he needed to shave twice a day. She felt
like a vulture swooping down greedily on every tiny
intimate detail of him and her tummy hollowed with
a sense of dread, for she had never felt so vulnerable.

Zahir focused on the fluid sway of her hips encased
in colourful silk as she moved ahead of him. He guessed
she had just stepped out of the shower and was naked beneath those swirling folds of fabric and he was assailed
by a slew of highly erotic images that sent a surge of lust
shooting straight to his groin. He gritted his even white
teeth and flung his arrogant dark head high. He knew
what he was doing; he knew exactly what he was doing
this time. He might have ditched his sense of honour but

he had made a decision he could live with. Nobody was perfect, nobody followed every rule... Imperfection had suddenly become newly acceptable to him.

Saffy turned round and regarded him expectantly, her gaze slanting out of a direct meeting with his shrewd eyes and focusing on his wide sensual mouth instead. Instantly she felt hunger flare like a storm in her pelvis and perspiration beaded her short upper lip as she fought the weakness and tried to crush it out. But her body, it seemed, had discovered a treacherous life all of its own and she was suddenly aware of the heaviness of her tender breasts and the straining, aching peaks.

'That five million you told me about?' she prompted with deliberate tartness of tone, keen for him to take his leave again.

'My London lawyer set up the fund with your solicitor. But five years ago nobody involved was aware that your solicitor was in the early stages of senile dementia and, sadly, he didn't do his job properly,' Zahir explained grimly. 'You were not informed about the fund as you should have been and when your solicitor took early retirement through ill health, his son took over his legal practice. When the son realised that you were ignorant of the money accumulating every month, he committed fraud.'

'*Fraud?*' Saffy parroted, her bright blue eyes widening.

'He's been syphoning off the funds for his own benefit ever since. I have put the matter in the hands of the police,' Zahir informed her grimly. 'I owe you an apology for accusing you of having excessively enriched yourself since our divorce.'

Saffy lifted her chin. 'Yes, you do.'

'In spite of everything, I did intend for you to have that money as security and I am very angry that you did not receive it,' he admitted shortly. 'It is possible that you would never have become a model had you known that you were already financially secure.'

Saffy blinked in surprise at that suggestion. 'I doubt that. Had I known about the fund, I would have refused to accept it. We were married for such a short time that I didn't feel that you owed me anything.'

'You were my wife and my responsibility. I felt differently,' Zahir disagreed with unblemished cool.

'If you'd still had a large financial stake in my future, I wouldn't have felt free to put our marriage behind me,' Saffy admitted with quiet dignity as she began moving back to the door with obvious intent. 'But since I didn't know about the fund, it hardly matters now. I'm just relieved you've managed to sort it out. Now, if that's all you have to say—'

'No, it's not all. I have something else I wish to discuss.'

Saffy froze in her tracks and slowly turned back to him. 'If it's anything to do with the recent past, it's unwelcome and I don't want to hear it.'

Zahir regarded her with glittering dark golden eyes. 'Tough,' he told her. 'I'm here and you'll listen.'

'Look, that kind of attitude may go down well in Maraban but it leaves me cold!'

'But I don't…leave you cold,' he affixed as if she might be in some doubt as to his meaning.

A flush of pink washed from her long slender throat up in a wave of burning mortification, for to have him throw that in her face was an affront of no mean order. 'I'm not listening, Zahir… I'm going to show you out. I want you to leave.'

Instead he stalked towards her like a prowling jungle cat cornering a prey. 'No, you don't. You're being stubborn. You don't like the tables being turned but you put this ball into my court—'

'No, I didn't!' Saffy exclaimed in angry vexation.

'You came to me willingly—'

'I said I wasn't going to talk about this!' Saffy flung back at him furiously.

Zahir sent the door behind her crashing shut with an imperious shove of one strong hand. 'I have a proposition I want you to consider—'

'No…*no.*' Saffy whipped up her hands to press them against her ears in desperate defiance. 'I'm not listening. You've got nothing to say that I could want to hear.'

Zahir grabbed her hands and yanked them down, retaining a firm hold on her wrists. 'I've already bought you an apartment here in London. You'll move out of this one into it and I will visit you there whenever I am free…'

As simple shock winged through Saffy in a tidal wave her hands went limp in his grasp and she stared up at him wide-eyed with astonishment and no small amount of incredulity. 'An apartment? What on earth are you suggesting?'

'That you leave your current lover and become mine,' Zahir spelt out with barely leashed ferocity. 'I don't want you here with him. I don't care what arrangement you have. I will only come to you if you are mine alone!'

Saffy blinked rapidly, processing his words in disbelief. 'You're insane. Five years ago, you divorced me and cast me off like an old shoe you'd outgrown!' she condemned rawly. 'And now you're asking me to be your mistress?'

Brilliant dark eyes narrowed and he freed her hands. 'That's an emotive label and rather outdated.'

'And yet you've got the nerve to suggest such a demeaning relationship might suit me?' Saffy hissed at him furiously.

'Yes, I have the nerve,' Zahir declared in a driven undertone, his accent very thick. 'I want you to the edge of madness but I won't share you with other men.'

'My goodness,' Saffy said in a sharp and brittle voice. 'Was I that good in the tent?'

'Stop it,' Zahir urged harshly, stroking a stern finger across her parted lips, leaving a tingle in the wake of his warning. 'Don't reduce us both to that level with that tongue of yours. There is no sin in us indulging ourselves in pleasure. Who would it harm? We would be discreet. I would spend as much time with you as I can find to spare.'

But Saffy was still stunned by what he was proposing. A mistress? A kept woman in the background of his life, a *dirty* secret? *Her?* He had to be kidding. Her pride and independence would never allow her to accept such a relationship. Of course, how could he know that? At eighteen she had been loving, clingy and needy and that was probably how he still saw her. Back then marriage and a man she loved had been the zenith of her ambitions. But the more she thought of it the insult of what he was prepared to offer her in the present cut very deep indeed and she could not credit that he would believe even for a second that she could agree to be any man's secret mistress!

'It really is time that you go,' Saffy snapped, throwing her head back, damp golden hair rippling back from her taut cheekbones. 'You've said what you wanted to say and my answer is no. No, no, *no!* I like my life just the way it is.'

'Look at me and tell me you don't want me,' Zahir growled.

And she looked and lingered on those lean, darkly handsome features and lost, blue eyes fearlessly clashing with smouldering gold, and then it was as if a knot were unfurling faster and faster inside her, unleashing a disturbing blast of emotions and responses that shook her inside out. But even then in the midst of that gathering storm she knew that no way would she ever sink low enough to become his mistress. Yes, she wanted him, but no, she would never take what he was offering because the price was too high.

Saffy parted her lips. 'I don't want you enough for that…'

Zahir glowered down at her. 'Liar.'

Saffy tossed her head. 'You can't bully me into giving you the answer you want—'

'I don't bully you. I have never bullied you,' Zahir countered wrathfully.

'You've very domineering.'

'You like it,' he told her with a roughened edge to his voice, lush black lashes low over his gaze as he watched the tip of her tongue snake out to moisten her lower lip.

'I like my men civilised,' Saffy shot back scornfully.

'But you still want me,' Zahir framed with hungry intensity.

'As I said...not enough to become your personal, private slut,' she spelt out succinctly, but her breathing pattern was fracturing, her tension so great as he came closer that it was like a tightening band constraining her lungs.

'Prove it,' he said, backing her up against the wall, winding long brown fingers into her golden hair to anchor her in place, and drew her head up.

Saffy trembled, pink flying into her cheeks. 'No kissing, no anything,' she warned him. 'I won't let you do this to me—'

And being Zahir, who had a lot in common with an express train when he was set on a goal, he simply ignored her, bending his head, nuzzling her throat, licking a delicate path along her collarbone with such erotic skill that the pulse there went crazy. Her hands knotted into fists at her side to prevent herself from touching him even while the lips he had so far ignored tingled and burned for attention.

'And how dare you offer me *that* option?' Saffy continued heatedly, her rancour on that point unforgotten.

'He who does not dare *loses*,' Zahir traded with assurance, welding his hard, demanding mouth to hers in an explosion of passion that sent her heart racing and the blood pumping insanely fast through her veins.

'What the heck are you playing at?' she gasped strickenly, appalled by the insidious weakness spreading through her lower limbs and the glow of heat and yearning firing up low in her pelvis.

'I'm not playing,' Zahir said thickly, returning to plunder her mouth, sliding his tongue in and out between her parted lips and then delving deep in a sensual assault that made tiny shudders rack her tall, shapely frame. He pressed her back against the wall and even through the barrier of the suit she could feel him hard and urgent and ready. 'I want you. I have wanted you every day since you left Maraban... I can't sleep for wanting you!'

And although words were easy to say and often empty, something still quickened and tightened inside Saffy's chest when he admitted that she exerted that much influence over him. Her robe came undone as he jerked it loose, sliding a hand below it to trail his fingers up her inner thigh. Instantly every sense went on red alert. In that moment she wanted him to touch her more than she had ever wanted anything and she went rigid with anticipation, unable to breathe for longing.

She burned; she *ached.* And then with one stroke of his clever fingers he found her and an agonised moan was wrenched from her as he toyed with her tender flesh, rubbing the tiny bud that controlled her until she strained against him, whimpering, quivering, helpless with need while he explored the slick, hot heat between her legs and she gasped under his marauding mouth. Time had no meaning for her. Indeed it felt as if the world had speeded up because she was so frantically impatient, every skin cell reaching for the climax her body was so desperate to experience.

Zahir paused and she heard the sound of a zip, the crackle of foil and she blinked like someone coming out of the dark into the light, but her hunger didn't abate even a little when she met stunning coal-black-fringed golden eyes alight with desire. She trembled, tried to reason and discovered that she was quite incapable of logic in the grip of the uncontrollable need clawing at her like a kind of madness…terrifying and overwhelming, utterly shameless in its single-minded focus.

'I cannot take you to another man's bed,' Zahir growled, snaking one arm round her waist to lift her off her feet. 'Wrap your legs round me,' he urged.

And she did, hungry for him to put his mouth back on hers, unbearably hungry for him to touch her again. Her arms locked round his neck to steady herself and he braced her against the wall while he angled his hips and lowered her until she felt the smooth, hot crown of his bold shaft pushing against her most tender flesh. Her eyes widened to their fullest, her head rolling back on her shoulders as he slowly, strongly pressed his passage up into her tight sheath. Her excitement went into a tail-spin as he stretched her with his fullness, his grunt of all-male satisfaction vibrating sexily in her ear. He angled her back, withdrew from her achingly tender flesh and then brought her down again hard, sending shock-waves of sensation pounding through her lower body.

'You're so tight,' he growled through gritted teeth, repeating the movement until he was fully seated inside her. 'You feel *so* good. I would kill for this!'

'Don't stop!' she cried, shivering as another wild, exhilarating wave of pleasure-pain pulsed through her pelvis, pushing the excitement higher until it was all-consuming and she was battered by both frustration and uncontrollable need.

'I *couldn't*...' Zahir husked, positioning his hips, grinding against her and withdrawing before driving home again hard. Over and over he repeated that movement until she was literally roused to screaming point.

And the first throbbing upsurge of climax splintered through her like a lightning bolt then and she cried out as the successive spasms of intense pleasure rippled through her. He came with a shudder and a shout and slowly, gently, lowered her legs back down to the floor, which was unfortunate because her legs didn't want to hold her up. She tipped forward as he balanced her, hands strong on her slim shoulders, and he kissed her breathless in the interim before lifting his tousled dark head and saying with typical practicality, 'Where's the bathroom?'

She told him and had to stagger back against the wall to stay upright. She was feeling horribly dizzy. Shock was tearing through her every bit as powerfully as the orgasm had. He had had her against the wall and it had been hideously, horribly thrilling but she didn't want to accept that she had not only let that happen but urged him on to commit that sin. Her knees wanted to give way but she wouldn't let them. With shaking hands, she tied the sash on her robe and covered herself up. A little late, a snide voice remarked in her brain and she squashed it. Her body was still pulsing from his possession and she was weak as water, drained by disbelief at what she had allowed to take place between them.

'Are you OK?' Zahir asked huskily from the doorway.

Saffy shot him a look from below her tumbled hair that would have slaughtered a weaker man where he stood. 'Not really,' she answered truthfully.

'You're very pale—perhaps you should sit down.'

Saffy dropped down onto the nearest sofa, lowered her head and breathed in slow and deep while she fought to reclaim her composure. Her head was swimming, her skin damp with perspiration and she felt slightly sick.

'When would you like to move out?' Zahir enquired smoothly. 'Give me a date and I will have all the arrangements made for you. There will be no hassle, no inconvenience—'

'*Move out?*' Saffy questioned blankly. 'I'm not moving anywhere!'

'You can't continue to live here with McDonald.'

With unsteady hands Saffy caught up her trailing hair and shoved it back from her clammy face as she clumsily sat up. 'What just happened was a bad idea. A *really* bad idea and letting you keep me in an apartment somewhere as a mistress is never going to happen, Zahir. Just accept that.'

'I will not accept it.'

Saffy sprang up on a surge of temper and just as suddenly the room seemed to spin violently around her. Disorientated, she swayed sickly, so dizzy she couldn't focus and she couldn't combat the rising tide of darkness that engulfed her as she fainted.

With a sharp imprecation, Zahir snatched her limp body up from the wooden floor and he settled her down on the sofa. Saffy recovered consciousness quickly and blinked in confusion to find him on his knees beside her. 'What happened?'

'You just dropped where you stood,' Zahir breathed tautly. 'Did I hurt you? Are you ill?'

Her lashes fluttered in bemusement as she dimly registered the sound of the front door slamming. 'No,' she whispered weakly. 'But I think the real problem may be that I'm pregnant...'

'Pregnant?' Zahir exclaimed, his strong bone structure pulling taut below his olive skin. 'When did you get pregnant?'

'Oh, dear,' a familiar voice interposed from the door, which Zahir had left ajar. 'Is this one of those moments when I walk out and come back in making more noise so that you know that I'm here?'

'Cameron?' Saffy craned her neck and began to sit up as her flatmate stared at her anxiously from across the room. Her brain felt as lively as sludge. She had not meant to blurt out her suspicion that she might be pregnant; she had simply spoken her thoughts out loud and now felt exceedingly foolish. 'I fainted. I've never done that in my life before.'

'There's a first time for everything,' Cameron said soothingly.

'Pregnant,' Zahir said again as though he could not get past that single word, and he studied Cameron grimly. '*Your* child?'

'No, you can leave me out of this little chat. I bat for the other team,' Cameron confided with a wry smile. 'You need to make an urgent appointment with the doctor, Saffy.'

Zahir's brow indented. 'What do you mean?' he queried.

'I'm her gay best friend and you can only be Zahir,' Cameron responded ruefully. 'The guards at the front door and the limo flying the little flag parked outside are a dead giveaway.'

'You're gay?' Zahir murmured wrathfully, and he fixed brilliant dark golden eyes accusingly on Saffy. 'Why didn't you tell me that?'

'It was none of your business.'

'And the baby?' Zahir prompted tautly.

'Excuse me,' Cameron said quietly, and he walked back out of the room, carefully closing the door in his wake.

Sitting up then because she no longer felt light-headed, Saffy swung her feet down onto the floor and swivelled round to face Zahir. 'Look, I don't even know yet if I am pregnant,' she admitted heavily. 'I have a test but I haven't used it yet. My suspicions may just be my imagination.'

His face granite hard, Zahir studied her intently like a male struggling to concentrate on only one thing at a time. 'If he's gay, why do you live with him?'

'Because he's my friend and we both were keen to buy an apartment at the same time. We get on very well,' Saffy told him wryly, wishing she had bitten her tongue out of her head before letting drop the fact that she suspected that she might be pregnant, for such a threat—and she had no doubt that he would see it as a threat—would only create more stormy waves in her dealings with Zahir.

'If McDonald's gay, why do people believe you and he are a couple?' Zahir persisted.

Saffy sighed. 'Cameron was raised by elderly grand-parents and he's very attached to them. He doesn't think they could accept his sexuality and he says he won't come out of the closet until they're gone.'

'So, in the meantime he uses you for cover.'

'We use each other,' Saffy parried without hesitation. 'I get bothered less by aggressive men as long as Cameron appears to be part of my life. Now can we please leave my friend out of this discussion?'

Zahir gritted his even white teeth together. 'Pregnant,' he repeated afresh.

'Maybe, maybe not,' Saffy muttered wearily. 'Look, I'll go and do the wretched test now and we'll see if there's anything to worry about.'

'If it is true, how will we know whether or not it is mine?' Zahir demanded icily.

'Don't make me slap you, Zahir. I haven't the energy right now,' Saffy sighed unhappily, moving past him.

Long brown fingers snapped round her wrist to hold her still. 'Do you have any idea how major an event this could be for a man in my position?' he raked down at her.

'No and, right now, I don't want to think about it. I only want to find out if there is anything for us to worry about. You shouldn't have come here, Zahir. You should have kept your distance. What happened between us in Maraban ended there. You're screwing up my life,' Saffy condemned, dragging her arm angrily free.

'It won't be at an end if you're carrying my child.'

Without another word, Saffy trudged through the hall to the bathroom, retrieved the test kit from the cupboard and pulled out the instructions. Minutes later she stood at the window holding the wand, waiting to see the result. She still felt shell-shocked by the explosive passion that had erupted between them, had never dreamt that she could lose control of her own body to such an extent, had not even suspected that the desire for sex might so badly betray her principles. Of course it had not occurred to her either that she would see him again, that he would deliberately seek her out in London or tell her that he couldn't sleep for *wanting* her. At least she wasn't the only one of them tossing and turning sleepless in the dark of the night, she thought wretchedly. But without the smallest warning, everything had changed. She had believed she could shrug off their encounter in Maraban; she had tried to tell herself that she had used him. In short, she reflected painfully, she had told herself a whole lot of face-saving rubbish in an effort to persuade herself that she was fully in control of events and now reality was banging very loudly at her door.

Almost absent-mindedly she looked down at the wand in her hand and her entire body froze. She gulped in a breath, checked her watch, gazed down transfixed at the line that had formed just as the instructions had explained. Her legs suddenly felt so woolly she had to perch on the side of the bath. *Be careful of what you wish for*...for according to the test result, she was pregnant. For a split second a rush of joy consumed her and then she recalled Zahir's hard, forbidding expression and she groaned out loud, for nothing but complications lay ahead. Zahir and an accidental pregnancy would be a very dangerous combination: Zahir liked to plan everything; Zahir had to be in control; Zahir had been raised in a culture in which such a development was totally unacceptable, socially, morally and every other way there was.

Why, oh, why had she opened her silly mouth and told him? Regret touched her deep. Now whether she liked it or not he was involved and it would have been much better for both of them if he was not. She didn't want him involved. Even less did she want him to be hostile to her condition. She might never before have allowed herself to dream of having a baby, but she would never, ever have chosen to have a child by a man who couldn't possibly want either of them.

Saffy walked back into the living room where Zahir was drinking coffee—Cameron evidently having played host in her absence—and staring moodily out of the window. He didn't like cities: he felt claustrophobic in them. Why did she still remember that? Hearing her entrance, he swung round, stunning dark golden eyes shooting straight to her pale, tight features.

And he knew, that fast he knew, read the defensiveness there and the reluctance to get any closer to him. Why? Was she afraid of him now? Did she think that in some way he meant her harm? Her golden hair had dried into loose, undisciplined waves round her lovely oval face and her eyes were incredibly blue against her pallor. Even with strain etched in every line of her visage she was hauntingly beautiful.

'We do have something to worry about,' she confirmed.

Zahir released his breath in a slow hiss, not a muscle moving on his lean bronzed face. 'I thought you were taking the contraceptive pill.'

'You assumed I was. I saw no reason to tell you otherwise because I didn't think this situation would arise,' Saffy admitted doggedly, determined to be honest now because matters had become too serious for her to risk even half-truths.

'Why were you not taking precautions to protect yourself against this development?' he demanded.

'I had no reason to. I wasn't having sex with anyone, so you don't need to wonder whose child it is,' she told him tightly, colour mantling her cheekbones.

'Naturally I will wonder. I have no wish to offend you but I was certainly under the impression that you had other lovers,' Zahir countered flatly.

'Don't believe all that you read in the papers,' Saffy advised, lifting her head high, her blue eyes guarded.

'I don't but, even allowing for a fair amount of exaggeration and invented stories, there is room for me to doubt the likelihood that in one brief encounter I have fathered your child,' Zahir fielded very quietly.

'I didn't think it was very likely either, but we're both young and healthy, it was the wrong time of the month for me to have an accident and clearly you have killer sperm,' Saffy told him drily.

'Don't make a joke of it,' Zahir growled.

'I can't prove it's your baby until after it's born,' Saffy murmured ruefully. 'DNA testing is too risky during pregnancy. On the other hand you could think back sensibly to that day in the tent and appreciate that ironically you are the only lover I've *ever* had.'

Zahir frowned, winged ebony brows pleating above questioning dark as night eyes flaring with disbelief. 'That is not possible.'

'Forget the newspaper stories and your prejudices and think about it rationally,' Saffy urged with quiet dignity, determined not to allow him to continue to cherish doubts about who had fathered her child. 'You're not stupid—I know you're not. I was a virgin.'

All colour bled from below his olive-toned complexion as he stared back at her with smouldering golden force and she recognised the exact moment when he recalled the blood stains on the bed because he suddenly swore in Arabic, tore his stunned gaze from hers and half swung away from her, his lean brown hands clenching into fists. 'If that is true, I have greatly wronged you,' he bit out rawly.

'We wronged each other a long time ago,' Saffy cut in. 'I *chose* to share that bed with you. It was my decision and this is my...er, problem.'

'If it's my child, it's mine too and I don't see our child as a problem,' Zahir retorted with a harsh edge to his dark deep voice. 'We'll remarry just as soon as I can arrange it.'

'Remarry?' Saffy gasped in wonderment. 'You have to be joking!'

'Our child's future is too serious to joke about and it can only be secured through marriage.'

'And we all know how that turned out the last time,' Saffy returned doggedly, fighting to think logically because his proposal had shaken her to her very depths. Was he serious? Was he really serious?

'When my father died and I took the throne, everything changed in Maraban,' Zahir declared levelly. 'We would be able to lead normal lives now. You're pregnant. Of course, I want to marry you.'

Saffy was reeling from a dozen different reactions:

disbelief, scorn, anger, frustration among them. Zahir was set on taking charge as usual. He wasn't reacting on a personal level, he was reacting as a public figure, keen to hide an embarrassing mistake within the respectability of marriage.

'I don't want to marry you just because I'm pregnant.'

'And what do you think your child would want?' Zahir shot that icily controlled demand back at her. 'If you don't marry me, you will deprive that child of a father and of the status in life he or she has a right to enjoy. Without marriage, the child will have to remain secret and it will be almost impossible for me to establish a normal relationship with him or her.'

In one cool statement, Zahir had given Saffy a lot to think about, but then faster than the speed of light her child had gone from being a line on a test wand to a living, breathing being, who might well question her decisions at a later date. For the first time she appreciated that she could not continue to put her own wants and needs first because, whatever she chose to do, she would, one day, have to take responsibility for the choices she had made on her child's behalf.

'We could get married just to ensure that the baby was legitimate…and then get another divorce,' she suggested tautly.

Brilliant dark eyes flamed golden as flames. 'Is that really the very best you can offer? Is the prospect of being my wife again such a sacrifice?'

Saffy studied the floor. She thought of the wicked forbidden delight of his passion, recognising that on that level everything between them had radically changed. She looked up, feeling the instant mesmeric pull of him the moment she saw his lean dark face. Her heart hammered inside her, her mouth running dry.

'Couldn't you give our marriage a second chance?' Zahir asked huskily.

'It's too soon to consider that,' Saffy argued. 'The first thing I need to do now is see my doctor and confirm that I *am* pregnant. Then we'll decide what to do. Look at this from my point of view. When you arrived here, you asked me to be your mistress…now suddenly you're talking marriage, but I don't want to get married purely because you accidentally got me pregnant.'

Zahir surveyed her with stormy intensity and the atmosphere thickened as though laced with cracked ice. 'I believe in fate, not accidents. What is meant to be will be.'

Saffy rolled her eyes, compressed her lips and stood up. 'You shipped me out to the desert for seduction, not fatherhood. You brought this roof down over our ears— you sort it out!'

'Marriage will sort it out,' he contended stubbornly.

'Oh, if only it were that simple.'

'But it is.' Before she could even guess his intention, he had closed a hand over hers. His brilliant gaze sought and held hers by sheer force of will. 'Right now, it's the best choice you can make. Let go of the past. Trust me to look after you and my child. I will not let you down.'

'And would you agree to a divorce at a later date?'

Saffy prompted shakily, more impressed than she wanted to be by his promise of good intentions.

'If that's what you wanted, if you were unhappy as you were before, yes,' Zahir agreed grittily, not choosing to add the unpleasant realities that would accompany any such decision on her part. Complete honesty was not possible. What really mattered was getting that ring back on her finger and securing their child's future. 'This is not about us, this is about our child, what he or she needs most.'

'If you really mean that...' Saffy drew in a ragged breath, terrified of the confusing thoughts teeming through her head. She was trying very hard to put the welfare of her child first and not muddy the waters with the bitterness of the past and the insecurity of the present. He would keep his promise: she knew that. On that level she trusted him and she quite understood that he wanted their child to have the very best start in life possible. They owed their child that chance.

'I do,' Zahir confirmed levelly.

'Then on that basis, I agree.' So great was the stress of making that announcement that Saffy felt lightheaded again as all the little devils in her memory banks began queuing up to remind her of how vulnerable she would be if she put herself in Zahir's power again.

Zahir released her hand. 'I'll organise it.'

He got as far as the door before Saffy called him back to say tautly, 'I want a *proper* wedding.'

'Meaning?' Zahir sought to clarify.

'No hole-in-the-corner do in the embassy for me this

time,' Saffy spelled out with scorn. 'I want a bridal gown and a family occasion with my sisters as bridesmaids and all the rest of the wedding hoopla.'

Taken aback by the admission, Zahir literally paled.

'Those are my terms and I won't budge on them,' Saffy completed doggedly.

CHAPTER SEVEN

'ARE YOU REALLY sure about doing this?' Kat looked tense and anxious and Saffy immediately felt guilty.

What had she been thinking of when she dragged her family into all of this? A shotgun wedding, no less. Her sister, Kat, didn't need the stress but she had insisted on organising the wedding within the space of one incredibly short week and had proven that if sufficient money was thrown at a challenge, it could be done. Saffy studied her reflection in the mirror. Her gorgeous designer wedding dress was a classic, nipped in at the waist for shape and falling in fluid folds to her satin-clad feet. She wasn't wearing a veil: the hairdresser had piled her hair up and topped it with the magnificent sapphire and diamond tiara Zahir had sent to her. Matching drop earrings sparkled with every movement she made.

'Saffy?' the attractive redhead pressed. 'You know, it may be your wedding day but it's still not too late to change your mind. You don't *have* to marry Zahir. You don't have to do this to please anybody.'

Looking reflective, Saffy breathed in deep. 'I really do want to give our baby the chance to have two parents. None of us ever had that. My sisters and I had you and you were a brilliant stand-in Mum,' she told Kat warmly. 'But I'd like to try it the old-fashioned way before I try to go it alone.'

Kat frowned. 'You're not in a very optimistic mood for a new bride.'

'I'm being realistic. Zahir will commit to being a father—I know that about him and I respect him for it. If marriage works for us, it works, and if it doesn't work, at least I'll have tried,' Saffy muttered ruefully.

'I just can't believe you got involved with him again. It's like fatal attraction without the bunny boiler. I mean, five years ago Zahir broke your heart and I don't want him doing it again.' Her sister sighed unhappily. 'Mikhail has checked him out and he says Maraban is stable now and that Zahir seems to be one of the good guys.'

'I could've told you that,' Saffy interrupted heatedly.

'And there's no sleazy stories about him either,' Kat added in a suitably quiet undertone. 'Obviously there's been women but not in the kind of numbers you need to worry about.'

Saffy ground her teeth together in silence, wishing that her Russian billionaire brother-in-law had minded his own business when it came to Zahir. Even as she thought it she knew she was wronging the man. Undoubtedly Kat's concerns about her sister's bridegroom had prompted Mikhail's investigation into Zahir's reputation. 'He would never be sleazy,' Saffy declared, suppressing her recollection of that invitation to be his mistress.

'Are you upset about Emmie refusing to come today?' Kat asked ruefully.

'No.' Saffy lied sooner than add additional worry to Kat's caring heart. 'I can understand her not wanting to get into a bridesmaid's frock when she's so pregnant and I can also understand her saying that she's not in the mood.'

'Some day soon, you two need to sit down and talk and sort out the aggro between you.'

'Easier said than done with Emmie always avoiding me like the plague,' Saffy countered ruefully. 'I phoned her and said I understood her not wanting to be a bridesmaid but would love her to come just as a guest and she said she wasn't feeling well enough to travel.'

'Well, she has had a pretty tough time being pregnant, so that probably wasn't a lie,' Kat conceded. 'It makes me wonder if I'm wise to be considering IVF in case that kind of sickness and nausea in pregnancy runs in the family.'

'I'm not feeling sick…not yet, anyway,' Saffy pointed out bracingly, smiling as Topsy bounced into the room, bubbling with excitement in her glittering green bridesmaid's dress and quite unaware of the serious chat her older sisters had been involved in. It seemed natural to the three sisters that neither Saffy's mother nor her father were taking part in the coming ceremony. Saffy had had virtually nothing to do with her mother, Odette, or her father since they had abandoned her to foster care when she was twelve years old. Her parents had divorced when she was much younger and the bitterness of their estrangement had had an inevitable effect on her father's attitude to his twin daughters. He had left them behind and moved on. Although Kat had encouraged Saffy to foster a forgiving attitude towards their mother, Saffy had too many memories of childhood neglect to do so. Odette simply wasn't a loving parent and never had been.

The wedding took place at the church only a few doors down from Kat and Mikhail's London home. The church's rather gloomy interior had been transformed with an abundance of white and pink flowers and knotted ribbons. Saffy walked down the aisle on Cameron's arm, her heart banging like a drum at a rock concert when she finally got close enough to see Zahir's imperious dark head at the altar. How did he feel about this? How did he *really* feel? Throughout the past crazy busy week while she packed up her life in London her only contact with Zahir had been by phone. She had rung him after the doctor had confirmed her pregnancy. He had rung her several times to find out about the wedding schedule. There had been nothing intimate about those exchanges.

She had also ploughed through a half-dozen frustrating meetings with her agent and various clients as the reality of her condition forced the need for urgent rethinks on previously planned shoots. A couple of clients had taken the opportunity to drop her because her pregnancy meant that she was in breach of contract.

Desert Ice, however, had retained her services because they were more than halfway through their campaign. She was grateful for that because it was mainly her earnings from the cosmetics company that funded the orphanage she supported.

Zahir's stunning black-fringed golden eyes met hers as she drew level with him and she felt painfully vulnerable, which she didn't like at all. Unfortunately wounding memories of their first wedding were assailing her, reminding her of a day when she had not had a doubt in the world about becoming a wife, had indeed innocently overflowed with feelings of love and happiness. The wedding ring slid onto her finger and she breathed in deep, conscious that Zahir retained a hold on her hand. It was done, the die was cast, she told herself soothingly. What was she afraid of happening? What was there to fear now? That he didn't love her—well, she knew he didn't love her, didn't she? Unfortunately the awareness that he was marrying her to give their baby a name and a home was no more welcome to her heart or her pride.

On their passage back down the aisle, Zahir pressed a supportive hand to her spine. 'You feel very shaky,' he admitted when she cast him an enquiring glance.

And it was true, she did feel shaky, had ridden roughshod over her misgivings to marry him, trying at every step to put her child's needs ahead of her own.

Zahir participated in the photographs in silence. Sapphire was pale as death and silent and her family, aside of the little bouncy one in green, who had smiled brightly at him, were clearly hostile and suspicious. No doubt her family had taken their cues from Sapphire. She didn't want to be married to him again; he could feel it in the tension that gripped her every time he touched her. That made him angry and bitter, roused memories better left buried. But he had royally screwed up by allowing his primal instincts to triumph and there was always a price to be paid for recklessness, he reminded himself darkly. He had got her back. That was, at least, a beginning, and only time would tell whether or not she would continue to hold the threat of a divorce like a gun to his head.

'You look stunning,' Zahir told her belatedly as she scrambled into the limo that would whisk them from the church to the embassy to undergo a Muslim marriage ceremony. 'How are you feeling?'

'I'm not ill, only pregnant,' Saffy countered defensively, wishing he hadn't reminded her of her condition, reluctant to be viewed as in any way in need of special treatment.

The second ceremony was brief, witnessed by embassy officials and a posed photograph was taken afterwards. They returned to Mikhail and Kat's house where a reception was being held in the ballroom. After the wedding breakfast, they circulated. Surrounded by the familiar faces of the models she often worked with, Saffy began to relax a little, bearing up well to comments about how quiet she had been about her supposed long-term relationship with Zahir and striving to behave more like a normal bride.

'Of course, I shouldn't mention it,' trilled Natasha,

a six-foot-tall Ukrainian blonde, well on her way to supermodel status. 'But Zahir was mine first.'

It was said so quietly and with such a sunny smile
that it took several seconds for that spiteful confession
to sink in on Saffy. She stared back into Natasha's very
pale blue eyes and murmured, 'Really?' as politely as if
the other woman had commented on the weather.

'Yes, a couple of years ago now. A fling at a film festival,' Natasha confided with a little shrug of a designer-
clad shoulder. 'But he was hard to forget.'

'Yes,' Saffy acknowledged, passing on as soon as she
could into less aggressive company, anger licking like
fire at her composure. Mine first? No, he had been hers,
her husband and then her ex-husband before he became
anyone else's. But the truth that he had sought amusement in other beds could still slash like a knife turning
in her breast. She glanced back at Natasha, beautiful
and reputedly sexually voracious, struggling not to picture Zahir entwined in her arms, and the nausea she had
never experienced until that moment turned her stomach into a washing machine and sent sickness hurtling
up her throat. Her skin clammy with perspiration, she
rushed off to the cloakroom and made it just in time.
She was horribly sick and it took a few minutes for her
to freshen up and lose the unsteadiness that afflicted
her in the aftermath.

When she emerged, Topsy was waiting for her. 'Are
you OK? Zahir saw you leaving and asked me to check.'

Zahir didn't miss much, Saffy reflected wretchedly.

'I think I just got bitten by morning sickness.' And a very tall shrewish blonde.

But Saffy was no fan of ducking reality and she knew she had to deal with life as it was. Zahir had been with other women when he was no longer married to her and that was his business, not hers. His past was his own, just as hers would have been had she lived a little more dangerously since their first marriage. But unfortunately there had not been a cure for the fact that she had still found Zahir and her memory of him far more attractive than other men. What did that say about her? He was like a habit she had never managed to shake, her one and only fantasy, and the men who had pursued her over the years had never managed to cause her a single sleepless night. With the exception of Zahir, she had never pined for a phone call or a smile from a man, had truly never contrived to rouse that much interest, and perhaps that was why she had fallen so easily back into bed with him. Was it a kind of persistent physical infatuation? Had he somehow spoiled her for other men? She stared at him as she crossed the floor of the ballroom.

He was lithe, powerfully built and supremely sophisticated in his light grey morning suit with his luxuriant ebony hair fanning back from his brow; his dark deep-set eyes were riveting in his lean, bronzed face. He was drop-dead gorgeous and always had been a very hard act to follow. But as her body stirred with responses far removed from nausea, her breasts swelling and peaking beneath her bodice and a dull ache expanding in her pelvis, she was furious with herself for being so susceptible to a male who neither loved nor even truly wanted her.

'What's wrong?' Zahir asked softly.

'Why would anything be wrong?' she traded tartly, ice in her cool scrutiny and edging her voice. 'You tell me...film festival two years ago, Ukrainian blonde by the name of Natasha, ring any bells?' That scornful and provocative question just leapt off Saffy's tongue before she was even aware she was going to voice it.

The faintest hint of colour edged Zahir's chiselled cheekbones but his dark golden gaze did not waver from hers. Indeed if anything he stood a little straighter. 'I will never lie to you.'

Even when you should, she almost screamed at him, wanting, needing to know and yet fearing what knowing more would do to her.

'There weren't many and there was nothing serious,' Zahir breathed in a harsh undertone. 'This is not a conversation I want to have on our wedding day.'

'It's not something I want to talk about either!' Saffy launched back at him, her eyes a very bright blue lit with anger.

His stubborn jaw line squared. 'Before you judge me, ask yourself if you have any idea of what state I was in after our divorce.'

Saffy came over all defensive. 'How would I know?'

'When you're ready to tell me what changed you out of all recognition in the bedroom, I'll tell you why I did what I did.' His brilliant dark eyes glittered. It was a challenge, blunt and simple, and it only made Saffy angrier than ever.

He had divorced her. *He* had made that choice. He could not expect her to accept the consequences or feel responsible for a situation that had not been of her making. As for what had changed her into a normal sexually able woman, that was not something she was willing to share with him. It was too private, too personal, might well affect the way he looked at her and that very possible outcome made her cringe.

'Are you two actually arguing?' Kat came up to demand in dismay.

'We always did have a fiery relationship,' Zahir admitted.

'Not so different from our own,' Kat's husband, Mikhail, teased his wife. 'It takes time to adjust to living with another person.'

'Time and buckets of patience,' Zahir added, an authoritative look stamped on his lean dark face that only made Saffy want to slap him hard.

'Your guests are waiting for the bride and groom to start the dancing,' Kat informed them more cheerfully.

Saffy wasn't in the mood to dance, especially not with Natasha smirking at the side of the floor, but she owed her sister too much to risk upsetting her and she gave way with good grace.

Zahir was a great dancer with a natural sense of rhythm but Saffy felt as if someone had welded an iron bar to her spine and she was stiff in the circle of his arms, holding herself at a distance. Glimpses of Natasha watching them did not improve her mood. Yes, she had known he had made love to other women, but actually having a face to pin to one of those anonymous women was another turn of the torture screw. She had never thought of herself as the jealous type and now she was finding out different. Once Zahir had been hers, entirely hers, and even though things had gone wrong in the bedroom she had rather naively trusted him not to stray. Now she was wondering crazy things, such as how she compared to his other lovers, and she was regretting her lack of experience and her honesty on that score. Yet how could she have lied when her child's paternity hinged on telling the complete truth? That reminder cooled the fizz in her blood, settled her down and made her seek another topic of conversation.

'I thought you might have invited your brother and sister and possibly even Azel to the wedding,' she remarked gingerly.

'One of Hayat's children is in hospital with complications following on from a bout of measles. Akram is standing in for me at an OPEC meeting and my sister-in-law, Azel, no longer lives with us. She remarried last year and now lives in Dubai,' Zahir explained. 'You will meet what remains of my family tomorrow.'

'I'll look forward to it,' Saffy said politely. 'Do they know about the baby?'

'Only my siblings. When we chose to marry in such haste, it made sense to be honest,' Zahir said wryly.

Hot pink burned like a banner across her cheeks at the thought that his strictly raised siblings might assume that she was a total slut for succumbing so quickly and easily to their brother's attractions.

'You know, when you blush, the tip of your nose turns pink as well,' Zahir husked. 'It's cute as hell.'

'You know what happened in the desert...the baby,' Saffy said sharply. 'It's *all* your fault.'

A sizzling, utterly unexpected smile played across Zahir's wide sensual mouth and startled her. 'I know. But out of it I gained a very beautiful wife and we have a baby in our future and I can't find it within my heart to regret anything we did.'

Her eyes prickled and she blinked rapidly, knowing that her acid and pointless comment had not deserved so generous a response. Suddenly her tension gave and she rested her head down on his broad shoulder, drinking in and loving the familiar scent of him—warm clean male laced with an evocative hint of sandalwood. She was momentarily weak with the sheer amount of emotion pumping through her and so confused, still so desperately confused about what she felt, what she truly thought. With every passing moment, her feelings seemed to swing to one side and then violently to the other. So much had happened between them in such a short time frame that she was mentally all over the place.

Saffy was half asleep by the time they left for the airport. She had changed into a very elegant shift dress and jacket almost the same colour as her eyes and let her hair down to flow round her shoulders in a golden mane. Relaxation was infiltrating her for the first time that day.

Drowsily she studied the platinum ring on her finger. They were married again: she couldn't quite believe it.

'I think I'll sleep all the way to Maraban,' Saffy told him apologetically as they boarded the private jet.

'It's been a long day and it is after midnight,' Zahir conceded wryly. 'But first there's something I'd like to tell you.'

Alert to the guarded note in his dark deep drawl, Saffy felt her adrenalin start to pump. The jet took off and drinks were served. She undid her belt, let the stewardess show her into the sleeping compartment where she freshened up, and then she rejoined Zahir, made herself comfortable and sipped her fresh orange juice. 'So?' she prompted quietly, proud of her patience and self-discipline while she wondered what he had to unveil. 'What is it?'

Zahir straightened his broad shoulders and settled hard dark eyes on her without flinching. 'I've bought the Desert Ice cosmetics company.'

CHAPTER EIGHT

SAFFY BLINKED IN astonishment, for of all the many surprises she had thought Zahir might want to disclose that one staggering confession had not figured. She set down her glass and stood up, her mind in a bemused fog. 'You bought the company? But why? Why the heck would you do that?'

'It *was* a good investment.' Zahir loosed a sardonic laugh that bluntly dismissed that explanation. 'But I bought it only for your benefit. I knew the company had a cast-iron contract with you and I didn't want anyone putting pressure on you while you were pregnant.'

Eyes slowly widening, Saffy stared back at him in rampant disbelief, while she wondered what strings he had pulled to learn the contract terms she had been on with the company. 'I can't believe that you would interfere in my career to that extent!' she admitted in stunned disbelief, anger steadily gathering below the surface of that initial reaction. 'Nobody was putting pressure on me at the meeting I attended with their campaign manager this week.'

Cynicism hardened Zahir's expressive mouth, making him look inexpressibly tough in a way far different from the younger man she remembered. It was a look that was hard, weathered and unapologetic and she refused to be intimidated by it. 'Naturally not. By that time, I was the new owner, so of course there was no pressure. They can film your face as much as they like while you're pregnant but they'll be doing it in Maraban.'

'In...*Maraban?*' Saffy parroted as though he had suggested somewhere as remote as the moon.

'I don't want you forced to travel thousands of miles round the globe now that you're pregnant. It would be too stressful for you.'

'And what would you know about that?' Saffy demanded hotly. 'What do you know about what a pregnant woman needs?'

'I don't want you exhausted,' Zahir asserted grimly. 'I appreciate that the baby is a development that wasn't planned or, indeed, expected, but adjustments have to be made to your working schedule.'

'You're not the boss of me!' Saffy hissed back at him in helpless outrage. 'You know, the one phrase I heard you speak most clearly was, *"I don't want..."* This is about you, your need to clip my wings and control me. Isn't it enough that I married you? What about what I want? What about what I need? This isn't all about you!'

'I'm not trying to control you.' Eyes now smouldering with anger, Zahir gazed back at her, his hard jaw line set at an unyielding angle. 'But the security needs alone that are now required to ensure your safety would be impossible to maintain in some of the exotic locations where you have recently travelled.'

'I don't have security needs!' Saffy flung at him in a bitterly aggrieved tone of fury. 'It's taken me five years to build my career and I didn't get where I am by being difficult!'

Zahir didn't bat a single absurdly long eyelash. He stared steadily back at her, those twin black fringes round his remarkable eyes merely adding to the intensity of his scrutiny. 'As my wife, you have security needs. Just as I could be a target, you could be as well. I will not allow your headstrong spirit to tempt you into taking unnecessary risks. This is not about your career. This is about you accepting that your new status will demand lifestyle changes. You are no longer Sapphire Marshall, you are a queen.'

'I don't want to be a queen!' Saffy sobbed in a passionate rage at the logic he was firing at her. Memories were flooding back to her of long-buried quarrels during which she had raged while Zahir shot down her every argument with murderous logic and practicality. 'You never told me that. I just thought I'd be your wife, your consort, your plus one or whatever you want to call it!'

'The last queen was my mother, who died when my younger brother was born,' Zahir commented grimly. 'It is time you saw sense. You can't have thought you could marry me and ignore who and what I am.'

Saffy was so worked up she wanted to scream. Over the past week she had thought of many, many things, like dresses and wedding breakfasts and guest lists and babies, but not once had she pondered her future status in Maraban. In fact she hadn't wanted to think about Maraban at all because once she had been very unhappy there.

'I didn't think about it,' Saffy muttered in indignation, furious with him, wondering in a rage how on earth he had broken the news about the Desert Ice company and then contrived to roll over his indefensible interference in her career to put her on the defensive with the news that she was apparently a queen. 'I don't want to be a queen. I'm sure I'm not cut out for it. In fact I bet I'm totally unsuitable to be royal.'

'With that attitude you probably will be,' Zahir shot back at her with derision. 'I think you tried harder at eighteen to fit in than you are willing to try now as an adult.'

Saffy's lush mouth dropped open as temper exploded in her like a grenade. 'I was a doormat at eighteen, a total stupid doormat! I wanted to please you. I wanted to please your family. I was so busy trying to be something I'm not—*and* getting no thanks for it! I had no space to be me!'

'Times have changed. Maraban has been transformed and brought into the twenty-first century. But I have changed as well,' Zahir breathed on a taut warning note, his gaze burning gold in its force. 'I will tell you now how things are and I won't keep secrets from you again.'

'*Secrets?*' Saffy shot back at him jaggedly, entrapped by that one word of admission, her nervous tension seizing on it. '*What secrets?*'

'Five years ago, I kept a lot from you in an attempt to protect you. I didn't want to hurt you but this time I will employ no lies and no half-truths. I will tell it like it is…'

Other women, Saffy was thinking in despair, a sharp wounding pain piercing her somewhere in the chest region. What else could he be talking about? When he had found no satisfaction in the marital bedroom he had gone elsewhere. Maybe out to that remote desert palace where his late father had kept his personal harem, *very* discreet. Hey, Saffy, you dummy, a little voice piped up at the back of her mind…maybe he wasn't on army manoeuvres all those times he was gone. Maybe he was off the leash having fun, the kind of fun you couldn't give him then. And what shook Saffy most at that moment was that instead of confronting him on that score and demanding an explanation, she instead wanted to stay silent and withdraw, conserve some dignity, protect herself from painful revelations that she did not at that moment feel strong enough to bear. Every atom of ESP she possessed urged her to leave the past where it belonged.

Saffy lifted her golden head. 'I'm tired. I'm going to bed but thanks for making our wedding night almost as dreadful as the first we had,' she murmured with stinging scorn.

And she saw right then in his lean darkly handsome face that he had forgotten it was their wedding night. And really that said it all, didn't it? She had already travelled from being the object of intense desire to being the pregnant wife, apparently shorn of attraction.

Zahir gritted his teeth and resisted the urge to talk back to her in a similar vein. Had she really thought he would stage their wedding night on a plane when she was exhausted and already under strain from all the challenges of the past weeks? He suffered a hollow sensation of horror even recalling that first catastrophic wedding night, her sickness, fear and distress, his own incomprehension and sense of defeat. She had been too young, far too young and naïve at eighteen, he knew that now. Guilt assailed him as Saffy ducked into the cabin, her lovely face taut and pale awakening memories he would have done anything to avoid. So much for honesty, so much for trying to clear the air, he reflected bitterly.

That last comment of hers had been a low blow, Saffy conceded in shame. It wasn't either of their faults that their first wedding night had been catastrophic and he had been incredibly kind and patient and understanding even though she knew he didn't understand any more than she did then what was wrong with her. Hitting out at him like that had been unjust, a mean retaliation to the reality that Zahir had made her feel small and stupid with his talk of security concerns and queens. She didn't look much like a queen, she thought wretchedly, studying herself with wet pink eyes in the mirror, noting the mascara and eyeliner smudged from tears. She had panicked when he mentioned that because she was so terrified of not meeting his expectations again. Hadn't she *already* done that to him once? She didn't want to let him down or embarrass him but what did she know about being royal? Certainly she had learned absolutely nothing during their last marriage when only the servants knew she existed and she was virtually the invisible woman.

He didn't love her, didn't want her, probably had no faith in her ability to act like a royal wife either, Saffy thought painfully, tears streaming down her cheeks as she forced her convulsed face into a pillow. Why did she care so much about what he thought of her? Why did it hurt so much that she felt she couldn't stand it? And why more than anything in the world did she now want him to come in and put his arms round her to comfort her the way he had once done without even thinking about it? She had married him to give their baby a better start in life. That was the only reason and she didn't know why she was getting so worked up, sobs shuddering through her body like a storm unleashed on her without warning.

I am not in love with him. I am *so* not in love with him, she told herself urgently. That is not why I'm suddenly looking for more from him than he ever promised to deliver. And in that guarded state of mind she finally fell asleep.

The stewardess wakened her with breakfast and the announcement that the plane would be landing in an hour. Noting that she had slept alone in the bed, Saffy lifted her chin, knowing he had spent the night in one of the reclining seats. Why was she wondering whether he had been unfaithful to her when they had last been married? What did it matter? How was that relevant?

The last thing she needed was to get bound up in the problems of a long-dead past. They weren't the same people any more. Showered and elegantly attired in a print dress and a fine cashmere cardigan, she emerged from the sleeping compartment, feeling as brittle as bone china.

Zahir, sheathed in the beige and white pristine desert robes that accentuated his height and undeniably exotic attributes, gave her a smile that was a masterpiece of civility while wishing her good morning. She almost laughed but, once again, their shared past rattled like a skeleton locked in a cupboard: Zahir was superb at plastering over the cracks and pretending nothing had happened and that last night's divisive dispute had not occurred. Time and time again he had done that to her when they were first married when she tried to have serious talks with him and he shrugged them off, changed the subject, refused to be drawn. Stop it, *stop it*, she urged her disobedient brain, determined not to bring those memories of his evasiveness into the present when so much else had altered.

'We had a row,' she reminded him out of pure spite and resentment of his poise.

'I should never tackle a serious conversation after midnight when we're both tired.' His eyes glittered with unexpected raw amusement and the sheer primal attraction of him in that instant sent a flock of butterflies dancing in her tummy and clenched her muscles tight somewhere a great deal more intimate. Pink flushed her cheeks as he sipped at his coffee, the very image of cool control and sophistication. 'Coffee?'

Saffy served herself from the coffee pot on the table and sat down. 'What you said—'

Zahir shifted a fluid brown hand in a silencing motion. 'No, leave it. It was the wrong time and we have all the time in the world now.'

Saffy tried to steel herself to resist the command note in that assurance and then wondered if perhaps he was right. In any case, did she want confessions if what she suspected was true? Did she really want to stir up the past and perhaps damage the future relationship they might have before this marriage even got off the ground? Such patience, such careful concern felt unfamiliar to her in Zahir's presence, for once she had said whatever she liked to him with absolutely no lock on her tongue. And she wanted that freedom back, she recognised dimly, wanted it back almost more than she wanted anything.

'It's not like you to be so quiet.'

'The Queenie bit pulverised me,' she muttered tightly.

'You're more than up to the challenge,' Zahir asserted smoothly. 'You're accustomed to being in the public eye and right now you look…*wonderful.*'

'Do I?' Saffy hated the sound of that question, her gaze welded to his in search of falsehood, fake flattery, the smallest hint of insincerity.

'You always did and still do. And sadly, although it shouldn't matter, such beauty does impress people,'

Zahir murmured ruefully. 'I've never understood why you're not vain.'

'Other people work and train to do much more important and necessary things than I do but I got where I am because of my face and figure, not my brain or my skills,' Saffy pointed out flatly. 'It's not something to boast about.'

'But you're so much more—you always were,' Zahir declared, reaching for her fingers where they curled in discomfiture on the table top and enclosing them in his warm hand. 'And in Maraban, you will be able to show how much more you are capable of.'

'What does that mean?' Saffy prompted, touched by that hand round hers, energised by the conviction with which he spoke.

'That the woman who gives most of her earnings to an orphanage in Africa will have free rein to raise funds for good works in my country. Yes, I found out about that fact, quite accidentally through your crooked solicitor,' Zahir admitted. 'It made me feel very proud of you.'

Saffy tensed and reddened, wary of praise on the score of one of her biggest secrets. 'The children had so little and I wanted to help them. It made my career seem less superficial when I could feel that I had a worthwhile cause to work for.'

A wary sense of peace had settled over her by the time the plane landed at Maraban's splendid new airport. But when she stepped out of the plane to the music being played by a military band, and a smiling older man stepped up to bow and address Zahir while a lit-

tle girl in a fancy dress stepped nervously forward to
present a bouquet of flowers to Saffy, she realised that
he had been right to warn her that her life would radically change. Zahir introduced her and the man bowed
very low. He was the prime minister of Maraban. A
discovery that startled Saffy and embarrassed her, for
she knew she should have spent more time boning up
on the changes in the country that was to be her new
home. She had assumed Zahir was a feudal king like his
late father, but evidently Maraban now had an elected
government as well.

The little girl was the prime minister's daughter and
spoke English and Saffy, always at her best with children, bent down to chat to her, suddenly wondering
whether the child she carried would be a boy or a girl.
A little boy with Zahir's amazing eyes and love of the
outdoors and action. Or a little girl, who liked to experi-
ment with hair and make-up and clothes. Or a mix of
both of them, which would be much more likely, Saffy
acknowledged abstractedly.

A limousine carried them through the city streets,
lined on either side by excited crowds, peering at the
car. 'Do I have to wave or anything?' she asked uneasily.

'No, only smile to look as happy as a bride is popu-
larly supposed to be,' Zahir murmured with a wry note
in his dark deep voice, and she suspected that he was
recalling the night they had just spent apart.

'Your people seem to be celebrating the fact that
you've got married,' Saffy remarked.

'People are reassured by the concept of family and

continuity, as long as it doesn't include a man like my late father,' Zahir imparted drily, and then turned to look at her. 'Why do you never mention yours? I noticed he was not at the wedding and didn't like to ask because you never ever mentioned him five years ago. Is he dead?'

'No. Alive with a second wife and family. His divorce from my mother was very bitter,' Saffy confided. 'And he hasn't had anything to do with me since I was twelve years old when I did something...' her voice slowed and thickened with distress '...something he couldn't forgive.'

His black brows drew together and he regarded her keenly. 'What could you have done that would excuse such an outright rejection from a father of his own child? I can't believe you did anything worthy of such a punishment.'

Saffy was very pale and she compressed her lips. 'Then you'd be wrong.'

'Tell me...you can't give me only half of the story.'.

It was her second most shameful secret, Saffy reflected wretchedly, but one that there was no reason for her to keep from him as he was part of her family now and everyone else knew the facts. 'As you know, life was pretty rough where I grew up and my sisters and I were often left without supervision, so of course we got in with the wrong crowd,' she confided tightly, her skin already turning clammy with never-forgotten shame and guilt. 'I went joyriding in a stolen car with my twin. I didn't steal it *or* drive it but the car crashed. Her leg was badly damaged and she was left disabled and scarred for several years afterwards. She went through hell as a teenager. Luckily she was able to have surgery when she was older and she can walk normally again now. But the joyriders were my friends first and it was my fault. I'm the older twin and I should have been looking after her.'

'Saffy...' and it was the very first time he had used the family diminutive of her name, which made his intervention all the more effective as she turned her head in surprise, her clouded blue eyes meeting his. 'You were twelve years old. You did something wrong and you paid a heavy price—'

'No, *Emmie* did—' Saffy protested vehemently. 'Every morning for years she had to wake up and see her identical twin, walking, unscarred, *perfect* and, even though she's completely healed now, she's never been able to forgive me for what she went through during that period of her life. We both know I was to blame and that it should have been me who got hurt.'

'But you *were* hurt,' Zahir murmured gently. 'She was hurt in the body and you were hurt in the mind. You've carried the guilt for what happened ever since, haven't you?'

Tears were swimming in Saffy's eyes and she didn't trust herself to speak, so she nodded vigorously in agreement. All those years she had stood by watching her twin suffer, first in a wheelchair, then on crutches, struggling to fit in with other teenagers when she couldn't play sport or dance or do almost anything that they could.

'Accidents happen,' Zahir continued. 'You learned from the experience, didn't you?'

Saffy nodded wordlessly, a soundless sob thickening her throat and making it impossible to swallow.

'So what did your father do?'

'He said…he said I was evil and that he didn't want to know me any more.'

'And how did he treat Emmie?'

'He cut her out of his life as well. So, you see, that was my fault too.'

'No. He was a father and perhaps he used your mistakes as an excuse to absolve himself of responsibility for his twin daughters. No decent man would stay away from an injured child merely to punish her sibling.'

That was a truth that had evaded Saffy all her life to that point and it shook her because when Zahir put the episode in that light, she saw his view of it and it altered her own. Her father had conveniently rejected both his daughters. Although Emmie had been hurt, he hadn't even visited her in hospital, nor had he intervened when the twins were forced to enter foster care because their mother refused to take further responsibility for them. It had been Saffy's sister, Kat, who had been the three sisters' saviour, giving them a proper home and a loving caring environment, the first any of them had ever known.

'I appreciate you viewing the episode that way,' Saffy breathed in a muffled undertone. 'But Emmie can't see it like that. She still doesn't want anything to do with me.'

'As I've never met her, you'll have to talk to her about that. Put it out of your mind now,' Zahir urged, stunning dark golden eyes welded to her troubled face, a smile slashing his wide sensual mouth. 'and stop blaming yourself for something that was outside your control.'

Her spirits picked up as if a bubble of happiness had been released inside her. He knew what she had done and it hadn't shocked him or made him see her as a cruelly irresponsible and selfish person. And most miraculously of all, he had made her feel better with one smile. She gazed back at him, her heart thumping hard inside her chest, an agony of feeling squeezed tight inside her. She wanted so badly to touch him, could feel her breasts heavy, the tender tips straining inside her bra while a warm honeyed heat built between her legs. It was pure lust, she told herself defensively, watching his eyes flame gold, and lust was a practical basis for a practical marriage.

'If we weren't in view of hundreds of people, you would be horizontal,' Zahir purred hungrily, the erotic note in his sensual drawl tugging at her senses.

'As you said, we have all the time in the world,' Saffy burbled, relieved that he could still respond to her, *want* her. 'I did think that the way you behaved yesterday meant that, now that I'm pregnant, I had lost my appeal,' she told him baldly.

Zahir laughed with rich appreciation. 'Is that a joke?'

Saffy stiffened. 'No.'

'Knowing that's my baby inside you makes me want you more than ever,' he breathed with a husky sensual edge to his voice, surveying her in a way no woman could have misunderstood or doubted, his hunger unashamed.

Although her colour heightened, Saffy relaxed, reassured that she was still an object of desire. In reality, she wanted a great deal more from him, she acknowledged inwardly, but it was early days and she could be patient. After all, she loved him. She couldn't lie to herself any longer about that. She had married him because she wanted to be his wife again, not only because of the child she carried. She wasn't quite the clear-headed, unselfish person she had pretended to be inside her own mind, putting her child's needs first. She wanted Zahir, she *loved* Zahir, and somehow she was going to make their marriage work so well that he found her indispensable. Furthermore, she wasn't going to cripple herself with wounding suspicions about other women, past infidelities or indeed anything from that era, she swore fiercely to herself. This marriage was a new beginning, not a rerun of mistakes and misunderstandings made long ago.

CHAPTER NINE

THE ROYAL PALACE was a vast building dating back hundreds of years and extended and renovated by every successive generation of Zahir's family. Even from the outside Saffy could see changes everywhere she looked because the massive courtyard fronting the palace entrance, once a parking area for military vehicles and limousines, had been transformed into beautiful gardens full of graceful trees being industriously watered to keep them healthy in the heat. Glorious flowering shrubs bloomed in every direction and fountains fanned water to cool the air in terraced seating areas. The gardeners at work fell still and lowered their heads respectfully as the limo passed by. When the late King Fareed had driven past, everyone had fallen down on their knees at his insistence and she was relieved that Zahir had clearly brought an end to that kind of exaggerated subservience.

'It looks so different,' she commented as the limo drew up outside the huge arched entrance. 'Much more welcoming.'

'It's so big we initially thought of knocking it down

and constructing something more fit for purpose. After all, I don't live like my father with hundreds of servants and guards, but it *is* an historic building and, since the family only requires part of it to actually live in, the government uses one wing and official events are staged here. We will still have total privacy though,' he asserted. 'Don't worry about that. And, of course, you'll be free to redecorate and do anything you like with our wing of the palace. I want you to feel at home here this time.'

Saffy decided that she would pretty much come to like and accept any place Zahir called home. Besides, their baby had been conceived in a tent. A palatial tent, to be sure, but a tent nonetheless. Her lush mouth quirked at the recollection. That was a secret that would probably never be shared.

The domestic staff greeted them at the end of the long hall and she was given more flowers, which were in turn taken from her as if she could not be expected to carry anything for herself. Zahir closed a relaxed hand round hers and walked her into a big reception room where a man and a woman awaited them.

'Hayat…' Saffy greeted his sister, several years his senior, warmly, registering that the delicate youthful brunette she had once met was now a more rounded woman in her thirties, but she still had the same warm, friendly smile. Hayat was quick to kiss her on both cheeks and offer good wishes. Saffy had never got to know the older woman that well because when she had first been married to Zahir, Hayat and her husband had been living in Switzerland.

'And since he was only a boy when you last met him, this is my younger brother Akram.'

She would have known Zahir's brother immediately by his close resemblance to her husband, but she was not impervious to the look of hostility in his rather set face as he murmured a strictly polite welcome that was neither sociable nor encouraging. But Saffy kept the smile on her face, reminding herself that it was early days and that, after the divorce five years earlier, Akram might consider her a particularly bad match for his brother, the king. Or maybe Akram was less than impressed by the fact that she was already pregnant, although if that was the case he ought to remember that conception took two people, not one, she thought ruefully.

Zahir carried her off again, one hand closed round hers as if he was keen to retain physical contact and, certainly, she had no objection retaining that connection. She had never been in the wing of the palace he took her to, was happy to be invited to explore and was pleasantly surprised by how contemporary the décor was there. Back in the old dark days of King Fareed's occupation, the parts of the palace she had known had rejoiced in a preponderance of over-gilded furniture, brightly coloured wallpaper, fussy drapes and half-naked statues. But now all that was tasteless and garish had been swept away as though it had never been.

'Did your father ever live here?' she asked awkwardly.

'No,' Zahir said succinctly. 'I didn't want to occupy his wing at the front…too many bad memories. It's government offices now.'

'This is beautiful,' Saffy confided, brushing back filmy drapes and opening French windows that led out into a spacious garden courtyard full of lush colourful plants. 'It will be perfect for the baby to play in.'

'One last place to show you,' Zahir murmured, tugging her impatiently back indoors to walk her down the corridor, while she tried to compute the sheer number of rooms that she now had the right to regard as part of her new home. He flung open the double doors at the foot like a showman. 'Our room. I had it freshly decorated.'

Our room, she repeated inwardly, thinking that phrase, which once had unnerved her, now had a good, solid, reassuring sound to it. The big room was breathtaking in the morning sunshine, furnished with a simply huge bed dressed in white and covered with more pillows and cushions than anyone would ever want to move before slipping between the sheets. Masses of white flowers filled several vases and perfumed the air with their abundance. The effect was light, bright and designer chic. Twin bathrooms led off the bedroom, one with a family-sized Jacuzzi in the corner.

'I'm already picturing you in there,' Zahir muttered huskily from behind her, his breath warming her cheek as he settled his lean hands on her rounded hips.

'Are you indeed?' Sliding round to look up at him, Saffy lifted her hands to his face and curved them to his exotic cheekbones. Dear heaven, those eyes of his got to her every time, she conceded dizzily as he bent his handsome dark head and circled her lush mouth slowly, teasingly with his own and her heart skipped a beat. 'I'll only get in with company.'

His cell phone hummed and Zahir winced. 'Hold that thought,' he urged, digging it out of his pocket to speak in his own language.

And that fast the moment of intimacy was over. He inclined his head at an apologetic angle and told her that something needed his attention and he would see her later. Saffy suppressed her disappointment, conceding that their lives would often be interrupted by his duties and knowing she would have to get used to the fact. She returned to exploring their wing of the palace. A manservant brought her luggage. There was a complete dream of a clothing closet installed in the room next door and she smiled, smoothing shoe shelves and glancing into what could only be custom-built units. Knowing Zahir must have ensured that so much was prepared for her in advance gave her a warm feeling deep down inside.

A maid brought her tea and tiny cakes and she sat out in the tranquil courtyard garden below the shade of the palm trees, enjoying the fading afternoon heat and the play of shadows through the palm fronds. For the first time in a long time she felt at peace. Acknowledging her feelings for Zahir had eased her worst insecurities and put paid to her frantic changes of mood because now she knew what lay behind her reactions. They were husband and wife and she was carrying their first child and she was happy. Happy, she thought wryly, unable to recall when she had last felt so happy or indeed an intensity of any emotion: only around Zahir. Had she always still loved him? Had it been his haunting image that prevented her from ever experiencing a strong attraction to another man? Regardless of what had happened between them, she had retained past memories of Zahir that were still clear as day in her mind. He had referred to her once as his 'first love' and she knew she wanted to be his first and *only* love, but the clock still couldn't be turned back. And nor in many ways would Saffy have wanted to achieve that impossibility, not if it meant returning to the uninformed, bewildered teenager she had been, incapable of consummating her marriage and having to live within the confines of the repressive regime of the late King Fareed.

Zahir phoned her full of apologies to say that he could not join her before dinner. He reappeared, vital and startlingly handsome, to study her where she sat reading on the terrace. She smiled at him, blue eyes sparkling, and his winged brows pleated in surprise. 'I thought you'd be furious with me for leaving you alone all afternoon,' he admitted ruefully.

And Saffy laughed. 'I'm not eighteen any more,' she reminded him gently. 'And I understand that you have responsibilities you can't escape.'

'But not the very first day you arrive. In that spirit, I have blocked off two weeks at the end of the month purely for us,' Zahir told her, his features suddenly very serious in cast. 'We can travel, stay here, do whatever you like, but there will no other demands on our time.'

Saffy was impressed that he had already foreseen the necessity for them to formally make space in their schedules to spend time together as a couple. It was an effort and an opportunity he had not tried to organise five years earlier and she appreciated it. A pretty fabulous three-course meal was served to them in the dining room. There was evidently a chef in charge of the kitchens and one out to impress. While they ate, Zahir shared his ambition to promote Maraban as a tourist destination and he asked her if she would be interested in helping to put together a public relations film to show off some of Maraban's main attractions.

'We have beaches, archaeological sites, mountains,' Zahir told her persuasively. 'You could present it. You're accustomed to being in front of the cameras.'

'Not in a speaking role, at least only occasionally.' But Saffy was pleased to be offered the chance to do something useful. 'I haven't been to any of those places though.'

Zahir frowned at the unspoken reminder that his father's determination to conceal their marriage had left her virtually imprisoned within the palace walls. 'Your eyes will be fresh then, your observations and expectations more realistic. We have a lot to learn about what tourists want. We don't have many marketing people here,' he confided. 'In fact Maraban would still be floundering and trapped in past mistakes if thousands of our former citizens hadn't responded to my appeal to come home after my father's regime fell. Many professionals returned from abroad to enable us to tackle the challenge of bringing our country into the twenty-first century.'

'It's wonderful that people chose to come back and help,' Saffy murmured, loving the gravity of his lean strong face, the warmth and concern he could not hide when he spoke about the country of his birth.

'But not half as wonderful as having you here with me again,' Zahir countered, dark golden eyes welded to her as he rose from his chair. 'Will you come to bed with me now, Your Majesty?'

'Call me Queenie—I'm never going to get used to the other. In answer to your question, I don't know...' Saffy angled her head to one side, pretending to think it over even though her heart was racing like a marathon runner's. 'Last night you were a no-show.'

Faint colour darkened his cheekbones. 'On board our flight, I didn't think I'd be welcome.'

'Put it this way—I wouldn't have kicked you out of bed,' Saffy confided, turning pink.

With a flashing smile of satisfaction, Zahir crossed the room and snatched her bodily up off the carpet into his arms to carry her down the corridor, a process accompanied by much giggling from Saffy. Halfway towards their bedroom he started kissing her and an arrow of sweet, piercing heat slivered between her thighs, smothering her amusement and awakening her body to desire.

'Being alone with you is all I've thought about all

day,' Zahir admitted, settling her down on the gigantic bed, which she noted was already clear of cushions and turned down in readiness for their occupation. Evidently the staff might be well acquainted with the habits of newly married couples.

As he cast off his robes and she kicked off her shoes Saffy smiled at his honesty. 'One-track mind.'

'*Always*...with you.' Zahir nuzzled against her slender throat, kissing and licking a sensitive spot below her ear that made her quiver and tightened her sensitive nipples. Then he groaned. 'I need a shave—'

Saffy grabbed him before he could spring back off the bed. '*Not* right now,' she told him squarely.

Zahir laughed. 'I don't want to scratch you.'

'Face facts. I won't agree to you going anywhere right at this minute,' Saffy told him, smoothing appreciative palms up over his broad muscular chest and then down very, very slowly and appreciatively over his six-pack abs. 'This is my time and I'm holding on tight to you.'

In the moonlight, Zahir's lean features were taut. 'You mean that?'

Saffy's fingers trailed daringly lower and closed around his bold erection.

With a roughened groan of satisfaction, Zahir flung himself back against the pillows. 'You're absolutely right. Nothing would move me right now.'

Saffy leant over him, her mane of hair trailing across his abdomen. He said something in Arabic. She pressed her lips to the tiny brown disc of a male nipple and moved in a southerly direction, taking her time

as she kissed and stroked her way down his beautiful
bronzed body.

'This is our wedding night…' Zahir muttered thickly.
'I should be doing this to you.'

'My turn later…right now, I'm in charge,' Saffy whispered just before she found him with her mouth and
his hands lodged firmly into her hair, his hips rising to
assist her, and an exclamation of intense pleasure was
wrenched from him. Proud of her own boldness, no longer ashamed of the desire he roused in her, Saffy was
thoroughly enjoying herself.

She loved having him in her power, revelled in every
response he couldn't control and experienced a deep
sense of achievement when he could no longer stand
her teasing caresses and he dragged her up to him and
flipped her over to ravage her lush lips with an almost
savage kiss.

Making love to Zahir turned her on and no sooner
had he registered that fact than he rose over her, all
masculine, dominant power and energy, and thrust
his engorged shaft into the silky wet tightness of her
inner channel. She cried out in delight and then he was
moving and stretching her, ramping up her level of excitement to an almost unbearable degree. It had never
occurred to her that slow and deep could be as thrilling as fast and hard, but he wouldn't let her urge him
on and control the pace.

'No, this we do *my* way,' Zahir growled, flexing his
hips, sending a shiver of exquisite sensitivity over her

entire skin surface, her nipples straining as he shifted position and angle to torture her more.

He kept her straining on the edge of climax for a long time and the ripples of growing excitement were engulfing her like a flood when, in receipt of one final driving thrust, she found a wild, scorching release that shattered her into shaking, sobbing weightlessness, utterly drained by the joy of the experience. She lay there for a long time afterwards, wrapped in his arms, steeped in pure pleasure, marvelling that they were together again.

'Now perhaps you'll consider telling me what or *who* transformed you in the bedroom from the terrified girl I remember into the woman you are now,' Zahir urged in a roughened undertone that nonetheless shockwaved through her like a sudden clap of thunder.

In receipt of that request, a little shudder of repulsion travelled through Saffy's suddenly ferociously tense body. No, she could not do that; no, she could not risk sharing what had happened to her lest it destroy the new bonds they had created. She could feel him waiting for her to speak, literally *willing* her to speak in that dreadful expectant silence. As the silence continued and she failed to respond the strong, protective arms wrapped round her tensed, loosened and then carefully withdrew and he shifted his lean, powerful body away from hers, forging a separation between them that she could feel aching through every fibre she possessed.

Zahir wasn't giving her a choice and he wasn't about to conveniently drop the subject for the sake of peace either, she recognised wretchedly. He wanted to know;

he was determined to know and he had a will of iron that would chip away at her obstinacy day after day. He wouldn't let it go and the distance that would create between them would provide fertile ground in which suspicion might well fester. Would he then start to doubt that he was truly her baby's father? Would he wonder if he had really been her only lover?

Stinging tears stung Saffy's eyes and trickled down her cheeks in the darkness. He was always so honest; he never seemed afraid of anything, never seemed to worry about how other people saw him. Why couldn't she be the same? Why couldn't she just spill it all out and stop worrying about how it might damage his view of her? But Saffy couldn't find an answer to the never-tell-anyone barrier that existed inside her mind. The therapist had had a lot of trouble getting her to talk and finally she had had hypnotherapy to overcome what she was too afraid and ashamed to remember, and only then, in possession of full knowledge, had she found it possible to move forward...

CHAPTER TEN

BREAKFAST FOR SAFFY and Zahir the following morning was an almost silent affair. Zahir, being Zahir of course, was scrupulously polite and yet in every glance, every intonation Saffy imagined she heard condemnation, suspicion, doubt that she could be trusted as he believed he should be able to trust his wife. Nausea stirred in her stomach as she contemplated the piece of toast clasped between her fingers and with a stifled apology she fled for the nearest bathroom to lose what little she had eaten.

Afterwards, weak and with hot, perspiring skin she lay down on the bed, relishing the restorative coolness of the air conditioning wafting over her.

Zahir strode through the bedroom door, stunning dark golden eyes intent on the picture she presented. 'With all the flowers surrounding you here you look like the Sleeping Beauty…'

Saffy parted pink lips. 'But this doesn't feel like a fairy tale,' she whispered apologetically because if there had ever been a romantic male, it was Zahir. And how on earth could a romantic male ever come to terms with something as ugly as her biggest secret?

'I've phoned Hayat's obstetrician.'

'Why the heck did you do that?'

'You're sick. You need medical attention,' Zahir informed her with a stubborn angle to his jaw line.

'Being sick in early pregnancy is very common and not something to make a fuss about,' Saffy countered steadily.

'I shouldn't have tired you out last night,' Zahir responded tight-mouthed, his beautiful eyes shaded by his outrageously lush black lashes.

Saffy thrust her hands down onto the mattress to lift herself up into sitting position. 'That's got nothing to do with this—this is only my body struggling to adapt to being newly pregnant and it's normal.'

'I will stop worrying only when the doctor tells me to do so. I'm responsible for looking after you,' Zahir asserted, unimpressed by her argument. 'And while I realise that you're not feeling like it, you must make an effort to eat some breakfast to keep your strength up.'

And the boss has spoken, Saffy tagged on in silence to that speech as Zahir stalked out of the door again. He did *care* that she wasn't feeling well, she assured herself ruefully. It wasn't love but it was concern, but for how long would she even retain that hold on him if she continued to keep her secrets? Naturally he was curious, naturally sooner or later he would need to know the truth about her past. For the first time she accepted that telling Zahir the truth was unavoidable and a bridge she would eventually have to cross.

Zahir's sister, Hayat, accompanied the consultant, who had tended her through her pregnancies. A well-built older man with a studious manner, he was calm and practical and exactly what Saffy needed to reinforce her belief that a little nausea was not serious cause for concern.

'The baby's father is very worried about your health,' the doctor declared. 'It is a challenge of civility to tell a king he must not worry unduly.'

Hayat was waiting outside to ask Saffy to join her for tea. Dressed in a light summer dress in shades of blue, Saffy accompanied her sister-in-law to the rear of the palace complex where she and her husband and children lived. Her husband, Rahim, was a senior doctor at the city hospital and their three little girls occupied much of Hayat and Saffy's conversation until a maid arrived to take the children out to the gardens to play.

Tea with tiny sweet cakes was served on a shaded balcony.

'My brother needs to learn to say no,' Hayat told Saffy firmly. 'The same day he brings you home a bride he was immediately dragged into some government squabble about security concerns and forced to abandon you. You will quickly discover that Zahir doesn't know how to say no to the demands made on his time.'

Saffy simply smiled, warmed by the frank tongue that Hayat appeared to share with her brother. 'Zahir was always very conscientious. Thank you for being so welcoming, Hayat. I appreciate it.'

'I know how much you and Zahir went through when you were married five years ago and our people now have a very good idea as well,' Hayat commented, her brown eyes level and serious. 'Zahir was wise when he chose to issue a public statement, admitting that he was remarrying the woman whom his father once forced him to divorce.'

Saffy stiffened in surprise at that revelation. 'I had no idea there had been any statement made about our marriage!' she exclaimed.

'Or that now my brother, the king, is forced to tell *lies* in public to protect *you?*' another louder voice interposed from the doorway behind them and both women's heads whipped around in astonishment at the interruption.

'Akram!' Hayat snapped in a warning tone at her youngest brother before turning back to Saffy with her face flushed and her expression uneasy to say, 'Please excuse me for a moment.'

But Zahir's volatile kid brother had worked up too much of a head of steam to be denied the confrontation with his brother's wife that his temper clearly craved. He concentrated his attention on Saffy, who was already starting to rise from her chair in dismay. 'You walked out on my brother—you *deserted* him after all he had endured to keep you as a wife against our father's wishes!' he accused with loathing. 'Zahir was imprisoned, tortured and beaten for your benefit and then you threw your marriage away by divorcing him when he needed your loyalty most!'

Her expression distraught, Hayat was pleading with her angry brother to keep quiet while simultaneously yanking on his arm in an unsuccessful effort to physically drag him away.

Saffy could barely part her numb lips. She was in serious shock from Akram's ringing condemnation of her behaviour. And what on earth was he talking about? Imprisoned, tortured, *beaten? Zahir?*

'I will deal with this…' and another more familiar voice intervened, cutting across the row going on between Hayat and Akram with commanding force.

Trembling, Saffy focused on Zahir where he stood like a bronzed statue in the centre of the light, airy reception room, coldly surveying his squabbling siblings. He spoke in his own language at length to Akram and Hayat backed off, dropping her head apologetically. Whatever Zahir told his brother, Akram turned his head in consternation to stare back at Saffy with frowning disbelief. He took a half-step towards her and muttered uncomfortably, 'I am very sorry. It seems I got everything wrong.'

'Yes, Zahir divorced me,' Saffy pointed out ruefully.

'Even so, I should never have spoken to you in that way or approached you in a temper. It was not my business,' Akram mumbled, his face very flushed, his discomfiture in Zahir's thunderous presence pronounced. 'Over the years it seems I reached the wrong conclusions and, as my brother has reminded me, I was never party to the true facts of what happened between you.'

An uneasy silence fell. Zahir was still glaring angrily at his kid brother.

'No harm done,' Saffy said awkwardly, keen to dispel the tension. 'I assume that Zahir has told you what really happened and that you no longer think so badly of me. Now, if you would all excuse me...'

'Where are you going?' Zahir demanded.

'Only for a walk. I'd like to be alone for a while,' she muttered tightly.

'I will accompany you,' Zahir pronounced.

'No...I only want a minute alone,' Saffy whispered pleadingly, because she was thinking about what Akram had hurled at her and reaching the worst possible conclusions. Zahir had been punished by his father for defying him by marrying her? Why had that possibility never occurred to her before? Why had she been so wrapped up in her own misery that it had never occurred to her that Zahir might be dealing with bad things too? But, imprisoned, tortured, beaten...surely not? Was that possible? Would his father have subjected his son to such brutal intimidation? According to his reputation, King Fareed had been responsible for many atrocities. She thought of Zahir's appallingly scarred back and a sense of cold fear of the unknown and of such cruelty infiltrated her. But if Zahir had suffered like that, why hadn't he told her?

When Saffy actually focused enough to recognise where her wandering feet had carried her, she realised that she was back in the old part of the palace where she had once lived. She walked down a dim corridor and cast open the door of the room that had once been theirs. It shook her that it was still furnished the same, untouched by time or alteration, and she walked in with a compulsive shiver of remembrance of the past.

A thousand images engulfed her all at once and she reeled from memories of Zahir watching her with wary eyes, his silences, sudden absences and his refusal to answer questions. Had he been hiding stuff from her that she should have guessed? Was Akram telling the truth? She couldn't bear that suspicion, wasn't sure she could ever live with any discovery that painful…

'I should have had this place cleared…' Zahir murmured from behind her. 'But I used to come here to think about you.'

Saffy turned round, her face pale as milk, her eyes nakedly vulnerable. 'When? After the divorce? I think you need to start talking, Zahir…and maybe I do too,' she acknowledged unevenly.

'After I married you, my brother Omar asked me if I was insane to challenge our father to that extent,' Zahir admitted with curt reluctance. 'But at first I genuinely had no idea what I was dealing with: Omar had protected me too much. He kept a lot of secrets. I was the younger son, the junior army officer, and I wasn't part of the inner circle of people who knew what a monster my father had become on a diet of unfettered power.'

'So, you must have regretted marrying me rather quickly,' Saffy assumed, searching the lean strong features she loved for every passing nuance of expression and sinking down on the edge of the bed where she had often cried her heart out with loneliness.

His handsome mouth hardened. 'I only ever regretted the unnatural lifestyle which our marriage inflicted on you. I had no regrets on my own behalf.'

'That's a kind thing to say but it can't be the way you really felt.'

'I loved you more than life,' Zahir breathed starkly. 'My mistake was in rebelling against my father and bringing you back here to become the equivalent of a hostage. I should have married you and left you in London where you would be safe, but I was too selfish to do that.'

Loved you more than life. The declaration rippled through her like an unexpected benediction, steadying her nerves. 'I loved you too. You weren't selfish. I wouldn't have agreed to being left behind in London.'

'But you didn't know what you were getting into here any more than I did.' Face grave, Zahir compressed his lips. 'Omar had been married five years and he still had no child. Our father was impatient to see the next generation in the family born.'

'That must have put a lot of pressure on Omar and Azel.'

'More on Omar for the lack of fertility was his, *not* hers but I didn't learn that until shortly before Omar... *died*.' He spoke that last word with curious emphasis. 'My older brother's secret was that he had discovered he was unable to father a child and he was afraid to tell our father lest he was passed over in the succession stakes in favour of me. Omar was always the ambitious one,' Zahir told her heavily. 'Unfortunately for him, our father had run out of patience. He demanded that Omar either set Azel aside or take a second wife.'

Saffy was shocked. 'And that was the background to *our* marriage?'

'Our father was doubly enraged when I married you without permission because my marriage to a suitable woman would have been the next step on his agenda.'

'And of course I got in the way of his plans,' Saffy completed. 'Yet you thought he would eventually accept me.'

'I was wrong,' Zahir admitted grittily. 'I was much more naïve than I thought I was about what our father was really like. I never dreamt he would be as vicious with his sons as he was to some of our people. How adolescent was such innocence in a grown man?'

'Everybody wants to think the best of their parents,' Saffy told him with rueful understanding. 'I don't blame you for getting it wrong.'

'The year we were married was the year my father went over the edge. Although I was unaware of it, he had become a regular drug user and suffered from violent rages. From the first day you arrived he wanted me to divorce you...and the sensible act would have been to surrender to greater force, but I was never sensible about you.'

Her heart was beating in what felt uncomfortably like the foot of her throat. 'Greater force?' she queried suspiciously. 'If even half of what Akram suggested happened to you, I have the right to know about it. *Were* you imprisoned? Tortured? *Beaten?*'

Zahir stared levelly back at her, not a muscle moving on his bronzed handsome face, his mouth an unsmiling line. 'I could curse Akram, though he spoke out of ignorance. This is a conversation I never wanted to have with you…'

Saffy was trembling. 'You're telling me that your father—your own father—did do that stuff to you?' she prompted sickly. 'That you weren't away on army manoeuvres when you disappeared for weeks on end?'

Zahir gave confirmation with a grudging jerk of his chin.

And Saffy just closed her eyes, because all of a sudden she couldn't bear to look at him when she had excelled at being such a blind, childish fool all the months they had been man and wife the first time around. He had reappeared after those apparent military trips, filthy, often visibly bruised and cut, always having lost weight…and not once had she questioned the condition he was in, not once had she suspected that he had been brutally ill-treated while he was away from her and prevented from returning from her. In her little cocoon the very fact he was a prince had made entertaining such a suspicion too incredible to even consider. She had assumed that soldiers led a rough and ready life and that such trips were organised to be as realistic and tough as real warfare. And he had never told her, never once breathed a word of what was being done to him, never once sought her sympathy or support…

'Why didn't you tell me?' she asked thickly, tears thickening her throat and creating a huge lump there.

'I didn't want to upset you. There was nothing you could have done to stop it. Omar was correct. I should never have brought you to Maraban. Our father was a madman and he was out of control, incapable of accepting any form of opposition. It was all or nothing and once I defied him he was determined to break me.'

'And all over *me*…all because you married me,' Saffy muttered, her distress growing by the second as she looked back on her colossally ignorant and oblivious self at the age of eighteen. Little wonder he had ducked her questions, embraced silence, never knowing when he would be with her or torn from her side again.

'That whole year you were the only thing that kept me going,' Zahir informed her harshly. *'Look at me.'*

'No!' Saffy unfroze finally and flew upright. 'I have to think about this on my own!'

As she tried to brush past him he closed a hand round a slim forearm. 'I told you I would tell no more lies or half-truths but I never wanted you to know about that period of my life!'

'Oh, I know that…Mr Macho-I-suffer-in-silence!' Saffy condemned chokily, her increasing distress clawing at her control. 'So when you came back here to me after suffering gross mistreatment and allowed me to shout at you and complain that I was bored and lonely?

Just what I need to know to feel like the biggest bitch ever created!'

And, tears streaming down her distraught face, Saffy fled, in need of privacy. How could he do that to her? How could he not have told her? How could he have allowed her to find out all that from his resentful brother? She had known King Fareed wasn't a pleasant or popular man, but she had had no idea that he was a drug-abusing tyrant capable of torturing his own son if he was disobedient! What an idiot she must have been not to have guessed that something so dreadful was going on! How could she ever forgive herself for that? *You were the only thing that kept me going.* Why was he still trying to make her feel better by saying that sort of rubbish? He'd been stuck in a virtually sexless marriage while being regularly punished for rebelling against his father's dictates. And not once had she suspected anything. Was she stupid, utterly stupid, to have been so unseeing?

Saffy took refuge in their new bedroom, which was comfortably removed from the suffocating memories of the older accommodation they had once occasionally shared. She was remembering the condition of Zahir's back, thinking, although she didn't want to, of him being whipped, beaten up, *hurt* and all on her behalf. Zahir with his pride and his intrinsic sense of decency! She ran to the bathroom and heaved but nothing came up and she hugged the vanity unit to stay upright, surveying her tousled reflection with stricken accusing eyes.

How could you not know? How could you not see what he was going through?

'This is why I never wanted you to know. I didn't want to see you hurt because all of it was my fault...'

Saffy spun round. He stood in the doorway, lean and bronzed and gorgeous in black jeans and a white shirt, so much the guy she loved and admired and cared about. 'How was it your fault?' she scissored back at him incredulously.

'I married you. I brought you back here with me. I placed both of us in a foolish and vulnerable position,' Zahir stated grimly. 'I will never forgive myself for that.'

'You should've divorced me the minute the punishments started!' Saffy launched back at him. 'How could you be so stubborn that you went through that just for me?'

A faint shadow of a smile that struck her as impossible in the circumstances curved his wide sensual mouth. 'I loved you...I couldn't give you up.'

'I wouldn't have let you go through that if I'd known! How could you still want me?' she sobbed in disbelief. 'I wasn't even able to give you sex!'

'The sex was the least of it. Believe me, at the time, consummating our marriage was not my biggest challenge.' His stunning golden eyes lowered from her shaken face and he held out a hand until she grasped it, allowing him to pull her closer. 'But I couldn't seek help or advice for us either. Had anyone known we had those problems my father would have had yet another reason to want you out of my life...'

Saffy dragged in a quivering breath, still reeling from what she had learned. Eyes wet, she pushed her face against his shoulder, drinking in the scent of his sun-warmed flesh, the faint evocative tang that was uniquely his, which made her feel vaguely intoxicated. She was addicted to him, so pathetically *addicted*. 'Thank heaven you finally had the sense to divorce me and give the dreadful man what he wanted.'

'That was probably the one and only unselfish thing I ever did while I was married to you, the only thing I *ever* did solely for you and not for me,' Zahir muttered roughly above her down-bent head, his lips brushing across her brow in a calming gesture. 'I'm not the saint you seem to think. I made appalling errors of judgement.'

Her forehead furrowing, she looked up at him 'Such as?'

'Bringing you into Maraban five years ago,' he specified. 'Three months after Omar's death, I found out that he had been murdered...'

'What?' Shattered by that statement, she stared up at him.

'One of the generals told me the truth because the most senior army personnel were becoming nervous about my father's reign of terror. Omar was beaten up by my father's henchmen and he died from a head injury. The car crash was simply a cover-up. It was then that I realised that my father really had gone beyond the hope of return,' Zahir revealed rawly.

'Oh…my…word,' Saffy framed sickly. 'Are you sure?'

'One hundred per cent.' Zahir compressed his lips. 'That's when I appreciated that keeping you in Maraban was sheer insanity when my father wanted rid of you. I didn't have the power to protect you. I was putting your life at risk by refusing to divorce you. I was making you a target in my father's eyes. I'm ashamed it took Omar's death to make me accept that if I couldn't keep you safe, I *had* to let you go….'

Saffy's heart was beating very loudly in her eardrums and she drifted dizzily away from him on weak legs to drop heavily down on a sofa in the corner of their room. 'So, that's why the divorce came out of nowhere at me. You honestly thought I was in danger. Why didn't you tell me the truth then, Zahir?'

'The truth would have terrified you and I was ashamed that I could not even keep myself safe, never mind my wife. But that was also the moment that, in losing you, my father finally lost my loyalty. I could never have forgiven him for what he had done to Omar, but losing you was excruciating,' he completed gruffly, dropping down on his knees in front of her and momentarily lowering his dark head down onto her lap. 'You have no idea how much I loved you, what strength it took to give you up, knowing, having to accept that it was the *only* thing I could do…'

As he admitted that stinging tears were rolling down Saffy's face. She had never dreamt that she could feel such pain on someone else's behalf and yet when Zahir talked of how much it had hurt to divorce her, it was as if a giant black hole of unhappiness opened up inside her and cracked her heart right down the middle. Her fingers delved into his luxuriant black hair, delving, smoothing. 'I loved you too…I loved you so much. I don't think I even understood how much I needed you in my life until we were forced apart,' she confided jaggedly.

'I tried to contact you after my father died and the fighting was finished,' Zahir told her grimly as he lifted his handsome dark head and leapt back upright to pace restively. 'I spoke to your sister, Kat.'

Saffy was stunned. 'She didn't tell me.'

Zahir grimaced. 'Kat pleaded with me to leave you alone. She said you had just got your life back together, that you were working, making friends and that the last thing you needed was to see me again,' Zahir recalled, tight-mouthed at the recollection.

Saffy felt as if someone had walked over her grave. How could the sister she loved have got her so wrong? The divorce had broken her heart but she had still loved Zahir and would have moved heaven and earth to see him again. 'She shouldn't have interfered.'

'On that score we'll have to disagree.' Zahir surprised her with that response. 'Sadly, even though I didn't like what Kat had to say, she was right.'

'No, she was wrong,' Saffy contradicted.

'You were far too young to deal with what I was dealing with then on top of the other problems we had and Maraban had. You needed the time to live the normal life you should have enjoyed before we married,' Zahir contended. 'I can see that now but I couldn't see it at the time. I simply wanted you back the minute it would have been safe to bring you back...'

Tears trickled down Saffy's cheeks. 'I would've come back to you,' she whispered shakily.

'You would've walked away from those magazine covers and your face everywhere?' Zahir prompted dubiously.

'Yes, it was never that important to me. It was the means to make a living and not be a burden on my sister.'

Zahir bent down and grasped her hands to raise her. 'But we work better now because we're older and wiser.'

A shadow crossed her lovely face. 'And, of course, you're much more experienced.'

He paled, his strong bone structure tightening. 'After our *mutual* failure, I was afraid I had become...impotent. I had lost all confidence,' he confided in a grudging undertone, tension and shame etched in every line of his strong face. 'I knew I had to get past my obsession with you because you were no longer mine. My father sent me abroad before the civil war broke out. Ironically he was trying to reward me for divorcing you...'

Saffy lifted her fingers and gently smoothed the stubborn angle of his jaw. 'It's all right. I can't say I don't mind because that would be a lie, but I understand why it happened.'

His beautiful dark eyes narrowed and centred intently on her solemn face. 'Then isn't it time you explained how that miracle happened for you? You insist there hasn't been another man but—'

'That was the truth.' Her wandering fingers strayed to his wide sensual lower lip to silence him. 'I wanted to be normal in the bedroom and I went to see a specialist to find out what was wrong with me. I was told that I suffered from a condition called vaginismus, which is an involuntary tightening of the pelvic muscles, often triggered by some trauma in the past. My inability to relax, the panic attacks when you tried to touch me were all part of it,' she explained, doggedly pushing herself on to spill what had lain behind her deepest vulnerability. 'I went for therapy but it wasn't until I had hypnotherapy that I discovered what had triggered my phobia about that part of my body...'

Zahir held her back from him, his shrewd gaze welded to her troubled face and the sheen of perspiration already dampening her upper lip. 'Tell me—there should be nothing you can't tell me.'

'I was abused by one of my mother's boyfriends when I was a child,' Saffy framed shakily, tears welling up in her eyes because she could not bring herself to look and see how he was reacting to that unsavoury news. 'I suppose I was lucky he didn't rape me, but then he was never able to get me alone for very long. He threatened me. He said that if I told Mum, she wouldn't believe me, and he said Emmie and Topsy would have to take my place.'

Zahir swore in his own language and gripped her

shoulders. 'Please tell me that you went to your mother for help.'

A taut expression set Saffy's face. 'I did but my abuser was right—Mum refused to believe me and punished me for even opening the subject. My abuser was a well-off professional man with a name for being a womaniser and there was no way my mother was going to give him up or suspect him on only the strength of my word.'

Zahir pushed up her chin. 'What age were you?'

'Seven.' Saffy gazed up into his furious eyes and shivered. 'I couldn't stop him, Zahir, but I knew it was wrong.'

Zahir almost crushed her in his arms. 'Is that the impression I'm giving you? That it was somehow your fault that some filthy pervert abused your trust? That's *not* how I feel. I'm furious the bastard got away with it, furious your mother wouldn't listen to you, furious I wasn't there to prevent it happening in the first place!' he spelt out in a savage undertone.

'You're angry.'

'But *not* with you, with the people who have hurt you and let you down, even though I'm one of their number,' he muttered, his breathing fracturing as he scooped her up and brought her carefully down on the bed with him, holding her close to every line of his long, lean physique. 'Facing the fact that you'd been abused must have been very difficult for you.'

'Apparently it's quite common for children to suppress memories of that kind of assault,' Saffy whispered unevenly, reassured by the solid thump of his heart against her breast and the reality that he was hugging her without demonstrating any symptoms of revulsion towards her. 'I felt horrible but, on one level, it was a relief to find out what had made me the way I was. I knew I'd never be able to have another relationship until I could overcome my problems.'

'I wish I'd known. What treatment did you have?'

'I had loads of supportive counselling and then a physical intervention,' Saffy explained hesitantly. 'I had muscle relaxants injected to prevent the contractions and a dilator was inserted while I was still unconscious. For a long time I slept with it inserted overnight...' As Zahir looked down at her, her face was burning. 'I had to learn to accept my own body and to touch myself. I'd always avoided that without ever wondering why. I assumed I was just very fastidious, I didn't know I suffered from an actual phobia until we got married and it all went wrong. But after I had completed the treatment I did hope to find a lover once I'd worked through all the recovery steps.'

'And why didn't you do that?' Zahir demanded, stunning dark golden eyes pinned to her. 'I shouldn't have thought that would have been a challenge.'

'You'd be surprised. I not only wanted a man who attracted me, but also one whom I *cared* something about. Having waited so long and gone through so much to find the answer to my problems, I didn't want just anyone!' Saffy explained with spirit. 'Unfortunately the right guy didn't appear. To most of the men I met, I would only have been a trophy. I wanted more than that from a man. I believed I deserved more than that.'

His lush black lashes semi-screened his glittering scrutiny, colour lying in a hard line along his fabulous cheekbones. 'Then how on earth did you contrive to settle for me again?'

Saffy stiffened. 'I was still very attracted to you… don't know why,' she dared to pronounce, watching his amazing eyes smoulder at that challenge into glowing golden flames. 'I told myself that being with you didn't mean anything to me emotionally and that I was simply using you to get rid of my virginity.'

Zahir nodded very slowly and then bent his head to steal a kiss that made her head spin, and her fingers clutched frantic handfuls of his luxuriant black hair. The pressure of his mouth combined with the penetration of his tongue was an intoxicating thrill, so that when he lifted his head again, separating them, she frowned.

'I told myself a lot of lies that night in the tent as well. I couldn't admit how I still felt about you,' he confided with a hard twist of his mouth. 'In fact in the time we were divorced I had grown unreasonably and unjustly bitter.'

'Bitter?' she queried.

'Bitter that I'd loved and lost you and that you appeared to be having a hell of a good time without me. Even worse, I couldn't forget you,' he confessed harshly. 'There you were in my sister's magazines, which she was always leaving lying around, seemingly enjoying a party lifestyle with various different men. I was angry and jealous… There, I have said it at last! I wanted you back from the moment I lost you and I never changed towards you. I loved you five years ago and I love you even more now…'

'You…*do?*' Saffy was enchanted by that admission and the ferocious fervent force with which he spoke and studied her.

'I love you and I always will.' Zahir groaned because the wife he adored was not a patient woman and she was stroking her hand down his taut, powerful thigh with rousing intent.

'I love you too… I didn't stop loving you either,' Saffy confided. 'But I was too proud to admit that. At first, I wanted you to believe I'd had other lovers.'

'It wouldn't have mattered if you had had. I would still love you. I've grown up too,' Zahir declared. 'Circumstances tore us apart.'

'But you brought us back together again.' Saffy scored a fingernail along the rippling muscle of one thigh, loving his instant response to her provocation. 'You kidnapped me.'

'I also asked you to be my mistress. I'm ashamed of that,' he said bluntly. 'But I wanted you any way I could get you… I couldn't face losing you again but my behaviour was inexcusable.'

Saffy stared down at him and suddenly grinned, unable to hide her amusement. 'But that behaviour was very much *you*. You can't fight what you are inside: direct, bold, passionate. I couldn't believe you still wanted me that much after our disastrous year together.'

'I honestly did believe that it was *I* who had failed *you* in the bedroom,' Zahir told her tautly. 'I assumed my clumsiness and ignorance had scared you, that I'd hurt you, given you a *fear* of intimacy.'

'No…no, it wouldn't have mattered who I was with, it would have been the same, but another man might not have had your patience,' she argued, her eyes not leaving his for a second as, drawn like a moth to a flame, she slowly lowered her mouth to his. 'You were very kind and understanding when you must have been hugely sexually frustrated.'

It was Zahir's turn to smile. 'No, you took care of me in other ways and I had few complaints.'

Saffy tensed. 'Doesn't knowing about the…er… abuse turn you off?'

'No, it makes you even more worthy of being the love of my life. I know how strong you must be to have got through that and dealt with it.' With gentle fingers he smoothed a stray strand of golden hair from her brow. 'I know how hard I had to work coming to terms with what was done to me while I was imprisoned by my father…'

'I still can't stand the thought of that,' she admitted chokily, her eyes filming over.

'Omar and I were raised like spoilt little rich kids with titles. Being powerless and a victim taught me a lot that I needed to learn for the benefit of others,' Zahir delivered wryly, rolling over to slide a long, hard thigh between hers and nudge her knees apart. 'I want to make love to you…I want to know that you're mine forever.'

Loving the weight of him against her, Saffy gave him

a teasing smile. 'I hope you do appreciate that you will be stuck with me for ever.'

'I was terrified that that might not be the case,' Zahir sliced in, claiming a hungry driving kiss that left her breathless. 'Afraid that you were keeping your options open and planning to ask me for a divorce some day.'

'As long as you can kiss me like that, you're pretty safe,' Saffy teased, watching heat flare in his gaze.

He made love to her with all the scorching passion of his temperament and when she finally subsided in the strong circle of his arms, alight with happiness and the glorious aftermath of incredible physical pleasure, she snuggled close to him. 'I'm not going anywhere away from you ever again,' she swore vehemently.

Zahir grinned, splayed long fingers over her still-flat tummy and gently stroked it. 'So, you'll sleep in a tent with me next time I ask?'

'As long as it has electric and hot and cold running water,' Saffy specified. 'You're really happy about the baby, aren't you?'

A slashing smile scythed across his lean bronzed features. 'Of course I'm excited about the baby, the next generation. We'll be a family as I always dreamt. I still remember the first time I saw you in that store,' he confided huskily. 'And people don't believe in love at first sight.'

'I do...' Lacing her fingers into his thick, tousled black hair, Saffy looked up into his gorgeous eyes with a heart beating like a drum. 'And after what we've been through together and apart, I also believe that a love like that can last for ever...'

'For ever,' Zahir repeated, wrapping both arms round her and pulling her close, knowing that, having lost her once, he would never take the smallest risk of losing her again.

Two years on from that conversation, Saffy soothed her son, Karim, as he fell off his toddler bike for at least the third time and roared with temper and frustration. As soon as his mother set him down again on his sturdy little legs, Karim streaked back to the bike, determined to master the art of riding it so that he could race around the gardens in the company of his female cousins. As she watched her little boy tell the bike off for not doing his bidding, she laughed.

'He doesn't give up easily,' her sister, Kat, commented.

'No, he's like Zahir in that.' Saffy smiled at her sibling, loving the fact that she and Mikhail had come to stay with them in Maraban but aching for the couple at the same time. Kat had recently gone through IVF in Russia in an attempt to conceive but, sadly, the procedure hadn't worked. In another month the couple were set for a second try and Saffy was praying that the treatment would deliver a successful result, for if any woman deserved a child of her own it was Kat, who had raised her three sisters with so much love and support.

'The servants wait on him hand and foot,' Kat commented. 'You'll have to watch that.'

'I do. He tidies up his own toys. Zahir doesn't want him spoiled the same way he was.'

'The way your husband spoils you?' Kat laughed, secure in the knowledge that Saffy was deliriously happy in Maraban.

'Spoiling me gives Zahir a kick,' Saffy confided with a grin, thinking of the vast selection of jewels and luxuries she was continually showered in.

More importantly, Saffy had found a real role to keep her busy in her husband's country. She had participated in making a promotional film of Maraban and had impressed everybody with her skill as a presenter. But then she had thoroughly enjoyed the personalised tour of the various sites of interest with Zahir by her side and had become almost as knowledgeable about his country of birth as he was in the process. The warm welcome of the locals had increased her identification with Maraban as her new home. She had got involved with local charities, now sat on the board of the newest hospital in the city and regularly visited educational institutions. But most precious of all on her terms had been spending an entire week with Zahir and Karim at the orphanage school in South Africa, which she had long supported.

As a rule she usually went to London to see her sisters. Topsy was at university, studying hard and rarely free for more than a weekend, but Emmie often visited London to shop and the twins now got together as often as they could contrive it. Rediscovering her relationship with her sister meant a great deal to Saffy and the process was helped by the reality that both women now had much more in common.

Zahir strode through the door with Mikhail a mere step in his wake. Kat's husband, a Russian billionaire, was currently advising the Marabani government on how best to invest the oil revenues that kept the country afloat. Zahir swept his son off the bike a split second before the child fell again.

'He won't stop trying,' Saffy told her handsome husband. 'He won't give up. He's so like you.'

'But he has your eyes and impatience,' Zahir remarked appreciatively as he set his squirming son down again and watched him head straight back to the demon bike that still wouldn't do what he wanted it to do.

Zahir linked his fingers with Saffy and walked her out onto the terrace. Overhead the sun was sinking in a peach and orange blaze of colour and soon they would sit down to dinner by candlelight and talk long into the night. Just for a moment, even though she was very much enjoying having her sister and her husband as guests, she wished she were alone with Zahir.

He looked down at her with smouldering dark golden eyes and butterflies leapt in her tummy and her mouth ran dry. 'We should get dressed for dinner,' he murmured lazily.

A smile tugging at her lush lips, Saffy leant back against his lean powerful body in an attitude of complete trust, knowing they would end up in bed, loving the fact that he found it as hard to keep his hands off her as she did him. She was deliriously happy in her mar-

riage and Karim's arrival had enriched and deepened the
ties between her and Zahir. 'I love you,' she whispered.

'I love you too,' Zahir purred, pressing his mouth
hungrily to the base of her throat and making her shiver
against him.

* * * * *

Emir promised pleasure. He promised forgetfulness. And for however short a time the prospect of that seemed preferable right now to doing battle endlessly on every front.

How would it feel to have this big man hold her and have those strong hands bring her pleasure?

She must have swayed towards him, for the next thing she knew he was holding her in front of him.

'Why, Britt,' he said. 'If I'd known we could have arranged something before the meeting.'

He was blunter than she had ever been—blunter than she was prepared for—and breath shot out of her lungs as he dipped his head to brush her lips with his. Incredibly, she was instantly hungry, instantly frantic for more pressure, more intimacy, and for everything to happen fast.

He felt so good…so very good.

She wanted this. She needed it. And she forgot everything the moment his hands caressed her breasts. She wanted this—wanted him. She wanted, just for once in her life, to feel that she didn't have to be the leader, the fighter, that just this one time she could be a woman.

DIAMOND
IN THE DESERT

BY
SUSAN STEPHENS

First published in Great Britain 2013
by Mills & Boon, an imprint of Harlequin (UK) Limited.
Harlequin (UK) Limited, Eton House, 18-24 Paradise Road,
Richmond, Surrey TW9 1SR

© Susan Stephens 2013

ISBN: 978 0 263 90016 3

Harlequin (UK) policy is to use papers that are natural, renewable and recyclable products and made from wood grown in sustainable forests. The logging and manufacturing process conform to the legal environmental regulations of the country of origin.

Printed and bound in Spain
by Blackprint CPI, Barcelona

DIAMOND
IN THE DESERT

For all my wonderful readers
who love the mystery of the desert
and the romance of a sheikh.

CHAPTER ONE

MONDAY SEVEN A.M. on a cold, foggy day in London a breakfast meeting was being held by a powerful consortium set up to acquire the world's biggest diamond mine. The group of three men was led by Sheikh Sharif al Kareshi, a leading geologist otherwise known as the Black Sheikh, thanks to his discovery of vast oil lakes beneath the desert sands of Kareshi. Concealed lighting was set at the perfect level for reading the fine print on a contract, and the surroundings were sumptuous as befitted the ruling Sheikh of Kareshi in his London home. Seated with the sheikh at the table were two men of roughly the same age, that was to say, thirty-two. One was a Spaniard, and the other owned an island off southern Italy. All three men were giants in the world of commerce, and heartbreakers in the game of life. Colossal sums of money were being bandied about. The atmosphere was tense.

'A diamond mine beyond the Arctic circle?' the darkly glamorous Count Roman Quisvada remarked.

'Diamonds were discovered in the Canadian Arctic some years back,' Sharif explained, leaning back. 'Why not the European Arctic, my friend?'

All three men had been friends since boarding school in England, and, although they had all gone on to make individual fortunes, they were bound by friendship and trusted each other implicitly.

'My first pass over the findings suggests this discovery by Skavanga Mining could be even larger than we suspected,' Sharif went on, pushing some documents across the table to the other two men.

'And I hear that Skavanga boasts three sisters who have become known as the Skavanga Diamonds, which in itself intrigues me,' the dangerous-looking Spaniard commented as he peeled a Valencia orange with a blade as sharp as a scalpel.

'I'll tell you what I know, Raffa,' the sheikh promised his friend, better known as Don Rafael de Leon, Duke of Cantalabria, a mountainous and very beautiful region of Spain.

Count Roman Quisvada also sat forward. Roman was an expert in diamonds, with laboratories that specialised in cutting and polishing high-value stones, while Raffa owned the world's largest and most exclusive chain of high-end retail jewellers. The Black Sheikh, the Italian count, and the Spanish duke had the diamond business sewn up.

There was just one loose end, Sharif reflected, and that was a company called Skavanga Mining. Owned by the three sisters, Britt, Eva and Leila Skavanga, along with the girls' absentee brother, Tyr, Skavanga Mining had reported the discovery of the largest diamond deposits ever recorded. He was on the point of going to Skavanga to check out these reports for himself.

While he was there he would check out Britt Skavanga, the oldest sister, who was currently running the company, Sharif mused as he drew a photograph towards him. She looked like a worthy opponent with her clear grey eyes, firm mouth and the tilt of that chin. He looked forward to meeting her. A deal with the added spice of down time in the bedroom held obvious appeal. There was no sentiment in business and he certainly wasted none on women.

'Why do you get all the fun?' Roman complained, frowning when Sharif told the other men about his plan.

'There are plenty to go round,' he reassured them dryly as the other two men studied the photographs of the sisters. Glancing at Raffa, he felt a momentary twinge of something close to apprehension. The youngest sister, whom Raffa was studying, was clearly an innocent, while Raffa was most certainly not.

'Three good-looking women,' Roman commented, glancing between his friends.

'For three ruthless asset strippers,' Raffa added, devouring the last piece of orange with relish. 'I look forward to stripping the assets off this one—'

Raffa's dark eyes blackened dangerously as Sharif gathered the photographs in. Sharif hardly realised that he was caressing the photograph of Britt Skavanga with his forefinger while denying Raffa further study of Leila, the youngest sister.

'This could be our most promising project to date,' the man known to the world as the Black Sheikh commented.

'And if anyone can land this deal, Sharif can,' Roman remarked, hoping to heal the momentary rift between his friends. He could only be thankful their interest wasn't in the same girl.

Raffa's laugh relaxed them all. 'Didn't I hear you have some interesting sexual techniques in Kareshi, Sharif? Silken ties? Chiffon blindfolds?'

Roman huffed a laugh at this. 'I've heard the same

thing. In the harem tents it's said they use creams and potions to send sensation through the roof—'

'Enough,' Sharif rapped, raising his hands to silence his friends. 'Can we please return to business?'

Within seconds the Skavanga girls were forgotten and the talk was all of balance sheets and financial predictions, but in one part of his mind Sharif was still thinking about a pair of cool grey eyes and a full, expressive mouth, and what could be accomplished with a little expert tutelage.

An absolute monarch, bred to a hard life in the desert, Sharif had been trained to rule and fight and argue at council with the wisest of men—women being notable by their absence, which was something he had changed as soon as he took over the country. Women in Kareshi had used to be regarded as ornaments to be pampered and spoiled and hidden away; under his rule they were expected to pull their weight. Education for all was now the law.

And who would dare to argue with the Black Sheikh? Not Britt Skavanga, that was for sure. Staring at Britt's photograph and seeing the steely determination so similar to his own in her eyes only reinforced his intention to check out all the assets in Skavanga personally. Britt possessed the generous, giving mouth of a concubine, with the unrelenting gaze of a Viking warrior. The combination aroused him. Even the severity of the suit she was wearing intrigued him. Her breasts thrusting against the soft wool stirred his senses in a most agreeable way. He adored severe tailoring on a woman. It was a type of shorthand he had learned to read many years ago. Severe equalled repressed, or possibly a player who liked to tease. Either way, he was a huge fan.

'Are you still with us, Sharif?' Raffa enquired with

amusement as his friend finally pushed Britt's photograph away.

'Yes, but not for long as I will be leaving for Skavanga in the morning, travelling in my capacity of geologist and advisor to the consortium. This will allow me to make an impartial assessment of the situation without ruffling any feathers.'

'That's sensible,' Raffa agreed. 'Talk of the Black Sheikh descending on a business would be enough to send anyone into a panic.'

'Have you ever *descended* on a tasty business prospect without devouring it?' Roman enquired, hiding his smile.

'The fact that this mysterious figure, conjured by the press and known to the world as the Black Sheikh, has never had a photograph published will surely be an advantage to you,' Raffa suggested.

'I reserve judgement until we meet again when I will be in a position to tell you if the claims that have been made about the Skavanga Diamonds are true,' Sharif said with a closing gesture.

'We can ask for no more than that,' his two friends agreed.

'Well, clearly, I must be the one to meet him,' Britt insisted as the three sisters sat round the interestingly shaped—if not very practical, thanks to the holes the designer had punched in it—blonde wood kitchen table in Britt's sleek, minimalist, barely lived-in penthouse.

'Clearly—why?' Britt's feisty middle sister, Eva, demanded. 'Who says you have the right to take the lead in this new venture? Shouldn't we all have a part in it? What about the equality you're always banging on about, Britt?'

'Britt has far more business experience than we have,' the youngest and most mild-mannered sister, Leila, pointed out. 'And that's a perfectly sensible reason for Britt to be the one to meet with him,' Leila added, sweeping anxious fingers through her tumbling blonde curls.

'Perfectly sensible?' Eva scoffed. 'Britt has experience in mining iron ore and copper. But diamonds?' Eva rolled her emerald eyes. 'You must agree the three of us are virgins where diamonds are concerned?'

And Eva was likely to remain a virgin in every sense if she kept on like this, Britt thought, fretting like a mother over her middle sister. Eva had been a glass-half-empty type of person for as long as Britt could remember and sadly there were no dashing Petruchios in Skavanga to prevent Eva from turning into a fully-fledged shrew. 'I'm going to deal with this—and with him,' she said firmly.

'You and the Black Sheikh?' Eva said scornfully. 'You might be a hotshot businesswoman here in Skavanga, but the sheikh's business interests are global—and he runs a country. What on earth makes you think you can take a man like that on?'

'I know my business,' Britt said calmly. 'I know our mine and I'll be factual. I'll be cool and I'll be reasoned.'

'Britt's very good at doing stuff like this without engaging her emotions,' Leila added.

'Really?' Eva mocked. 'Whether she can or not remains to be seen.'

'I won't let you down,' Britt promised, knowing her sisters' concerns both for her and for the business had prompted this row. 'I've handled difficult people in the past and I'm well prepared to meet the Black Sheikh. I realise I must handle him with kid gloves—'

'Nice.' Eva laughed.

Britt ignored this. 'We would be unwise to underestimate him,' she said. 'The ruler of Kareshi is known as the Black Sheikh for a very good reason—'

'Rape and pillage?' Eva suggested scathingly.

Britt held her tongue. 'Sheikh Sharif is one of the foremost geologists in the world.'

'It's a shame we couldn't find any photographs of him,' Leila mused.

'He's a geologist, not a film star,' Britt pointed out. 'And how many Arab rulers have you seen photographs of?'

'He's probably so ugly he'd break the camera,' Eva muttered. 'I bet he's a nerd with pebble glasses and a bristly chin.'

'If he is he would be easier for Britt to deal with,' Leila said hopefully.

'A ruler who has moved his country forward and brought peace sounds like a decent man to me, so, whatever he looks like, it doesn't matter. I just need your support. Fact: the minerals at the mine are running out and we need investment. The consortium this man heads up has the money to allow us to mine the diamonds.'

There was a silence as Britt's sisters accepted the truth of this and she breathed a sigh of relief when they nodded their heads. Now she had a chance to rescue the mine and the town of Skavanga that was built around it. That, together with all the fresh challenges ahead of her, made her meeting with the so-called Black Sheikh seem less of a problem.

She was feeling slightly less sanguine the following day.

'Serves you right for building up your hopes,' Eva said as the girls gathered in Britt's study after hearing her groan. 'Your famous Black Sheikh can't even be bothered to meet with you,' Eva remarked, peering over Britt's shoulder at the email message on the computer screen. 'So he's sending a representative instead,' she scoffed, turning to throw an I-told-you-so look at Leila.

'I'll get some fresh coffee,' Leila offered.

Eva's carping was really getting on Britt's nerves. She'd been up since dawn exchanging emails with Kareshi. It was practically noon for her, Britt reflected angrily as Leila brought the coffee in. Her sisters loved staying in the city with her, but sometimes they forgot that, while they could lounge around, she had a job to do. 'I'm still going to meet with him. What else am I going to do?' she demanded, swinging round to confront her sisters. 'Do you two have any better ideas?'

Eva fell silent, while Leila gave Britt a sympathetic look as she handed her a mug of coffee. 'I'm just sorry we're going back home and leaving you with all this to deal with.'

'That's my job,' Britt said, controlling her anger. She could never be angry with Leila. 'Of course I'm disappointed I won't be meeting the Black Sheikh, but all I've ever asked for is your support, Eva.'

'Sorry,' Eva muttered awkwardly. 'I know you got landed with the company when Mum and Dad died. I'm just worried about what's going to happen now all the commodities are running out. I do realise the mine's sunk without the diamonds. And I know you'll do your very best to land this deal, but I'm worried about you, Britt. This is too much on your shoulders.'

'Stop it,' Britt warned, giving her sister a hug. 'Whoever the Black Sheikh sends, I can deal with him.'

'It says that the man you're to expect is a qualified geologist,' Leila pointed out. 'So at least you'll have something in common.' Britt's degree was also in Geology, with a Master's in Business Management.

'Yes,' Eva agreed, trying to sound as optimistic as her sister. 'I'm sure it will be fine.'

Britt knew that both her sisters were genuinely concerned about her. They just had different ways of showing it. 'Well, I'm excited,' she said firmly to lift the mood. 'When this man gets here we're another step closer to saving the company.'

'I wish Tyr were here to help you.'

Leila's words made them all silent. Tyr was their long-lost brother and they rarely talked about him because it hurt too much. They couldn't understand why he had left in the first place, much less why Tyr had never contacted them.

Britt broke the silence first. 'Tyr would do exactly what we're doing. He thinks the same as us. He cares about the company and the people here.'

'Which explains why he stays away,' Eva murmured.

'He's still one of us,' Britt insisted. 'We stick together. Remember that. The discovery of diamonds might even encourage him to return home.'

'But Tyr isn't motivated by money,' Leila piped up.

Even Eva couldn't disagree with that. Tyr was an idealist, an adventurer. Their brother was many things, but money was not his god, though Britt wished he would come home again. She missed him. Tyr had been away too long.

'Here's something that will make you laugh,' Leila said in an attempt to lift the mood. Pulling the newspaper towards her, she pointed to an article in the newspaper that referred to the three sisters as the Skavanga Diamonds. 'They haven't tired of giving us that ridiculous nickname.'

'It's just so patronising,' Eva huffed, brushing a cascade of fiery red curls away from her face.

'I've been called worse things,' Britt argued calmly.

'Don't be so naïve,' Eva snapped. 'All that article does is wave a flag in front of the nose of every fortune-hunter out there—'

'And what's wrong with that?' Leila interrupted. 'I'd just like to see a man who isn't drunk by nine o'clock—'

This brought a shocked intake of breath from Britt and Eva, as Leila had mentioned something else they never spoke about. There had long been a rumour that their father had been drunk when he piloted the small company plane to disaster with their mother on board.

Leila flushed red as she realised her mistake. 'I'm sorry—I'm just tired of your sniping, Eva. We really should get behind Britt.'

'Leila's right,' Britt insisted. 'It's crucial we keep our focus and make this deal work. We certainly can't afford to fall out between us. That article is fluff and we shouldn't even be wasting time discussing it. If Skavanga Mining is going to have a future we have to consider every offer on the table—and so far the consortium's is the only offer.'

'I suppose you could always give the sheikh's representative a proper welcome, Skavanga style,' Eva suggested, brightening.

Leila relaxed into a smile. 'I'm sure Britt has got a few ideas up her sleeve.'

'It's not my sleeve you need to worry about,' Britt commented dryly, relieved that they were all the best of friends again.

'Just promise me you won't do anything you'll regret,' Leila said, remembering to worry.

'I won't regret it at the time,' Britt promised dryly.

'Unless he truly is a boffin with pebble glasses—in which case I'll just have to put a paper bag over his head.'

'Don't become overconfident,' Eva warned.

'I'm not worried. If he proves difficult I'll cut a hole in the ice and send him swimming. That will soon cool his ardour—'

'Why stop there?' Eva added. 'Don't forget the birch twig switches. You can always give him a good thrashing. That'll sort him out.'

'I'll certainly consider it—'

'Tell me you're joking?' Leila begged.

Thankfully, Britt's younger sister missed the look Britt and Eva exchanged.

CHAPTER TWO

BRITT WAS UNUSUALLY nervous. The breakfast meeting with the Black Sheikh's representative had been arranged for nine and it was already twenty past when she rushed through the doors of Skavanga Mining and tore up the stairs. It wasn't as if she was unused to business meetings, but this one was different for a number of reasons, not least of which was the fact that her car had blown a tyre on the way to the office. Changing a tyre was an energetic exercise at the best of times, enough to get her heart racing, but the circumstances of this meeting had made her anxious without that, because so much depended on it—

'I'll show myself in,' she said as a secretary glanced up in surprise.

Pausing outside the door to the boardroom, she took a moment to compose herself. Eva was right in that when their parents were killed Britt had been the only person qualified to take over the company and care for her two younger sisters. Their brother was... Well, Tyr was a maverick—a mercenary, for all they knew. He had been a regular soldier at one time, and no one knew where he was now. It was up to her to cut this deal; there was no one else. The man inside the boardroom could save the company if he gave a green light to the consortium.

And she was late, an embarrassment that put her firmly on the back foot.

Back foot?

Forget that, Britt concluded as the imposing figure standing silhouetted against the light by the window turned to face her. The man was dressed conventionally in a dark, beautifully tailored business suit, when somehow she had imagined her visitor would be wearing flowing robes. This man needed no props to appear exotic. His proud, dark face, the thick black hair, which he wore carelessly swept back, and his watchful eyes were all the exotic ingredients required to complete a stunning picture. Far from the bristly nerd, he was heart-stoppingly good-looking, and it took all she'd got to keep her feet marching steadily across the room towards him.

'Ms Skavanga?'

The deep, faintly accented voice ran shivers through every part of her. It was the voice of a master, a lover, a man who expected nothing less than to be obeyed.

Oh, get over it, Britt told herself impatiently. It was the voice of a man and he was tall, dark and handsome. So what? She had a company to run.

'Britt Skavanga,' she said firmly, advancing to meet him with her hand outstretched. 'I'm sorry, you have me at a disadvantage,' she added, explaining that all she had been told was that His Majesty Sheikh Sharif al Kareshi would be sending his most trusted aide.

'For these preliminary discussions that is correct,' he said, taking hold of her hand in a grip that was controlled yet deadly.

His touch stunned her. It might have been disappointingly brief, but it was as if it held some electrical charge that shot fire through her veins.

She wanted him.

Just like that she wanted him?

She was a highly sexed woman, but she had never experienced such an instant, strong attraction to any man before.

'So,' she said, lifting her chin as she made a determined effort to pitch her voice at a level suitable for the importance of the business to be carried out between them, 'what may I call you?'

'Emir,' he replied, more aloof than ever.

'Just Emir?' she said.

'It's enough.' He shrugged, discarding her wild fantasy about him at a stroke.

'Shall we make a start?' He looked her up and down with all the cool detachment of a buyer weighing up a mare brought to market. 'Have you had some sort of accident, Ms Skavanga?'

'Please, call me Britt.' She had completely forgotten about the tyre until he brought it up, and now all she could think was what a wreck she must look. She clearly wasn't making an impression as an on-top-of-things businesswoman, that was for sure.

'Would you like to take a moment?' Emir enquired as she smoothed her hair self-consciously.

'No, thank you,' she said, matching his cool. She wasn't about to hand over the initiative this early in the game. 'I've kept you waiting long enough. A tyre blew on my way to the office,' she explained.

'And *you* changed it?'

She frowned. 'Why wouldn't I? I didn't want to waste time changing my clothes.'

'Thank you for the consideration.' Emir dipped his head in a small bow, allowing her to admire his thick, wavy hair, though his ironic expression suggested that

Emir believed a woman's place was somewhere fragrant and sheltered where she could bake and quake until her hunter returned.

Was he married?

She glanced at his ring-free hands, and remembered to thank him when he pulled out a chair. She couldn't remember the last time that had happened. She was used to fending for herself, though it was nice to meet a gentleman, even if she suspected that beneath his velvet charm Emir was ruthless and would use every setback she experienced to his advantage.

No problem. She wasn't about to give him an inch.

'Please,' she said, indicating a place that put the wide expanse of the boardroom table between them.

He had the grace of a big cat, she registered as he sat down. Emir was dark and mysterious compared to the blond giants in Skavanga she was used to. He was big and exuded power like some soft-pawed predator.

She had to be on guard at all times or he would win this game before she even knew it had been lost. Business was all that mattered now—though it was hard to concentrate when the flow of energy between them had grown.

Chemistry, she mused. And no wonder when Emir radiated danger. The dark business suit moulded his athletic frame to perfection, while the crisp white shirt set off his bronzed skin, and a grey silk tie provided a reassuring sober touch—to those who might be fooled. She wasn't one of them. Emir might as well have been dressed in flowing robes with an unsheathed scimitar at his side, for seductive exoticism flowed from him.

She looked away quickly when his black gaze found hers and held it. *Damn!* She could feel her cheeks blazing. She quickly buried her attention in the documents in front of her.

Britt's apparent devotion to her work amused him. He'd felt the same spark between them that she had, and there was always the same outcome to that. He generally relied on the first few minutes of any meeting to assess people. Body language told him so much. Up to now Skavanga had not impressed him. It was a grey place with an air of dejection that permeated both the company and the town. He didn't need the report in front of him to tell him that the mineral deposits were running out, he could smell failure in the air. And however good this woman was at running the business—and she must be good to keep a failing company alive for so long—she couldn't sell thin air. Britt needed to mine those diamonds in order to keep her company alive, and to do that she needed the consortium he headed up to back her.

The town might be grey, but Britt Skavanga was anything but. She exceeded his expectations. There was a vivid private world behind those serious dove grey eyes, and it was a world he intended to enter as soon as he could.

'You will relate our dealings verbatim to His Majesty?' she said as they began the meeting.

'Of course. His Majesty greets you as a friend and hopes that all future dealings between us will bring mutual respect as well as great benefit to both our countries.'

He had not anticipated her sharp intake of breath, or the darkening of her eyes as he made the traditional Kareshi greeting, touching his chest, his mouth and finally his brow. He amended his original assessment of Britt to that of a simmering volcano waiting to explode.

She recovered quickly. 'Please tell His Majesty that I welcome his interest in Skavanga Mining, and may I also welcome you as his envoy.'

Nicely done. She was cool. He'd give her that. His senses roared as she held his gaze. The only woman he knew who would do that was his sister, Jasmina, and she was a troublesome minx.

As Britt continued to lay out her vision of the future for Skavanga Mining he thought there was a touching innocence about her, even in the way she thought she would have any say once the consortium took over. Her capable hands were neatly manicured, the nails short and unpainted, and she wore very little make-up. There was no artifice about her. What you saw was what you got with Britt Skavanga—except for the fire in her eyes, and he guessed very few had seen that blaze into an inferno.

'You must find the prospect of mining the icy wastes quite daunting after what you're used to in the desert,' she was saying.

He returned reluctantly to business. 'On the contrary. There is a lot in Skavanga that reminds me of the vastness and variety of my desert home. It is a variety only obvious to those who see it, of course.' As much as he wanted this new venture to go ahead, he wanted Britt Skavanga even more.

As hard as she tried to concentrate, her body was making it impossible to think, but then her body seemed tuned to Emir's. She even found herself leaning towards him, and had to make herself sit back. Even then his heat curled around her. His face was stern, *which she loved,* and his scent, spicy and warm, sandalwood, maybe, it was a reminder of the exotic world he came from. Her sisters had already teased her mercilessly about Kareshi supposedly being at the forefront of the erotic arts. She had pretended not to listen to such nonsense, especially when they insisted that the people of Kareshi had a potion they used to heighten sensation. But she'd heard them. And now she was wondering if anything they'd said could be true—

'Ms Skavanga?'

She jerked alert as Emir spoke her name. 'I beg your pardon. My mind was just—'

'Wandering? Or examining the facts?' he said with amusement.

'Yes—'

'Yes? Which is it?'

She couldn't even remember the question. The blood rush to her cheeks was furious and hot, while Emir just raised a brow and his mouth curved slightly.

'Are you ready to continue?' he said.

'Absolutely,' she confirmed, sitting up straight. She was mad for this man—crazy for him. No way could she think straight until the tension had been released.

'There are some amendments I want to discuss,' he said, frowning slightly as he glanced up at her.

She turned with relief to the documents in front of her.

'I need more time,' she said.

'Really?' Emir queried softly.

She swallowed deep when she saw the look in his eyes. 'I don't think we should rush anything—'

'I don't think we should close any doors, either.'

Were they still talking about business? Shaking herself round, she explained that she wouldn't be making any decisions on behalf of the other shareholders yet.

'And I need to take samples from the mine before I

can involve the consortium in such a large investment,' Emir pointed out.

He only had to speak for alarm bells to go off in every part of her body, making it impossible to think about anything other than long, moonlit nights in the desert. Not once since taking over at Skavanga Mining had she ever been so distracted during a meeting. It didn't help that she had thought the Black Sheikh's trusted envoy would be some greybeard with a courtly air.

'Here is your copy of my projections,' she said, forcing her mind back to business before closing her file to signify the end of the meeting.

'I have my own projections, thank you.'

She bridled at that before reminding herself that just a murmur from the Black Sheikh could rock a government, and that his envoy was hardly going to be a pushover when it came to negotiations.

'Before we finish, there's just one here on the second page,' he said, leaning towards her.

'I see it,' she said, stiffening as she tried to close her mind to Emir's intoxicating scent. And those powerful hands...the suppleness in his fingers...the strength in his wrists...

He caught her staring and she started blushing again. This was ridiculous. She was acting like a teenager on her first date.

Exhaling shakily, she sat back in the chair determined to recover the situation, but Emir was on a roll.

'You seem to have missed something here,' he said, pointing to another paragraph.

She never missed anything. She was meticulous in all her business dealings. But sure enough, Emir had found one tiny thing she had overlooked.

'And this clause can go,' he said, removing it with a strike of his pen.

'Now, just a minute—' She stared aghast as Emir deconstructed her carefully drawn-up plan. 'No,' she said firmly. 'That clause does not go, and neither does anything else without further discussion, and this part of the meeting is over.'

He sat back in his chair as she stood up, which explained why she wasn't ready for him moving in front of her to stand in her way.

'You seem upset,' he said. 'And I don't want the first part of our meeting to end badly.'

'Bringing in investors is a big step for me to take—'

'Britt—'

Emir's touch on her skin was like an incendiary device, but the fact that his hand was on her arm at all was an outrage. 'Let me go,' she warned softly, but they both heard the shake in her voice. And surely Emir could feel her trembling beneath his touch. He must feel the heated awareness in her skin.

He murmured something in his own language. It might as well have been a spell. She turned to look at him, not keen to go anywhere suddenly.

'It seems to me we have a timing problem, Britt. But there is a solution, if you will allow me to take it?'

Emir's eyes were dark and amused. At first she thought she must have misunderstood him, but there was no mistake, and the solution he was proposing had been in her mind for some time. But surely no civilised businessman would be willing to enter into such a risky entanglement within an hour of meeting her?

As Emir's hand grazed her chin she moved into his embrace, allowing him to turn her face up to his. This was no meeting between business colleagues. This was a meeting between a man and woman who were hot for each other, and the man was a warrior of the desert.

Emir promised pleasure. He also promised a chance to forget, and, for however short a time, the prospect of that seemed preferable at this moment to doing battle endlessly on every front. How would it feel to have this big man hold her and bring her pleasure? She must have swayed towards him, for the next thing she knew he was holding her in front of him.

'Why, Britt,' he said with amusement. 'If I'd known how badly you wanted this I'm sure we could have arranged something before the meeting.'

Emir's blunt approach should have shocked her— annoyed her—but instead it made her want him all the more, and as he brushed her lips with his she found herself instantly hungry, instantly frantic, for more pressure, more intimacy, and for everything to happen fast.

But Emir was even more experienced than she had realised, and now he took pleasure in subjecting her to an agonising delay. As the clock ticked, the tension built and he held her stare with his knowing and faintly amused look. She guessed Emir knew everything about arousal, and could only hope it wouldn't be long before he decided she had suffered enough. She voiced a cry of relief when he cupped her face in his warm, slightly roughened hands, and another when her patience was rewarded by a kiss that began lightly and then brutally mimicked the act her body so desperately craved.

It was in no way subjugation by a powerful man, but the meeting of eager mates, a fierce coupling between two people who knew exactly what they wanted from each other, and as Emir pressed her back against the

boardroom table and set about removing her clothes she
gasped in triumph and began ripping at his.

He tossed her jacket aside. She loosened his tie and
dragged it off, letting it drop onto the floor. As he ripped
her blouse open she battled with the buttons on his shirt.
She exclaimed with pleased surprise when he lifted her
and she clung to him as he stripped off her tights and
her briefs. Suddenly it was all about seeing who could
rid themselves of any barriers first. She was mindless
sensation—hot flesh brushing, touching, cleaving, in
a tangle of limbs and hectic breathing, while Emir remained calm and strong, and certain. He felt so good
beneath her hands...so very good—

*Too good! You have never felt like this about a man
before—*

Danger! This man can change your life—

*You won't walk away from this with a smile on your
face—*

Using sheer force of will, she closed off her annoy-
ing inner voice. She wanted this. She needed it. This
was her every fantasy come true. Even now as Emir
took time to protect them both she saw no reason not
to follow her most basic instinct. Why shouldn't she?
Emir was—

Emir was enormous. He was entirely built to scale.
Was she ready for this?

He made her forget everything the moment he caressed her breasts. Moaning, she rested back and let him
do what he wanted with her. Just this once she wanted
to feel that she didn't have to lead or fight. Just this
once she could be the woman she had always dreamed
of being—the woman who was with a man who knew
how to please her.

And I wonder what he thinks about you—

To hell with what he thinks about me, she raged silently.

To hell with you, don't you mean?

CHAPTER THREE

BRITT WAS BEAUTIFUL and willing and he had needs. Willing? She was a wild cat with a body that was strong and firm, yet voluptuous. Her breasts were incredible, uptilted and full, and he took his time to weigh them appreciatively, smiling when she groaned with pleasure as he circled her nipples very lightly with his thumbnails. She was so responsive, so eager that her nipples had tightened and were thrusting towards him, pink and impertinent, and clearly in need of more attention. He aimed to please. Kissing her neck, he travelled down, part of him already regretting that they had wasted so much time. She shuddered with desire as he blazed a trail through the dust she had collected when she changed her tyre. 'You're clean now,' he said, smiling into her lust-dazed eyes.

She laughed down low in her throat in a way he found really sexy, and then weakened against him as she waited for him to continue his sensory assault.

'Shall I take the edge off your hunger?' he offered.

'Yours too,' she insisted huskily.

'If that's what you want, you tell me what you'd like.'

Her gaze flicked up and her cheeks flushed pink. She wasn't sure whether to believe him or not.

'I'm serious,' he said quietly.

'Please—'

As she appealed to him he decided that the time he had allowed for this visit to Skavanga wouldn't be enough. He ran his fingers lightly over her beautiful breasts before moving on to trace the swell of her belly. Lifting her skirt, he nudged her thighs apart. She made it easy for him, so he repaid her gesture by delicately exploring the heated flesh at the apex of her thighs. When she whimpered with pleasure it was all he could do to hold back. So much for his much-vaunted self-control, he mused, as Britt thrust her hips towards him, trying for more contact. He wanted nothing more than to take her now. Clutching his arms, she tilted herself back against the table, moaning with need. Opening her legs a little more for him, she showed him a very different woman from the one in the starchy photograph he had examined in London, but this was the woman he had suspected Britt was hiding all along.

'You're quite clinical about this, aren't you?' Britt panted in a rare moment of lucidity as he watched her pleasure.

Duty could do that to a man. He never let himself go. Growing up the second son of the third wife had hardly been to his advantage as a youth. He had been forced to watch the cruelty inflicted on his people by those closer to the throne than he was on a daily basis. So, yes, he was cold. He'd had to be to overthrow tyrants that were also his relatives. There was no room now in his life for anything other than the most basic human appetite.

'Don't make me wait,' Britt was begging him.

She needn't worry. His preference at this moment was to please her.

This was insane. Emir was cold, detached—and the

sexiest thing on two legs. He was frighteningly distant,
but she was lost in an erotic haze of his making. She
needed more—more pressure, more contact—more of
him. The more aloof he was, the more her body cried out
to him. The ache he'd set up inside her was unbearable.
She had to have more of his skilful touches—

An excited cry escaped her throat when she felt the
insistent thrust of his erection against her belly. She
rubbed herself shamelessly against it, sobbing with pleasure as each delicious contraction of her nerve endings
gave some small indication of what was to come. Emir's
hard, warrior frame was even more powerful than she
had imagined, and yet he used his hands so delicately in
a way that drove her crazy for him. Lacing her fingers
through his thick black hair, she dragged him close. He
responded by cupping the back of her head to keep her
in place as he dipped down and plundered her mouth.
Sweeping the table clear, he lifted her and balanced
her on the edge. Moving between her legs, he forced
them apart with the width of his body. 'Wrap your legs
around me,' he commanded, pushing them wider still.

She had never obeyed a man's instructions in her life,
but she rushed to obey these. Resting her hands flat on
the table behind her, she arched her spine, thrusting
her breasts forward, while Emir reared over her, magnificent and erect.

Like a stallion on the point of servicing a mare?
With far more consideration than that—
Are you sure?

She was sure that any more delay would send her
crazy. She was also sure that Emir knew exactly what
he was doing.

'Tell me what you want, Britt,' he demanded fiercely.
'You know what I want,' she said.

'But you must tell me,' he said in low, cruel voice.

Her throat dried. The harsher he got, the more arousing she found it. No one had ever pushed her boundaries like this before. And she had thought herself liberal where sex was concerned? She was a novice compared to Emir.

She had also thought herself emotion-free, Britt realised, but knew deep in her heart that something had changed inside her. Even when she plumbed the depths of Emir's cold black eyes she wanted to be the one to draw a response from him—she wanted to learn more about him, and in every way.

'Say it,' he instructed.

Her face blazed red. No one spoke to her like that— no one told her what to do. But her body liked what was happening, and was responding with enthusiasm. 'Yes,' she said. 'Yes, please.' And then she told him exactly what she wanted him to do to her without sparing a single lurid detail.

Now he was pleased. Now she got through to him. Now he almost smiled.

'I think I can manage that,' he said dryly. 'My only concern is that we may not have sufficient time to work our way through your rather extensive wish list.'

On this occasion, she thought. 'Perhaps another time,' she said, matching him for dispassion. But then she glanced at the door. How could she have forgotten that it was still unlocked? Just as she was thinking she must do something about it, Emir touched her in a way that made it impossible for her to move.

'Don't you like the risk?' he said, reading her easily.

She looked at him, and suddenly she loved the risk.

'Hold me,' he said softly. 'Use me—take what you need.'

She hesitated, another first for her. No one had ever given her this freedom. She moved to do as he said and found it took two hands to enclose him.

'I'm waiting,' he said.

With those dangerous eyes watching her, she made a pass. Loving it, she made a second, firmer stroke—

Taking control, Emir caught the tip inside her. She gasped and would have pulled away, but he cupped her buttocks firmly in his strong hands and drew her slowly on to him. 'What are you afraid of?' he said, staring deep into her eyes. 'You know I won't hurt you.'

She didn't know him at all, but for some reason she trusted him. 'I'm just—'

'Hungry,' he said. 'I know.'

A sound of sheer pleasure trembled from her throat. She had played games with boys before, she realised, but Emir was a man, and a man like no other man.

'Am I enough for you?' he mocked.

She lifted her chin. 'What do you think?'

He told her exactly what he thought, and while she was still gasping with shock and lust he kissed her, and before she could recover he thrust inside her deeply to the hilt. For a moment she was incapable of thinking or doing, and even breathing was suspended. This wasn't pleasure, this was an addiction. She could never get enough of this—or of him. The sensation of being completely inhabited while being played by a master was a very short road to release.

'No,' he said sharply, stopping her. 'I'll tell you when. Look at me, Britt,' he said fiercely.

On the promise of pleasure she stared into Emir's molten gaze. She would obey him. She would pay whatever price it took for this to continue.

He was pleased with her. Britt was more responsive

than even he had guessed. She was a strong woman who made him want to pleasure her. He loved the challenge that was Britt Skavanga. He loved her fire. He loved her cries of pleasure and the soft little whimpers she made when he thrust repeatedly into her. What had started as a basic function to clear his head had become an exercise in pleasuring Britt.

'Now,' he whispered fiercely.

He held her firmly as she rocked into orgasm with a release so violent he trusted his strength more than the boardroom table and held her close, though he could do nothing about the noise she was making, which would probably travel to the next town, and so he smothered it with a kiss. When he let her go, she gasped and called his name. He held her safe, cushioning her against the hard edge of the table with his hands as he soothed her down. Withdrawing carefully, he steadied Britt on her feet before releasing her. Smoothing the hair back from her flushed, damp brow, he stared into her dazed eyes, waiting until he was sure she had recovered. The one thing he had not expected was to feel an ache of longing in his chest. He had not expected to feel anything.

'Wow,' she whispered, her voice muffled against his naked chest.

He liked the feeling of Britt resting on him and was in no hurry to move away. If she had been anyone else the next move would have been simple. He would have taken her back to Kareshi with him. But she was too much like him. There would be no diamond mine, no town, no Skavanga Mining, without Britt. Just as he belonged in Kareshi, she was tied here. But still he felt a stab of regret that he couldn't have this exciting woman. 'Are you okay?' he murmured as she stirred.

She lifted her chin to look at him, and as she did this

she drew herself up and drew her emotions in. As she pulled herself together he could almost see her forcing herself to get over whatever it was she had briefly felt for him.

'There are two bathrooms,' she informed him briskly. 'You can use the one directly off the boardroom. I have my own en suite attached to my office. We will reconvene this meeting in fifteen minutes.'

A smile of incredulity and, yes, admiration curved his lips as he watched her go. She walked across the room with her head held high like a queen. It might have seemed ridiculous had anyone else tried it, but Britt Skavanga could pull it off.

He showered down quickly in the bathroom she had told him about, and was both surprised and pleased by the quality of the amenities until he remembered that Britt had a hand in everything here. There were high-quality towels on heated rails, as well as shampoo, along with all the bits and pieces that contributed to making a freshen-up session pleasurable. Britt hadn't forgotten anything—at which point a bolt of very masculine suspicion punched him in the guts. Had she done this before? And if so, how many times?

And why should he care?

He returned to the boardroom to find Britt had arrived before him. She looked composed. She looked as if nothing had happened between them. She looked as she might have looked at the start of the meeting if she hadn't been forced to change a tyre first. She also looked very alone to him, seated beneath the portraits of her forebears, and once again he got the strongest sense that duty ruled Britt every bit as much as it ruled him.

They both imagined they were privileged and, yes, each was powerful in their own way, but neither of them could choose what they wanted out of life, because the choices had already been made for them.

She hated herself, *hated herself* for what she had done. Losing control like that. She hadn't even been able to meet her sex-sated reflection in the bathroom mirror. She had weakened with Emir in a way she must never weaken again. She put it down to a moment of madness before she closed her heart. But as her mind flashed back to what they'd done, and the remembered feeling of being close to him, for however short a time, she desperately wanted more—

She would just have to exercise more control—

'Is something distracting you, Britt?' Emir demanded, jolting her back to the present.

'Should there be something?' she said in a voice that held no hint that Emir was the only distraction.

'No,' he said without expression.

They deserved each other, she thought. But she was curious all the same. Did he really feel nothing? Didn't his body throb with pleasurable awareness as hers did? Didn't he want more? Didn't he yearn to know more about her as she longed to know more about him? Or was she nothing more than an entertainment between coffee breaks for Emir?

And rumour had it she was the hardest of the Skavanga Diamonds?

What a laugh!

Tears of shame were pricking her eyes. She could never make a mistake like this again—

'Hay fever,' she explained briskly when Emir glanced suspiciously at her.

'In Skavanga?' he said, glancing outside at the icy scene.

'We have pollen,' she said coldly, moving on.

She wasn't sure how she got to the end of the second half of their meeting, but she did. There was too much hanging on the outcome for her to spoil the deal with a clouded mind. So far so good, Britt concluded, wrapping everything up with a carefully rehearsed closing statement. At least she could tell her sisters that she hadn't been forced to concede anything vital, and that Emir was prepared to move on to the next stage, which would involve a visit to the mine.

'I'm looking forward to that,' he said.

There was nothing in his eyes for her. The rest of Emir's visit would be purely about business—

And why should it be anything else?

She hated herself for the weakness, but she had expected something—some outward sign that their passionate encounter had made an impression on him… but apparently not.

'Is that everything?' Emir said as he gathered up his papers. 'I imagine you want to make an early start in the morning if we're going to the mine.'

The mine was miles away from anywhere. The only logical place for them to stay was the old cabin Britt's great-grandfather had built. It was isolated—there were no other people around. Doing a quick risk-assessment of the likely outcome, knowing the passion they shared, she knew she would be far better off arranging for one of her lieutenants to take him…

But Emir would see that as cowardice. And was she frightened of him? Could she even entrust the task of taking him to the mine to anyone else? She should be there. And maybe getting him out of her system once and for all would allow her to sharpen up and concentrate on what really mattered again.

'I would like to make an early start,' she said, 'though I must warn you there are no luxury facilities at the cabin. It's pretty basic.' Somehow, what Emir thought about the cabin that meant so much to her mattered to her, Britt realised. It mattered a lot.

Emir seemed unconcerned. 'Apart from the difference in temperature, the Arctic is another wilderness like the desert.'

'My great-grandfather built the cabin. It's very old–'

'You're fortunate to have something so special and permanent to remember him by.'

Yes, she was, and the fact that Emir knew this meant a lot to her.

They stared at each other until she forced herself to look away. This was not the time to be inventing imaginary bonds between them. Better she remembered Eva's words about a true Nordic welcome to contain this warrior of the desert. It would be interesting to discover if Emir was still so confident after a brush with ice and fire.

CHAPTER FOUR

HE LEARNED MORE about Britt during the first few hours of their expedition than he had learned in any of the reports. She was intelligent and organised, energetic and could be mischievous, which reminded him to remain on guard.

She had called him at five-thirty a.m.—just to check he was awake, she had assured him. He suspected she hadn't slept after their encounter, and guessed she was hoping he'd had a sleepless night too. He gave nothing away.

It couldn't strictly be called dawn when her Jeep rolled up outside his hotel, since at this time of year in Skavanga a weak grey light washed the land for a full twenty-four hours. Only Britt coloured the darkness when she sprang down and came to greet him. He was waiting for her just outside the doors. Her hair gleamed like freshly harvested wheat and she had pulled an ice-blue beanie over her ears to protect them from the bitter cold. Her cheeks and lips were whipped red by the harshest of winds, and she was wearing black polar trousers tucked into boots, with a red waterproof jacket zippered up to her neck. She looked fresh and clean and bright, and determined.

'Britt—'

'Emir.'

Her greeting was cool. His was no more than polite, though he noticed that the tip of her nose was as red as her full bottom lip and her blue-grey eyes were the colour of polar ice. She gave him the once-over, and seemed satisfied by what she saw. He knew the drill. He might live in the desert, but he was no stranger to Arctic conditions.

'Was the hotel okay?' she asked him politely when they were both buckled in.

'Yes. Thank you,' he said, allowing his gaze to linger on her face

She shot him a glance and her cheeks flushed red. She was remembering their time in the boardroom. He was too.

She drove smoothly and fast along treacherous roads and only slowed for moose and for a streak of red fox until they entered what appeared to be an uninhabited zone. Here the featureless ice road was shielded on either side between towering walls of packed snow. She still drove at a steady seventy and refused his offer to take over. She knew the way, she said. She liked to be in control, he thought. Except when she was having sex when she liked him to take the lead.

'We'll soon be there,' she said, distracting him from these thoughts.

They had been climbing up the side of a mountain for some time, leaving the ice walls far behind. Below them was a vast expanse of frozen lake—grey, naturally.

'The mine is just down there,' she said when he craned his neck to look.

He wondered what other delights awaited him. All he could be sure of was that Britt hadn't finished with him yet. She liked to prove herself, so he was confident the test would include some physical activity. He looked forward to it, just as he looked forward to a return bout with her in the desert.

Emir seemed utterly relaxed and completely at home in a landscape that had terrified many people she had brought here. She knew this place like the back of her hand, and yet, truthfully, had never felt completely safe. Knowing Emir, he had probably trialled every extreme sport known to man, so what was a little snow and ice to him?

'Penny for them,' he said.

She made herself relax so she could clear her mind and equivocate. 'I'm thinking about food. Aren't you?'

She was curious to know what he was thinking, but as usual Emir gave nothing away.

'Some,' he murmured.

She glanced his way and felt her heart bounce. She would never get used to the way he looked, and for one spark of interest from those deceptively sleepy eyes she would happily walk barefoot in the snow, which was something Emir definitely didn't need to know.

'The food's really good at the mine,' she said, clinging to safe ground. 'And the catering staff will have stocked the cabin for us. The food has to be excellent when people are so isolated. It's one of the few pleasures they have.'

'I wouldn't be too sure about that,' he said dryly.

'There are separate quarters for men and women,' she countered promptly—and primly.

'Right.' His tone was sceptical.

'You seem to know a lot about it,' she said, feeling a bit peeved—jealous, maybe, especially when he said,

'It's much the same for people who work in the desert.'

'Oh, I see.'

'Good,' he said, ignoring her sharp tone and settling back. 'I'm going to doze now, if you don't mind?'

'Not at all.'

Sleep? Yeah, right—like a black panther sleeps with one eye open. There was no such thing as stand down for Emir.

Emir could play her at her own game, and play it well, Britt realised as she turned off the main road. She could be cool, but he would be cooler, and now there was no real contact between them as he dozed—apparently—which she regretted. He wanted her to feel this way—to feel this lack of him, she suspected.

'Sorry,' she exclaimed with shock as the Jeep lurched on the rutted forest track. The moment's inattention had jolted Emir awake and had almost thrown them into the ditch.

'No problem,' he said. 'If you want me to drive...?'

'I'm fine. Thank you.' She'd heard that the ruler of Kareshi was introducing change, but not fast enough, clearly. Emir probably resented her running the company too. He came from a land where men ruled and women obeyed—

She gasped as his hand covered hers. 'Take it easy,' he said, steadying the steering wheel as it bounced in her hands.

'I've been travelling these roads since I was a child.'

'Then I'm surprised you don't know about the hazards of melting snow.'

He definitely deserved a session in the sauna and a dip in the freezing lake afterwards, she concluded.

'We're nearly there,' she said.

'Good.'

Why the smile in his voice? Was he looking forward to their stay at the isolated cabin? She squirmed in her seat at the thought that he might be and then wondered angrily why she was acting this way. It was one thing bringing her city friends into the wilderness for a rustic weekend, but quite another bringing Emir down here when there could only be one outcome—

Unless he had had enough of her, of course, but something told her that wasn't the case. She'd stick with her decision to enjoy him and get him out of her system, Britt concluded, explaining that the nearest hotel was too far away from the mine to stay there.

'You don't have to explain to me, Britt. I like it here. You forget,' Emir murmured as she drew to a halt outside the ancient log cabin, 'the wilderness is my home.'

And now she was angry with him for being so pleased with everything. And even angrier with herself because Emir was right, the wilderness was beautiful in its own unique way, she thought, staring out across the glassy lake. It was as if she were seeing it for the first time. Because she was seeing it through Emir's eyes, Britt realised, and he sharpened her focus on everything.

'This is magnificent,' he exclaimed as they climbed down from the Jeep.

She tensed as he came to stand beside her. Her heart pumped and her blood raced as she tried not to notice how hot he looked in the dark, heavy jacket and snow boots. Emir radiated something more than the confidence of a man who was sensibly dressed and comfortable in this extreme temperature. He exuded the type of strength that anyone would like to cling to in a storm—

He looked downright dangerous, she told herself sensibly, putting a few healthy feet of fresh air between them. But the lake was beautiful, and neither of them was in any hurry to move away. It stretched for miles and was framed by towering mountains whose jagged peaks were lost in cloud. A thick pine forest crept up these craggy slopes until there was nothing for the roots to cling to. But it was the silence that was most impressive, and that was heavy and complete. It felt almost as if the world were holding its breath, though she had to smile when Emir turned to look at the cabin and an eagle called.

'I'll grab our bags,' he said.

As he brushed past her on his way to the Jeep she shivered with awareness, and then smiled as she walked towards the cabin. She was always happy here—always in control. There would be no problems here. She'd keep things light and professional. Here, she could put what had happened between them in the boardroom behind her.

Emir caught up with her at the door, and his first question was how far was it to the mine? With her back to him, she pulled a wry face. Putting what had happened behind her was going to be easier than she had thought. They hadn't even crossed the threshold yet and Emir's mind was already set on business.

Which was exactly what she had hoped for—

Was it?

Of course it was, but she wasn't going to pretend it didn't sting. Everyone had their pride, and everyone wanted to feel special—

Hard luck for her, she thought ruefully.

'So, how far exactly is it to the mine?' he said. 'How long will it take by road?'

'Depending on the weather?' She turned the key in the lock. 'I'd say around ten minutes.'

'Is there any chance we can take a look around today, in that case?' Emir asked as he held the door for her.

He was in more of a hurry than she'd thought. Well, that was fine with her. She could accommodate a fast turnaround. 'The mine is a twenty-four-hour concern. We can visit as soon as you're ready.'

'Then I'd like to freshen up and go see it right away—if that's okay with you?'

'That's fine with me.' She had to stop herself laughing at the thought that she had never met anyone quite so much like her before.

As she used to be, Britt amended, before Emir came into her life. Taking charge of her bag, she hoisted it onto her shoulders. 'Welcome,' she said, walking into the cabin.

'This is nice,' Emir commented as he gazed around.

He made everything seem small, she thought, but in a good way. The cabin had been built by a big man for big men, yet could be described as cosy. On a modest scale, it still reflected the personality of the man who had built it and who had founded the Skavanga dynasty. With nothing but his determination, Britt's great-grandfather had practically clawed the first minerals out of the ground with his bare hands, and with makeshift tools that other prospectors had thrown away. There was nothing to be ashamed of here in the cabin. It was only possible to feel proud.

'What?' Emir said when he caught her staring at him.

'You're the only man apart from my brother who makes me feel small,' she said, managing not to make it sound like a compliment.

'I take it you're talking about your brother, Tyr?'

'My long-lost brother, Tyr,' she admitted with a shrug.

'I can assure you the very last thing on my mind is to make you feel small.'

'You don't—well, not in the way you mean. How tall are you, anyway?'

'Tall enough.'

She could vouch for that. And was that a glint of humour in Emir's eyes? Maybe this wouldn't be so bad, after all. Maybe bringing him to the cabin wasn't the worst idea she'd ever had. Maybe they could actually do business with each other *and* have fun.

And then say goodbye?

Why not?

'Are you going to show me to my room?' Emir prompted, glancing towards the wooden staircase.

'Yes, of course. '

Ditching her bag, she mounted the wooden stairs ahead of him, showing Emir into a comfortable double bedroom with a bathroom attached. 'You'll sleep in here,' she said. 'There are plenty of towels in the bathroom, and endless hot water, so don't stint yourself—and just give me a shout if you need anything more.'

'This is excellent,' he called downstairs to her. 'Thank you for putting me up.'

'As an alternative to having you camp down the mine?' She laughed. 'Of course, there are bunkhouses you could use—'

'I'm fine here.'

And looking forward to tasting some genuine Nordic hospitality, she hoped, tongue in cheek, as she glanced out of the window at the snow-clad scene.

'Britt—'

'What?' Heart pounding, she turned. Even now with all the telling off she'd given herself at the tempting thought of testing out the bed springs, she hoped and smiled and waited.

'Window keys?' Emir was standing on the landing, staring down at her. 'It's steaming hot in here.'

Ah… 'Sorry.'

She stood for a moment to compose herself and then ran upstairs to sort him out. The central heating she'd had installed was always turned up full blast before a visit. She could operate it from her phone, and thoughts of turning it down a little had flown out of the window along with her sensible head thanks to Emir. 'I suggest you leave the window open until the room cools down.' Fighting off all feelings about the big, hard, desirable body so very close to her, she unlocked the window and showed him where to hang the key.

'This is a beautiful room, Britt.'

The room was well furnished with a thick feather duvet on the bed, sturdy furniture, and plenty of throws for extra warmth. She'd hung curtains in rich autumnal shades to complement the wooden walls. 'Glad you think so.'

Now she had to look at him, but she lost no time making for the door.

'Are these your grandparents?'

She did not want to turn around, but how could she ignore the question when Emir was examining some sepia photographs hanging on the wall?

'This one is my great-grandfather,' she said, coming to stand beside him. The photographs had been hung on the wall to remind each successive generation of the legacy they had inherited. Her great-grandfather was a handsome, middle-aged man with a moustache and a big, worn hat. He was dressed in leather boots with his heavy trousers tucked into them, his hands were gnarled and he wore a rugged jacket, which was patched at the elbows. Even the pose, the way he was leaning on a spade, spoke volumes about those early days. Family and Skavanga Mining meant everything to her, Britt realised as she turned to leave the room.

She had to ask Emir to move. Why was he leaning against the door? "Excuse me…"

Straightening up, he moved aside. Now she was disappointed because he hadn't tried to stop her. What was wrong with her? She had brought a man she was fiercely attracted to to an isolated cabin. What did she think was going to happen? But now she wondered if sex with Emir would get him out of her system. Would anything?

At the top of the stairs she couldn't resist turning to see if he was still watching her.

Something else for her to regret. And what did that amused look signify—the bed was just a few tempting steps away?

And now the familiar ache had started up again. They were consenting adults who made their own agenda, and, with the mine open twenty-four seven, it wasn't as if they didn't have time—

And if she gave in to her appetite, Emir would expect everything to be on his terms from hereon in—

'I'll take quick a shower and see you outside in ten,' she called, running up the next flight of stairs to her own room in the attic. Slamming the door, she rested back against it. Saying yes to Emir would be the easiest thing in the world. Saying no to him required cast-iron discipline, and she wasn't quite sure she'd got that.

She had to have it, Britt told herself sternly as she showered down. Anything else was weakness.

Britt's bedroom was one of three at the cabin. She

had chosen it as a child, because she could be alone up here. She had always loved the pitched roof with its wealth of beams, thinking it was like something out of a fairy tale. When she was little she could see the sky and the mountains if she stood on the bed, and when she was on her own she could be anyone she wanted to be. Over the years she had collected items that made her feel good. Her grandmother had worked the patchwork quilt. Her grandfather had carved the headboard. These family treasures meant the world to her. They were far more precious than any diamonds, but then she had to remember the good the diamonds could do—for Skavanga, the town her ancestors had built, and for her sisters, and for the company.

She had to secure Emir's recommendation to his master, the Black Sheikh, Britt reflected as she toyed with some trinkets on the dressing table. They were the same cheap hair ornaments she had worn as a girl, she realised, picking them up and holding them against her long blonde hair so she could study the effect in the mirror. She hadn't even changed the threadbare stool in front of the dressing table, because her grandmother had worked the stitches, and because it was a reminder of the girl Britt had been, like the books by her bedside. This was a very different place from her penthouse in the centre of Skavanga, but the penthouse was her public face while this was where she kept her heart.

And to keep it she must cut that deal to her advantage—

With a man as shrewd as Emir in the frame?

She had never doubted her own abilities before, Britt realised as she wandered over to a window she could see out of now without standing on the bed. Skavanga

Mining had meant everything to her parents, but they hadn't been able to keep it—

Because her father was a drunk—

She shook her head, shaking out the memory. Her parents had tried their best—

Leaving little time for Britt and her siblings.

So she had picked up a mess. Lots of people had to do that. And somehow she would find a way to cut a favourable deal with the consortium.

Staring out of the window drew her gaze to the traditional sauna hut, sitting squat on the shore of the lake. With its deep hat of snow and rows of birch twigs switches hanging in a rack outside the door, it brought a smile to her face as she remembered Eva's teasing recommendation—that she bring Emir into line here. There were certainly several ways she could think of to do that. If only there weren't a risk he might enjoy them too much...

Seeing Emir's shadow darkening the snow outside, she quickly stepped back from the window. Tossing the towel aside, she pulled out the drawers of the old wooden chest and picked out warm, lightweight Arctic clothing—thermals, sweater, waterproof trousers and thick, sealskin socks. She resented the way her heart was drumming, as if she were going out on a date, rather than showing a man around a mine so he could make vast sums of money for his master out of generations of her family's hard work. She also hated the fact that Emir had beaten her to it downstairs. She was endlessly competitive. Having two sisters, she supposed. Determined to seize back the initiative, she knocked on the window to capture his attention, and when she'd got his attention she held up five fingers to let him know she'd be down right away. Almost. She'd brush her hair and put some lip gloss on first.

Traitor.

Everyone likes to feel good, Britt argued firmly with her inner voice. This has nothing to do with Sharif.

He had the cabin keys as well as the keys to the Jeep, and was settled behind the wheel by the time Britt appeared at the door. Climbing out, he strolled over to lock the cabin. She held out her hand to take charge of the keys.

'I'll keep them,' he said, stowing them in the pocket of his lightweight polar fleece.

Britt's crystal gaze turned stony.

'I'm driving too,' he said, enjoying the light floral scent she was wearing, which seemed at complete odds with the warrior woman expression on her face.

She was still seething when she swung into the passenger seat at his side. 'I know where we're going,' she pointed out.

'Then you can guide me there,' he said, gunning the engine. 'I'll turn the Sat Nav off.'

She all but growled at this.

'Why don't you let me drive?' she said.

'Why don't you direct me?' he said mildly, releasing the brake. 'It doesn't hurt to share the load from time to time,' he added, which earned him an angry glance.

They drove on in silence down the tree-shrouded lane. He noticed she glanced at the sauna on the lakeside as they drove past. He guessed his trials might begin there. The sauna was all ready and fired up. She wasn't joking when she'd said the people at the mine looked after her. The consortium would have to work hard to win hearts and minds as well as everything else if they were going to make this project a success. Perhaps they needed Britt's participation in the scheme more than he'd thought at first.

The snow was banked high either side of the road. The tall pines were bowed under its weight. The air was frigid with an icy mist overhanging everything. Snow was falling more heavily by the time they reached the main road. It had blurred the tyre tracks behind them and kept the windscreen wipers working frantically. 'Left or right?' he said, slowing the vehicle.

'If you'd let me drive—'

He put the handbrake on.

'Left,' she said impatiently.

As he swung the wheel Britt tugged off her soft blue beanie and her golden hair cascaded down. If she had been trying to win his attention she couldn't have thought up a better ruse, he realised as the scent of clean hair and lightly fragranced shampoo hit him square in the groin. He smiled to himself when she tied it back severely as if she knew that he liked it falling free around her shoulders. The fact that Britt didn't want to flaunt her femininity in front of him told him something. She liked him and she didn't want him to know.

'You must be tired,' he said, turning his thoughts to the stress she was under. It wasn't easy trying to salvage the family business, as he knew only too well. Whether it was a town or a country made no difference when people you cared about were involved. Her thoughts were with all the people who depended on her, as his were with Kareshi.

'I'm not as fragile as you seem to think,' she said, turning a hostile back on him as she stared out of the window.

She wasn't fragile at all. And if Britt tired at any

point, he'd be there. Crazy, but somehow this woman
had got under his skin—and he had more than enough
energy for both of them.

CHAPTER FIVE

EMIR HAD WHAT was needed to take the mine to the next level summed up within the first half hour of him visiting the immense open-cast site. Digging down into the Arctic core would require mega-machines, as well as an extension to the ice road in order to accommodate them, and that would take colossal funding.

With such vast sums involved he would oversee everything. Second in command—second in anything—wasn't his way. Britt was beginning to wonder how Emir managed to work for the sheikh—until he handed over the car keys.

As she thanked him she couldn't have been more surprised and wondered if she had earned some respect down the mine? She had known the majority of the miners most of her life, and got on with everyone, and, though her brother Tyr would have been their first choice, she knew that in Tyr's absence the miners respected her for taking on the job. Some of them had worked side by side with her grandfather, and she was proud to call them friends. She would do anything to keep them in employment.

Emir broke the silence as she started the engine. 'Once I've had the samples tested, we can start planning the work schedule in earnest.'

'I'm sure you won't be disappointed with the result of the test. I've had reports from some of the best brains in Europe, who all came to the same conclusion. The Skavanga mine is set to become the richest diamond discovery ever made.' If they could afford to mine the gems, she added silently. But surely now Emir had seen the mine for himself he wouldn't pull back. *He mustn't pull back.*

She tensed as he stretched out his long legs and settled back. 'So what do you think of the mine now you've seen it? Will you put in a good report? I have had other offers,' she bluffed in an effort to prompt him.

'If you've had other offers you must consider them all.'

Emir had called her bluff and left her hanging. Who else did he think could afford to do the work? It was the consortium or nothing. 'I would have liked Tyr to be involved, but we haven't seen him for years.'

'That doesn't mean he isn't around.'

'I'll have a word with our lawyers when we get back—to see if they can find him. I imagine you'll need to consult with your principal before making the next move?' She glanced across, but the only fallout from this was a heart-crunching smile from Emir. She turned up the heating, but there was ice in her blood. The fact remained that only three men had the resources to bring the diamonds to the surface.

'Why don't you stop by the sauna?' Emir suggested as she shivered involuntarily.

She was shivering, but at the thought of all the battles ahead of her.

Battles she hadn't looked for in a job she didn't want—

No one must know that. No one would *ever* know

that. She had accepted responsibility for the mine because there was no one else to do so, and had no intention of welching on that responsibility now. 'The sauna sounds like a good idea. I'm sure you'll enjoy it—'

'I'm sure I will too.'

It would be interesting to see if Emir felt quite so confident by the time they left the sauna.

Shock at the sudden dramatic change in temperature as they climbed out of the Jeep rendered them both silent for a few moments. The sky was uniform grey, though the Northern Lights had just begun to sweep across the bowl of the heavens as if a band of giants were waving luminescent flags. It was startling and awe-inspiring and they both lifted their heads to stare. The air was frigid, and mist formed in front of their mouths as they stood motionless as the display undulated above them.

The ice hole was probably frozen solid, Britt realised as the cold finally prompted them to move. They kept a power saw at the hut and that would soon sort it out. The sauna hut looked like a gingerbread house with a thick white coat of snow. It was another of her special places. Taking a sauna was a tradition she loved. It was the only way to thaw out the bones in Skavanga. And it was a great leveller as everyone stripped to the buff.

'No changing rooms?' Emir queried.

'Not even a shower,' she said, wondering if he was having second thoughts. 'We'll bathe in the lake afterwards.'

'Fine by me,' he said, gazing out across the glassy skating rink the lake had become.

As his lips pressed down with approval her attention was drawn to his sexy mouth. There wasn't much about Emir that wasn't sexy, and she couldn't pretend

that she wasn't looking forward to seeing him naked.
So far their encounters had been rushed, but there was
no rushing involved in a traditional sauna. There would
be all the time in the world to admire him.

She left him to open the locked compartment where
the power saw was kept, but Emir wasn't too happy
when she started it up. She turned, ready to give him a
lecture on the fact that she had been cutting holes in the
ice since she was thirteen, and stalled. That man could
take his clothes off faster than anyone she knew. And
could cause a ton of trouble just by standing there. How
was she supposed to keep her gaze glued to his face?

'I'll cut the ice. You go inside. The sauna's been lit
for some time. It should be perfect. Just ladle some more
water on the hot stones—'

She hardly needed steam at this point, Britt reflected
as Emir pushed through the door and disappeared. He
was a towering monument to masculinity.

*And she was going to share some down time with
him?*

She'd always managed to do so before with people
without leaping on top of them—

And they all looked like Emir?

None of them looked like Emir.

Having cut the hole in the ice, she stripped down
ready for the sauna. She kept her underwear on. She'd
never done that before. Not that it offered much protection, but she felt better. And maybe it sent a message.
If not, too bad; for the first time she could remember
ever, she felt self-conscious, so the scraps of lace helped
her, if no one else.

She found Emir leaning back on the wooden bench,
perfectly relaxed, and perfectly naked as he allowed

the steam rising from the hot stones on the brazier to roll over him.

She sat down in the shadows away from him, but couldn't settle.

'Too hot?' he asked as she constantly changed position.

Try, overheating...

And that was something else he didn't need to know. Emir's eyes might be closed, but she suspected he knew everything going on around him. If she needed proof of that, his faint smile told her everything. And as if she needed any more provocation with those hard-muscled legs stretched out in front of him, and his best bits prominently displayed—should she be foolish enough to take a look. She transferred her gaze to his face. His eyelashes were so thick and black they threw crescent shadows across his cheekbones, while his ebony brows swept up like some wild Tartar from the plains of Russia...

Or a sheikh...

Waves of shock and faintness washed over her, until she told herself firmly to give that overactive imagination of hers a rest. 'I'm going outside to cool off.'

Emir went as far as opening one eye.

'I'm going for a swim in the swimming hole—'

'Then I'm coming with you—'

'No need,' she said quickly, needing space.

Too late. Emir was already standing and taking up every spare inch in the hut. Regret at her foolishness replaced the shock and faintness. They should have said goodbye in Skavanga. She could have sent a trusted employee to the mine.

Could you trust anyone else to do this deal but you?

Whatever. There had to be an easier way than this.

'You can't go swimming in an ice lake on your own,' Emir said firmly, as if reading her.

'I've been swimming in the lake since I was a child.'

'When you were supervised, I imagine.'

'I'm old enough to take care of myself now.'

'Really?'

Emir's mockery was getting to her. And what did he think he was looking at now?

Oh... She quickly crossed her arms over her chest.

'I'm coming anyway,' he said, still with a flare of amusement in his eyes.

So be it, she thought, firming her jaw. In fairness, the golden rule at the cabin was that no one *ever* went swimming in the frozen lake alone. But did Emir have to tower over her to make his point?

He grabbed a towel on his way out, which he flung around her shoulders. 'You'll need it afterwards,' he said.

She gave him a look that said she didn't need his help, especially not here, and then gritted her teeth as she thought about the icy shock to come.

Running to the lake, she tossed her towel away at the last minute and jumped in before she had chance to change her mind.

She might have screamed. Who knew what she did or said? Once the icy water claimed her, rational thought was impossible. She was in shock and knew better than to linger. She was soon clambering out again—only to find Emir standing waiting for her with a towel.

'You didn't need to do that.'

He tossed the towel her way without another word, and then dived into the lake before she could stop him. She ran to the edge, but there was no sign of him— just loose ice floating. Panic consumed her, but just as

she was preparing to jump in after him he emerged.
Laughing.

Laughing!

Emir had barely cracked a smile the whole time he'd
been in Skavanga, and *now* he was laughing?

She repaid the favour by tossing him a clean towel,
which he wrapped around his waist. She didn't wait
to see how securely he fixed it. She just pelted for the
sauna and dived in. Emir was close behind and shut
the door.

'Amazing,' he said, like a tiger that, finding itself in
the Arctic, had played with polar bears and found it fun.

He shook his head, sending tiny rainbow droplets of
glacier flying around the cabin like the diamonds they
were both seeking.

'You enjoyed it, I see?' she said as the spray from
him hissed on the hot stones.

'Of course I enjoyed it,' he exclaimed. 'I can think
of only one thing better—'

She could be excused for holding her breath.

'Next you rub me down with ice—'

Before it melted? She doubted that was possible.

'I definitely want more,' he said, glancing through
the window.

Oh, to be a frozen lake, she thought.

As Emir settled back on the wooden bench and
closed his eyes she realised she was glad he had embraced her traditions, which led on naturally to wondering about his. She had to stop that before her thoughts
took a turn for the seriously erotic.

'You love this place, don't you?' he said.

'It means a lot to me,' she admitted, 'as does the
cabin.'

'It's what it represents,' Emir observed.

Correct, she thought.

'If I lived in Skavanga, I'd come here to recharge my batteries.'

Which was exactly what she did. She sometimes came to the cabin just for a change of pace. It helped her to relax and get back in the race.

And it was high time she stopped finding points of contact between them, Britt warned herself, or she'd be convincing herself that fate was giving her a sign. There was no sign. There was no Emir and Britt. It seemed they got on outside sex and business, but that was it.

'What are you thinking?' he said.

She was resting her chin on her knees when she realised Emir was staring at her.

'Why don't you take your underwear off?' he suggested. 'You can't be comfortable in those soggy scraps.'

'They'll soon dry out,' she said, keeping her head down.

Out of the corner of her eye she saw him shrug, but his expression called her a coward. And he was right. She was usually naked before she reached the door of the sauna—and she'd had sex with this man. Plus, she was hardly a vestal virgin in the first place. But somehow with Emir she felt exposed in all sorts of ways, and her underwear was one small, tiny, infinitesimal piece of armour—and she was hanging onto it. 'I'm going outside,' she announced.

'Excellent. I'm ready for my ice rub, Ms Skavanga.'

'Okay, tough guy, bring a towel. And don't blame me if this is too hard core for you.' Her grand flounce off was ruined by the sight of Emir's grin.

She had used to swim through the snow when she was a little girl—or pretend to—and so she plunged straight in. It wasn't something you stopped to think about. The shock was indescribable. But there was pleasure too as all her nerve endings shrieked at once. The soft bed of snow was cold but not life threatening. It was invigorating, and wiped her mind clean of any concerns she had—

But where was Emir?

She suddenly realised he wasn't with her. Springing up, she looked around. Nothing—just silence and snow. She called his name. Still nothing.

Had he gone back to the hut?

She ran to the window and peered in. It was empty.

The lake—

Dread made her unsteady on her feet as she stumbled towards the water, but then she gusted with relief...and fury as his head appeared above the surface. 'You're mad,' she yelled. 'You never go swimming in the lake on your own. What if something had happened to you?'

'You stole my line,' he said, springing out. 'I'm flattered you'd care.'

'Of course I'd care,' she yelled, leaning forward hands on hips. 'What the hell would I tell your people if I lost you in a frozen lake? Don't you dare laugh at me,' she warned when Emir pressed his lips together. 'Don't you—'

'What?' he said sharply. Catching hold of her arms, he dragged her close, but she saw from his eyes that he was only teasing her. 'Didn't I tell you I wanted more?' he growled.

His brows rose, his mouth curved. She could have stamped on his foot—much good it would do her in bare feet. They stared at each other for a long moment, until finally she wrestled herself free. 'You're impossible! You're irresponsible and you're a pig-headed pain in the neck.'

'Anything else?'

'You deserve to freeze to death!'

'Harsh,' he commented.

Wrapping both towels around her, she stormed off.

'You're a liability!' she flashed over her shoulder, unable to stare at the gleaming lake water streaming off his naked body a moment longer.

'Come back here. You haven't fulfilled your part of the bargain.'

She stopped at the door to the sauna. Emir's voice was pitched low and sent shivers down her spine. This was another of those 'what am I doing here?' moments...

And as soon as she turned she knew. There was nowhere else on earth she'd rather be. 'My part of the bargain?' she queried.

'Ice,' he said, holding her gaze in a way that shot arousal through her.

'I can't believe you haven't had enough yet.'

'I haven't had nearly enough.'

Those black eyes—that stare—that wicked, sexy mouth—

'You asked for this,' she said, scooping up a couple of handfuls.

She was right about ice melting on Emir. Even now, fresh from the lake, he was red hot, and as the ice scraped across his smooth, bronzed skin it disappeared beneath the warmth of her hands, leaving her with no alternative but to explore the heat of his body.

'That's enough,' she said, stepping back the instant her breathing became ragged. She had been wrong to think she could do this—that she could play with this man—toy with him—amuse herself at his expense. Emir was more than a match for her, and the strength she'd felt beneath her hands had only confirmed her thoughts that his body was hard, while hers was all too soft and yielding.

She didn't need to see his face to know he was smiling again as she went back to the sauna hut. Her hands were trembling as she let herself in, and hot guilt rushed through her as she curled up on the bench with her knees tucked under her chin and her arms wrapped tightly round them. By the time Emir walked in, she had put safety back at the top of her agenda. 'Let me know if you plan any more solo trips in the lake. Forget the sheikh—I don't even have a contact number for your next of kin.'

'Your concern overwhelms me,' Emir said dryly as he poured another ladle of water onto the hot stones.

'Where are you going now?' she said as he turned for the door.

'To choose which birch switch I would like to use,' he said as if she should have known. 'Would you care to join me?'

Talk about a conversation stopper.

CHAPTER SIX

SHE WAS TWISTED into a ferment of lust. Her heart was beating like a drum as she watched Emir selecting a birch twig switch. She loved that his process of elimination was so exacting. She loved that he examined each bunch before trying them out on his muscular calves. Each arc through the air…each short, sharp slap against his skin…made her breath catch. Her head was reeling with all sorts of erotic impressions, though she couldn't help wondering if he ever felt the cold. She had grabbed a robe and fur boots before exiting the hut and was well wrapped up.

He started thrashing his shoulders. This was like an advanced lesson in how to watch, feel and suffer—from the most intense frustration she had ever known.

'What do you think?' His dark eyes were full of humour.

'I think I'll leave you to it,' she said, shaking her head as if to indulge the tourist in him.

'Why so prudish, suddenly?' Emir challenged as she turned to go.

Yes. Why was she so strait-laced with Emir when thrashing the body with birch twigs was a normal part of the traditional sauna routine in Skavanga?

'Don't you want to try it?' Emir called after her with amusement in his voice.

She stopped, realising that however high she raised the bar he jumped over it and raised it yet more for her.

Where would this end?

'I can do it any time,' she said casually. He didn't need to know she was shivering with arousal rather than cold as she headed for the door. She swung it open and the enticing warmth with the mellow scent of hot wood washed over her.

'It's not like you to run away from a challenge, Britt.'

She hadn't closed the door yet. 'You don't know anything about me.'

'Are we going to debate this while our body temperatures drop like a stone?'

His maybe. 'You could always join me in the sauna...' she suggested.

'Or you could join me with the birch twigs.' As Emir laughed she made her decision.

'In your dreams. And you might want to put some clothes on,' she added, heading for the sauna hut.

Slamming the door behind her, she leaned back against it, exhaling shakily. Damn the man! Did nothing faze him? She had dreamed of meeting her match, but now she'd met him she wasn't so sure it was such a good idea. They were too similar—too stubborn—too set on duty—too competitive—too everything.

It was too exhausting!

Flopping down on the bench, she closed her eyes, but that didn't help to blank out the fact that a connection of some sort, that wasn't sex, was growing between them. Crashing into the hut in a blast of energy and frigid air, Emir exclaimed, 'Make room for me,' before she could progress this thought.

'Close the door!'

'Wuss,' he murmured in a way that made her picture his sexy mouth curved in that half-smile.

'I don't like the cold,' she muttered, hugging her knees and burying her face so she didn't have to look at him.

'You could have fooled me! But I guess you'd love the desert,' he said.

She went very still and then forced herself to reach for the ladle so she didn't seem too impressed by this last comment.

'You can't still be cold?' Emir commented as she ladled water onto the hot stones. 'That's enough!'

The small hut was full of steam. She had been ladling the water on autopilot, trying not to think about the possibility of travelling to the desert with Emir, and in doing so was threatening to steam them alive. 'Sorry.' She lifted her shoulders in a careless shrug. 'I got carried away.'

'You certainly did,' Emir agreed as he towelled down.

'It's a long time since I've done the whole sauna ritual thing. I'd forgotten—'

'What fun it was?' Emir interrupted.

'How cold you get,' she argued, picking up the ladle again.

He laughed and took it from her. 'That's enough,' he said as their hands brushed. 'Sit down.' He towered over her, blocking out the light. 'If you want to raise the temperature, just ask me.'

'Very funny.' She glanced up.

Emir shrugged and smiled faintly, making her glad she was wearing a towel. He had no inhibitions, and, in fairness, most people went naked in the sauna, but that only worked if they had no sexual interest in each other.

'How about I build a fire in the fire pit outside?' Emir suggested. 'You don't want to be cooped up in here much longer.'

She had always enjoyed sitting round a blazing fire surrounded by snow and ice, and it would be one heck of a lot safer than this intimate space. 'That's a great idea.'

'I'll call you when I'm ready.'

You do that, she thought, banking Emir's sexy smile.

Her heart thumped on cue when he rapped on the door. Sliding off the bench, she went outside to join him. Emir had built an amazing fire…roaring hot and set to last.

'Nights in the desert can be freezing,' he explained. 'And in some parts a fire is essential to keep mountain lions away. We have amazing wildlife,' he added as she sat down and stretched her feet out. 'Kareshi is a country of great contrasts. We have big modern cities as well as a wilderness where tribal traditions haven't changed in centuries.'

Why was he telling her this? Was he serious about her visiting Kareshi? They were staring at each other again, Britt realised, turning away to pretend interest in the fire. There was no point in getting any closer to Emir when their relationship, such as it was, wasn't going anywhere. Lifting his chin, he stared at her as if he were expecting her to say something. Who knew that Britt Skavanga, lately hotshot businesswoman, as her sisters liked to teasingly call her, could feel so awkward, even shy?

Maybe you should get out of the office more often.

Maybe she should, Britt thought wryly, lacking the

energy for once to argue with her contrary inner voice.
Emir had gone quite still, she noticed.

'Do you see them?' he said, looking past her into
the trees.

'The deer? Yes,' she murmured. A doe and a fawn
were watching them from the safety of the undergrowth.
'They're so beautiful,' she whispered, hardly daring to
breathe. 'I always feel close to nature here,' she confided in another whisper.

'As I do in the desert,' Emir murmured back.

There was that connection thing again. It was there
whether she liked it or not. And now she stiffened, remembering the warning her mother had given her when
Britt was a child. Now she understood why her mother
had said the things she had, but as a little girl she had
thought her father loud rather than violent, and playful,
rather than bullying. Now she knew he'd been a drunk
who had prompted her mother to warn all her daughters that men kept you down. Her girls were going to
be warriors who went out into the world and made their
own way. Britt had grown up with the determination
that no man would ever rule her engraved on her heart.
And Emir was a forceful man...

His touch on her arm made her flinch, but then she
realised he was pointing to the deer watching them. The
animals were considering flight, and she wondered if it
was Emir's inner stillness holding them. Their brown
eyes were wide in gentle faces, and though Emir had
moved closer to her he kept space between them, which
made her feel relaxed. He had that sort of calming
aura—which didn't mean she wasn't intensely aware
of him. It was a special moment as they watched the
deer watching them. It was as if humans and animals
had come together briefly.

'What an amazing encounter,' she breathed as the deer turned and picked their way unhurriedly back through the maze of trees into the depth of the forest.

'Now I'm certain you'd love the desert,' Emir said, turning to smile at her. 'Many think it's just a barren space—'

'But we know better?'

He huffed a laugh, holding her gaze in a way that said he was glad she had understood.

'Maybe one day I'll make it to the desert,' she said, trying not to care too much.

'I'll make sure of it,' Emir said quietly. 'If this deal goes through I'll make sure you visit Kareshi.'

'I'd love to,' she exclaimed impulsively.

How much longer are you going to wear your heart on your sleeve? Britt wondered as Emir flashed her an amused glance and raised a brow. But she could see that a whole world of possibility was opening up, both for her and for Skavanga, and she couldn't pretend that the thought of visiting an emerging country where the vigorous young ruler had already done so much for his people didn't excited her.

'I want you to see what the money from the diamonds can accomplish,' Emir remarked.

Yes, there were benefits for both their countries. 'I will,' she said, more in hope than expectation. 'I think you miss Kareshi,' she added in an attempt to shift the spotlight onto him.

'I love my country. I love my people. I love my life in Kareshi. I love my horses—they're a real passion for me. I breed pure Arabs, though sometimes I strengthen the line of my breeding stock with Criolla ponies from the Argentine pampas.'

'You play polo?'

'Of course, and many polo players are my friends. You will have heard of the Acosta brothers, I'm sure.'

She had heard of the Acosta brothers. Who hadn't? 'I learned to ride at the local stable,' she admitted. 'Just old nags compared to the type of horses you're talking about, but I loved it all the same. I love the sense of freedom, and still ride whenever I get the chance.'

'Something we have in common,' he said.

Something else, she thought, inhaling steadily. Friendships were founded on sharing a passion for life, and there was no doubt that they were opening up to each other. So much for her mother's warning. And, yes, it was dangerous to reveal too much of yourself, but if you didn't, how could you ever get close to anyone?

She had to face facts. Once he had collected the information he needed, Emir would go home—and inviting her to Kareshi was probably just talk. Making her excuses, she stood up to go. Emir stood too.

'No birching?' he asked wryly.

She gave him a crooked smile. 'I'm warm enough, thanks to you.'

'That's right,' he called after her as she walked away. 'You probably deserve a good birching—probably even want it. But you're not getting it from me—'

Britt shook her head in wry acceptance, but Emir didn't turn around as she huffed a laugh. He didn't need to. There was a new sort of ease between them—an understanding, almost.

He caught her at the door of the hut, and, lifting a switch from the rack, he shot her a teasing look. 'Are you quite sure?'

'Certain,' she said, but there was laughter in both their eyes.

Laughter that died very quickly when Emir ran the

switch of twigs very lightly down between her breasts and over her belly to the apex of her thighs. She was instantly aroused and couldn't move, even had she wanted to. She remained motionless as he increased the pressure just enough, moving the bunched twigs with exactly the right degree of delicacy. Her breath came out in a noisy shudder, and all this time Emir was holding her gaze. His eyes told her that he knew exactly what she wanted him to do. Her breathing stalled when he used the switch to ease her legs apart.

'Why deny yourself, Britt?'

'Because I need to get inside where it's warm,' she said lightly, pulling herself together.

Physically, she yearned for everything Emir could give her, Britt realised as she quickly shed her underwear, while emotionally she was a wreck. She felt such a strong connection to him, and knew she would never be able to ignore those feelings—

Better she end this now.

He joined her in the hut. That was a foregone conclusion. The stag didn't abandon the doe when it was cornered. The stag knew what the doe wanted and tracking it was part of the game. They sat opposite each other with the hot stones sizzling between them, and, leaning back, Emir gave her a look—just a slight curve at the corner of his sexy mouth.

'What?' she said, knowing he could hardly have avoided noticing that she was naked.

'Now we get really hot,' he said.

CHAPTER SEVEN

As Emir's familiar warmth and scent flared in her senses and his arms gathered her in, Britt felt a new energy flooding through her. She even spared a foolish moment to wish it could always be like this—that he was really hers, and that these strong arms and this strong body would sometimes take over so she could take time out occasionally. But that was so ridiculous she had no difficulty blanking it out. She took one last look at a world where desire for a man could grow into friendship, and where that friendship could grow into love. That was just childhood fantasy. She'd settle for lust.

Holding her face between his hands, Emir made her look at him. Gazing into the burning stare of a man who knew so much about her body made it easy to forget her doubts. Her face must have shown this transition, because he brushed her lips with his. And from there it was an easy slide into a passionate embrace that ended with Emir manoeuvring her into a comfortable position on the bench—which just happened to be under him.

'Is there any part of this you don't like?' he said, smiling down at her.

She liked everything—too much—and at what risk to her heart? Right now she didn't care as another part of Britt Skavanga, warrior woman, chipped off and floated away. At one time sex was little more than a normal function for her, like eating or sleeping, but now...

Now that wasn't nearly enough.

But Emir's hands were distracting her, and as he traced the line of her spine she embraced the feelings inside her. They were so strong she could hardly ignore them. She wanted this man. She wanted him so badly. She wanted to be one with him in every way. Unfortunately, Emir's approach to sex was much like hers had used to be, and being on the receiving end of that was very different from doling it out. But then her mind filled with pleasure as his lips caressed her neck. He knew just how to work her hot spots until she softened against him and relaxed. She had always taken the lead in the past—she had been the one who knew what she was doing and where she was going, the one who was completely in control—but with Emir there was no control. She was his.

'I love your body,' he said as she writhed beneath him.

'I love yours too.' How could she not?

Emir was built on a heroic scale. She doubted she had ever met a bigger man. There wasn't a spare inch of unnecessary flesh on his hard, toned body, and each muscle was clearly delineated after his strenuous physical exercise in the lake. He was every bit the soldier, the fighter, the leader, yet he had the most sensitive hands. She groaned as he massaged her scalp with his fingertips.

'What do you want, Britt?' he murmured.

'Do you really need me to answer that?'

'I like you to tell me,' he said.

Emir's voice had the power to arouse her almost as

much as the man himself. Raising her chin, she took a deep breath and then told him what she wanted.

'So open your legs wider,' he said.

Her first thought was, No. I can't do that—not while you're looking down at me.

'Wider,' he said.

She wanted this. He excited her—

'Wider still…'

'I can't—you're merciless—'

'Yes, I am,' he agreed in the same soft tone.

'Enough,' she begged him, reaching out. She needed human contact. She needed closeness more than anything. She needed a kiss—a tender kiss. She still longed for the illusion that they were close in every way, Britt realised, feeling a pang of regret for what could never be.

He had never seen anything more beautiful than Britt at this moment, when every part of her was glowing and aroused. His desire to be joined to her was overwhelming, but something as special as this could not be rushed. It must be appreciated and savoured. One of the so-called erotic secrets of Kareshi was nothing more than this lingering over pleasure. Making time for pleasure was a so much a national pursuit he had been forced to persuade the Kareshi people to balance their country's business needs against it, but he would never wish these old traditions to die out. In fact, he had every intention of fostering them, and as Britt reached for him he took her wrists in a firm grip. 'Not yet,' he whispered.

'Don't you want me?' she said, arching her back as she displayed her breasts to best advantage.

She had no idea how much.

He held her locked in his stare as she sat up. He even

allowed her to lace her fingers through his hair, binding him to her. Britt was easy to read. She was already on the edge. Intuition had always helped him in the past—in all sorts of situations, and now this. With Britt he mastered his own desires by channelling his thoughts into all the things that intrigued him about her.

'How can you bear to wait?' she complained.

'I bear it because I know what's best for you,' he said. 'I know what you need and I know the best way to give it to you.'

'How do you know?' she said, writhing with impatience.

On the sexual front that was all too obvious, but knowing Britt wasn't so hard. She was the oldest child, always trying to do her best, the lab-rat for her sisters, the one who would have been given the strictest upbringing by her parents. Britt was used to bearing the weight of responsibility on her shoulders, and with duties at home and then duties in the business she hadn't had much time to explore life, let alone discover the nuances of sex and how very good it could be.

'So, how did you like our Nordic traditions?' she murmured against his mouth.

Distracted, he brushed a kiss against her lips. 'I like them a lot. I'd like to know more. I'd like to know more about you—'

The look of surprise on her face almost broke the erotic spell for him, and then she said with touching honesty, 'I'd like to know more about you and your country.'

'Maybe you will.'

Closing his eyes, he inhaled her wildflower scent, and realised then that the thought of never smelling it again was unthinkable. He was still on guard, of course.

There was still a business deal to do and it would be unwise to underestimate Britt Skavanga. She was everything he had been warned to expect...and so much more.

When Emir kissed her she was glad of his arms supporting her, because he didn't just kiss her breath away, he kissed her thoughts away too. It felt so good to drop her guard and lose herself in sensation, shut out the business robot she had become. It was good to feel sensation spreading in tiny rivers of fire through her veins, and even better to feel Emir's erection resting heavily against her thigh, because that said he wanted her as much as she wanted him. She groaned with anticipation when he nudged her thighs apart. Moving between them, he started teasing her with delicate touches until she thought she would go mad for him.

'Wrap your legs around me,' he instructed, staring deep into her eyes.

'Don't make me wait,' she warned, but in a way she was glad when he soothed her with kisses and caresses first. She cried out and urged him on. There were no certainties other than the fact that she was being drawn deeper into a dangerous liaison with him.

As if sensing her unease, he took her face in his big, warm hands and drugged her with kisses. Gentle to begin with, they grew deeper and firmer as the embers inside her sparked and flared. She loved it when he took possession of her mouth, and loved it even more when he took possession of her body. She loved being held so firmly. She loved the powerful emotions inside her.

'Have you changed your mind?' he said as she tried to rein them in.

She denied this, and then he did something so amazing she couldn't have stopped him if she had tried. A shaking cry escaped her throat as he sank slowly deep inside her. She could never be fully prepared for Emir. The sheer size of him stole the breath from her lungs. He was such an intuitive lover. He understood every part of her and how she responded. He knew her limits and never stepped over them, while his hands and mouth worked magic. Today he was using the seductive language of Kareshi—soft and guttural, husky and persuasive—to both encourage and excite her. It must have succeeded because she found herself pressing her legs wide for him with the heel of her palms against her thighs.

'Good,' he approved, thrusting even deeper.

She cried out his name repeatedly as he moved rhythmically and reliably towards the inevitable conclusion. But suddenly some madness overcame them, and control was no longer possible as they fought their way to release.

She was still shuddering with aftershocks minutes later. Her internal muscles closed around him gratefully, to an indescribably delicious beat.

Neither of them spoke for quite a while. They had both experienced the same thing—something out of the ordinary, she thought as Emir stared down at her. At last his eyes were full of everything she had longed to see.

'I take it you enjoyed that?' he murmured, and, withdrawing gently, he helped her to sit up.

'And you?' she said, resting her cheek against his chest.

'I have one suggestion—'

She glanced up.

'Next time we try a bed.'

His grin infected her. 'Now there's a novel thought,'

she agreed, but after she had rested on him for a moment or two harsh reality intruded and she remembered who she was, who he was, and the parts they played in this drama.

Lifting her chin, she put on the old confident face. 'Don't get ahead of yourself, mister. I sleep alone.'

'Who mentioned sleeping?' Emir argued.

'Do you always have to show such perfect good sense?'

'With you, I think I do,' he said, smiling, unrepentant.

Emir was probably the one man she was prepared to take instruction from, Britt concluded as she showered down later in her en-suite bathroom at the cabin, if only because the pay-off was so great. And she wasn't just thinking about the sexual pay-off, but the pay-off that was making her sing and waltz around the bathroom like a fruit-loop—the pay-off that made her feel all warm and fuzzy inside—and optimistic about the future—about everything. She felt suddenly as if anything could happen—as if the boundaries of Skavanga and her job had fallen away, leaving a world full of possibility. And the desert kingdom of Kareshi was definitely the stand out country in that world waiting to be discovered.

Of course, she must visit Emir's homeland as he had suggested. If the deal went through it would be wrong to accept the consortium's investment without wanting to know as much as she possibly could about the benefits the diamonds would bring to both countries. Perhaps there could be reciprocal cultural and educational opportunities—anything was possible. She longed to get stuck into it—to get out of the office and meet people at last. Her mind was blazing with ideas. No dream seemed too far-fetched.

Showering down after his unique encounter with Britt, Sharif's thoughts were arranged in several compartments. The first was all to do with Britt the businesswoman. She was meticulous and had held the company together when many would have failed. Her attention to detail was second to none—as he had learned when it had taken him several hours, rather than the usual five minutes, to pore over her first agenda and find a hole. She was clear-headed and quick-thinking in her business life—

And an emotional mess when it came to anything else.

Her life was tied up in duty, but she wanted it all. He guessed she heard the clock ticking, but she didn't know how to escape from her work long enough to find the fulfilment she craved—the satisfaction of raising her own family and extending her sphere of influence in the workplace too. She did everything she could to support her sisters while they studied and campaigned for this and that, but they didn't seem to stop and think that Britt deserved some fulfilment too.

And neither should he, he reminded himself. He had one duty, one goal, and one responsibility, which was to the men who had come in with him on this deal. Business always came first, because business fed improvements in Kareshi, and only then could he afford to pause to wonder if there was anything missing from his life—

Britt?

Any man would be missing a woman like Britt in his life. She was exceptional. She was an intriguing mix of control and abandonment, and it seemed to him that the only time Britt let go was during sex, which made cutting the best deal possible a challenging prospect, but not impossible.

Business, always business, he thought, towelling down. He liked that Britt was part of that business. He had always loved a challenge and Britt was a challenge. Securing the towel around his waist, he picked up his razor to engage in the one battle he usually lost. His beard grew faster than he could shave it off, but at least the ritual soothed him and gave him time to think.

Shaking his head as if that could shake thoughts of Britt out of it, he rinsed his face and raked his thick, unruly hair into some semblance of order. The deal was a tantalising prospect and he would bring it in. Between them he and his friends had the means and the skill and the outlets necessary to transform dull, uncut diamonds into sparkling gems that would shimmer with fire as they shivered against a woman's skin. Britt believed she held all the cards, and could cut the better deal, but he held the joker.

Stepping into jeans, he tugged on a plain back top, and fastened his belt before reaching for the phone. Some decisions were harder to take than others, and this was harder than most. Britt had all the instincts of a man inside the body of a woman, but she had a woman's emotions, which held her back when it came to clear thinking in a deal like this where family was involved. He wished he could protect her from the fallout from this call, but his duty was clear. This wasn't for him alone, but for the consortium, and for Kareshi. In the absence of her brother, Britt led her tribe as he did, making her a worthy adversary. He just had to hope she could handle this new twist in the plot as competently as she had coped with other obstacles life had thrown at her.

He drummed his fingers impatiently as he waited for the call to connect. Three rings later the call was answered. He hesitated, which was definitely a first for him, but the die had been cast on the day he had sat down to research the share structure of Skavanga Mining and had discovered that the major shareholder was not in fact the three sisters, but their missing brother, Tyr Skavanga. More complicated still was that, for reasons of his own, Tyr didn't want his sisters to know where he was. Having given his word, Emir would have to keep that from Britt even though Tyr's long-distance involvement in the deal would swing the balance firmly in the consortium's favour.

'Hello, Tyr,' he said, settling down into what he knew would be a long call.

CHAPTER EIGHT

HE WAS PACKING? *Emir was packing?* She had come downstairs after her shower expecting to find him basking in front of a roaring fire—which he would have banked up, perhaps with a drink in hand and one waiting for her on the table. She had anticipated more getting-to-know-you time. That was what couples did when they'd grown closer after sex...

And they had grown closer, Britt reassured herself, feeling painfully obvious in banged-up jeans, simple top and bare feet. She felt as if, in this relaxed state, all her feelings were on display. And all those feelings spoke of closeness and intimacy with Emir. She had dressed in anticipation of continuing ease between them. She had dressed as she would dress when her sisters were around. And now she felt vulnerable and exposed. And utterly ridiculous for having let her guard down so badly.

How could she have got this so wrong?

She watched him from the doorway of his bedroom as Emir folded his clothes, arranging them in a bag that he could sling casually over his shoulder. He must have known she was standing there, but he didn't say a word. The chill seemed to creep up from the floor and consume her. Even her face felt cold.

What had gone wrong?

What was wrong was that Emir didn't care and she had refused to see that. He had come here to do a job and his job was done. He had taken samples for analysis and had seen the mine for himself. He had weighed her up and interviewed her colleagues. His only job now was to pack up and leave. What had she been? An unexpected bonus on the side? She had no part to play in Emir's plans, he'd made that clear. Why had she ever allowed herself to believe that she had? All that talk of Kareshi and the desert was just that—talk.

Her throat felt tight. Her mouth was dry. She felt numb. Anything she said in this situation would sound ridiculous. And what was the point of having a row when she had no call on this man? She had enjoyed him as much as he had enjoyed her. Was it his fault if she couldn't move on?

All this was sound reasoning, but reason didn't allow for passion, for emotion—for any of the things she felt for Emir. And out of bitter disappointment at his manner towards her—or rather his lack of...anything, really—came anger. What had he meant by staring into her eyes and suggesting they should take sex to the bedroom next time? Was that concern for her? Or was Emir more concerned about getting grazes on his knees? She had laughed with and trusted this man. Everything had changed for her, because she'd thought... Because she'd thought...

She didn't have a clue what she'd thought, Britt realised. She only knew she had given herself completely to a man, something she'd never done before, and now, just as her mother had predicted, she was paying the price. But she would not play the role of misused mistress and give him the chance to mock.

'You're leaving?' she said coolly. 'Already?'

'My job here's done,' Emir confirmed, straightening up. He turned to face her. 'My flight plan is filed. I leave right away.'

When did he file his flight plan? Immediately after making love to her?

'Do you have transport to the airport?' She wasn't so petty she would let him call a cab. She would take him to the airport if she had to.

'My people are coming for me,' he said, turning back to zip up his bag.

Of course. 'Oh, good,' she said, going hot and cold in turn as she chalked up the completeness of his plan as just one more insult to add to the rest. He'd had sex with her first and then had called his people to come and get him. He'd used her—

As she had used men in the past.

Her heart lurched as their eyes met. Mistake. Now he could see how badly she didn't want him to go.

'I have to report back to the consortium, Britt,' he said, confirming this assumption.

'Of course.' She cleared her throat and arranged her features in a composed mask. She had never been at such a disadvantage where a man was concerned. But that was because she had never known anyone like Emir before and had always prided herself on being able to read people. She had not read him. They were like two strangers, out of sync, out of context, out of time.

She stood in embarrassed silence. With no small talk to delay him, let alone some siren song with which to change his mind, she could only wait for him to leave.

'Thank you for your hospitality, Britt,' he said, shouldering the bag.

Her hospitality? Did that include the sex? Her face

was composed, but as Emir moved to shake her hand she stood back.

Emir didn't react one way or the other to this snub. 'I'll wait for test results on the samples, and if all goes well you will hear from my lawyers in the next few weeks.'

'Your lawyers?' Her head was reeling by now, with business and personal thoughts hopelessly mixed.

'Forgive me, Britt.' Emir paused with his hand on the door. 'I meant, of course, the lawyers acting for the consortium will be in touch with you.'

Suddenly all the anger and hurt inside her exploded into fury, which manifested itself in an icy question. 'And what if I get a better offer in the meantime?'

'Then you must consider it and we will meet again. I should tell you that the consortium has been in touch with your sisters, and they have already agreed—'

'You've spoken to Eva and Leila?' she cut in. He'd done that without speaking to her? She couldn't take any more in than she already had—and she certainly couldn't believe that her sisters would do a deal without speaking to her first.

'My people have spoken to your sisters,' Emir explained.

'And you didn't think to tell me?' *They didn't think to tell me?* She was flooded with hurt and pain.

'I just have.' A muscle flicked in his jaw.

'So all the time we've been here—' Outrage boiled in her eyes. 'I think you'd better go,' she managed tensely. Suddenly, all that mattered was speaking to her sisters so she could find out what the hell was going on.

Meanwhile, Emir was checking round the room, just to be sure he hadn't forgotten anything, presumably. He didn't care a jot about her, she realised with a cold rush of certainty. This had only ever been about the deal. How convenient to keep her distracted here while the consortium's lackeys acted behind her back. How very clever of Emir. And how irredeemably stupid of her.

'If you've left anything I'll send it on,' she said coldly, just wanting him to go.

How could her heart still betray her when Emir's brooding stare switched to her face?

'I knew I could count on you,' he said as her stupid heart performed the customary leap.

Emir's impassive stare turned her own eyes glacial. 'Well, you've got what you wanted from me, so you might as well go. You'll get nothing else here.'

The inky brows rose, but Emir remained silent. She just hoped her barb had stabbed home. But no.

'This is business, Britt, and there is no emotion in business. I wish I could tell you more, but—'

'Please—spare me.' She drew herself up. 'Goodbye, Emir.'

She didn't follow him out. She wouldn't give him the satisfaction. She listened to him jog down the stairs, while registering the tenderness of a body that had been very well used, and heard him stride across the main room downstairs where they had been so briefly close. It was as if Emir were stripping the joy out of the cabin she loved with every step he took, and each of those departing steps served as a reminder that she had wasted her feelings on someone who cared for nothing in this world apart from business.

Apart from her sisters and Tyr, that had been how she was not so very long ago, Britt conceded as the front door closed behind Emir.

She hadn't even realised she had stopped breathing

until she heard a car door slam and she drew in a desperate, shuddering breath.

There were times when he would gladly exchange places with the grooms who worked in his stables and this was one of them, but harsh decisions had to be made. He thought he could feel Britt's anguished stare on his back as he held up his hand to hail the black Jeep that had come to collect him. His men would take him back to the airport and his private jet. His mind was still full of her when he climbed into the passenger seat and they drove him away. It was better to leave now before things became really complicated.

Her sense of betrayal by Emir—and, yes, even more so by her sisters—was indescribable. And for once both Eva and Leila were out of touch by phone. She had tried them constantly since Emir had left, prowling around the cabin like a wounded animal, unable to settle or do anything until she had spoken to them. Even her beloved cabin had let her down. It failed to soothe her this time. She should never have brought Emir here. He had tainted her precious memories.

Not wanting to face the fact that she had been less than focused, she turned on every light in the cabin, but it still felt empty. There was no reply from her sisters, so all she could do was dwell on what she'd seen through the window when he'd left—Emir climbing into a Jeep and being driven away. She'd got the sense of other big men in the vehicle, shadowy, and no doubt armed. Where there were such vast resources up for grabs, no one took any chances. She had been kidding herself if she had thought that bringing investors in would be easy to handle. She was up against a power-

ful and well-oiled machine. She should have known
when each man in the consortium was a power in his
own right, and she was on her own—

So? Get used to it! There was no time for self-pity.
This was all about protecting her sisters, whatever
they'd done. They weren't to blame. They had no idea
what it took to survive in the cut-throat world of business—she didn't want them to know. She would protect
them as she always had.

She nearly jumped out of her skin when the phone
rang, and she rushed to pick it up. Mixed feelings when
she did so, because it was Eva, her middle and least
flexible sister, calling. 'Eva—'

'You rang?' Eva intoned. 'Seven missed calls, Britt?
What's going on?'

Where to begin? Suddenly, Britt was at a loss, but
then her mind cleared and became as unemotional as
it usually was where business was concerned. 'The
man from the consortium just left the cabin. He said
you and Leila signed something?' Britt waited tensely
for her sister to respond, guessing Eva would be doing
ten things at once. 'So, what have you signed?' Britt
pressed, controlling her impatience.

'All we did was give permission for the consortium's
people to enter the offices to start their preliminary investigations.'

'Why didn't you speak to me first?'

'Because we couldn't get hold of you.'

And now she could only rue the day she had left Skavanga to show Emir the mine.

'We thought we were helping you move things on.'

Britt could accept that. The sooner the consortium's
accountants had completed their investigations, the
sooner she could bring some investment into Skavanga

Mining and save the company. 'So you haven't agreed to sell your shares?'

'Of course not. What do you take me for?'

'I don't want to argue with you, Eva. I'm just worried—'

'You know I don't know the first thing about the business,' Eva countered. 'And I'm sorry you got landed with it when our parents died. I do know there are a thousand things you'd rather do.'

'Never mind that now—I need to help people at home. I'm coming back—'

'Before you go, how did you get on with him?"

'Who?' Britt said defensively.

'You know—the man who was at the mine with you—the sheikh's man.'

'Oh, you mean Emir.'

'What?'

'Emir,' Britt repeated.

'Well, that's original,' Eva murmured with a smile in her voice. 'Did the Black Sheikh come up with any more titles to fool you, or just the one?'

Britt started to say something and then stopped. 'Sorry?'

'Oh, come on,' Eva exclaimed impatiently. 'I guess he was quite a man, but I can't believe your brain has taken up permanent residence below your belt. You know your thesaurus as well as anyone: emir, potentate, person of rank. Have I rung any bells yet?'

'But he said his name was—' Hot waves of shame washed over her. She was every bit as stupid as she had thought herself when Emir left, only more so.

'Since when have you believed everything you're told, Britt?' Eva demanded.

Since she met a man who told her that his name was Emir.

She had to speak to him. She would speak to him, Britt determined icily, just as soon as she had finished this call to her sister.

'You haven't fallen for him, have you?' Eva said shrewdly.

'No, of course not,' Britt fired back.

There was a silence that suggested Eva wasn't entirely convinced. Too bad. Whatever Britt might have felt for Emir was gone now. Gone completely. Finished. Over. Dead. Gone.

'You should have taken him for a roll in the snow so you could both cool down.'

'I did,' she admitted flatly. 'He loved it.'

'Sounds like my kind of guy—'

'This isn't funny, Eva.'

'No,' Eva agreed, turning serious. 'You've made a fool of yourself and you don't like it. Turns out you're not the hotshot man-eater you thought you were.'

'But I'm still a businesswoman,' Britt murmured thoughtfully, 'and you know what they say.'

'I'm sure you're going to tell me,' Eva observed dryly.

'Don't get mad, get even.'

'That's what I was afraid of,' Eva commented under her breath. 'Just don't cut off your nose to spite your face. Don't screw this deal after putting so much effort into it.'

'Don't worry, I won't.'

'So what are you going to do?' Eva pressed, concern ringing in her voice.

For betraying her—for allowing his people to approach her sisters while Britt and he were otherwise engaged?

'I'm going to follow him to Kareshi. I'm going to track him down. I'm going to ring his office to try and find out where he is. I'll go into the desert if I have to. I'm going to find the bastard and make him pay.'

CHAPTER NINE

KARESHI...

She was actually here. It hardly seemed possible. For all her bitter, mixed-up thoughts when it came to the man she had called Emir and must now learn to call His Majesty Sheikh Sharif al Kareshi, Britt couldn't help but be dazzled by her first sight of the ocean of sand stretching away to a purple haze following the curve of the earth. She craned her neck, having just caught sight of the glittering capital city. It couldn't stand in greater contrast to the desert.

Just as her thoughts of the man the world called the Black Sheikh couldn't have stood in starker contrast to the universal approval the man enjoyed. How could he fool so many people? How could he fool her?

That last question was easily answered. Her body had done that for her, yearning for a man when it should freeze at the very thought of him—if she had any sense.

As the city came into clearer view and she saw all the amazing buildings she got a better picture of the Black Sheikh's power and his immense wealth. It seemed incredible that she was here, and that His Majesty Sheikh Sharif had been her lover—

That she had been so easily fooled.

'The captain has switched the seat-belt sign on.'

'Oh, yes, thank you,' she said glancing up, glad of the distraction. Any distraction to take her mind off that man was welcome.

Having secured her belt, she continued to stare avidly out of the window. Her life to date hadn't allowed for much time outside Skavanga, and from what she could see from the plane Kareshi couldn't have been more different. The thought of exploring the city and meeting new people was exciting in spite of all the other things she had to face. An ivory beach bordered the city, and beyond that lay a tranquil sea of clear bright blue, but it was the wilderness that drew her attention. The Black Sheikh was down there somewhere. His people had told her this in an attempt to put her off. They didn't know her if they thought she would be dismayed to learn His Majesty was deep in the desert with his people. She would find him and she would confront him. She had every reason to do so, if only to learn the result of the trials on the mineral samples he had taken from the mine. She suspected he would agree to see her. His people were sure to have told him that she had been asking for him and, like Britt, the Black Sheikh flinched from nothing.

Another glance out of the window revealed a seemingly limitless carpet of umber and sienna, gold and tangerine, and over this colourful, if alien landscape the black shadow of the aircraft appeared to be creeping with deceptive stealth. The desert was a magical place and she was impatient to be travelling through it. Would she find Sheikh Sharif? The ice fields of Skavanga were apparently featureless, but that was never completely true, and where landmarks failed there was always GPS. Tracking down the ruler of Kareshi would be a challenge, but not one she couldn't handle.

* * *

Shortly after she reached the hotel Britt received a call from Eva to say that one of their main customers for the minerals they mined had gone down, defaulting on a payment to Skavanga Mining, and leaving the company dangerously exposed. It was the last thing she needed, and her mind was already racing on what to do for the best when Eva explained that the consortium had stepped in.

'I think you need to speak to the sheikh to find out the details.'

'That's my intention,' Britt assured her sister, feeling that the consortium's net was slowly closing over her family business.

As soon as she ended the call she tried once again to speak to a member of the sheikh's staff to arrange an appointment as a matter of urgency. Audience with His Majesty was booked up for months in advance, some snooty official informed her. And, no, His Majesty had *certainly not* left any message for a visitor from a *mining* company. This was said as if mining were some sleazy, disreputable occupation.

So speaks a man who has probably never got his hands dirty in his life, Britt thought, pulling the phone away from her ear. She had been placing calls non-stop from her bedroom for the past two hours—to Sharif's offices, to his palace, to the country's administrative offices, and even to her country's diplomatic representative in the city.

Okay. Calm down, she told herself, taking a deep breath as she paced the room. Let's think this through. There was a number she could call, and this really was a wild card. Remembering Emir telling her about his love of horses, she stabbed in the number for His Majesty's stables.

The voice that answered was young and female and it took Britt a couple of breaths to compute this, as her calls so far had led Britt to believe that only men worked for the sheikh and they all had tent poles up their backsides.

'Hello,' the pleasant female voice said again. 'Jasmina Kareshi speaking...'

The Black Sheikh's sister! Though Princess Jasmina sounded far too relaxed to be a princess. 'Hello. This is Britt Skavanga speaking. I wonder if you could help me?'

'Call me Jazz,' the friendly voice on the other end of the line insisted as Jazz went on to explain that her brother had in fact been in touch some time ago to warn her that Britt was due to arrive in the country.

'How did he find out?' Britt exclaimed with surprise.

'Are you serious?' Jazz demanded.

Jazz's upbeat nature was engaging, and as the ruler of Kareshi's sister proceeded to tell Britt that her brother knew everything that was going on in Kareshi at least ten minutes before it happened Britt got the feeling that in different circumstances Jazz and she might have been friends.

'As he's not here, I'm supposed to be helping you any way I can,' Jazz explained. 'I can only apologise that it's taken so long for the two of us to get in touch, but I've been tied up with my favourite mare at the stables while she was giving birth.'

'Please don't apologise,' Britt said quickly. She was just glad to have someone sensible to talk to. 'I hope everything went well for your horse.'

'Perfectly,' Jazz confirmed, adding in an amused

tone, 'I imagine it went a lot better for me and my mare than it did for you without a formal introduction to my brother's stuffy staff.'

Diplomacy was called for, Britt concluded. 'They did what they could,' she said cagily.

'I bet they did,' Jazz agreed wryly.

This was really dangerous. Not only had she fallen for the Black Sheikh masquerading as Emir, but now she was starting to get on with his sister.

'My brother's in the desert,' Jazz confirmed. 'Let me give you the GPS—'

'Thanks.'

Jazz proceeded to dispense GPS coordinates for a Bedouin camp in the desert as casually as if she were directing Britt to the local mall. Britt was able to draw a couple of possible conclusions from this. Sharif had not wanted his staff to know about the connection between them—possibly because as she was a woman in a recently reformed and previously male-dominated country they wouldn't treat her too well. But at least he had entrusted the news of her arrival to Jazz. She'd give him the benefit of the doubt this one time. Just before signing off, she checked with Jazz that the car hire company she had decided on had the best vehicles for trekking in the desert.

'It should be the best,' Jazz exclaimed. 'Like practically everything else in Kareshi, my brother owns it.'

Of course he did. And he thought Skavanga Mining was in the bag too. Not just an investment, but a takeover. There was no time to lose. Having promised to keep in touch with Jazz, she cut the line.

She had a moment—a fluttering heart, sweaty palms moment—when she knew it would have been far safer to deal with the Black Sheikh from a distance, preferably half a world away in Skavanga. Sharif was too confident for her liking, telling his sister about Britt's arrival in Kareshi as if he knew all her arrangements. According to Jazz it was very likely that he did, Britt reasoned, more eager than ever to get into the desert to confront him. And this time she would definitely confine their talks to business. She might be a slow learner, but she never made the same mistake twice.

He wasn't surprised that Britt had decided to track him down in the desert. He would have been more surprised if she had remained in Skavanga doing nothing. He admired her for not taking anything lying down. Well, almost anything, he mused, a smile hovering around his mouth. He did look forward to taking her on a bed one day.

Stretching out his naked body on the bank of silken cushions in the sleeping area of his tent, he turned his thoughts to business. Business had always been a game to him—a game he never lost, though with Britt it was different. He wanted to include her. He knew about the customer going bankrupt leaving Skavanga Mining in the lurch. He also knew there was nothing Britt could have done about it even had she been in Skavanga, though he doubted she would see it that way. He had been forced to get in touch with Tyr again to fast-track the deal, and with Britt on her way to the desert maybe he would get the chance to put her straight. He didn't like this subterfuge Tyr had forced upon him, though he could understand the reasons for it.

He rose and bathed in the pool formed by an underground stream that bubbled up beside his sleeping quarters. Donning his traditional black robes, he ran impatient hands through his damp black hair. Jasmina had contacted him to say that Britt had landed safely and would soon be joining him. Not soon enough, he thought as one of the elders of the tribe gave a discreet cough from the entrance to the tent to attract his attention.

A tent was a wholly inadequate description for the luxurious pavilion in which this noble tribe had insisted on housing him, Sharif reflected as he strode in lightweight sandals across priceless rugs to greet the old man. A simple bivouac would have been enough for him, but this was a palatial marquee fitted out as if for some mythical potentate. It was in fact a priceless ancient artefact, full of antique treasures, which had been carefully collected and preserved over centuries by the wandering tribesmen who kept these sorts of tents permanently at the ready to welcome their leader.

The elder informed him that the preparations for Britt's arrival were now in place. Sharif thanked him with no hint of his personal thoughts on his face, but it amused him to think that an experienced businesswoman like Britt had shown no compunction in attempting to throw him off stride by introducing him to a variety of Nordic delights. It remained to be seen how she would react when he turned the tables on her. How would she like being housed in the harem, for instance?

The elderly tribesman insisted on showing him round the harem tent set aside for Britt. It was a great deal more luxurious than even Sharif's regal pavilion, though admittedly it was a little short on seating areas. The large, luxuriously appointed space was dominated by an enormous bank of silken cushions carefully arranged into the shape of a bed enclosed by billowing white silk curtains. The harem tent had one purpose and one purpose only—a thought that curved his lips in a smile, if only because Britt would soon realise where she was staying, and would be incensed. Teasing her was one of his favourite pastimes. How long was it going to take her to realise that?

Thanking his elderly guide, he ducked his head and left the tent. Pausing a moment, he soaked in the purposeful bustle of a community whose endless travels along unseen paths through a wilderness that stretched seemingly to infinity never failed to amaze him. He didn't bring many visitors to the desert, believing the change from their soft lives in the city to the rigours of life in an encampment would be too much for them, but Britt was different. She was adventurous and curious, and would relish every moment of a challenge like this.

Spending time with his people was always a pleasure for him. It gave him a welcome break from the constant baying of the media—to see his face, to know his life, to know him. And, more importantly, it gave him the chance to live alongside his people and understand their needs. On this visit the elders had asked for more travelling schools, as well as more mobile clinics and hospitals. They would have them. He would make sure of it.

No wonder he was passionate about the diamond deal, Sharif reflected as some of the children ran up to him, clustering around a man who, in their eyes, was merely a newcomer in the camp. He hunkered down so they were all on eye level, while the children examined his prayer beads and the heavily decorated scabbard of his *khanjar*, the traditional Kareshi dagger that he wore at his side.

This was his joy, he realised as he watched the children's dark, inquisitive eyes, and their busy little hands as they examined these treasures. They were the future of his country, and he would allow nothing to put a dent in the prospects of these children. He had banished his unscrupulous relatives with the express purpose of allowing Kareshi to grow and flourish, and he would support his people with whatever it took.

He was still the warrior Sheikh, Sharif reflected as the children were called away for supper. His people expected it of their leader, and it was a right that he had fought for, and that was in his blood. But he did have a softer side that he didn't show the world, and that side of him longed for a family, and for closeness and love. He hadn't known that as a child. He hadn't even realised that he'd missed it until he spent more time here in the desert with his people. What he wouldn't give to know the closeness they shared...

He stopped outside the tent they had prepared for Britt, and felt a rush of gratitude for the heritage his people had so carefully preserved. As he fingered the finely woven tassels holding back the curtains over the opening his thoughts strayed back to Britt. They had never really left her.

It wasn't as if she hadn't changed a tyre before—

Famously, she had changed one on the very first day she had met Sharif. But that had been on a familiar vehicle with tools she had used before, and on a hard surface, while this was sand.

As soon as she raised the Jeep on the jack, it slipped and thumped down hard, narrowly missing her feet. Hands on her hips, she considered her options. It was a beautiful night. The sky was clear, the moon was bright, and she had parked in the shadow of a dune where she was sheltered from the wind. It was lovely—if she could just calm down. And, maybe she shouldn't have set out half cock with only the thought of seeing Emir/Sharif again in her head. But she was where she was, and had to get on with it.

She had never seen so many stars before, Britt realised, staring up. What a beautiful place this was. There was no pollution of any kind. A sea of stars and a crescent moon hung overhead. And there was no need for panic, she reasoned, turning back to the Jeep. She had water, fuel, and plenty of food. The GPS was up and running, and according to that she was only around fifteen miles away from the encampment. The best thing she could do was wait until the morning when she would try again to wedge the wheels and stop them slipping. As a sensible precaution, and because she didn't want Jazz to worry, she texted Sharif's sister: *Flat tyre. No prob. I'll sleep 4WD then change it am and head 2 camp.*

A reply came through almost immediately: *I hve yr coordinates. Do u hve flares? Help o—*

The screen blanked. She tried again. She shook the phone. She screamed obscenities at it. She banged it on her hand and screamed again. She tried switching it off and rebooting it.

It was dead.

So what had Jazz meant by that last message? Help was on its way? Or help off-road in the middle of the desert at night was out of the question?

Heaving a breath, she stared up, and blinked to find the sky completely changed. Half was as beautiful as the last time she looked, which was just a few seconds ago, while the other half was sullen black. A prickle of unease crept down her spine. And then a spear of fright when she heard something...the rushing sound of a ferocious wind. It was like all her childhood nightmares come at once. Something monstrous was on its way—

what, she couldn't tell. The only certainty was that it was getting closer all the time.

Her hands were trembling, Britt realised as she buttoned the phone inside the breast pocket of her shirt. Not much fazed her, but now she wished she had a travelling companion who knew the desert. Sharif would know. This was his home territory. Sharif would know what to do.

The elders had invited him to eat with them around the campfire. The respect they showed him was an honour he treasured. Here in the wildest reaches of the desert he might be their leader, but he could always learn from his people and this was a priceless opportunity for him to speak to them about their concerns. They talked on long into the night, and by the time he left them he was glad he could bring them good news about renewed investment and the realisation of their plans. He didn't go straight back to his tent. He felt restless for no good reason other than the fact that the palm trees seemed unnaturally still to him, as if they were waiting for something to happen. He had a keen weather nose and tonight the signs weren't good. He stared up into the clear sky, knowing things could change in a few moments in the desert.

He paced the perimeter of the camp and found himself back at the harem tent where Britt would be housed when she arrived. His mood lightened as he dipped his head to take a look inside. He could just imagine her outraged reaction when she realised where she was staying. He hoped she would at least linger long enough to enjoy some of the delights. The surroundings were so sumptuous it seemed incredible that they could exist outside a maharaja's palace, let alone in the desert. Like his own pavilion, hers had been cleverly positioned around the underground stream. The water was clear and warm and provided a natural bathing pool in a discreetly closed off section of the tent. Solid gold drinking vessels glinted in the mellow light of brass lanterns, while priceless woven rugs felt rich and soft beneath his sandaled feet. The heady scent of incense pervaded everything, but it was the light that was so special. The candles inside the lanterns washed the space with a golden light that gave the impression of a golden room. It certainly wasn't a place to hold a business meeting. This tent was dedicated entirely to pleasure, a fact he doubted Britt would miss. He tried not to smile, but there was everything here a sheikh of old might have required to woo his mistress. The older women of the tribe had heard a female visitor was expected and had approached him with their plan; he couldn't resist.

Would their Leader's friend be pleased to experience some of the very special beauty treatments that had been passed down through generations?

Absolutely, he had replied.

Would she enjoy being dressed in one of the precious vintage robes they had lovingly cleaned and preserved; a robe they carried with them in their treasure chest on their endless travels across the desert?

He didn't even have to think about that one. He was sure she would.

And the food...Would she enjoy their food? Could they make her sweetmeats like the old days; the sort of thing with which the sheikhs of old would tempt their... their...

Their friends? he had supplied helpfully.

'I'm sure she would,' he had confirmed. He had yet to meet a woman who would refuse a decent piece of cake.

His acceptance of all these treats for Britt had put smiles into many eyes, and that was all he cared about.

Their final assurance was that if their sheikh would honour them by entertaining a female visitor in their camp, they would ensure he did so in the old way.

Perfect, he had said, having some idea of what that might entail. He couldn't think of anything his visitor would enjoy more, he had told them.

Imagining Britt's expression when she was treated as a prized concubine was thanks enough, but there was a serious element to this mischief. The older women guided the young, and it was imperative to have them onside so they embraced all the educational opportunities he was opening up to women under his rule. Kareshi would be different—better for all in the future, and on that he was determined.

The peal of the phone distracted him from these musings. It was his sister Jasmina, calling him to say that Britt had decided not to wait until the morning to travel into the desert, but with all the confidence of someone who believed she knew the wilderness—every wilderness—Britt had insisted on setting out by road, just a couple of hours ago.

Issuing a clipped goodbye to his sister, he went into action. No wonder he'd felt apprehensive. Here with tents erected against the shield of a rock face people were safe, but if the weather worsened out in the desert, and Britt was lost—

All thoughts of Britt in connection with the harem tent shot from his mind. She knew *her* wilderness, not his!

Striding back into the centre of the camp, he was already securing the headdress called a *howlis* around his face and calling for his horse, while his faithful people, seeing that he meant to leave the camp, were gathering round him. They had no time to lose. If a sandstorm was coming, as he suspected, and Britt was alone on treacherously shifting sand, all the technology of a modern age wouldn't save her.

Calling for a camel to carry the equipment he might need, he strode on towards the corral where they were saddling his stallion. Springing onto its back, he took the lead rope from the camel and lashed it to his tack. He wasted no time riding away from the safety of the camp at the head of his small troupe, into what Britt would imagine was the most beautiful and tranquil starlit night.

Where had the romance of the desert gone? She had almost been blasted away in a gust of sand in a last attempt to change the tyre. What was it about her and tyres? And this wasn't fun, Britt concluded, raking her hand across the back of her neck. Sand was getting everywhere. Eddies of sand were exfoliating her face while more sand was slipping through the smallest gap in her clothes.

Did she even stand a chance of being found? Britt wondered, gazing around, really frightened now. Visibility was shrinking to nothing as the wind blew the sand about, and the sky was black. She couldn't even see the stars. She had never felt more alone, or so scared. Battling against the wind, she made it to the back of the Jeep and locked her tools away. Shielding her eyes, she opened the driver's door and launched herself inside. The wind was so strong now it was lifting the Jeep and threatening to turn it over. She had never wished for Sharif more. She couldn't care less about their differences right now. She just wanted him to find her.

She had checked the weather before setting out, but could never have imagined how quickly it could change. There was nothing to see out of the window. She changed her mind about Sharif finding her. It was too dangerous. She didn't want him to risk his life. But she just couldn't sit here, helpless, waiting to buried, or worse... She had to remain visible. If the Jeep were buried she would never be found.

There was a warning triangle in the boot—and a spade handle. And the very last thing she needed right now was a bra. She could make a warning symbol. And there were flares in the boot.

Downside? She would just have to brave the storm again.

The wind was screaming louder than ever and the sand was like an industrial rasp. But she was determined—determined to live, determined to be seen, and determined to do everything in her power to ensure that happened.

Once she had managed to get everything out of the back of the Jeep, securing the warning triangle to the handle of the spade with her bra was the easy part. Finding a way to fix it onto the Jeep wasn't quite so simple. She settled for wedging it into the bull bars, and now she had to get back into the shelter of the vehicle as quickly as she could or she would be buried where she stood.

Closing the door, she relished the relative silence, and, turning everything off, she resigned herself to the darkness. She had to conserve power. There was nothing more she could do for now but wait out the storm and hope that when it passed over she would still be alive and could dig her way out.

CHAPTER TEN

DISMOUNTING, SHARIF COVERED his horse's face with a cloth so he could lead it forward. Attached to his horse by a rope was the camel loaded down with equipment. The camel's eyelashes provided the ultimate in protection against the sand, while he had to be content with narrowing his eyes and staring through the smallest slit in his *howlis*. His men had gathered round him, and so long as he could see the compass he was happy he could lead them to Britt's Jeep. When all else failed magnetic north saved the day.

As they struggled on against the wind he sent up silent thanks that Jasmina had been able to text him Britt's last coordinates, but a shaft of dread pierced him when he wondered if he would reach her in time.

He *had* to reach her in time. He had intended to test Britt as she had tested him in Skavanga when she arrived in the desert, but not like this.

What would she think when he appeared out of the storm? That a bandit was coming for her? It only occurred to him now that she had never seen him in robes before. That seemed so unimportant. He just prayed he would find her alive. He had left the encampment battening down for what was essentially a siege. Custom dictated the tribe pitch their tents at the foot of a rock face to allow for situations like a sandstorm. The best he could hope for where Britt was concerned was that she'd had enough sense to stay inside her vehicle. She wouldn't stand a cat in hell's chance outside.

The scream of the wind was unbearable. It seemed never ending. It was as if a living creature were trying every way it knew how to reach her inside the Jeep. Curled up defensively with her hands over her ears, she knew that the electrics were shot and the phone was useless. The sand was already halfway up the window. How much longer could she survive this?

What a rotten end, she thought, grimacing at the preposterous situation in which she found herself. She could only feel sorry for the person who had to drag her lifeless body out of the Jeep—

She Would Not Die Like This.

Throwing her weight against the driver's door, she tried to force it open, but it wouldn't budge—and even if it had, where was she going?

Flares were her last hope, Britt reasoned. She had no idea now if it was day or night, and before she could set off a flare she needed something to break the window.

Climbing over the seats, she found everything she needed. The vehicle was well equipped for a trek in the desert. There were flares and work gloves, safety goggles, a hard hat, and heavy-duty cutters, as well as a torch and a first-aid kit. Perfect. She was in business.

He had almost given up hope when he saw the flare flickering dimly in the distance. Adrenalin shot through his veins, giving him the strength of ten men and the resolve of ten more. He urged his weary animals on and his brave men followed close behind him. He couldn't

be sure it was Britt who had let off the flare until he
saw the warning triangle she had fixed onto the top of
a spade handle with a bra, and then he smiled. Britt
was ever resourceful, and any thought he might have
had about her setting off into the desert at night without a proper guide seemed irrelevant as he forged on,
his lungs almost exploding as he strained against the
wind. Nothing could keep him back. Sharp grains of
sand whirled around him, but the robes protected him
and the *howlis* did its job. Just thinking about Britt and
how frightened she must be made his discomfort irrelevant. His only goal was to reach her—to save her—to
protect her—to somehow get her back to the camp—

If she were still alive.

He prayed that she was, as he had never prayed before. He prayed that he could save her as he sprang down
from his horse, and started to work his way around the
buried Jeep. The vehicle was buried far deeper than he
had imagined, and, worse, he couldn't hear anything
against the wind. Was she alive in there? With not a
moment to lose he yanked at the windscreen with his
men helping him. Britt had already loosened it to let
off the flare—

And then he saw her. Alive! Though clearly unconscious. She had managed to free the rubber seal on the
glass and had forced it out far enough to let off the flare,
but in doing so had allowed sand to pour in and fill the
vacuum, almost burying her. He waved his men back.
It wasn't safe. Too many of them and the Jeep might
sink further into the sand or even turn over on top of
them, killing his men and burying Britt. He would not
let anyone else take the risk of pulling her out.

He dug with his hands, and with the spade he had
freed from the bull bars of the Jeep. He was desper-

ate to reach her—frantic to save her. It was the longest
hour of his life, and also his greatest triumph when he
finally sliced through Britt's seat belt with the *khanjar*
at his side, and lifted her to safety in his arms.

To say she was bewildered would be putting it mildly.
She had woken up to find herself transported from a
nightmare into a Hollywood blockbuster, complete with
sumptuous Arabian tent and billowing curtains, with
not a grain of sand to be seen. Added to which, there
were women clustering around what passed for her bed.
Dressed in rainbow hues, they looked amazing with
their flowing gowns and veils. At the moment they were
trying to explain to her in a series of mimes that she
had been barely conscious when their leader carried
her into the camp. At which point it seemed they had
to pause and sigh.

She must have been asleep for ages, Britt realised,
staring around. The bed on which she was reclining was
covered in the most deliciously scented cushions, and
was enclosed by billowing white curtains, which the
women had drawn back. She felt panicked for a moment
as she tried to take it all in. Was this the encampment
Jazz had told her about—or was she somewhere else?

And then it all came flooding back. The terrifying
storm— The sickening fear of being buried alive. Her
desperate attempt to set off a flare, not knowing if anyone would see it—

Someone had. She squeezed out a croak on a throat
that felt as if it had been sandpapered, and the women
couldn't understand a word she said, anyway, so the
identity of her rescuer was destined to remain a mystery.

The women were instantly sympathetic and rushed
to bring her drinks laced with honey, and one of them

indicated an outdoor spa, which Britt could now see was situated at the far end of the tent.

And what a tent! It was more of a pavilion, large and lavishly furnished with colourful hangings and jewel-coloured rugs covering the floor. Burnished brass lanterns decorated with intricate piercing cast a soft golden glow, while the roof was gathered up in the centre and had been used to display a number of antique artefacts. She was still staring up in wonder when the women distracted her. They had brought basins of cool water and soft towels, and, however much she indicated that she could sort herself out, they insisted on looking after her and bathing all her scratches and battle wounds.

It was a nice feeling to be made so welcome. Thanking the women with smiles, she drank their potions and accepted some of their tiny cakes, but she couldn't lie here all day like some out-of-work concubine. She was badly in need of a sugar rush to kick her into gear. And those little cakes were delicious. She was contentedly munching when she suddenly remembered Jazz. Sharif's sister must be out of her mind with worry—

Thank goodness she had a signal. She quickly stabbed in: *safe @camp. sorry if i frightnd u! lost a day sleeping! talk soon* J

A message came back before she had chance to put the phone away: *relieved ur safe. Look fwd 2 mtg u b4 long!* ☺

Britt smiled as she put the phone down again. She looked forward to that meeting too. And now the women were miming that she should come with them. She hesitated until they pointed towards the spa again, but the thought of bathing in clean, warm water was irresistible.

She was a little concerned when the women started giggling as they drew her out of the bed and across the rugs towards the bathing pool, especially when they started giggling and then sighing in turn. Were they preparing her for the sheikh? Was she to be served up on a magic carpet with a honey bun in her mouth?

Not if she could help it.

She asked with gestures: 'Did your sheikh bring me here?' She tried to draw a picture with her hands of a man who was very tall and robed, which was about all she could remember of her rescuer—that and his black horse. She must have kept slipping into unconsciousness when he brought her back here. 'The Black Sheikh?' she suggested, gazing around the golden tent, hoping to find something black to pounce on. 'His Majesty, Sheikh Sharif al Kareshi…?'

The women looked at her blankly, and then she had an idea. She sighed theatrically as they had done.

Exclaiming with delight, they smiled back, nudging each other as they exchanged giggles and glances.

She left a pause to allow for more sighs while her heart thundered a blistering tattoo. So it was very likely that Emir or Sharif, or whatever he was calling himself these days, had rescued her. Her brain still wasn't functioning properly, but it seemed preferable to be in the tent of someone she knew, even if that someone was the Black Sheikh.

She allowed the women to lead her into the bathing pool. She didn't want to offend them and what was the harm of refreshing herself so she could start the new day and explore the camp? The women were keen to pamper her outer self with unguents, and her inner self with fresh juice. One of them played a stringed instrument softly in the background, while the scent rising from the warm spring water was divine. Relaxing back in the clear, warm water, she indulged in a little dream in which she was a young woman lost in the desert who had been rescued by a handsome sheikh—

She *was* a young woman lost in the desert who had been rescued by a handsome sheikh!

And however she felt about him, the first thing she had to do was thank Sharif for saving her life. She had to forget all about who had done what to whom, or how angry she had been about his people's interference in the business, and start with that. She could always tell him what she thought about his high-handed ways afterwards. Sharif had risked his life to save her. Compared to that, her pride counted for nothing.

The women interrupted her thoughts, bringing her towels, which they held out like a screen so she could climb from the pool with her modesty intact. They quickly wrapped her, head to foot, and she noticed now that the sleeping area had already been straightened, and enough food to feed an army had been laid out.

Was she expecting visitors?

One visitor?

Her heart thundered at the thought.

As they led her towards the bed of cushions she caught sight of the lavender sky, tinged with the lambent gold of a dying sun. The women insisted she must lie down on a sheet while they massaged her skin with soothing emollients to ease the discomfort of all the cuts and bruises she had sustained during her ordeal. The scent of the cream was amazing and she couldn't ever remember being indulged to this extent. Being prepared for the sheikh indeed...

She was a little concerned when, instead of her own clothes, the women showed her an exquisite gown in flowing silk. 'Where are my clothes?' she mimed.

One of the women mimed back that Britt's clothes were still wet after having been washed.

Ah... 'Thank you.'

She bit her lip, wondering how the rest of this night would play out, but then decided she would just have to throw herself into the spirit of generosity being lavished on her by these wonderful people. And the gown was beautiful, though it had clearly been designed for someone far more glamorous than she was. In ice blue silk, it was as fine as gossamer, and was intricately decorated with silver thread. It was the sort of robe she could easily imagine a sheikh's mistress wearing. But as there were no alternatives on offer...

One of the women brought in a full-length mirror so Britt could see the finished effect. The transformation was complete when they draped a matching veil over her hair and drew the wisp of chiffon across her face, securing it with a jewelled clip. She stood for a moment staring at her reflection in amazement. At least she fitted in with the surroundings now, and for perhaps the first time ever she felt different about herself and didn't long for jeans or suits. She had never worn anything so exotic, or believed she had the potential to project an air of mystery. I could be the Sheikh's diamond, she thought with amusement.

She tensed as something changed in the tent...a rustle of cloth...a hint of spice...

She turned to find the women backing away from her.

And then she saw the man. Silhouetted with his back against the light, he was tall and powerful and dressed in black robes. A black headdress covered half his face, but she would have known him anywhere, and her body yearned for her lover before her mind had chance to make a reasoned choice.

'So it was you...' Even as she spoke she realised how foolish that must sound.

His Majesty, Sheikh Sharif al Kareshi, the man known to the world as the Black Sheikh, and known to her before today as Emir, loosened his headdress. Every thought of thanking him for saving her life, or condemning him for walking out on her without explaining why, faded into insignificance as their stares met and held.

'Thank you for saving my life,' she managed on a throat that felt as tight as a drum.

She was mad with herself. The very last thing she had intended when she first set out on this adventure was to be in awe of Sharif. She had come to rail at him, to demand answers, but now she was lost for words and all that seemed to matter was that they were together again. 'You risked your life for me—'

'I'm glad to see you up and well,' he said, ignoring this. Removing his headdress fully, he cast the yards of heavy black silk aside.

'I am very well, thanks to you.'

Dark eyes surveyed her keenly. 'Do you have everything you need?'

As Sharif continued to hold her stare her throat seemed to close again. She felt horribly exposed in the flowing, flimsy gown and smoothed her hands self-consciously down the front of it.

'Relax, Britt. We're the same people we were in Skavanga.'

Were they? Just hearing his voice in these surroundings seemed so surreal.

'You've had a terrible ordeal,' he pointed out. 'Why don't you make the most of this break?'

'Your Majesty, I—'

'Please—' he stopped her with the hint of a smile '—call me Sharif.' He paused, and then added, 'Of course, if you prefer, you can call me Emir.'

The laughter in his eyes was quickly shuttered when she drew herself up. 'There are many things I'd like to call you, but Emir isn't one of them,' she assured him. 'This might not be the time to air grievances—after all, you did save my life—'

'But you're getting heated,' he guessed.

'I am curious to know why you found it necessary to deceive me.'

'I conduct my business discreetly.'

'Discretion's one thing—deception's another.'

'I never deceived you, Britt.'

'You didn't explain fully, did you? I still don't know why you left in such a hurry.'

'Things moved faster than I expected, and I wasn't in a position to explain them to you.'

'The Black Sheikh is held back? By whom?'

'I'm afraid I can't tell you that.'

'Isn't that taking loyalty too far?'

'Loyalty can never be taken too far,' Sharif assured her. 'Just be satisfied that your sisters were not involved and that everything I've done has been for the sake of the company—'

'And your deal.'

'Obviously, the consortium is a consideration.'

'I bet,' she muttered. 'I'm glad you find this amusing,' she added, seeing his eyes glinting.

'I don't find it in the least amusing. When a company defaults on a payment risking the livelihoods of families who have worked for Skavanga Mining for generations, I did what I could to put things right as fast as I could, and while you were still in the air flying to Kareshi to see me.'

She knew this was true and blushed furiously beneath her veil. She was used to being on top of things—at work and with her sisters. She was also used to being told all the facts, and yet Sharif was holding something back for the sake of loyalty, he had implied—but loyalty to whom?

It hardly mattered. He wasn't going to tell her, Britt realised with frustration. 'Okay, I'm sorry. Maybe I did overreact, but it still doesn't explain why you couldn't have said something before you left the cabin.'

'I'm not in the habit of explaining myself to anyone.'

'You don't say,' she murmured.

'It's just how I am, Britt.'

'Accountable to no one,' she guessed.

The Black Sheikh dipped his head.

'Well, whatever you've done, or haven't done, thank you—' She was on the point of thanking him again for saving her life, when Sharif held up his hands.

'Enough, Britt. You don't have to say it again.' Glancing towards the curtained sleeping area, he added, 'And you should take a rest.'

Her mind had been safely distracted from the sumptuous sleeping area up to now, and she stepped back, unconsciously putting some distance between herself and Sharif. She needed time to get her thoughts in order. Better do something mundane, she decided, drawing back the curtains. Task completed, she turned to face Sharif, who made her the traditional Kareshi greeting, touching his chest, his mouth and finally his brow.

'It means peace,' he said dryly. 'And you really don't have to stand in my presence, Britt.'

'Maybe I prefer to—'

'And maybe, as I suggested, you should take a rest.'

Now was not the time to argue, so she compromised, sitting primly on the very edge of one of the deep, silk-satin cushion. 'I apologise for putting you to so much trouble,' she said, gesturing around. 'I had no idea a storm was coming, or that it would close in so quickly. I did do my research—'

'But you couldn't wait to come and see me a moment longer?' he suggested dryly.

'It wasn't like that.' It was like that, Britt admitted silently.

She watched warily as Sharif prowled around the sleeping area, his prayer beads clicking at his waist in a constant reminder that she was well out of her comfort zone here. She stiffened when he came to sit with her—on the opposite side of the cushions, true, but close enough to set her heart racing. And while she was dressed in this flimsy gown, a style that was so alien to her in every way, she couldn't help feeling vulnerable.

'The women gave me this gown to wear while they were washing my clothes,' she felt bound to explain.

'Very nice,' he said.

Very nice was an understatement. The gown was glo-riously feminine and designed to seduce—which she could have done without right now. Her sisters would laugh if they could see her. Britt Skavanga backed into a corner, and now lost for words.

CHAPTER ELEVEN

'I AM GLAD you have been given everything you need,' Sharif said, glancing round the sumptuous pavilion.

'Everything except my clothes.' Britt was becoming increasingly aware that the gown the women had dressed her in was almost sheer. 'I believe my own clothes will soon be here.' She had no idea when they were arriving, or even if they would ever arrive. She only knew that her body burned beneath Sharif's stare as his lazy gaze roved over the diaphanous gown—she had never longed for a business suit more.

Sharif's lips tugged a little at one corner as if he knew this.

Turning away, she ground her teeth with frustration at the position she found herself in. Of course she was grateful to Sharif for saving her, but being housed in the harem at the sheikh's pleasure was hardly her recreation of choice—

She had to calm down and accept that a lot had happened in the past twenty-four hours and she was emotionally overwrought. The temptation to do exactly as Sharif suggested—relax and recline, as he was doing—was overwhelming, but with his familiar, intoxicating scent washing over her—amber, patchouli and sandalwood, combined with riding leather and clean, warm man—she couldn't be answerable for her own actions if she did that. Business was her safest option. 'If I'd seen a photograph of you before you came to Skavanga, I wouldn't have mixed you up with Emir and maybe we could have avoided this mess, and then you wouldn't have been forced to risk your life riding through the storm to find me.'

'I don't make a habit of issuing photographs with business letters. And as it happens, I did see a photograph of you, but it wasn't a true representation.'

'What do you mean?' she asked.

'I mean the photograph showed one woman when you are clearly someone very different.'

'In what way?'

Sharif smiled faintly. 'You're far more complex than your photograph suggests.'

She pulled a face beneath the veil, remembering the posed shot. She had been wearing a stiff suit and an even stiffer expression. She hated having her photograph taken, but had been forced to endure that one for the sake of the company journal.

'Well, I haven't seen a single photograph of you in the press,' she countered.

'Really?' Sharif pretended concern. 'I must remedy that situation immediately.'

'And now you're mocking me,' she protested.

He shrugged. 'I thought we agreed to call a truce. But if there's nothing more you need—'

'Nothing. Thank you,' she said stiffly as he turned to go. Her body, of course, had other ideas. If she could just keep her attention fixed on something apart from Sharif's massive shoulders beneath his flowing black robe, or those strong tanned hands that had given her so much pleasure—

'I'll leave you to rest,' he said, getting up.

'Thank you.'

And now she was disappointed?

He was leaving while her body was on fire for him.

Yes. And she should be glad, Britt told herself firmly. A heavy pulse might be throbbing between her legs, but this man was not Emir—and Emir had been dangerous enough—this man was a regal and unknowable stranger, who could pluck her heart from her chest and trample it underfoot while she was still in an erotic daze. She stood too and, lifting her chin, she directed a firm stare into his eyes. Even that was a mistake. Lust ripped through her, along with the desire to mean something to this man. For a few heady seconds she could think of nothing but being held by him, kissed by him, and then, thankfully, she pulled herself round.

'This is wonderful accommodation and I can't thank you enough for all you've done for me. Your people are so very kind. They let me sleep, they tended to my wounds, they—'

'They bathed you?' Sharif supplied.

The way his mouth kicked up at one corner sent such a vivid flash of sensation ripping through her she almost forgot what she was going to say. 'I...I had a bath,' she admitted in a shaking voice that was not Britt Skavanga at all.

'They spoiled you with soothing emollients, and that's so bad?'

'They did,' she agreed, wishing he would look anywhere but into her eyes with that dark, mocking stare. And every time she nodded her head, tiny jewels tinkled in a most alluring way—she could do without that too!

'The women have dressed you for their sheikh,' Sharif observed.

And now she couldn't tell if he was joking or not. Her chest was heaving with pent-up passion thanks to her desire deep down to be angry—to have a go. *He can't talk to you like that!* She wasn't a canapé to whet his appetite—a canapé carefully prepared and presented to the sheikh for him to sample, then either swallow or discard.

'They have prepared you well,' Sharif said, showing not the slightest flicker of remorse for this outrageous statement. 'Would you rather they had brought you something ugly to wear?' he demanded when her body language gave away her indignation. 'Moral outrage doesn't suit you, Britt,' he went on in the same mocking drawl. 'It's far too late for that. But I must say the gown suits you. That shade of blue is very good with your eyes...'

So why wasn't he looking into her eyes?

Straightening up, she wished her jeans and top were dry so she could bring an end to this nonsense.

And yet...

And yet she was secretly glad that Sharif's gaze was so appreciative. Why else would she stand so straight? Why were her lips parted, and why was she licking them with the tip of her tongue? And why, for all that was logical, was she thrusting her breasts out when her nipples were so painfully erect?

'It's a very pretty dress,' she agreed coolly.

'Our desert fashions suit you,' Sharif agreed.

She shivered involuntarily as he reached out to run the tip of his forefinger down the very edge of her veil. There was still a good distance between them, but no distance could be enough.

And now her thoughts were all erotic. Perhaps Sharif saving her life had added a primitive edge to her feelings towards him. The desire to thank him fully, and in the most obvious way, was growing like a madness inside her. Thank goodness for the veil.

'I'll call back later—when you've had a rest,' he said.

She watched without saying anything as Sharif drew the gauzy curtains around the sleeping area. She reminded herself firmly that she might be dressed like the sugar plum fairy, but she had no intention of dancing to his tune. She was here for business, and business alone. She had to be wary of this man. Sharif had spoken to her sisters without telling her. He had taken mineral samples from the mine, and yet he hadn't had the courtesy to share the results of the tests with her. This might be a seductive setting, she reasoned angrily as the curtains around the sleeping area blew in the warm, early evening breeze, and Sharif was certainly the most seductive of men, but, grateful or not, she still wanted answers, and he had a lot of explaining to do.

He was back? She tried not to care—not to show she cared. She must have failed miserably as breath shot out of her when he dragged her close. This was not even the civilised businessman—this was the master of the desert. There was no conversation between them, no debate. And there was quite definitely no thought of business in Sharif's eyes. There was just the determination to master her and share her pleasure.

'Well, Britt?' Sharif demanded, holding her in front of him. 'You had enough to say for yourself in Skavanga. You must have something to say to me now. Why did you really come to Kareshi when you could have wired your test results and I could have done the same? When you could have laid out your complaints against me in an email message without making this trip?'

Why had she listened to Eva? Eva was hot-headed

and impetuous, and was always getting herself into some sort of trouble, while Britt was cool and meticulous, and never allowed emotion to get in the way.

How had this happened?

'Why are you really here?' Sharif pressed mercilessly, smiling grimly down into her eyes. 'What do you need from me?'

He knew very well what she needed from him. She needed his hands on her body, and his eyes staring deep into hers. She needed his scent and heat to invade her senses, and his body to master hers—

His senses raged as Britt pressed her body against his. This was his woman. This was the woman he remembered and desired. This was the fierce, driven woman he had first met in Skavanga, the woman who took what she wanted and rarely thought about it afterwards.

'Sharif?'

Could it be possible that he didn't want that part of her? he marvelled as Britt spoke his name. Did that wildcat bring out the worst in him? Loosening his grip on her arms, he let her go. When he had first entered the pavilion he had seen the tender heart of a woman he had started to know in Skavanga—the vulnerable woman inside the brittle shell—the woman he had walked away from before he could cause her any hurt.

'Sharif, what is it?'

He stared down and saw the disappointment in her eyes. And why shouldn't Britt expect the worst when he had walked out on her before?

Everything had been so cut and dried in the past. He'd fed his urges and moved on, but he had never met a woman like this before. He had never realised a woman could come to mean so much to him. The feelings raging inside him when he had found Britt alive were impossible to describe. All he could think was: she was still in the world, and thank God for it. But he had a country to rule and endless responsibilities. Did he make love to her now, as he so badly wanted to do, or did he save her by turning and walking away?

'It's not like you to hesitate,' she murmured.

'And it's not like you to be so meek and mild,' he countered with an ironic smile. 'What shall we do about this role reversal?'

'You're asking me?' she queried, starting to smile.

He closed his eyes, allowing her scent and warmth and strength to curl around his core, clearing his mind. He prided himself on his self-control, but there was will power and then there was denial, and he wasn't in the mood to deny either of them tonight. He wanted Britt. She wanted him. It was that simple. Above all, he was a sensualist who never ate merely because he was hungry, but only when the food was at its best. Britt thought she knew everything about men and sex and satisfaction, but it would be his pleasure to teach her just how wrong she was.

'What are you doing?' she said as he led her back through the billowing curtains.

Settling himself on the silken cushions, he raised a hand and beckoned to her.

'What the hell do you think this is?' she said.

'This is a harem,' he said with a shrug. 'And if you don't like that idea you might want to step out of the light.'

'I'll stand where I like,' she fired back.

His shrugged again as if to say that was okay with him. It was. There wasn't one inch of Britt that wasn't beautifully displayed or made even more enticing by the fact that she was wearing such an ethereal gown and standing in front of the light. He let the silence hang for a while, and then, almost as if it were an afterthought, he said, 'When the women brought that gown, didn't they bring you any underwear?'

Her gasp of outrage must have been heard clearly in Skavanga.

'You are totally unscrupulous,' she exclaimed, wrapping the flimsy folds around her.

'I meant no offence,' he said, having difficulty hiding his grin as he eased back on the cushions. 'I was merely admiring you—'

'Well, you can stop admiring me right now.'

'Are you sure about that?'

'Yes, I'm sure. I feel ridiculous—'

'You look lovely. Now, come over here.'

'You must be joking.'

'So stand there all night.'

'I won't have to,' she said confidently, 'because at some point you'll leave. At which time I will settle down to sleep on *my* bed.'

Britt looked magnificent when she was angry. Proud and strong, and finely bred, she reminded him of one of his prized Arabian ponies. And this was quite a compliment coming from him. Plus, a little teasing was in order. Hadn't she put him through trials by fire and ice in Skavanga? Britt had done everything she could think of to unsettle him while he was on her territory, but now the tables were turned she didn't like it. 'Come on,' he coaxed. 'You know you want to—'

'I know I don't,' she flashed. 'Just because you saved my life doesn't give you droit de seigneur!'

'Ah, so you're a virgin,' he said as if this were news to him. 'When did that happen?'

Her look would have felled most men. It suggested she would like to bring the curtains and even the roof down on his head. She was so sure he had styled himself on some sheikh of old, she couldn't imagine that beneath his robes he was the same man she had met in Skavanga. He should get on with proving that he was that man, but he was rather enjoying teasing her. Helping himself to some juice and a few grapes, he left Britt to draw back a curtain to scan the tent, no doubt searching for another seating area. She wouldn't find one, and he had no intention of going anywhere.

'There's nowhere else to sit,' she complained. 'Until you go,' she added pointedly.

He shrugged and carried on eating his grapes. 'Formal chairs are not required in the harem—so there is just this all-purpose sleeping, lounging, pleasuring area, where I'm currently reclining.'

'Don't remind me! I don't know what game you're playing, Sharif, but I'd like you to leave right now.'

'I'm not going anywhere. This is my camp, my pavilion, my country—and you,' he added with particular charm, 'are my guest.'

'I treated you better than this when you were my guest.'

He only had to raise a brow to remind Britt that she had treated him like a fool, and was surprised when he had turned the tables on her at the lake.

'I came to do business with you,' she protested, shifting her weight from foot to foot—doing anything rather than sit with him. 'If you had stuck around long enough for us to have a proper discussion in Skavanga, I wouldn't even be here at all.'

'So that's what this is about,' he said. 'It still hurts.'

'You bet it does.'

He had left at the right time and, though he wouldn't betray Tyr's part in the business, he wanted to reassure her. 'Well, I'm sorry,' he said. 'It seems I must learn to explain myself in future.'

'Damn right you should,' she said, crossing her arms.

'I'm just so glad you're here—and in one piece.'

'Thank you for reminding me,' she said wryly. 'You know I can't be angry with you now.'

They were both in the same difficult place. They wanted each other. They both understood that if you laid the bare facts on the table theirs was not a sensible match. The only mistake that either of them had made was wanting more than sex out of this relationship.

'So maybe we can be friends?' she said as if reading his mind. 'Except in business, of course,' she added quickly.

'Maybe,' he said. 'Maybe business too.'

After a long pause, she said, 'So, tell me about the tent. Do your people always provide you with a harem tent—just in case?'

'In case of what?' he prompted, frowning.

'I think you know what I mean—'

'Come and sit with me so I can tell you about it. Or don't you trust yourself to sit close to me?' he added, curbing his smile.

She chose a spot as far away from him as possible. Again he was reminded of his finely bred Arabian ponies, whose trust must be earned. Britt was as suspicious as any of them. 'Remember the deer,' he said.

'The deer?' she queried.

'Remember the deer in Skavanga and how relaxed we were as we watched them?'

'And then you'll tell me about the tent?'

'And then I'll tell you about the tent,' he promised.

She hardly knew Sharif, and they sat in silence until—yes, she remembered the deer—yes, she began to relax.

'This pavilion is a priceless artefact,' he said. 'Everything you see around you has been carefully preserved—and not just for years, but for centuries by the people in this camp and by their ancestors. It is a treasure beyond price.'

'Go on,' she said, leaning forward.

'You may have guessed from the lack of seating that this pleasure tent is devoted to pursuits that allow a man or a woman to take their ease. Pleasure wasn't a one-sided affair for the sheikhs. Many women asked to be considered for the position of concubine.'

'More fool them.'

'What makes you say that?' he asked as she removed the veil from her hair.

She huffed. 'Because I would never be seduced so easily.'

'Really?'

'Really.'

'It's a shame your nipples are such a dead giveaway.'

She looked down quickly and, after blushing furiously, she had to laugh.

'Shall I go on?'

'Please…'

'After yet another day of struggles beneath the merciless sun,' he declaimed as if standing in an auditorium, 'fighting off invaders—hunting for food—the sheikh would return…'

'Drum roll?'

He laughed. 'If you like.'

'How many women did he return to?'

'At least a football team,' he teased. 'Maybe more.'

'Sheikhs must have been pretty fit back then.'

'Are you suggesting I'm not?'

She met his eyes and smiled and he thought how attractive she was, and how overwhelmingly glad he would always be that he'd found her in time to save her. He went on with his storytelling. 'Or, maybe there could be just one special woman. If she pleased the sheikh one woman would be enough.'

'Lucky her!' Britt exclaimed. 'Until the sheikh decides to increase his collection of doting females, I presume?'

She amused him. And he liked combative Britt every bit as much as her softer self. 'Your imagination is a miraculous thing, Britt Skavanga.'

'Just as well since it allows me to anticipate trouble.'

'So, what's the difference between my story and the way you have treated men in the past? You think of yourself as independent, don't you? You're a woman who does as she pleases?'

'You bet I am.'

'No one forced any of the sheikh's women to enter the harem. They did so entirely of their own accord.'

'And no doubt considered it an honour,' she agreed, flashing him an ironic look.

'But surely you agree that a woman is entitled to the same privileges as a man?'

'Of course I do.'

Where was this leading? Britt wondered. Why did she feel as if Sharif was backing her into a corner? Perhaps it was his manner. He was way too relaxed.

'So if you agree,' he said with all the silky assurance of the desert lion she thought him, 'can you give me a single reason why you shouldn't take your pleasure in the sheikh's pavilion…like a man?'

Her mouth opened and closed again. The only time

she was ever lost for words was with Sharif, Britt realised with frustration. He was as shrewd as he was dis-
tractingly amusing, and was altogether aware of how
skilfully he had backed her into that tight little corner.
He was in fact a pitiless seducer who knew very well
that, where he might have failed to impress her with
the fantasy of the harem tent, with its billowing curtains and silken cushions, or even the rather seductive
clothes they were both wearing, he could very quickly
succeed with fact. She had always been an ardent believer in fact.

CHAPTER TWELVE

SHE COULD HARDLY believe that Sharif had just given her a licence to enjoy him in a room specifically created for that purpose. Crazy. But not without its attraction, Britt realised, feeling her body's eager responses. But she would be cautious. She had heard things about Kareshi. And she liked to be in control. What if she didn't like some of these pleasures Sharif was hinting at? Her gaze darted round. She started to notice things she hadn't seen before. They might be ancient artefacts, as Sharif described them, but they were clearly used for pleasure.

She drew in a sharp, guilty breath hearing him laugh softly. 'Where are you now, Britt?' he said.

Caught out while exploring Planet Erotica, she thought. 'I'm in a very interesting tent—I can see that now.'

'Very interesting indeed,' Sharif agreed mildly, and he made no move to come any closer. 'So I have laid you bare at last, Britt Skavanga?'

'Meaning?' she demanded, clutching the edges of her robe together.

'Have I challenged your stand only to find it has been erected on dangerously shifting sand?' Sharif queried with a dangerous glint in his eyes. 'I've offered you the freedom of the harem—the opportunity to take your pleasure like a man—and yet you are hesitating?'

'Maybe you're not as irresistible as you think.'

'And maybe you're not being entirely truthful,' he said. 'What do you see around you, Britt? What do your prejudices lead you to suppose? Do you think that women were brought here by force? Do you look around and see a prison? I look around and see a golden room of pleasure.'

'That's because you're a sensualist and I'm a modern woman who's got more sense.'

'So quick sex in a corner is enough for you?'

'I deplore this sort of thing.'

The corner of Sharif's mouth kicked up. 'You're such a liar, Britt. You have an enquiring mind, and even now you're wondering—'

'Wondering what?'

'Exactly,' he said. 'You don't know.'

'That's no answer to that.'

'Other than to say, you're wondering if there can be pleasure even greater than the pleasure we have already shared. Why don't you find out? Why don't you throw your prejudices away? Why don't you open your mind to possibility and to things we *modern-thinking* people may not have discovered if they hadn't been treasured and preserved by tribes like this.'

'There can't be much that hasn't been discovered yet,' she said, gasping as she snatched her hand away when Sharif touched it.

'Did you feel that?' he said.

Feel it? He had barely touched her and her senses had exploded.

'And this,' he murmured, lightly brushing the back of her neck.

Her shoulders lifted as she gave a shaky gasp. 'What is that? The sensation's incredible. What's happening to me?'

'This is happening to you.' Sharif explained, gesturing towards the golden dish of cream the women had used to massage her skin. 'This so-called magic potion has been passed down through the generations. Not magic,' he said, 'just a particular blend of herbs. Still…'

They had a magical effect, Britt silently supplied. The scratches she had acquired during her ordeal in the desert had already vanished, she realised, studying her skin. She shivered involuntarily as Sharif's hand continued its lazy exploration of the back of her neck, moving through her hair, until she could do no more than close her eyes and bask in the most incredible sensation.

'They put lotion on your scalp as well as on your body, and that lotion is designed to increase sensation wherever it touches.'

And they touched practically every part of her, she remembered, though the women had taken great care to preserve her modesty. She looked at Sharif, and saw the amusement in his eyes. So he thought he'd won again.

She stood abruptly, and became hopelessly entangled in her gown.

'I've heard of veils being used as silken restraints and even as blindfolds,' Sharif remarked dryly, 'but why would you need those when you can tie yourself in knots without help from anyone? Here—let me help you…'

She had no alternative but to rest still as Sharif set about freeing her.

She wasn't prepared for him being so gentle with her, or for her own yearning to receive more of this care. She wanted him—she had always wanted him.

She was still a little tense when he unwound the fine

silk chiffon gown—exposing her breasts, her nipples, her belly, her thighs, with just a wisp of fabric covering the rest of her. She concentrated on sensation, glad that Sharif was in no rush. Everything he did was calculated to soothe and please her. He took time preparing her, which she loved. She loved his lack of haste, and his thoroughness, and knew she could happily enjoy this for hours. Sharif's hands were such delicate instruments of pleasure, and so very knowing where she was concerned.

'And now the rest of you,' he said in a tone of voice that was a husky sedative.

Each application of cream brought her to a higher level of arousal and awareness, so that when he slipped a cushion beneath her hips, she understood for the first time what they were for, and applauded their invention. And when he dipped his hands in the bowl of cream a second time, warming it first between his palms...

And when he touched her...

'Good?' he murmured.

'Do you really need me to answer that?'

And at last he touched her where she was aching for him to touch, but his attention was almost clinical in its brevity.

'Not yet,' he soothed when she groaned in complaint.

He sat back, and she heard him washing his hands in the bowl of scented water and then drying his hands on a cloth. 'You need time to appreciate sensation, and I'm going to give you time, Britt.'

She sucked in a shocked breath. Words failed her. Being on the ball in the office was very different from being...on the sheikh's silken cushions.

'Why confine yourself to once or twice a night?' Sharif said, his eyes alive with laughter.

She didn't know whether to be outraged or in for the journey. When would she ever get another chance like this, for goodness' sake? And with Sharif's dark gaze drawing her ever deeper into his erotic world, and the knowing curve of his mouth reassuring her, there was only one reality for her, and that was Sharif.

'And now you have a job to do,' he said, breaking the dangerous spell. Removing the cushions, he carefully eased her legs down.

'What?' she said, wondering if this was the moment to admit to herself that she would walk on hot coals if that was what it took to have Sharif touch her again.

She followed his gaze to the dish of cream.

Desert robes were intended to come off with the least amount of trouble, Britt discovered as she loosened the laces on the front of Sharif's robe. As it dropped away to reveal his magnificent chest she realised that she might have found the sight of such brute force intimidating had she not known that Sharif was subtle rather than harsh and, above all, blessed with remarkable self-control.

She was glad when he turned on his stomach and stretched out. She wasn't sure she was ready for the whole of naked Sharif just yet. This warrior of the desert was a giant of a man with a formidable physique. Using leisurely strokes, she massaged every part of him, though had to stop herself paying too much attention to his buttocks. They might be the most perfect buttocks she had ever seen on a man, buttocks to mould with your hands—to sink your teeth in—but there was only so much cream to spare, she reflected wryly as he turned. 'Did I say you could move?'

'Continue,' he murmured, settling onto his back.

Okay, so she could do this—and with Sharif watching, if she had to. Hadn't they both seen each other naked in the snow? And was she going to turn her back on Sharif's challenge? Because that was what this was. She had acted big-time girl-around-town, and now he'd called her bluff as she'd called his at the ice lake. He'd come through that with flying colours—flying them high and proud.

How could she ever forget?

She took her time scooping up more cream in her hands and spent ages warming it until she really couldn't put off what had to be done any longer. She began with his chest, loving the sensation as she spread the cream across his warm, firm flesh. She moved on down his arms, right to his fingertips where she spent quite a lot of time lavishing care and attention on hands that were capable of dealing the most extreme pleasure—and gasped with shock when Sharif captured her hands and guided them down. They exchanged a look: his challenging and hers defiant.

He won.

Thank goodness.

Sharif had creamed her intimately and she would do the same for him...

Maybe they both won.

She took her time to make certain that every thick, pulsing inch of him was liberally coated with the cream. She was breathless with excitement at the thought of having all of that inside her—

'So, Britt,' he said, distracting her momentarily. 'You're beginning to see the benefit in delay.'

'And what if I am?' she said carelessly.

'Don't pretend with me,' Sharif warned, stretching out, totally unconcerned by his nudity.

As well he might be, she thought, admiring him in silence.

'So what do you think of my golden room of pleasure?' he demanded.

'Not bad,' she agreed. She'd come across perks in business before, but none like this.

'So you like it?' he said with amusement.

'It's fascinating,' was as far as she was prepared to commit. 'Okay, so it's fabulous,' she admitted when he gave her a look.

'But?' he queried.

'It's got such a vibe of forbidden pleasure—how can anyone be here without feeling guilty?'

'Do you feel guilty?'

Actually, no. The cream was beginning to do its work. 'It's just that this is the sort of place where anything could happen...'

'What are you getting at, Britt?'

Her throat tightened. 'I'd like to hear about all the possibilities,' she said.

And so Sharif told her about the various uses of the hard and soft cushions, and the feathers she had been wondering about. She blushed at his forthright description.

'What about your sauna in Skavanga?' Sharif countered, seeing her reaction to his explanation. 'What about your birch twig switches?'

'They are used for health reasons—to get the blood flowing faster.'

She wasn't going to ask any more questions, because she wasn't sure she was ready to hear Sharif's answers.

'Ice and fire,' he murmured, staring at her.

They held that stare for the longest time while decisions were being made by both of them. Finally, she knelt in front of him, and, reaching up, cupped his face in her hands. That thanks she had intended to give him for saving her life was well overdue. Leaning forward, she kissed him gently on the lips.

Sharif's lips were warm and firm. They could curve with humour or press down in a firm line. Both she loved, but now *she* wanted to both tempt and seduce. She increased the pressure and teased his lips apart with his tongue, but just as she began kissing him more deeply Sharif swung her beneath him and pinned her down.

'All that trouble I've gone to with you, Britt Skavanga,' he complained, smiling against her mouth, 'and all you really want is this—'

She let out a shocked cry as Sharif lodged one powerful leg between her thighs, allowing her to feel just how much he wanted it too.

'All you want is the romance of the desert and the sheikh taking you. Admit it,' he said.

'You are impossible.'

'And you are incredible,' he murmured, drawing her into his arms.

'I do want you,' she admitted, still reluctant to give any ground.

'Well, isn't that convenient?' Sharif murmured. 'Because I want you too.'

This teasing was all the more intense because she knew where it was leading. She knew Sharif wouldn't pull back, and nor would she. Somehow her legs opened wider for him, and somehow she was pulling her knees back and pressing her thighs apart and he was testing her for readiness, and catching inside her—

And she was moving her hips to capture more of him, only to discover that the cream had most definitely done its work. One final thrust of her hips and she claimed him completely. When Sharif took her firmly to the hilt, she lost control immediately. She might have called his name. She might have called out anything. She only knew that when the sensation started to subside he took her over the edge again and again.

They were insatiable. No thrust was too deep or too firm, no pace too fast, or too deliciously slow. Her cries of pleasure encouraged Sharif and he made her greedy for more. He never seemed to tire. He never seemed to tire of drawing out her pleasure, either, and each time was more powerful than the last, until finally she must have passed out from exhaustion.

'Welcome to my world, Britt Skavanga,' was the last thing she heard him say before drifting contentedly off to sleep.

CHAPTER THIRTEEN

HE WATCHED BRITT sleeping, knowing he had been searching for a woman like this all his life. *And now he'd found her, he couldn't have her?* Britt would never agree to be his mistress. And when he married—

When he married?

Yes, Sharif's thoughts where Britt was concerned were every bit as strong as that. Selfishly, he hoped she felt the same way about him. But he had always believed when he married it should be for political reasons, for the good of his country. He'd never been much interested before. His council had pressed him into giving advantageous matches consideration, but he'd never had an appetite for the task. He wanted a woman who excited him—a woman like Britt.

Warm certainty rushed through him as he brushed a strand of hair away from Britt's still-flushed face. He would find a way. The Black Sheikh could always find a way. He would never ask Britt to give up her independence. No one knew better than he that privilege came with a price, and that price was freedom to do as he pleased, but with a woman like Britt anything was possible.

Or, was it? Britt was exceptional and could do great things in life. She deserved the chance to choose her own path, while his was cast in stone. And then there was Skavanga Mining, and all the subterfuge with her brother...

He exhaled heavily as business and personal feelings collided. The consortium needed Britt's expertise in the mining industry as well as her people skills, but would she stay with the company when the consortium took over? She had been running the company up to now, so it would take some fine diplomacy on his part to keep Britt on board. Could he find something to soften the blow for her?

His dilemma was this: while he cared deeply for Britt, his loyalty could only be fixed in one direction, and his was firmly rooted in the consortium.

The phone flashing distracted him. It was Raffa to say he had been forced to move money into Skavanga Mining on the recommendation of their financial analysts. Britt could only see this as another plot, when in fact what Raffa had done had saved the company.

'Our money men are already swarming on Skavanga Mining, and we need you on the ground to reassure everyone that the changes don't mean catastrophe,' Raffa was saying.

'What about Tyr?' And the grand reunion he had been planning for Britt.

'Tyr can't be there—'

'What do you mean, Tyr can't be there?' He cursed viciously. Having Tyr in Skavanga in person would have softened the blow for Britt when she discovered Tyr's golden shares had swung the ownership of the company into the hands of the consortium. But now—how was he going to explain Tyr's absence without betraying Britt's brother as he had promised faithfully not to do?

He had to get back to Skavanga Mining right away to sort this out—and he could only do that without Britt's newly discovered emotions getting in the way, which meant returning to Skavanga without her. Thankfully, his jet was always fuelled. 'I'll be there in fourteen hours,' he said, ending the call.

Glancing at Britt, he knew there was no time to waste, and by the time he had woken her and explained as gently as he could about Tyr coming into the equation it could all be over in Skavanga. This was one emergency she would definitely want to be part of, but it was better if he prepared the ground first, and then sent the jet back for her.

She woke cautiously and her first thought was of Sharif. She didn't want to wake him as it was barely dawn. The first thin sliver of light was just beginning to show beneath the entrance to the tent. She stretched luxuriously, and, still half asleep, reached out to find him...

The empty space at her side required she open one eye. The initial bolt of surprise and disappointment was swiftly replaced by sound reasoning. He must have gone riding. It was dawn. It was quiet. It was the perfect time of day for riding. Groaning with contentment, she rolled over in the bed of soft silken cushions, and, clutching one, nestled her face into it, telling herself that it still held Sharif's faint, spicy scent. He'd held her safe through the night, and the pleasure they'd shared was indescribable. The closeness between them was real, and she was content, a state she couldn't claim very often. This encouraged her to dream that one day they might work side by side to create something special, something lasting, and not just for Skavanga, but for Kareshi too.

She stilled to listen to the muffled sounds of the encampment coming to life for another day. She could hear voices calling somewhere in the distance and cooking vessels clanking against each other, and then there

was the gentle pop and fizz of the water in her bathing pool as it bubbled up from its warm underground
source. Everything was designed to soothe the senses.
Everything was in tune with her sleepy, mellow mood.
She wasn't too warm or too cold, and her body felt deliciously well used by a man who made every day a
special day, an exciting day.

Yes, she was a contented woman this morning, Britt
reflected as she stretched languorously on her silken
bed, and she couldn't ever remember feeling that way
before—

She jumped up when the phone rang.

'Leila?'

She sat bolt upright. When her younger sister called
it was invariably good news. Leila didn't have a grouchy
bone in her body and had to be one of the easiest people
in the world to get along with, and Britt was bursting to
share the news about her growing closeness with Sharif.
'It's so good to hear your voice—'

An ominous silence followed.

'Leila, what's wrong?' Britt realised belatedly that
if it was dawn in the desert it was the middle of the
night in Skavanga.

'I don't know where to start.' Leila's voice was soft
and hesitant. 'We're in trouble. You have to come home,
Britt. We need you.'

'Who's in trouble? What's happened?' Britt pressed
anxiously. Her stomach took a dive as she waited for
Leila to answer.

'The company.'

As Leila's voice tailed away Britt glanced at the empty
side of the bed. 'Don't worry, I'm coming straight home.'

She was already off the bed and launching herself
through the curtains with her brain in gear. 'Hang on

a minute, Leila.' Grabbing a couple of towels from the stack by the pool, she wrapped them around her and ran to the entrance of the pavilion where she saw a passing girl and beckoned her over. Smiling somehow, she gestured urgently for her clothes, before retreating back into the privacy of the pavilion.

'Okay, I'm here,' she reassured her sister. 'So tell me what's going on.'

The pause at the other end of the line might have been a few seconds, but it felt like for ever. 'Leila, please,' Britt prompted.

'The consortium has taken over the company,' Leila said flatly.

'*What?*' Britt reeled back. 'How could they do that? I had the confidence of all the small shareholders before I left.'

'But we don't have enough shares between us to stave off a takeover, and they've bought some more from somewhere.'

'The consortium's betrayed our trust?' Which meant Sharif had betrayed her. 'I don't believe it. You must have got it wrong—'

'I haven't got it wrong,' Leila insisted. 'Their money men are already here.'

'In the middle of the night?'

'It's that critical, apparently.'

While she was in a harem tent in the desert!

Had nothing changed? Had she learned nothing? Sharif had walked away from her again—distracted her again. And this time it all but destroyed her. For a moment she couldn't move, she couldn't think.

'I'm sorry if I shocked you,' Leila said.

Shock?

'I'm sorry that you've had to handle this on your

own,' Britt said, forcing her mind to focus. 'I'll be there just as soon as I can get a flight.'

She had been stupidly taken in, Britt realised. Sharif had betrayed her. By his own admission, nothing was signed off without the Black Sheikh's consent. He must have known about the share deals all along.

'There's one thing I don't get,' she said. 'How can the deal be done when the family holds the majority share-holding? You didn't sell out to him, did you?'

'Not us,' Leila said quietly.

'Who then?'

'Tyr...Tyr has always had more shares than we have. Don't you remember our grandmother leaving him the golden shares?'

Shock hit her again. Their grandmother had done something with the shares, Britt remembered, but she had been too young to take it in. 'Is Tyr with you? Is he there?' Suddenly all that mattered was seeing her brother again. Tyr had always made things right when they were little— Or was that just her blind optimism at work again? She couldn't trust her own judgement these days.

'No. Tyr's not here, Britt. Neither Eva or I has seen him. The only thing I can tell you is that Tyr and the Black Sheikh are the main forces behind this deal,' Leila explained, hammering another nail into the coffin of Britt's misguided dream. 'The sheikh has got his law-yers and accountants swarming all over everything.'

'He didn't waste any time,' Britt said numbly. While she had been in bed with Sharif, he had been seeing the deal through and speaking to her brother. This had to be the ultimate betrayal, and was why Sharif hadn't been at her side when she woke this morning. He was already on his way to Skavanga. What could she say to Leila— to either of her sisters? Sorry would never cover it.

'It's such a shock,' Leila was saying. 'We still can't believe this is happening.'

There was no point regretting things that couldn't be changed, Britt reasoned as she switched quickly to reassuring her sister. 'Don't worry about any of this, Leila. Just stay out of it until I get back. I'll handle it.'

'What about you, Britt?'

'What about me?' She forced a laugh. 'Let me go and pack my case so I can come home.'

She had been betrayed by her feelings, Britt realized as she ended the call. She was to blame for this, no one else. And now it was up to her to make things right.

She spun around as the tent flap opened, but her hammering heart could take a break. It was the smiling women with her clothes. And whatever type of man their master was, these women had been nothing but kind to her. Greeting them warmly, she explained with mime that although she would love to spend more time with them, she really couldn't today.

It was as if she had never been away, Britt reflected as the cab brought her into the city from the airport. But had the streets always been so grey? The pavements were packed with ice and with low grey cloud overhead everything seemed greyer than ever. After the desert, she reasoned. This was her home and she loved it whatever the climate might be. This harsh land was where she had been born and bred to fight and she wasn't about to turn tail and run just because the odds were against her. Nothing much frightened her, she reasoned as the cab slowed down outside the offices of Skavanga Mining. Only her heart had ever let her down.

Her sisters were waiting for her just inside the glass entrance doors. Whatever the circumstances she was

always thrilled to see them. Knowing there was no time
to lose, she had come straight to the office from the airport with the intention of getting straight back in the
saddle. Thank goodness she'd had a non-crease business suit and stockings in her carry-on bag. She needed
all the armour she could lay her hands on.

'Together we stand,' Britt confirmed when they finally pulled apart from their hug.

'Thank God you're here,' Eva said grimly. 'We're
overrun by strangers. We have never needed to show a
united force more.'

'Not strangers—people from the consortium,' Leila
reassured her. 'But he's here,' Leila added gently. 'I just
thought you should know.'

'Tyr's here?' Britt's face dropped as she realised from
Leila's expression who her sister was talking about.
'You mean Sharif is here,' she said softly. Better she
face him now than later, Britt determined, leading her
sisters past Reception towards the stairs. 'With his
troops,' Eva added as a warning.

Britt made no response. Troops or not, it made no
difference to her. She would face him just the same.
She could only hope her heart stopped pounding when
she did so.

How the hell had he got here ahead of her?

His private jet, of course—

Get your head together fast, Britt ordered herself
fiercely. She was strong. She could do this. She had to
do this. She had always protected her sisters and the
people who worked for Skavanga Mining. That was
her role in life.

Without it what was she?

Nothing had changed, she told herself fiercely.

'Don't worry,' she said. 'I can handle this.'

Eva was right. The first-floor lobby was bustling with people Britt didn't know. Sharif's people—the consortium's people—Sharif had moved them in already. Her temper flared at the thought. But she had to keep her cool. She had lost the initiative the moment she allowed her emotions to come into play, and that must never happen again.

So, Tyr definitely wasn't coming. Sharif had tried to persuade him, but now he put his phone away. Their conversation had been typical of the type Sharif had come to expect from the man who was a latter day Robin Hood. If a worthy cause had to be fought Tyr would drop everything and swing into action. He couldn't blame the man, not with everything that was going on in Tyr's life, but his presence here today would have softened the blow for Britt, whose arrival was imminent. Britt's campaign to save the company was on track, but a happy reunion with the brother she hadn't seen for years was not on the cards. So now she would just be bewildered by what she would see as Tyr's betrayal and his.

He pulled away from the window when he saw Britt's cab arrive. However angry she was he had to keep her on board. Skavanga Mining needed her—

He needed her—

He would protect her from further distress the only way he knew how, which was to say nothing about Tyr, just as he had promised, and allow the blame to fall on the ruthless Black Sheikh instead. He would live up to his reputation. Better she hated him than she blamed Tyr for throwing in his lot with the consortium. Tyr had seen it as the only way to save the company in a hurry, and Tyr was right, though Sharif didn't expect Britt to be so understanding; and with Tyr and the other two men in the consortium tied up half a world away, it was up to him to handle the takeover. There had been time to leave a brief message for Britt with the women at the encampment, and he hoped she'd got it. If not he was in for a stormy ride.

'Britt.' He turned the instant she entered the room. His response to her was stronger than ever. She lit up the room—she lit up his life. She forced him to re-evaluate every decision he had ever made, and he always came to the same conclusion. He would never meet another woman like her, but from her expression he guessed she hated him now. 'Wait for me outside,' she told her sisters in a cold voice that confirmed his opinion.

'Are you sure?' the youngest asked anxiously.

'I'm sure,' Britt said without taking her eyes off him.

She looked magnificent—even better than he re-membered. A little crumpled from the journey, maybe, but her bearing was unchanged, and that said every-thing about a woman who didn't know the meaning of defeat. He'd made a serious error leaving her behind in Kareshi. He should have brought her with him and to hell with the consequences. He should have known that Britt was more than ready for whatever she had to face. Her steely gaze at this moment was unflinching.

'Please sit down,' she said, and then she blinked as if remembering that he was in charge now.

'Thank you,' he said, making nothing of it.

Crossing to the boardroom table, he held out the chair for her and heard the slide of silk stockings as she sat down and crossed her legs. He was acutely aware of her scent, of her, but, despite all those highly feminine traits that she was unable to hide, she was ice.

He chose a chair across the table from her. They both

left the chairman's chair empty, though if Britt felt any irony in sitting beneath portraits of her great-grandfather, who had hacked out a successful mining company from the icy wastes with his bare hands, or the father who had pretty much lost the business in half the time it had taken his own father to build it up, she certainly didn't show it. As far as Britt was concerned, it was business as usual and she was in control.

Even now she felt a conflict inside her that shouldn't exist. She had entered the room at the head of her sisters, determined to fight for them to the end. But seeing Sharif changed everything. It always did. The man beneath that formal suit called to her soul, and made her body crave his protective embrace.

So she might be stupid, but she wasn't a child, she told herself impatiently. She was a grown woman, who had learned how to run this company to the best of her ability when it was thrust upon her, whether she wanted it or not. And nothing had changed as far as she was concerned. 'I called the lawyers in on my way from the airport.'

'There's no point in rushing to do that,' he said, 'when I can fill you in.'

'I prefer to deal with professionals,' she said.

He couldn't blame Britt for the bite in her tone. The way that things had worked out here meant she could only feel betrayed by him.

She searched his eyes, and found nothing. What would he find in hers? The same? If her eyes contained only half the anger and contempt she felt for him, then that would have to do for now. She could only hope the hurt and bewilderment didn't show at all.

'I'd be interested to hear your account of things,' she said coldly. 'I believe my brother's involved in some way.' For the first time she saw Sharif hesitate. 'Did you think I wouldn't find out?'

'In an ideal world I would have liked things to take their course so you could get used to the idea of Tyr's involvement. As it was he stepped in to prevent a hostile takeover from any other quarter.'

'And this isn't a hostile takeover?'

'How can it be when Tyr is involved?'

'I wouldn't know since I haven't heard from him.'

'He is still on his travels.'

'So I believe. I heard he took the coward's way out—'

'No one calls your brother a coward in my hearing,' Sharif interrupted fiercely. 'Not even you, Britt.'

Sharif's frown was thunderous and though she opened her mouth to reply something stopped her.

'You realise Tyr and I go back a long way?'

'I don't know all his friends,' she said. 'I still don't,' she added acidly.

Ignoring her barb, Sharif explained that Kareshi was one of the countries Tyr had helped to independence.

'With his mercenaries?' she huffed scathingly.

He ignored this too. 'With your brother's backing I was able to protect my people and save them from tyrants who would have destroyed our country.' He fixed her with an unflinching stare. 'I will never hear a wrong word said against your brother.'

'I understand that from your perspective, my brother has done no wrong. Tyr knows how to help everyone except his own family—'

'You're so wrong,' Sharif cut in. 'And I'm going to tell you why. If Tyr had added his golden shares to those you and your sisters own, the company would still go down. Add those shares to the weight of the consortium and the funds we can provide—not some time in the future, but right now—and you have real power. That's what your brother's done. Tyr has stepped in to save, not just you and your family, but the company and the people who work here.'

'So why couldn't he tell me that himself?'

'It's up to Tyr to explain when he's ready.' Sharif paused as if he would have liked to say something more, but then he just said quietly, 'Tyr's braver than you know.'

She felt as if she had been struck across the face. There was no battle to fight here. It had already been won.

'A glass of water?' Sharif enquired softly.

She passed an angry hand over her eyes, fighting for composure. She felt sick and faint from all the shocks her mind had been forced to accept. The structure of the business had changed—Tyr was involved, but he still wasn't coming home. And mixed into all this were her feelings for this man. It was too much to take in all at once.

Thrusting her chair back, she stood.

Sharif stood too. 'We want to keep you, Britt—'

'I need time—'

'The consortium could use your people skills as well as the mining expertise you have. At least promise me that you'll think about what I've said.'

'Ten minutes,' she flashed, turning from the table. She had to get out of here—now.

One foot in front of the other—how hard could that be?

That might be easy if she didn't know she had let everyone down. She allowed herself to become distracted and everything had changed. The company might have been thrust upon her, but she had given it all she'd got, and had intended to continue doing so for the rest of her working life. So much for that.

Bracing her arms against the sink in the restroom, she hung her head. She couldn't bear to look at her reflection in the mirror. She couldn't bear to see the longing for Sharif in her eyes. Everything he'd said made sense. He wasn't even taking over and booting her out. They wanted her to stay on, he'd said. And she wanted Sharif in every way a woman could want a man. She wanted them to have a proper relationship that wasn't just founded on sex. She had run the gamut of emotions with him, and had learned from it, but this was the hardest lesson of all: the man they called the Black Sheikh would stop at nothing to achieve his goal—even recruiting Britt's long-lost brother, if that got him where he wanted to be. And Sharif didn't even want the part of her she wanted to give, he wanted her people skills. The only way she could survive knowing that was to revert to being the Britt who didn't feel anything.

Sluicing her face down in cold water, she reached for a towel and straightened up. Now she must face the cold man in the boardroom whom she loved more than life itself, and the only decision left for her to make was whether or not she could stay on here and work for Sharif.

She could stay on. She had to. She couldn't abandon the people who worked here, or her sisters. And if that meant her badly bruised heart took another battering, so what? She would just have to return it to its default setting of stone.

CHAPTER FOURTEEN

BRITT RETURNED TO the boardroom to find Sharif pacing. Caught unawares, he looked like a man with the weight of the world on his back. For the blink of an eye she felt sorry for him. Who shared the load with Sharif? When did he get time off? And then she remembered their time in the desert and her heart closed again.

'There is a problem,' he said, holding her stony gaze trapped in his.

'Oh?' She felt for the wall behind her as wasted emotions dragged her down. She could fix her mind all she liked on being tough and determined, and utterly sure about where she wanted this to go, but when she saw him—when she saw those concerns she couldn't know about furrowing his brow and drawing cruel lines down each side of his mouth—she wanted to reach out to him.

She wanted to help him, and, even more than that, she wanted to stand back to back with Sharif to solve every problem they came across, and she wanted him to feel the same way she did.

'I've had to make some changes to my plans.'

'Trouble in Kareshi?' she guessed.

'A troublesome relation who was banished from the kingdom has returned in my absence and is trying to rally support amongst the bullies who still remain. It's a basic fight between a brighter modern future for all and a return to the dark days of the past when a privileged few exploited the majority. I must return. I promised my people that they would never be at the mercy of bullies again, and it's a promise I intend to keep.'

Sharif really did have the weight of the world on his shoulders. 'What can I do?' Britt said. Whatever had led them to this place was irrelevant compared to so many lives in jeopardy.

'I need your agreement to stay on here. I need you to do my job for me while I'm away. I need you to ease the transition so that no one worries about change unnecessarily. Will you do that for me, Britt?'

Sharif needed her. The people here needed her. And if he didn't need her in the way she had hoped he would, she still couldn't turn her back on him, let alone turn her back on the other people she cared about.

'I really need you to do this for me, Britt.'

Her heart hammered violently as Sharif came closer to make his point, but he maintained some distance between them, and she respected that. Her heart responded. Her soul responded. She could no more refuse this man than she could turn and walk away from her duties here. But there was one thing she did have to know. 'Am I doing this for you, or for the consortium?'

'You're doing it for yourself, and for your people, Britt, and for what this company means to them. Hold things together for me until I get back and we can get this diamond project properly under way and then you'll see the benefits for both our people.'

'How long will you be away?' The words were out before she could stop them, and she hated herself for asking, but then reassured herself that, as this concerned business, she had to know.

'A month, no more, I promise you that.'

The tension grew and then she said, 'I noticed a lot of new people were here when I arrived. Will you introduce me?'

Sharif visibly relaxed. 'Thank you, Britt,' he said. 'The people you saw are people I trust. People I hope you will learn to trust. They moved in with the approval of your lawyers and with your own financial director alongside them to smooth the path—'

'Of your consortium's takeover of my family's company,' she said ruefully.

'Of our necessary intervention,' Sharif amended. 'I hope I can give you cause to change your mind,' he said when he saw her expression. 'This is going to be good for all of us, Britt—and you of all people must know there's no time to waste. Winter in the Arctic is just around the corner, which will make the preliminary drilling harder, if not impossible, so I need your firm answer now.'

'I'll stay,' she said quietly. 'Of course, I'll stay.'

How ironic it seemed that Sharif was battling to keep her on. He was right, though, she could handle anything the business threw at her, but when it came to her personal life she was useless. She had no self-belief, no courage, no practice in playing up to men, or making them see her as a woman who hurt and cared and loved and worried that she would never be good enough to deserve a family of her own to love, and a partner with whom she shared everything

'And when you come back?' she said.

'You can stay or not, as you please. You can still have an involvement in the company, but you could travel, if that's what you want to do. I have business interests in Kareshi that you are welcome to look over.'

A sop for her agreement, she thought. But a welcome one—if a little daunting for someone whose life had always revolved around Skavanga. 'I'd be like you then, always travelling.'

'And always returning home,' Sharif said with a shrug. 'What can I tell you, Britt? If you want responsibility there is no easy way. You should know that. You have to take everything that comes along.'

'And when Tyr comes home?'

'I'm not sure that your brother has any interest in the business—beyond saving it.'

She flushed at misjudging her brother when she should have known that Tyr would have all their best interests at heart.

'And now I've got a new contract of employment for you—'

'You anticipated my response.' But she went cold. Was she so easy to read? If she was, Sharif must know how hopelessly entangled her heart was with his.

Sharif gave nothing away as he uncapped his pen. 'Your lawyers have given it the once-over,' he explained. 'You can read their letter. I've got it here for you. I'll leave you in private for a few moments.'

She picked it up as Sharif shut the door behind him. Her nerves were all on edge as she scanned the contents of the letter. 'This is the best solution,' jumped out at her. So be it. She drew a steadying breath, knowing there wasn't time for personal feelings. There never had been time. She had consistently fooled herself about that where Sharif was concerned.

Walking to the door, she asked the first person she saw to witness her signature and two minutes later it was done. She issued a silent apology to her ancestors. This was no longer a family firm. She worked for the consortium now like everyone else at Skavanga Mining.

Sharif returned and saw her face. 'You haven't lost anything, Britt. You've only gained from this.'

That remained to be seen, she thought, remembering Sharif leaving her in Kareshi and again at the cabin.

'I left a message for you in Kareshi,' he said as if picking up on these thoughts. 'Didn't you get it? The women? Didn't they come to find you?' he added as she slowly shook her head.

And then she remembered the women trying to speak to her before she left. She'd been in too much of a hurry to spare the time for them. 'They did try to speak to me,' she admitted.

'But you didn't give them chance to explain?' Sharif guessed. 'Like you I never walk away from responsibility, Britt. You should know I would always get a message to you somehow.'

And he was actually paying her a compliment leaving Skavanga Mining in her care. It was a compliment she would gladly park in favour of hearing Sharif tell her that he couldn't envisage life without her—

How far must this self-delusion go before she finally got it into her head that whatever had happened between them in the past was over? Sharif had clearly moved on to the next phase of his life. Why couldn't she?

'Welcome on board, Britt.'

She stared at his outstretched hand, wondering if she dared touch it. She was actually afraid of what she might feel. She sought refuge as always in business. 'Is that it?' she said briskly, turning to go. 'I really should put my sisters out of their misery.'

'They already know what's going on.'

'You told them?'

'Like you, I didn't want them to worry, so I told them what was happening and sent them home.'

'You don't take any chances, do you, Sharif?' She

stared into the dark, unreadable eyes of the man who had briefly been her lover and who was now her boss.

'Never,' he confirmed.

A wave of emotion jolted her as she walked to the door. Sharif's voice stopped her. 'Don't leave like this,' he said.

She turned her face away from him, unwilling to meet his all-seeing stare. The last thing she wanted now was to break down in front of him. Sharif must be given no reason to think she wasn't tough enough to handle the assignment he had tasked her with.

'Britt,' he ground out, his mouth so close to her ear. 'Please. Listen to me—'

She tried to make a joke of it and almost managed to huff a laugh as she wrangled herself free. 'I think I've listened to you enough, don't you?'

'You don't get it, do you?' he said. 'I'm doing this for you—I rushed here for you—to save the company. This isn't just for the consortium. Yes, of course we'll benefit from it, but I wanted to save your company for you. Can't you see that? Why else would I leave my country when there's trouble brewing?'

'I don't know,' she said, shaking her head. 'Everything's happened so fast, I just don't know what to think. I only know I don't understand you.'

'I think you do. I think you understand me very well.'

She would not succumb to Sharif's dark charm. She would not weaken now. The urge to soften against him was overpowering, but if she did that she was lost. She might as well pack up her job and agree to be Sharif's mistress for as long as it amused the Black Sheikh. 'I need to go home and see my sisters.'

'You need to stay here with me,' Sharif argued.

She wanted his arms around her too badly to stay. She

still felt isolated and unsure of herself. She, who took pride in standing alone at the head of her troops, felt as if the ground had been pulled away from her feet today.

'Are you frightened of being alone with me, Britt?' Cupping her chin, Sharif made her look at him and she stared back. He was a warrior of the desert, a man who had fought to restore freedom to his country, and who could have brushed her aside and taken over Skavanga Mining without involving her.

So why hadn't he?

'I asked you a question, Britt? Why won't you answer me?'

Sharif's touch on her face was so seductive it would have been the easiest thing in the world to soften in his arms. 'I'm not frightened of you,' she said, speaking more to herself.

'Good,' he murmured. 'That's the last thing I want.'

But if he could know how frightened she was of the way she felt about him, he would surely count it as a victory. And the longer Sharif held her like this, close yet not too close, the more she longed for his warmth and his strength, and the clearer it became that, for the first time in her life, being Britt Skavanga, lone businesswoman, wasn't enough.

'I've got an idea,' Sharif said quietly as he released her.

'What?' she said cautiously.

'I'd like you the think about working in Kareshi as well as Skavanga— Don't look so shocked, Britt. We live in a small world—'

'It's not that.' Her heart had leapt at the thought, but she still doubted herself, doubted her capabilities, and wondered if Sharif was just saying this to make her feel better.

'It's not that—' Her heart had leapt at the thought, even as doubt crowded in that for some reason Sharif just wanted to make her feel better.

'I have always encouraged people to break down unnecessary barriers so they can broaden their horizons in every way. I'm keen to develop talent wherever I find it, and I'd like you to think about using your interpersonal skills more widely. I know you've always concentrated on Skavanga Mining in the past, and that's good, but while I'm away— Well, please just agree to think about what I've said—'

'I will,' she promised as Sharif moved towards the door.

'One month, Britt. I'll send the jet.'

Anything connected with Sharif was a whirlwind, Britt concluded, her head still reeling as he left the room. He ruled a country— He was a warrior. He was a lover, but no more than that. But Sharif had placed his trust in her, and had put her back in charge of Skavanga mining where she could protect the interests of the people she cared about.

A month, he'd said? She'd better get started.

He had to give her time, he reasoned. He would see Britt again soon—

A month—

He consoled himself with the thought that in between times he could sort out his country and his companies—

To hell with all of it!

Without Britt there was nothing. He'd known that on the flight when every mile he put between them was a mile too far. Without Britt there was no purpose to any of this. What was life for, if not to love and be loved?

CHAPTER FIFTEEN

A MONTH WAS a long time in business, and Britt was surprised at how many of the changes were good. With new blood came new ideas, along with fresh energy for everyone concerned to fire off. The combination of ice and fire seemed to be working well at Skavanga Mining. The Kareshis brought interesting solutions for deep shaft mining, while nothing fazed workers in Skavanga who were accustomed to dealing with extreme conditions on a daily basis. Drilling was already under way, and even Britt's sisters had been reassured by how well everyone was getting on, and how much care, time and money the consortium was putting into preserving the environment. They had always taken their lead from Britt where business was concerned and so when she explained Sharif's plan to them, they were all for her trip to Kareshi—though their teasing she could have done without.

'Oh, come off it,' Eva insisted in Britt's minimalist bedroom at the penthouse, where the sisters were helping Britt to pack in readiness for the arrival of Sharif's jet the following day. 'We've seen him now. Don't tell me you're not aching to see your desert sheikh again.'

Aching? If a month was a long time in business, it was infinity when it came to being parted from Sharif.

'He isn't *my* desert sheikh,' she said firmly, ignoring the glances her sisters exchanged. 'And, for your information, this is a business trip.'

'Hence the new underwear,' Leila remarked tongue in cheek.

Business trip?

Business trip, Britt told herself firmly as the limousine that had collected her from the steps of the royal flight, no less, slowed in front of the towering, heavily ornamented golden gates that led into the courtyard in front of Sheikh Sharif's residence in his capital city of Kareshi. She had read during the flight that the Black Sheikh's palace was a world heritage site, and was one of the most authentically restored medieval castles. To Britt it was simply overwhelming. The size of the place was incredible. It was, in fact, more like a fortified city contained within massive walls.

It was one month since she had last seen Sharif. One month in which to prepare herself for pennants flying from ancient battlements, alongside the hustle and bustle of a thriving modern city—but she could never be properly prepared, if only because the contrast was just too stark. And those contrasts existed in the Black Sheikh himself. Respectful of traditional values, Sharif was a forward-thinker, always planning the next improvement for his country.

Excitement wasn't enought to describe her feelings. There was also apprehension. Until she saw Sharif's expression when he saw her again, she couldn't relax. She was prepared for anything, and was already steeling her heart—the same heart that was hammering in her ears as she wondered if Sharif would be wearing his full and splendid regalia—the flowing black robes of the desert king? Or would he be wearing a sombre tailored suit to greet a director of what he had referred to in the press as his most exciting project yet?

Exhaling shakily, she hoped the problems he had referred to in Kareshi had been resolved, because she was bringing him good news from the mine. They were ahead of schedule and there was a lot to talk about. Ready for their first business meeting, she had changed into a modest dress and jacket in a conservative shade of beige on the plane.

Her heart bounced as the steps of the citadel came into view. Somewhere inside that gigantic building Sharif was waiting.

Not inside.

And not wearing black robes, either, she realised as the limousine drew to a halt.

Sharif was dressed for riding in breeches, polo shirt and boots...breeches that moulded his lower body with obscene attention to detail...

'Welcome to my home,' he said, opening the car door for her.

His face was hard to read. He was smiling, but it could easily have been a smile of welcome for a business associate, newly arrived in his country. Forget business—forget everything—her heart was going crazy. 'Thank you,' she said demurely, stepping out.

He was just so damn sexy she couldn't think of anything else to say. Her mind was closed to business, and her wayward body had tunnel vision and could only see one man—and that was the sexy man who knew just how to please her. There was only one swarthy, stubble-shaded face in her field of vision, and one head of unruly, thick black hair, one pair of keenly assessing eyes, one aquiline nose, one proud, smooth brow, one firm, sexy mouth—

Pull yourself together, Britt ordered herself firmly as Sharif indicated that she should mount the steps ahead of him.

There were guards in traditional robes with scimitars hanging at their sides standing sentry either side of the grand entrance doors and she felt overawed as she walked past them into the ancient citadel. Every breath she took seemed amplified and their footsteps sounded like pistol shots in the huge vaulted space. Everything was on a grand scale. It was an imposing marble-tiled hall with giant-sized stained-glass windows. There were sumptuous rugs in all the colours of the rainbow, and the beautifully ornamented furniture seemed to have been scaled for a race of giants. She felt like a mouse that had strayed into the lion's den. The arched ceiling above her head seemed to stretch away to the heavens, and she couldn't imagine who had built it, or how the monstrous stone pillars that supported it had been set in place.

Attendants bowed low as Sharif led her on. Even when he was dressed in riding gear, authority radiated from him. He was a natural leader without any affectation, and—

And she was going there again, Britt realised, reining her feelings in. Each time she saw Sharif she found something more to admire about him, yet his insular demeanor irritated the hell out of her too, even if she accepted that hiding his feelings must be an essential tool of kingship.

'Do you like it?' he said, catching her smile.

She jolted back to full attention, realising that Sharif had been watching her keenly the whole time. 'I think it's magnificent,' she said as a group of men in flowing robes with curving daggers in their belts and prayer beads clicking in their hands bowed low to Sharif.

A hint of cinnamon and some other exotic spices cut the air, a timely reminder of just how far away from home she was, and how they still had quite a few issues to address. She wondered if Sharif would hand her over to some underling soon, leaving their discussions until later. She almost hoped he would to give her chance to get used to this.

'What's amusing you?' he said.

'Just taking it all in,' she said honestly. 'I'm a historic building fanatic,' she admitted, thinking that a safe topic of conversation. 'And this is one of the best I've seen.'

'The main part of the citadel was built in the twelfth century—'

As he went on she realised that Sharif really did mean to be her tour guide. She had no complaints. He was an excellent teacher, as she knew only too well.

He took her into scented gardens while her heart yearned for him to a soundtrack of musical fountains.

'We have always had some of the greatest engineers in the world in Kareshi,' he explained.

And some of the greatest lovers too, she thought. And what else but love could this exquisite courtyard have been designed for? Everything spoke of romance—the intricate mosaic patterns on the floor, the songbirds carolling in the lemon trees, and the tinkling water features. Surely it was the most romantic place on earth?

And as such was completely wasted on her, Britt concluded, as Sharif indicated that they should move on. 'I'll have someone show you your room,' he said.

So that was it. Tour over. Her heart lurched on cue as he raked his wild, unruly hair into some semblance of order. He probably couldn't wait to pass her over to someone else.

'Freshen up and then meet me in ten,' he said.

Oh...

'Unless you're too tired after your journey?'

'I'm not tired.'

'Good. Put something casual on. Jeans—'

She held back on the salute as a group of women clothed in flowing gowns in a multitude of colours appeared out of nowhere. She turned to look over her shoulder as they ushered her away, but Sharif had already gone.

'These are your rooms,' an older woman, who seemed in charge of the rest, explained as Britt gazed around in wonder.

'All of them?' she murmured.

'All of them,' the smiling woman explained. 'My name is Zenub. If you need anything you only have to ask—or call me.' And when Britt looked surprised, she added, 'This is an ancient building, but we have a very modern sheikh. There is an internal telephone system. This room leads into your dressing room and bathroom,' she explained, opening an arched fretted door that might have been made of solid gold, for all Britt knew. The door was studded with gems that seemed real enough, and probably were, Britt concluded, since Sharif had explained that every original feature inside the citadel had been faithfully restored to its former glory.

She was excited to discover that she had her own inner courtyard, complete with fountain and songbirds. The scent from a cluster of orange trees decorated with fat, ripe fruit was incredible while the fretted walls and covered walkways kept everything cool. It was just the type of place to invite exploration—the type of place to linger and to dream. Perhaps it was just as well she didn't have time.

'There are clothes in the wardrobe, should you need them,' Zenub told her as she ushered the other women out. 'And your suitcase is over here,' she added, indicating a dressing room with yet another glorious display of fresh flowers on one of the low-lying, heavily decorated brass tables. 'Please don't hesitate to call me if you need anything else.'

Britt smiled. 'I will—thank you. And thank you for everything you've done to make me so welcome.'

Amazing didn't quite cover this, Britt reflected as the women left her alone in what amounted to the most fabulous apartment. Every item must have been a priceless treasure, and it was only when she walked into the bathroom and smiled that she saw Sharif's hand in the restoration. The bathroom was state of the art too. There were the high-quality towels on heated rails, as well as fabulous products lined up on the shelves. If the harem pavilion in the desert had been a place of pure pleasure, this was sheer indulgence. It was just a shame she didn't have time to indulge. Another time, she mused ruefully, stepping into the shower.

She showered down quickly and dried off. Tying back her hair, she thought, Sharif stipulated casual, so she tugged on her jeans. A simple white tee and sneakers completed the outfit. A slick of lip gloss and a spritz of scent later and she was ready—for anything, she told herself firmly, leaving the room.

Except for the sight of Sharif wearing a tight black top that sculpted his muscular arms to perfection, and snug-fitting jeans secured by a heavy-duty belt, holding heaven in its rightful place.

And why had she never noticed he had a tattoo before? *She'd been otherwise engaged, possibly?*

'Hello,' she managed lamely, while her thoughts ran crazy stupid wild.

'Britt.' He looked her over and seemed pleased. 'You fulfilled the brief.'

'Yes, I did, boss.' She raised her chin and met the dark, appraising stare with a challenging grin.

'Shall we?'

She glanced at the imposing doors, either side of which stood silent guards whose rich, jewel-coloured robes and headdresses reminded her that this was an exciting land full of rich variety and many surprises. But not half as many surprises as the man standing next to her, Britt suspected as they jogged down the steps together. She stopped at the bottom of the steps and did a double take. 'A motorbike?'

Sharif raised a sexy, inky brow. 'I take it you've seen one before?'

'Of course, but—'

'Helmet?'

'Thank you.' She buckled it on.

And yes, there were outriders. And yes, there was an armoured vehicle that might have contained anything from a rocket launcher to a mobile café, but it wouldn't have mattered, because none of the following posse could keep up with Sharif.

Riding a bike was hot without any additional inducements, like jean-clad sheikhs she had to cling to. Sharif was a great rider. She felt safe and yet in terrible danger—in the most thrilling way. By the time he stopped the big machine outside the university he could have had her on the street.

Fortunately, Sharif had more control than she had

and led her through the beautifully groomed grounds, explaining that he wanted to talk to her before he introduced Britt to the students.

'You've got another idea,' she guessed.

'You know me so well,' he said, his dark eyes glinting.

I wish, she thought as Sharif ruffled his hair. 'So, what's it about?'

'We've talked about this before, in a way,' he said, perching on a wall and drawing her down beside him. 'If you agree, I'd like you to start thinking about plans to bring our two countries together by arranging exchange trips between students.'

'Is that why you've brought me here?'

'That's one reason, yes. I want you to see where your diamonds are going.'

She couldn't pretend she wasn't excited. Her world had always revolved around Skavanga, but now Sharif was offering her more—so much more and her heart soared with hope.

'You're the best person for the job,' he said. 'You'll be reporting to me, of course—'

'Oh, of course.' She tried to keep it light.

'Don't mock,' he warned.

He touched her cheek as he said this, and stared deep into her eyes. It was impossible to feel nothing. Impossible, but she tried not to show it.

'Your first task is to work on a way for our people to learn about each other's culture.'

And now the dam finally burst and she laughed. 'Birch twig switches and harem tents? That should go down well with the students—'

'Britt—'

'I know. I'm sorry. I think it's a wonderful idea.' And

she could tell that it meant a lot to Sharif. This wasn't a whim on his part; this was a declaration of sorts—and maybe the only one she would ever get. But they were close. Deep down she knew this. And she wasn't fooling herself this time, because Sharif was sharing some of the things closest to his heart with her, and when he squeezed her hand and smiled into her eyes, she knew how much this meant to Sharif and was honoured to be a part of it.

'You would have to come back to Kareshi, of course,' he said, frowning.

'Of course,' she said thoughtfully.

'Once the changes have been implemented in Skavanga and everything has settled down here, I want you to tour our universities and colleges with me—art galleries, concert halls and museums. I want to share everything with you, Britt.'

'For the sake of the exchange scheme,' she clarified, still lacking something on the confidence front.

'Absolutely,' Sharif agreed. 'We have some fascinating exhibits in the museums. You might even recognise some of them.'

'But you don't expect me to explain those to students, I hope?'

'I don't think they need any explanation, do you?'

She stared into Sharif's laughing eyes, remembering everything in the fabulous pavilion where she had lost her heart. It had never occurred to her that Sharif might have lost his too.

Or was she just kidding herself again?

CHAPTER SIXTEEN

HE STOOD BACK to watch Britt, wanting to remember every single detail as she met and mingled with the students for the first time. He wished then that he had been less preoccupied and more open from the start, so he could have showered her with gifts and told her how he felt about her. But he had been like Britt—all duty, with every hour of every day filled. They had both changed. He had maybe changed most of all when he had discovered that a month away from Britt was like a lifetime. He'd realised then how much she meant to him and had concluded that it must never happen again.

He wondered now if he'd ever seen her truly relaxed before. Britt Skavanga unmasked and laughing was a wonderful creation. She genuinely loved people and would be wasted behind a desk in an office.

They ate together with a crowd of students who swarmed around Britt. He was almost jealous. Their table was the noisiest, but she still got up and went around every table in the refectory, introducing herself and explaining the scheme she was already cooking in her head. It was as if there had never been a misunderstanding between them, he thought as she glanced over to him and smiled as if wanting to reassure him that she was enjoying this. One of the students commented that Britt came from a cold country, but she had a warm heart.

Cheesy, but she'd warmed his heart. How long had he been in love with her? From that first crazy day, maybe? He just hadn't seen it for what it was. But one of the nice things about being a sheikh was that he could pretty much follow his instinct, and his instinct said, don't let this woman go. He had everything in a material sense a man could want, but nothing resonated without Britt. He saw things differently through her eyes. She made every experience richer. He wanted her in his life permanently and that meant not half a world away. He wanted them to do more than plan an exchange scheme or run a company. He was thinking on a much wider scale—a scale that would encompass both their countries. A life together was what he wanted. He knew that now, and that could only benefit the people who depended on them, and for the first time he thought he saw a way to do it.

'Are you ready to go?' he whispered to Britt discreetly.

'Not really,' she admitted with her usual honesty, gazing round at all the people she hadn't had chance to meet yet.

'You can come back,' he promised. 'Remember—I've asked you to run this project, so you're going to be seeing a lot of these people.'

'But—'

As he held her stare she saw with sudden clarity exactly what he was thinking. Her own eyes widened as his gaze dropped to her mouth.

They were never going to make it back to the citadel. He lost the outriders a few streets away from the university and the security van went off radar in a maze of side-turnings in the suburbs. Britt yelled to ask him what he was he doing when he pulled into a disused parking lot earmarked for development.

'What do you think?' he yelled back, skidding to a halt.

The scaffolding was up and a few walls were built, but that was it. More importantly, no one was working on the site today. Dismounting, he propped the bike on its stand and lifted Britt out of the saddle.

'Is this safe?' she demanded when he backed her against a wall.

'I thought you loved a bit of danger?'

'I do,' she said, already whimpering as he kissed her neck.

He couldn't wait. Neither could she. Pelvis to pelvis with pressure, waiting was impossible. Fingers flying, they ripped at each other's clothes. Blissful relief as Britt's legs locked around his waist and her small strong hands gripped his shoulders. Anything else was unimportant now. They were together. She was ready for him—more than. Penetration was fast and complete. There was a second's pause when they both closed their eyes to savour the moment, but from then on it was all sensation. He cupped her buttocks in his hands to prevent them scraping on the gritty wall, as he kissed her. He groaned and thrust deep, dipping his knees to gain a better angle. Britt was wild, just as he liked her. He wanted to shout out—let the world know how he felt about this woman— How he'd felt without her, which was empty, lost, useless— And how he felt now—exultant. Nothing could ever express his frustration at how long it had taken him to realise that if they wanted each other enough, they would find a way to be together. And that it had to happen here in a parking lot—

'Sharif?' she said.

She was giving him a worried look he'd seen before; he knew she couldn't hold on. 'Britt...'

He smiled against her mouth, loving the tension that always gripped her before release. And now it was a crazy ride, hands clawing, chests heaving, wild cries, until, finally, blessed release. The best. It wasn't just physical. This was heart and soul. Commitment. He was committed to this woman to the point where even the direction his future took would depend on what she said now.

'Marry me,' he said fiercely. 'Marry me and stay with me in Kareshi.'

'Yes,' she murmured groggily in a state of content-ment, resting heavily against him. '*What?*' she yelped, coming down to earth with a bump.

'Stay with me and be my queen.'

'You *are* joking?'

'No,' he said, brushing her hair back from her face. 'I can assure you I'm not joking.'

'You're a king, proposing marriage in a car lot when you've just had me up against the wall?'

'I'm a man asking a woman to marry me.'

'Aren't you being a little hasty?'

'Crazy things happen in car lots and this has been at the back of my mind for quite some time.'

'Only at the back,' she teased him as he helped her to sort out her clothes. And then she frowned. 'Are you really sure about this?'

'I'm not in the habit of making marriage proposals in car lots, or anywhere else, so, yes, I'm sure. But you're right—' Going down on one knee in the dirt, he asked the question again.

'You *are* sure,' she exclaimed. 'But how on earth will we make this work?'

'You and me can't solve this? Are you serious?'

'But—'

'But nothing,' he said. 'You can travel as I do. You can use the Internet. I don't have any trouble staying in touch.'

'And you run a country,' she mused.

'I'm only asking you to run my life.' He shrugged. 'How hard can that be?'

She gave him a crooked smile. 'I'd say that could be quite a challenge.'

'A challenge I hope you want to take on?' he said, holding her in front of him.

'Yes.'

'I'd be surprised if you'd said anything else,' he admitted, returning the grin as he brushed a kiss against her mouth.

'You arrogant—'

'Sheikhs are supposed to be arrogant,' he said, kissing her again. 'I'm only fulfilling my job description.'

'So I'd be staying here in Kareshi with you?'

'Living with me,' he corrected her. 'And running a very important project—with me, not for me. You'll be working for both our countries, alongside me. We'll be raising a family together, and you'll be my wife. But none of this will take place *here*, exactly. I did have somewhere a little better than a parking lot in mind.'

'What about the harem?'

'I'll tell them to go home.'

'I meant the tent.'

'We'll keep it for weekends. So? What's your answer, Britt?'

'I told you already. Yes. I accept your terms.'

'How about my love?'

'I accept that too—and most willingly,' she teased him, her eyes full of everything he wanted to see. 'I love you,' she shouted, making a flock of heavy-winged birds flap heavily up and away from the scaffolding. 'And I don't care who knows it.'

'And I love you too,' he said, and, drawing her into his arms, he kissed her again. 'I love you more than life itself, Britt Skavanga. Stay with me and help me build Kareshi into somewhere we can both be proud of. And I promise you that from now on there will be no secrets between us.'

But then she frowned again and asked the question he knew was coming.

'How can I ever leave Skavanga?'

'I'm not asking you to leave Skavanga. I'm asking you to be my wife, which will give you more freedom than you've ever dreamed of. You can work alongside me and raise a family. You can be a queen and a director of a company. You can head up charities and run my exchange programmes for me. You can recruit the brightest and the best of the students you've just met. I'm asking you to be my wife, the mother of my children, and my lover. The only restrictions will be those you impose on yourself, or that love imposes on you. You'll find a balance. I know it. And if you want more time—you've got it.'

They linked fingers as they walked back to Sharif's bike. They were close in every way. Her hand felt good in his. She felt good with this man. She felt safe. She felt warm inside. She felt complete.

EPILOGUE

'THERE'S JUST ONE thing missing,' Britt commented wistfully as her sister helped her to dress on her wedding day in her beautiful apartment at the citadel in Kareshi.

'Tyr,' Leila guessed as she lifted the cloud of cobweb-fine silk chiffon that would be attached to the sparkling diadem that would crown Britt's flowing golden hair.

'Have you heard anything? Has Sharif said anything to you about Tyr?' Eva demanded, her sharp tone mellowed somewhat by the hairpins she was holding in her mouth. 'After all, Tyr is a major player in the consortium now.'

'Nothing,' Britt admitted, turning to check her back view in the mirror. 'Sharif shares everything with me, but he won't share that. He says Tyr will return in his own good time, and that Tyr will explain his absence then, and that we must never think the worst of him, because Tyr is doing some wonderful work—'

'Righting wrongs everywhere but here,' Eva remarked.

'You know he's already done that—fighting with Sharif to free Kareshi. And I trust Sharif,' Britt said firmly. 'If he says Tyr will explain himself when he feels the time is right, then he will. And if Sharif has given his word to Tyr that he won't say anything, then he won't—not even to me.'

'So, I suppose we have to be satisfied with that,' Eva commented, standing back to admire her handiwork. 'And I must say those diamonds are fabulous.'

'I'm glad they distracted you,' Britt teased.

'Well, they would, wouldn't they?' Eva conceded. 'And this veil…'

'Eva, I do believe you're looking wistful,' Britt remarked with amusement as her sister reached for Britt's dress. 'Are you picturing yourself on your own wedding day?'

Eva sniffed. 'Don't be so ridiculous. There isn't a man alive I could be interested in.' Eva chose not to notice the look her sisters exchanged. 'Now, let's get this dress on you,' she said. 'The way Sharif runs you ragged with all those projects he's got you involved in, it will probably drop straight off you again.'

As Leila sighed even Eva was forced to give a pleased and surprised hum. 'Well… Who knew you could look so girlie?' she said with approval, standing back.

'Only a sister,' Britt muttered, throwing Eva a teasing fierce look while Leila tut-tutted at their exchange.

'Eva!' Leila complained where her two sisters settled down for a verbal sparring match. 'You can't get into a fight with Britt on her wedding day.'

'More's the pity,' Eva muttered, advancing with the veil.

'The dress fits like a dream,' Leila reassured Britt.

'Stand still, will you?' Eva ordered Britt. 'How am I supposed to fix this tiara to your head?'

'With a hammer and nails, in your present mood?' Britt suggested, exchanging a grin with Leila.

But Eva was right in one thing—the past six months

had been hectic. She had overseen so many exciting new schemes, as well as flying back to Skavanga to manage the ongoing work there. And as if that wasn't enough, she had insisted on having a hand in the organisation of her wedding at the citadel. Some people never knew when to relax the reins, Sharif had told her, with the type of smile that could distract her for quite a while. She wouldn't have it any other way, Britt reflected. Life had never been so rich, and when the baby came…

Tracing the outline of her stomach beneath the fairytale gown, she knew she would keep on working until Sharif tied her to the bed. Actually—

'Man alert,' Leila warned before Britt had chance to progress this delicious thought.

'Don't worry, I won't let him in,' Leila assured her.

'Stand back, I'll handle this,' Eva instructed her younger sister. Marching to the door, her red hair flying, Eva swung it open. 'Yes?'

There was silence for a moment and Britt turned to see who could possibly silence her combative middle sister.

'Ladies, please excuse me, but the bridegroom has asked me to deliver this gift to his beautiful bride.'

The voice was rich, dark chocolate, and even Britt could see that the man himself was just as tempting. Eva was still staring at him transfixed as Leila stepped forward to take the ruby red velvet box he was holding out.

'Thank you very much,' Britt said politely, taking another look at the man and then at Eva. Which one would blink first? she wondered.

'It is my pleasure,' he said, switching his attention back to Britt. 'Count Roman Quisvada at your service…'

He bowed? He bowed. 'And this is my sister, Leila,'

she said, remembering her manners. 'And Eva...' Who, of course, had to tip her stubborn little chin and glance meaningfully from the count to the door.

'I can see you're very busy,' the handsome Italian said, taking the hint, his dark eyes flashing with amusement. 'I hope to spend more time with you later.'

'Was he looking at me when he said that?' Eva demanded huffily, her cheeks an attractive shade of pink, Britt thought, as Eva closed the door behind the count with a flourish.

'There's no need to sound so peeved,' Leila pointed out. 'He's hot. And he's polite.'

'I do like a man who's polite in the bedroom,' Britt commented tongue in cheek.

'Wow, wow, wow,' Leila whispered as Britt opened the lid of the velvet box. 'And there's a note,' she added as the three Skavanga sisters stared awestruck at the blue-white diamond heart hanging from a finely worked platinum chain; the diamond flashing fire in all the colours of the rainbow.

Britt read the note while her sisters read over her shoulder: *I hope you enjoy wearing the first polished diamond to come from the Skavanga mine. It's as flawless as you are. Sharif.*

'Cheese-ee,' Eva commented. 'And he doesn't know you very well.'

Britt shook her head as the three sisters laughed.

When she walked down the red-carpeted steps towards him, the congregation in the grand ceremonial hall faded away, and there was only Britt— Beautiful Britt. His bride. But she was so much more than that and they were so much more together than they were apart.

'You look beautiful,' he murmured as her flame-haired sister and the young one, Leila, peeled away.

Now there were just the two of them he didn't dare to look at her or he'd carry her away and to hell with everyone. It took all he'd got to repeat the vows patiently and clearly when all the time his arms ached to hold her. Britt's darkening eyes said she felt the same, and as she held his gaze to tease him she knew how that would test him.

His control was definitely being severely tested, but that was one of the things he loved about Britt. She challenged him on every front and always had.

And long may it continue, he thought, teasing her back by staring fixedly ahead.

Sharif in heavy black silk robes perfumed with Sandalwood and edged with gold was a heady sight.

And he was her husband...

Her husband, Britt reflected, feeling a volcanic excitement rising inside her. Could she contain her lust? Sharif was refusing to look at her and it was only when they were declared man and wife that he finally turned.

Now she knew why he'd refused to look at her. The fire in his eyes was enough to melt her bones. How was she going to stand this? How was she going to sit through the wedding breakfast?

The food was delicious, but even that wasn't enough of a distraction. The setting was unparalleled, but nothing could take her mind off the main event. Candles flickered in golden sconces, casting a mellow glow over the jewel-coloured hangings, making golden plates and goblets flash as if they were on fire, while crystal glasses twinkled like fireflies dancing through the night. It was a voluptuous feast, prepared by world-renowned chefs, but she wondered if it would ever end, and was surprised when Sharif stood up.

'Ladies and gentlemen,' he began in the deep husky

voice Sharif could use to seduce to command. 'The evening is young, and I urge you to enjoy everything to the full. Thank you all for coming to help us celebrate this happiest of days, but now I must beg you to excuse us—'

She still didn't quite understand until Sharif whistled up his horse and held out his hand to her. His black stallion galloped into the hall. As *coup de théâtre* went, she had to admit this one was unparalleled. As their guests gasped the stallion skidded to a halt within inches of its master, and the next thing she knew Sharif was lifting her onto the saddle and holding her safely in front of him.

She gasped as the stallion reared, his silken mane flowing like liquid black diamonds, as his flashing ebony hooves clawed imperiously at the air.

The instant he touched down again, Sharif gave a command in the harsh tongue of Kareshi, and the horse took them galloping out of the hall into a starlit night, and a future that was sure to fulfil all their desires.

* * * * *

A sneaky peek at next month…

MODERN™

INTERNATIONAL AFFAIRS, SEDUCTION & PASSION GUARANTEED

My wish list for next month's titles…

In stores from 21st June 2013:

☐ His Most Exquisite Conquest — Emma Darcy

☐ His Brand of Passion — Kate Hewitt

☐ The Couple who Fooled the World — Maisey Yates

☐ Proof of Their Sin — Dani Collins

☐ In Petrakis's Power — Maggie Cox

In stores from 5th July 2013:

☐ One Night Heir — Lucy Monroe

☐ The Return of Her Past — Lindsay Armstrong

☐ Gilded Secrets — Maureen Child

☐ Once is Never Enough — Mira Lyn Kelly

Available at WHSmith, Tesco, Asda, Eason, Amazon and Apple

Just can't wait?

Special Offers

Every month we put together collections and longer reads written by your favourite authors.

Here are some of next month's highlights— and don't miss our fabulous discount online!

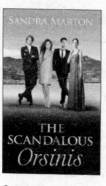

On sale 21st June

On sale 5th July

On sale 5th July

Save 20%
on all Special Releases

Find out more at
www.millsandboon.co.uk/specialreleases

Visit u
Online

0713/ST/MB4

MILLS & BOON®
Book Club

oin the Mills & Boon Book Club

Want to read more **Modern**™ books?
We're offering you **2 more** absolutely **FREE!**

e'll also treat you to these fabulous extras:

- 🌹 Exclusive offers and
  much more!

- 🌹 FREE home delivery

- 🌹 FREE books and gifts with our
  special rewards scheme

Get your free books now!

visit www.millsandboon.co.uk/bookclub
r call Customer Relations on 020 8288 2888

The World of Mills & Boon®

There's a Mills & Boon® series that's perfec
for you. We publish ten series and, with ne
titles every month, you never have to wait
long for your favourite to come along.

Blaze®
Scorching hot, sexy reads
4 new stories every month

By Request
Relive the romance with the best of the best
9 new stories every month

Cherish™
Romance to melt the heart every time
12 new stories every month

Desire™
Passionate and dramatic love stories
8 new stories every month

Mills & Boon® Online

Discover more romance at
www.millsandboon.co.uk

- 🌹 **FREE** online reads
- 🌹 **Books** up to one
  month before shops
- 🌹 **Browse our books**
  before you buy

...and much more!

For exclusive competitions and instant updates

 Like us on **facebook.com/millsandboon**

 Follow us on **twitter.com/millsandboon**

 Join us on **community.millsandboon.co.uk**

*Visit us
Online* Sign up for our FREE eNewsletter at
www.millsandboon.co.uk

WEB/M&B/R